PRAISE FOR THE FIRST BOOK IN THE SERIES

'A gritty and steamy post-apocalyptic novel. Written with an intentionally rough and raw pen, where every scene feels packed with the potential for explosion, this is a bold and gratifying read for action, romance, and dystopian fans of all kinds, especially those drawn to the darker edge of genre-hopping romance.'

Self-Publishing Review

'Harley is an entertaining character with sharp wit, excellent dialogue, and a thirst to prove she doesn't need the protection of others.'

Independent Book Review

BOOKS BY MARGOT DE KLERK

THE VAMPIRES OF OXFORD
Wicked Magic
Wicked Blood

THE IRON FISTS
Rise
Revolution
Redemption
Revenge

REDEMPTION
THE IRON FISTS

Margot de Klerk

COPYRIGHT

Copyright © 2023 Margot de Klerk

This is a work of fiction. Names, characters, business, events, and incidents are the products of the author's imagination. Any resemblance to actual persons, living or dead, or actual events is purely coincidental.

ISBN
978-1-9196213-8-8 (ebook)
978-1-9196213-9-5 (paperback)

Book Cover Design by MiblArt

To my kitties, who kept me company whilst I bullied Bas and Harley through this book.

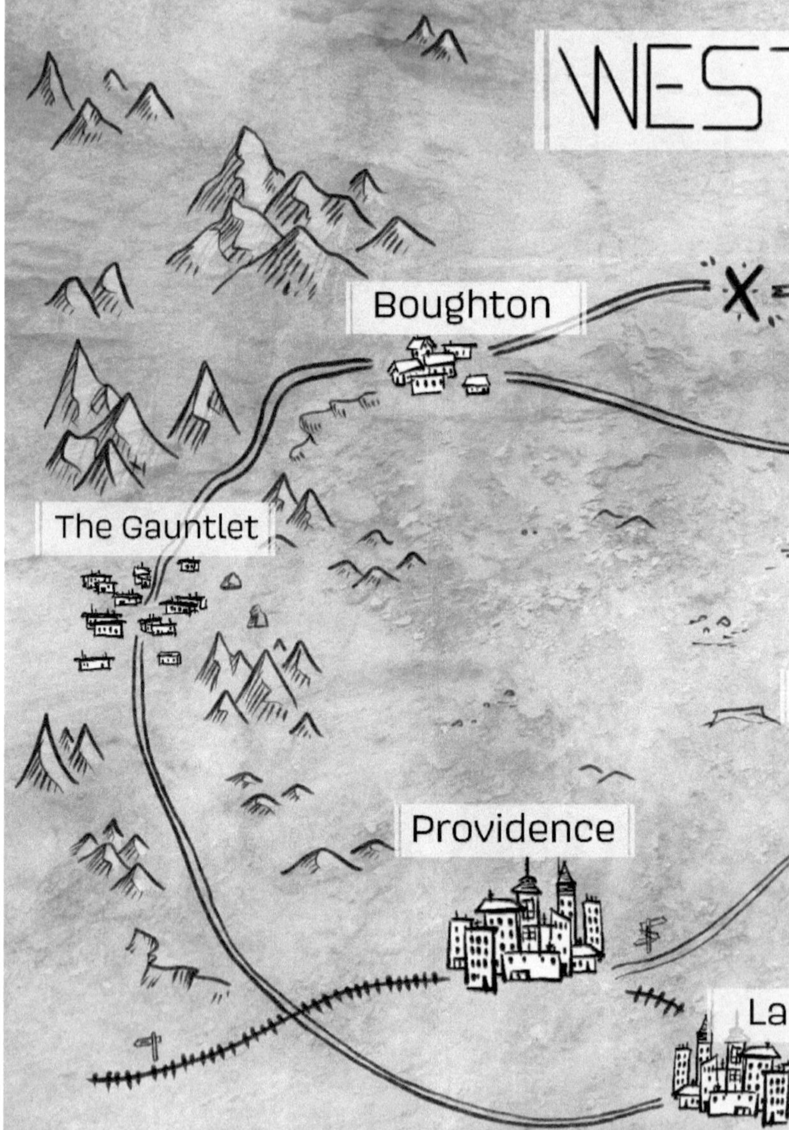

WEST
Boughton
The Gauntlet
Providence
La

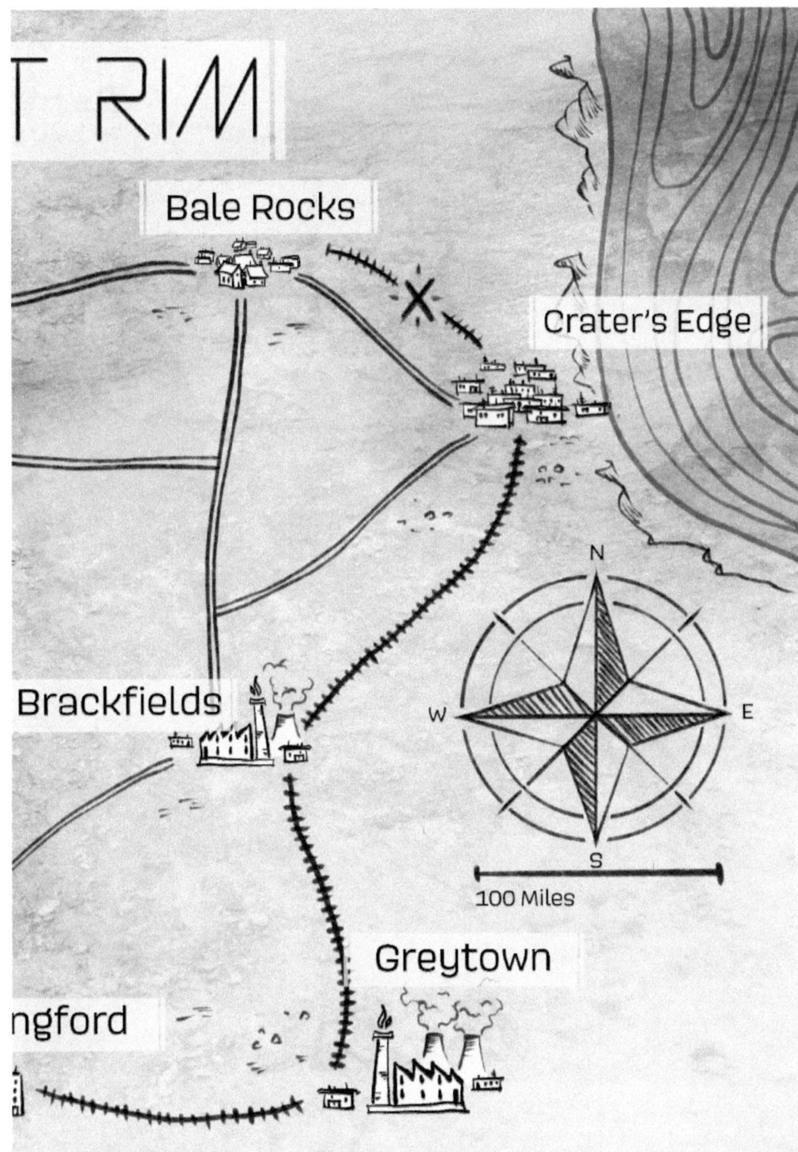
T RIM
Bale Rocks
Crater's Edge
Brackfields
N
W
E
S
100 Miles
Greytown
ngford

AUTHOR'S NOTE

Dear reader,

Welcome to REDEMPTION, the third book in my slow-burn post-apocalyptic romance series, The Iron Fists Series. Please note that this is not a standalone—you will need to read books one and two first.

As a reminder, here are the content warnings for the series:

- Violence, firearms usage, and gang warfare
- Drugs
- Swearing
- Sexual content, including non-consensual sex, consent under duress, and sexual harassment
- Slavery

If that's not your cup of tea—I totally understand! I have cleaner reads available as well. If you are interested in pursuing this, it's time to turn up the heat! I hope you enjoy Harley and Bas's adventures!

Thank you for sticking with me during this little adventure.

Margot

'He who seeks revenge should first dig two graves. One for himself.'
—Japanese proverb

ONE

SAVANNAH'S FACE WAS THE PICTURE of concentration—and irritation.

'I cannot believe you popped your stitches and didn't tell me,' she muttered. I could feel her angry breaths fluttering against my tense stomach. 'You are such an idiot. And—fucking relax, I don't want to hurt you.'

'Sorry.' I leant back a bit. 'Your breath is tickling me.'

'You are such a child.' Savannah sat back on her haunches, setting aside a pair of tweezers. 'Okay, I got the last of them. You're good to go. *Do not* dance on Saturday.'

'Why not? It won't rip open again, right?'

'The skin still needs to heal, Harley.' Savannah stood, peeled her latex gloves off, and marched to the sink to rinse her hands. 'Can't you wait tables or something instead? How are you even going to get there with the roads barricaded?'

'Theo will drive me.'

'Oh God, Theo's in town. That's *just* what I needed.'

I glared at her back. Standing, I adjusted my jumper to cover my stomach again. 'He's my best friend. You could be a bit nicer.'

'And when have you ever been nice about my friends?'

'I don't know any of your friends—'

'You know Maddock.' Savannah turned, scowling.

'You never introduce me to your friends,' I continued. 'If you mean Talbot, I refuse to be nice to him. He's a pig. And isn't Maddock leaving town?'

James Maddock was our downstairs neighbour. He'd been here since last summer, though he'd recently told me he was leaving—before I'd even managed to discover what he was in town for. To say he was acting strangely was an understatement.

'Greg's my boyfriend,' Savannah hissed. 'Show a little respect.'

Greg Talbot was a gang member and an arsehole. 'If you heard how he talked about you when you're not there, you wouldn't be so quick to defend him,' I snapped.

Savannah's lips twisted. She looked away, then abruptly stalked over and snatched up her first aid kit. 'I'm going to clear this up. I need to get to work.'

And she dodged. Again. For about the tenth time. Warning her did nothing—Savannah was determined to be stubborn.

'Thanks for taking the stitches out,' I muttered.

'Whatever.' She stomped off to the bathroom, leaving me alone in the main room of our dingy little flat.

It wasn't much, but it was ours. And, truth be told, I was grateful to still be there. A week ago, I'd been certain that I would have to leave town forever. But then the attack on the distillery had gone down. I wasn't quite sure of the details, but I knew the Iron Fists had managed to hold the distillery, and the Aces and the Black Hands seemed to have retreated from town.

For now, my and Theo's insane plot to kill Hannover was going unpunished.

I dreaded the moment that changed.

Since the attack, I had been isolated. I had received no information since I'd last seen Bas, Theo, and Ellery last Wednesday. Even Hardwick was missing in action; he hadn't shown up to our weekly meeting this Tuesday.

That was the main reason I was determined to dance in the bunker on Saturday. I needed information, desperately.

I had to find out whether anyone was coming for me.

I took up a spot in front of the sofa, the only area of the flat where I could stretch my arms out without hitting the walls, and started gently stretching. I'd skipped my exercises for a few days whilst the stitches had been in, but now I needed to get back in fighting shape as soon as possible.

Fifteen minutes later, I was in the splits position when Savannah marched past, dressed for work. She shot me a disapproving look.

'See you later!' I called.

She slammed the front door behind her. The lock thunked.

'Or not, then.'

Sighing, I abandoned my stretches and stood slowly. I meandered between the furniture and headed through the door to the bedroom that Savannah and I shared. The window was over her bed. I climbed on and peered outside, down to the training ground below.

Deserted.

I had checked every morning since Thursday last week, hoping Bas would appear for his usual morning workout.

He hadn't been a single time.

I'd never known him to miss a day.

The last time I'd seen Bas, he had shot Briggs in the head.

And it was my fault. I was the one who'd killed Tam, and Bas had protected my secret.

I'd been instructed to lay low and *keep my head down,* but every day that went past made me feel sicker with worry. I couldn't shake the feeling that Bas had got into terrible trouble.

I couldn't shake the feeling that I owed him my life again.

Groaning, I raked my fingers over my face, then clambered off the bed and went back to my stretches. Yesterday I'd sat at the window for a full hour. But I couldn't keep waiting for Bas forever. I'd see him on Saturday.

Until then, I had my own life to worry about.

After an early lunch, I headed to work. As I exited my building, I pulled my scarf over my head and ducked my neck to close the gap between my coat and my chin. A sharp, ruthless wind was blowing, chilling my extremities and coating my tongue and throat with the taste of dust.

A couple of flyers skittered across the empty street to join the other rubbish that was starting to pile up. There were no cars on our street; with one end of the street blocked by armed men, no one drove here anymore. Just like no one picked up the rubbish, and no one walked here at night.

We'd become a ghost street in a matter of hours.

The reason for the change was at the east end of the street. A sturdy beige four-by-four was parked diagonally across one side of the road, and the other half was blocked by a concrete barrier.

I had spent six hours in Ellery's flat last Wednesday, and by the time he and Bas had let me go, the army had moved in and taken over the centre of town.

I approached the blockade, my head lowered so the dust wouldn't blow in my eyes.

'Halt!'

A few dozen yards ahead of me, a woman stopped at the barricade. Two soldiers had climbed out of the vehicle, dressed head to toe in brown camo. Their faces were covered with balaclavas to keep the dust out of their lungs, and both had rifles slung over their shoulders.

I slowed my steps. Their words carried clearly to me on the wind.

'What's in the basket?'

'Just food!' the woman cried. 'That's it!'

'Show us.'

She set the basket on the ground, laid out a blanket, and began unpacking loaves of bread one by one. When she reached the bottom, one of the soldiers flicked his fingers. 'Lift the cloth.'

'There's nothing underneath!'

'If you want to get through, you'll do as you're told.'

The woman lifted the cloth covering the bottom of the basket. 'You see?'

'Fine.' One of the soldiers reached down and snatched a loaf, tearing a hunk off.

'Hey, that's mine!' the woman cried.

He shrugged, passing the rest of the loaf off to his colleague. 'Tax. Fine, you can pack your stuff up and get on. Next!'

He'd seen me lurking. Sighing, I started towards them again. The woman threw everything back in her basket with jerky movements. As I stopped beside her, I could hear her sobbing.

They waited until she was through the barricade before turning to me.

'Purpose?' Soldier One demanded. He was short and broad-shouldered, with narrow eyes.

'I work in the bar at the hotel,' I said. My voice was pitched very carefully to be neither provocative nor dismissive. I'd been going through this routine for a week, and I had learnt early on that they wanted trouble. It was better not to give them an excuse to make it.

'Yeah?' Soldier Two demanded. 'Ain't seen you through here before.'

'I work every day except Monday.'

Soldier Two's balaclava had fallen down. He had a whiskery blond beard and watery blue eyes. 'You giving us an attitude?'

'No, sir.' I tried to make my body language unthreatening—whatever the hell that meant.

'I think she's givin' us lip.' He glanced at Soldier One. 'Don't you?'

'Think she might be.' Soldier One waved at me with the hunk of bread between his dirty fingers. 'You got a weapon under that coat?'

'A knife.' I'd taken to leaving the gun Bas had given me at home, though it rankled not to have it on me. But according to the law set down by the mayor, carrying guns in town was illegal. And now the military was here to enforce his laws. I didn't want them to confiscate it.

'Show me.'

Gritting my teeth, I lifted my coat and pulled the knife out of its sheath. Soldier Two beckoned. With supreme reluctance, I relinquished the knife to him.

'This is awful nice for a serving girl.' He spun it between his fingers, then glanced at his colleague. 'You think she's having us on?'

'Be remiss of us not to check.' Soldier One flicked his fingers dismissively. 'Open the coat.'

You have got to be kidding me.

Biting my tongue against a myriad of sarcastic comments, I slowly unbuttoned my coat. Soldier Two shuffled his feet, staring hungrily at me. 'Hurry it up, girlie. We ain't got all day.'

You don't have anywhere else *to go.*

I kept my head down and opened my coat, revealing my jeans and jumper. I could *feel* their eyes on me, cloying and disgusting.

'Nice,' Soldier One jeered. 'Lift the top.'

I couldn't hold back. 'I'm not hiding weapons under my jumper!'

'You want to get to work or not, girlie?'

Fuck him! Swearing up a storm in my head, I grabbed the edge of my jumper and lifted it high enough that they could see my abs, not enough that he could see my bra. The soldiers leered openly at me.

I lowered my top. 'May I go now?' I asked as sweetly as I could. 'I don't want to be late.'

Soldier Two sighed wistfully, his beard ruffling. 'If you must. Ah, but… you can consider this confiscated.' He raised the knife.

Horror shot through me, followed by a healthy dose of fear. 'I need that!'

'Really?' He twirled it mockingly. 'Can't think what a lovely young lady would want a hunting knife for.'

I pressed my lips together. *Fucking arseholes. I hope they all get the runs from our water supply.*

But cursing them out, however satisfying, would not get me my knife back.

I dipped my head, affecting a scared voice. 'I need it for the gangs, sir. They come after the women…'

'You got us for that now, girlie.'

'But I live outside of the barricade… They come into our houses sometimes, and…'

'You work inside the barricade, love. I ain't buying that.'

Damnit. The guys who had been on the last few days had been much more sympathetic. They must have changed shifts.

Fuck.

'Can I at least… have it back and… put it back in my flat?' I chewed my lip, looking hopefully up at them through my hair.

'I don't think so, doll.' He smirked. 'Unless you wanna —'

Beep-beep!

A car horn shattered the silence of the street. I whirled around — a battered red car was approaching. The roar of the engine cut out as the old clunker rolled to a halt on the road beside me. The window lowered with a reluctant squeal to reveal the freckly face of Benny, the hotel's weapons check and general errand boy.

'Ey-up, boys.' He shot the two soldiers a grin. 'Don't mind if I pop through, do ya?'

'Benny!' I called.

'Who's that?' He squinted. 'Harley? You want a lift?'

Both soldiers moved closer to the car.

'No cars through without a permit,' Soldier Two said.

'I didn't need a permit yesterday.' Benny leant back in his seat, one hand on the steering wheel, the other slung over the open window. He looked perfectly relaxed, whilst I felt like I'd be sick from the tension alone.

'That's the rule,' Soldier Two said.

'Hey, you're Savage's brother, aren't ya?' Soldier One cut in. He glanced at his colleague. 'Don't worry, he's cool. He can go through.'

'So kind of ya, gents.' Benny waved to me. 'Come on, Harley. I'll give you a lift.'

'We ain't done with the lady,' Soldier Two protested.

'She works with me. You need a character reference?' Benny winked at me. 'Harley's good people. She works the bar at the Kranikovska —

wouldn't be half as successful without her.'

That was a gross overestimation of my abilities, but I certainly wasn't going to disagree.

'Fine, she can go,' Soldier One said in a long-suffering tone. 'Off ya get, lady.'

Wow, so gracious. Pasting a grateful smile on my face, I said, 'Thank you very much—'

'Don't you forget it,' he said over me.

I took a deep, calming breath. *Don't swear at him.* '—but may I please have my knife back?'

The soldiers exchanged irritated glances.

'I told you,' Soldier Two said, 'it's confiscated. No weapons past the barricade. Mayor's orders.'

'Those weren't the orders yesterday!'

'Well they are today.'

'Hey, hey now,' Benny interrupted smoothly. 'That's not fair. Harley here defuses all sorts of fights—and she's gotta look after herself and her family. You wanna tell the lady she's not allowed to look out for her kids?'

'You got kids?' Soldier One leered at me. I pressed my lips together and jerked my head in a movement that might have been interpretable as a nod. I didn't want to lie outright—but if it got me the knife back, I would.

'Just give her it back,' Benny said. 'It probably cost her a good portion of her wages.'

It would have if I had bought it. But I hadn't. I'd stolen it.

Soldier One was visibly hesitating, but Soldier Two dug his heels in. 'Orders are orders.'

'I'll put in a good word with my bro,' Benny said. 'I'm sure he'd want to know you guys are helping out the people of the town. You know how them bigwigs like the mayor can get, so jumped up on their own power they forget about the ordinary folk.'

Soldier Two scowled. 'Fine then.' He shoved the knife in my direction, blade first. I took it delicately. 'You tell him Dan and Mike are doing a fine job, yeah?'

'Of course,' Benny said cheerfully. 'Hop in, Harley.'

I rounded the car and climbed in, still clutching the knife in my hand. One of the soldiers jumped into their four-by-four and reversed it up onto the pavement so we could squeeze past.

Benny slammed his foot on the accelerator, and we took off amidst squealing tyres and the roar of the engine. 'Fucking pigs,' he muttered. 'They give you trouble?'

'No more than every other day.' My seatbelt was broken, so I held onto the overhead handle.

'I can give you a lift again tomorrow.' We'd left the barricade behind. Benny slowed the car to a more normal pace.

I bit my lip. 'I don't need you to do that.'

'Those guys aren't your friends, Harley.'

'Yeah, but—' I cut myself off, biting my tongue. He was right. And as I was learning, sometimes not asking for help made things worse. How much better off would I have been now if I'd just asked Theo for help straight away?

Or Bas?

Or even Ellery?

Yeah, it sucked to get help from men when they were at least half the problem. But I didn't have the power to solve every problem myself. And I was going to have to learn to pick my battles.

'Fine. Thanks for helping me.'

'Ooooh,' Benny sang. 'It's snowing in hell, yeah?'

'Shut up.'

'Harley Benoit just thanked me!' He laughed. 'Must be my birthday.'

'Fuck off, Benjamin.'

'Ooooh, not the full name! Noooo!'

I smacked him on the arm, but I was laughing too. 'I didn't know you had a brother in the military.'

'Two sisters and one brother,' he said. 'Fucking sucks, right? My bro's a big shot of some sort. Lieutenant, maybe? That's why they recognise me.'

'Seems pretty useful right now.'

'Eh, they'll get bored of us and fuck off back to Crater's Edge sooner or later, you'll see. The mayor ain't paying them enough to keep them interested in our little slice of hell.'

'I hope so,' I muttered.

Benny shot me a sidelong look. Smiling wryly, he steered his car onto, and across, the square. With the blockade keeping anyone from driving into town, no one was bringing their wares to the market. Not that they would be anyway, with the merchants' market on right now. Anyone who did want to sell was doing it out of the market hall down by the river, which was on the edge of the barricaded area.

There was nothing to stop us driving across the middle of the square.

A shiver ran down my spine as I looked out at the deserted marketplace.

'They'd better leave soon,' I repeated.

'Things will go back to normal,' Benny said confidently. 'Politicians come and go. We've been carrying on like this for decades.'

He was right, but I couldn't shake my uneasy feeling. Benny seemed to rationalise change much easier than I did.

I hadn't liked things the way they were, but I'd been comfortable with them. I had understood the rules.

Now… not so much.

Everything was up in the air.

Benny pulled up diagonally in front of the steps to the hotel and braked sharply. 'Hop out. I'll go park up.'

'Alright.' I swung my door open. 'Hey, Benny?'

'Mm-hmm?'

'Thanks. I owe you one.'

'Nah.' He shot me a toothy grin. 'Tom asked me to help out where I could. Just doing my job.'

'Well, thanks anyway.' I jumped down and slammed my door. Benny pulled away, his tyres squealing. Once he was gone, I climbed the stairs. Anna, the pretty bartender who usually shared shifts with me, was waiting just inside the door. As soon as I reached her, she grabbed my wrist and hauled me inside.

'Harley! There you are!'

'Hey.' I took my arm back, rubbing my wrist. 'What's wrong? I thought you were off today.'

'I'm staying at the hotel.' Abruptly, Anna threw her arms around me and buried her face in my hair. 'They keep coming here and demanding access to rooms and everything for free, so Tom said we had to stay to keep an eye on things. Oh, it's so bad, Harley.'

'Hey.' I rubbed her back, helplessness washing over me. Give me a handsy customer any day—they were way easier to deal with than upset friends. 'Hey, hey. It's okay.'

'I knew you'd say that.' Anna sniffled. 'You're so strong and… and you make things look so easy.'

I stifled a laugh. *The fuck you talking about?*
Me? Strong?

I felt quite the opposite most days.

'Shh-shh,' I crooned. Mercy of mercies, Anna's sobs began to abate. 'These things work out. We stick together and look out for each other, right? That's what Bale Rocks has always done.'

'I know,' Anna mumbled. She took a deep breath. 'I just get a bit… Sorry. It's been stressful.'

'I know.' I drew back, shooting her a weak smile which she returned wanly.

'You drove with Benny?'

'He picked me up at the barricade.' I headed for the double doors to the bar, waving to Lou, who was manning the front desk. 'They were being their typical selves.'

Lou mimed gagging.

'The soldiers are horrible,' Anna hissed. 'I hate them.'

Her vehemence took me by surprise; I hadn't realised Anna was capable of hate.

'Benny thinks they'll move on soon.' I entered the bar; it was empty, unsurprisingly. The hotel was full with the merchants at the moment, but we didn't see much of them because they spent the entire day at the market hall.

'I hope so.' Anna followed me behind the bar, watching as I tied my apron on. 'Tom asked me to speak to you.'

'Mm-hmm?' I said as I laid out my tray and put a jug under the water dispenser to fill.

'He's recommissioned a couple of rooms into dormitories for the staff to sleep in for a few nights. So you don't have to go through the barricade every day. I know some of the cleaning staff want to stay—I offered a spot to Kayla, but she said no. You know she works shifts in that casino…'

'She has her dad's shop, as well,' I said. 'She won't leave him.'

'But you'll stay, right?' Anna fiddled with the hem of her shirt, avoiding my eyes. 'It would be easier for you.'

'I…' I bit the inside of my cheek. It was obvious that she wanted me to say yes—but why? Anna and I worked together; we were friendly, but at the end of the day, we both went home to our own lives. I rarely saw her outside of working hours. It wasn't like her to show so much concern for my well-being.

Maybe it was just general uneasiness? Or maybe she wanted someone she knew to stay with her.

Tom was here, though.

But then, Tom was her uncle, and much older. Maybe she wanted a friend rather than a father figure.

I had to admit, it would be easier to stay inside the checkpoint. I wouldn't have to let some arsehole soldier frisk me every morning and night. I wouldn't have to worry about being arrested as a gang conspirator.

But it would put me on the opposite side of the checkpoint from Savannah, Theo, and Bas. I didn't know if I could cope with that.

And what would happen when I had to go to the bunker on weekends?

'I'll think about it,' I said carefully. 'I need to talk it over with Savannah first.'

'Oh.' Anna's face fell. 'Yeah, of course. That makes sense.'

'Sorry.'

'No, it's alright.' She pasted a brave smile onto her face. 'You have to look out for your sister.'

'Yeah.'

My smile felt brittle, as though my face might snap in half. I wasn't even lying to her, but my words felt so far from the truth. I had to stay outside the barricade because the gang members couldn't get in. As long as I was inside, I couldn't get news from them.

Which meant I wouldn't know if I was in danger.

Food had to be bought, meals had to be cooked, the flat had to be cleaned. Life went on, and so when I got off work that evening, I made my way down to the market hall. The merchants' market had been here a week, and they were going strong. Despite the military taking over, people still had to shop, and we still needed necessary supplies to weather the winter.

The market hall was on the north bank of the river, which marked the edge of the barricaded zone. The two bridges, two hundred yards east and west of the hall, were both impassable, blocked by army cars. Apart from that, no patrols were necessary. No one in their right mind would attempt to swim the river; if the current didn't carry them off, hypothermia would.

I bypassed the military field station which had been set up beside one of the bridges and entered the hall. In an instant, the desolation of the town vanished amidst the warmth and noise of dozens of people.

Children weaved between the legs of their parents, chasing one another and shouting. The merchants called out prices to passing customers. Dogs barked and chickens clucked. The heat came from the sheer number of people in there, even though it was ten-thirty at night. Many of the merchants only packed up at midnight; some, who sold drinks and refreshments, closed even later.

It was *alive*, in a way that nothing else was in Bale Rocks these days.

I meandered along the tables, browsing idly. I needed fabric and mending supplies, so I found my way to the west wall, where the clothing and fabric stalls were. A new hat wouldn't go amiss—I tried on a black knitted one and pursed my lips at the tarnished mirror.

'Fourteen NP,' the saleswoman said in a bored tone, 'or two for twenty-five.'

'Fourteen?' I echoed. That was daylight robbery!

'I'll get it for you.'

I twisted around in surprise. Theo strolled up, looking for all the world like he belonged there: baggy jeans, oversized denim jacket, hat pulled low over his ears. A total break from his usual uniform of black fatigues and combat boots.

'Theo!' I gasped. 'What are you doing here?'

'Buying you a hat.' He winked. 'Get one for Savannah, too.'

Theo had been my best friend since I was four. He was incredibly charming and handsome—with curly brown hair, dark brown eyes, and a tall, slender physique. Unfortunately, he was also a member of the Iron Fists.

Meaning that he should not be inside the barricade.

I pulled the hat off. 'We should go.'

'Harley, don't be silly.' Theo pulled his wallet out of his pocket and extracted a twenty and a five. He passed them over to the saleswoman, who was watching us through narrowed eyes. 'What colours do you want?'

'Black,' I said tersely.

'Black for you, purple for Sav.' Theo ran his fingers over the array of hats and selected a stylish purple one with a black lining. He handed both to me. 'Come on, let's go look at the coats.'

'I don't need a coat.'

'I do.'

He strolled off as though he didn't have a care in the world. I shot the hawker a tense smile and hurried after him. Theo paused in front of a rack of wool coats.

'Theo! You shouldn't be here!' I hissed, glancing around worriedly. 'What if someone sees—'

'I know, don't worry. I won't get caught.' He touched my hand, squeezing my fingers; invisible behind the rack of bulky coats. 'I wanted to check on you.'

'Checking on me is not worth getting shot if they see you,' I muttered out of the corner of my mouth. I couldn't stop my eyes from roving around, searching for armed men.

'Yes it is. Hey.' Theo abandoned the coats and turned to me, putting his hand on my cheek. 'Look at me, Harley.'

I glanced at him. His dark brown—almost black—eyes radiated sincerity as he stared down at me. His full lips quirked up. 'I can take care of myself. I'm worried about *you*. Are you safe?'

I couldn't hold his gaze. It was too intense.

Looking away, I muttered, 'No more or less than usual. Hannover hasn't made a move. Hardwick is laying low. The biggest annoyance is the soldiers.'

'They're giving you trouble?' Theo asked darkly.

'Not really,' I said hastily. 'They just like to throw their weight around. But I can handle them.' I didn't want Theo to go do something stupid.

'Hmm…' He turned back to the coats, putting his hands in the pockets to assess how deep they were. 'None of them have been asking questions about the gangs?'

'They search people's stuff, they confiscate weapons, they made me pull my top up—said they were looking for weapons, but they might have been checking me for tattoos.'

Theo shot me a sharp look. I shrugged. 'It's fine! Seriously. It's nothing worse than I've dealt with in the past.'

I took another covert look around the market hall, but it was packed.

No one was paying us any attention, except the salesman who was hoping we would buy one of his overpriced coats.

Theo extracted his hands from the pockets of a grey coat and took my hand, tugging me to the next stall, which sold jeans and overalls.

'I don't like them putting their hands on you,' he said lowly.

'Everyone puts their hands on women round here,' I reminded him.

'You can fight back against 'everyone',' Theo pointed out, unfolding a pair of jeans to assess them. 'You can't fight back against the army. They'll arrest you.'

'I can't fight back against the gangs, either. Unless you've forgotten that.'

'You have more of a chance, though.' He held the jeans up. 'These would look great on you.'

'My jeans can go another year with some repairs,' I said. 'And then I'll take your old ones, like I've done before.'

Theo grinned. 'So I can get them for me, then pass them on to you in a few years, you mean?'

'No!' I elbowed him. Theo chortled.

'Come with me in the changing room.' He snagged my elbow and guided me around to the back of the stall. 'Alright if I try these on?' he asked the salesman.

'No sex in my changing room, yeah?' the guy grunted.

'Mate, I'm gay.' Theo rolled his eyes and tugged me behind the curtain. I sniggered.

'There's not enough space back here to have sex, anyway. Not unless you want to get stabbed by a coat hanger.'

'You vastly underestimate my creativity.' Theo smirked, before turning his back on me so he could wiggle his trousers down. I studied the inside of the curtain.

When Theo spoke again, his voice was a barely audible whisper. 'I don't think you should come to the bunker on Saturday.'

'I have to. Hardwick—'

'—can fucking rot, for all I care. I don't want you in danger.'

'I know, I know, but I have to…' I trailed off, squirming. Theo turned around and stared at me with betrayal in his eyes.

'Is this because of Hardwick? Or because you want to see Bas?'

I looked away. 'Maybe a bit of both.'

'Harley…' Theo groaned.

'The jeans look nice,' I said.

'Fuck the jeans, Harley.'

'You wanted to try them on!'

Theo shook his head, already working them off again. 'For fuck's sake. Bas is bad news. You know that.'

'He shot Briggs for me. I—' *Owe him.*

'—don't owe him anything,' Theo said sternly, reading my mind like he always had when we were kids. 'He's a big boy. He made his own decision. You didn't ask him to do that. If he even so much as thinks of asking you to return the favour, I'm going to hang him by his own intestines.'

I shuddered. The threat was all the more visceral for the fact that Theo wasn't usually the type of person to engage in casual violence. He preferred flirting and manipulating people to threatening them. His weapons were charm and quick wits, not guns and knives.

Okay, that last one was a lie. He was handy with those weapons, too.

Even so.

He yanked the baggy atrocities he'd worn as a disguise on and folded the nice jeans over his arm.

'It's not like that.' I touched Theo's shoulder. 'Please let me handle Bas, okay?'

Theo bit his lip. His eyes were dark. 'Alright, but only because I trust you.'

'I know. Thank you.'

He reached past me, pushing the curtain open. I let him steer me back out.

'And because you're going to promise to come to me if you need help, immediately, from now on.'

I sighed.

'Promise me, Harley.' Theo's gaze was unrelenting. He paused next to a railing, as though checking out the jumpers, but he never looked away from me.

'If I promise, will you get out of here before someone catches you?'

'That would be the wrong reason to promise.' Theo grabbed my hand, lacing our fingers together. 'Promise me because you want to promise me, or don't promise at all.'

'I promise to come to you, within reason.' I kissed the back of his hand to lessen the blow of my half-promise. 'So long as you promise to let me stand on my own two feet.'

'I'm giving you the rope to hang me by.' Theo sighed. 'But yeah. I promise if you promise.' He leant in and kissed my forehead. 'I'm gonna pay and go. See you Saturday, baby.'

'Wouldn't miss it for anything.' I smiled weakly.

TWO

ON SATURDAY EVENING, I MET Theo a few streets north of the checkpoint.

It wasn't too easy to get around town by car at the moment—most of the main roads passed through the barricaded zone, and you could only get in if you proved you had a reason to drive in there. Theo, of course, couldn't pass the barricade at all—though I didn't doubt he could get into the centre if he really wanted to. Still, I certainly wasn't going to ask him to do it on my behalf.

Instead, I waited under the tattered awning of a barbershop, alert to every movement. If the streets were grotty in the centre of town, up here they were even worse: the majority of the ground-floor windows were boarded up, layers of graffiti covered the brick walls, and the only working streetlight in my vicinity flickered alarmingly. I wasn't alone on the street, either. I could see a dark figure sheltering in an alleyway across the road, and two men were standing in the doorway of a café, arguing in whispers.

I heard the roar of the car long before Theo rolled up and stopped beside me.

'You made it,' he said.

'Of course. They don't care about keeping me inside the barricade.' Rolling my eyes, I climbed up into the passenger seat.

'That might change,' Theo warned as I shut my door and put my seatbelt on.

'Hopefully not.' I flicked the radio on. 'This isn't your car.'

'Mine's at the garage.' Theo's tone was terse; I was pretty sure he blamed me for the damages his car had suffered when we went after Hannover. 'They have to replace the windscreen.'

'I am sorry about that.'

'It's not your fault.'

I gritted my teeth. He said that, but his tone was short, snippy, borderline angry.

With me.

I'd fucked up, there was no doubt about that. I was the one who had tried to save Rionach, the little girl who had been with Hannover. What else could I do? She was just a kid! But in doing so… I'd ignored the real threat.

And fucked up the whole plan.

I hated myself for it, too. If only I had stopped and thought about it. But it was too late now.

'I hope it gets fixed soon.'

Theo grunted noncommittally.

We weaved through the narrow streets in the north of town, making our way steadily eastwards, until we left the residential area behind. The dense, overcrowded apartment blocks gave way to ramshackle houses and sprawling grain farms—the source of the barley for the whiskey distillery, as well as the main producers of food for our town. Most of the farms had tall fences built around them, rigged with barbed wire and spikes to keep out thieves—human and animal alike.

North of the farmland, the wasteland began. Theo turned onto the narrow dirt track that led to the decommissioned train station and the entrance to the bunker.

'I wish you weren't going tonight,' he said, his voice mingling with the crooning of some Pre-Crash singer on the radio.

'I *can* look after myself for one night, Theo.'

'I know,' he muttered. 'But that doesn't mean you should have to.'

I stared out at the passing scenery—scrubby bushes and blocks of concrete turned silver by the moonlight. 'Are you worried Hannover will be there?'

'Hannover hasn't been seen in town since the strike,' Theo said. 'Ellery's pretty sure he managed to land a hit on him, so he's probably off nursing his wounds somewhere.'

'Oh.' That was an unexpected relief. Not that I generally enjoyed other people's pain, but the longer Hannover stayed away, the better for our town. Which… still didn't explain Theo's weird reluctance about me going to the bunker. 'Then what is it?'

'I just have a bad feeling.' Theo scowled. 'And I trust my gut—even if you don't.'

'Hey!' I pouted. 'I trust your gut, too.'

'You just don't want to listen to it.' He swerved around a block of concrete, and his headlamps illuminated the chain-link fence ahead of us.

I shrugged. 'We're here already. And maybe I'd rather see the danger than hide from it. I've always preferred knowing to not knowing.'

'I know.' Theo sighed. 'Can you blame me for wanting to keep you safe?'

'I guess not.' I toyed with the hem of my shirt. The stitching was coming loose. Just like it was on everything I owned.

Just like it felt like my life was coming unstuck.

Theo stopped the car. 'Well, there's nothing for it now, unless you're planning on waiting in the car until I leave.'

I shook my head and hastily climbed out.

'Are you fighting tonight?'

'Yep. I drew Maddock.'

'For real?'

Theo nodded. 'I hope you get to watch.'

'What time? I'll try and plan my break for then.'

'Around twelve forty-five.'

'Cool.' I might get lucky. I hadn't watched Theo fight in a while.

When we arrived in the main hall of the bunker, though, I discovered it bizarrely bereft of people.

'What's going on?' I whispered. 'Where is everyone?'

'It's been like this all week,' Theo murmured. 'It will heat up later, don't worry. Everyone is uneasy.'

I glanced up at him. He was frowning, and his jaw and shoulders were stiff, the tendons standing out on his neck.

'Theo…'

'Look,' he murmured. 'No—don't turn your head. Roped-off area by the far wall.'

Out of the corner of my eye, I glanced over. On the edge of the circle, the VIP area where the fighters could hang out, there was an extra roped-off area. Three men were sitting in it: a compact, weathered man with a shiny bald head; a tall man with brown skin and white hair; and a shorter man with curly blond hair and pink, wind-burnt skin.

I knew two of them. The first was Jackson, one of the most senior lieutenants of the Iron Fists.

'Who's the blond guy?' I whispered.

'Moncrief. One of the lieutenants.'

I sucked in a breath. Two lieutenants, and that only left the guy in the middle: tall, aged, and with a sombre expression.

Eduard Sayle.

The leader of the Iron Fists.

'What are they doing here?'

'I don't know,' Theo muttered, 'but it can't be good. Please will you head home?'

'I can't.'

'BENOIT!'

Carlos stormed over to us. He was the floor manager, a man as tall and beefy as an ox. He could throw a guy clean across the room without breaking a sweat. I cringed as he approached, his face red and spittle flying from his lips. 'Where were you last week?'

'Injured,' I said carefully.

'Oi! We aren't working you that hard. Didn't realise waitressing was such a dangerous job,' he sneered.

Fuck you too, Carlos, I thought sourly. 'It wasn't because of my job. Anyway, I'm better now, see? All good.' I did a cheeky little twirl. 'Don't worry, you'll get your usual cut.'

'I bloody well better. I don't put up with your cheek for nothing.'

He stomped off, calling over his shoulder, 'I want you on the floor in ten.'

'Sir, yes sir,' I muttered, scowling.

Theo snorted. ''Behn-waaah,'' he mocked.

'Shush, you.' I elbowed him. I didn't really care about Carlos, anyway. He talked big, but I'd never actually got in trouble with him. The worst he could do was cut my pay, which would suck, but it wasn't the end of the world.

No, I had much bigger worries.

I turned my gaze back on Sayle, Jackson, and Moncrief. I'd only seen Sayle in the bunker a handful of times during the years I'd danced here. He rarely showed his face, and it felt like bad news that he was here now.

What if they knew what I'd done?

Briggs popped into my head again, and my stomach turned. I was trying not to think about him.

I hadn't realised brains could splatter.

Until Bas had shot a man point blank. A man who'd been standing mere feet away from me.

I still remembered the sound his body had made when it hit the floor.

Which was weird, because at the time my ears had been ringing from the gunshot. I hadn't thought I'd heard it.

Briggs was the culmination of a problem I had made, and yet even after his death… I was still afraid.

If he had told anyone that I had killed Gabriel Tam—if anyone investigated Briggs's death—if Talbot decided to tell anyone else about my sins—

'You gonna stand there all night?'

I jerked my head up. Theo was watching me with a smirk that vanished when he saw my expression.

'What are you thinking of?'

I glanced around uneasily. 'Briggs,' I muttered.

Theo frowned. 'Don't,' he said tersely. 'It's taken care of.'

'But—'

'Trust me, Harley.'

'But what if he—'

'Harley.' Theo shook his head. 'Not here. We'll chat in the car later, okay?'

I nodded meekly. 'I'd better go change.'

'Alright.' Theo caught my hand and squeezed it. 'Break a leg.'

'You too.'

The crowd roared. I cringed.

In the cage, Theo landed a taunting punch on Maddock, before dancing out of his reach. Theo was an excellent fighter. He'd learnt to be flexible and fleet-footed as a dancer, and he put it to use in the ring.

I just hated watching him. What if he got hurt? What if something went wrong?

He was practically my brother. The thought of him being injured made me feel physically sick.

Unfortunately, I was the only one in the crowd who felt that way. All around me, people were screaming and shouting, waving fistfuls of cash as they placed bets.

Things had hotted up; Theo was right. Having the military in town didn't seem to be deterring our usual crowd—in fact, I was pretty sure some of the soldiers were here, too.

So much for the mayor's elite force of peacekeepers. They were just as corrupt as the rest of our town.

Theo dodged a blow and managed to get inside Maddock's guard, landing a punch that had the slighter man stumbling. I swallowed hard, clenching my hands around the railing I was leaning against. I was on the edge of the circle, out of sight of the cage and Carlos. Carlos had been on a rampage all evening—he'd almost made Lisette cry earlier.

The metal railing was imprinting on my fingers. I loosened my grip.

Theo and Maddock rushed together and apart, both as fluid as dancers, ducking and weaving as they dodged blows and threw their own. Maddock landed a glancing blow on Theo's chest. Theo staggered, and Maddock pressed his advantage, driving Theo up against the side of the cage with a volley of fast punches.

My heart leapt into my throat.

I'd always considered Theo to be one of the best fighters in the Iron Fists.

Maddock was better.

For every punch Theo landed, Maddock landed two more. For every blow Theo dodged, Maddock had a new offensive prepared.

Theo crashed to the floor. All around, spectators were screaming. My breath came in quick, frantic pants as Theo rolled, grappling with Maddock.

'Hey kitten.'

I jumped and twisted around, my arm digging into the railing. 'Diego! Fuck!'

''Ello.' Diego Bartholomew smirked. He was a handsome man, tall, with brown skin and dark curly hair, but he was smarmy. I'd gone to school with him, and he'd never missed the chance to make fun of the poor girl.

But now I knew one of his secrets.

'How's your toy boy doing?' I asked.

'Fucking fantastic.' His expression contorted into something vicious and unpleasant. 'Yours doesn't look like he's doing too hot.'

'Who, Theo?' I asked airily, even as my stomach tensed in time with the roar of the crowd. 'He can handle himself.'

'Can he? Looks to me like he's struggling.' Diego leant back against the railing, idly slithering an arm around me. I pulled away and wrinkled my nose.

'Keep your hands to yourself.'

Diego tipped his head back, chuckling. 'Considering what you're wearing, you sure are touchy.'

'Even if I was on the market, you wouldn't make my list of potential bedfellows.'

Oops. The moment the words were out of my mouth, the double meaning registered.

A slow grin crawled over Diego's face. 'So you're off the market, eh?' He crowded closer to me. I could smell his sweat, his cologne. 'Who's the lucky guy?'

'No one you know.' I edged away.

'*Re-e-eally?*' he drawled. 'I know a *lot* of people. Such as… the lovely mistress of Reverie, who tells *such* interesting stories.'

A chill ran down my spine. Reverie was the brothel I'd extorted Rodney Rochester into helping me break into so I could eavesdrop on Jackson three weeks ago. All fine and well; the mission had been a success—one of the few I could boast about these days. I didn't really need repercussions to show up now.

'She shouldn't be gossiping about her clients.'

'You're not her client, kitten.' Diego stroked a finger over my arm, raising goosebumps and transferring my body glitter onto his skin. 'I was *very* interested to hear who you arrived with, though.'

'Fuck off.'

Diego laughed. 'Such attitude in the eyes of defeat. Oh well, maybe I should tell Bas you're hanging out with his brother in a brothel, then. See what he thinks of it.'

'He knows.' I bit the words out tersely. I had to nip this in the bud right now before Diego went digging into why I'd been in the brothel. I didn't need rumours spreading—or worse, for the truth to get back to the wrong people.

Diego side-eyed me. 'Well, well, well. You are a naughty girl, Harley. Playing the brothers off against one another?'

I made a face. *Gross.*

'As if I'd do that. Piss off.'

A roar rose up around us, obliterating my words. I turned back to the cage—I'd totally forgotten about the fight.

It was over. Maddock jumped up, offering a hand to Theo.

Theo had lost.

He looked as shocked as I felt. I couldn't remember the last time Theo had lost.

What the hell had happened in there?

Diego could wait. I pushed off the railing and elbowed my way between mingling fighters towards the cage. Theo climbed out—he looked well enough; at least Maddock hadn't hurt him. I reached him as he stepped down from the dais.

'Theo!'

He turned, lowering the towel he'd been using to wipe his forehead. A tired smile pulled up his lips.

'Hey, Harley.'

'What happened? Are you okay?' I started to hug him, then pulled back at the last second. If he was injured and I'd missed it, I didn't want to make it worse. Instead, I looked him up and down, searching between the myriad of tattoos on his torso for any sign of injury. Several bruises were blossoming, especially across his ribcage.

'Fine.' Theo rolled his shoulders and grimaced. 'Ugh. I'll live. Ego's definitely bruised, though. Who knew Maddock had it in him?'

Not me.

'Come here, idiot.' I tugged his arm to bring him closer and hugged him. Theo immediately grabbed my shoulders.

'Woah! I'm gross, Harley.'

'What do you think I am?' It wasn't as though I was any stranger to being all sweaty. I pulled back and giggled. 'I got body glitter on you.'

Theo glanced down and sniggered. 'Shit, Carlos will try and put me on stage.'

I snorted. 'Bet the crowd would love that.'

At that moment, I caught a flash of red-brown hair on the other side of the cage. Someone turning away hurriedly.

A specific someone whom I'd been hoping to speak to: Bas.

'You can tell me about the fight after my shift, alright? I gotta go.'

'What?' Theo turned to follow my gaze. 'Harley!'

'I want to speak to him.'

Theo groaned. 'Fine, but I'm coming, too.'

'Great!' I darted off, hurrying around the cage, and almost clocking Maddock in the chest.

'Hey—sorry—congrats,' I blurted out.

'Harley!' he called. 'I've been meaning to speak to you—'

'Later!'

Bas had seen me. He turned and vanished into the back rooms. *Ah-ah, buster. You're not getting away.*

I cleared the crowd and hastened into the hallway. Bas disappeared around the corner.

'BAS!' I shouted. 'WAIT!'

I rounded the corner and slammed straight into him.

'Oof!'

He grabbed my shoulder to steady me, staring stonily down at me. 'Harley.'

Bas cut a formidable figure. I always seemed to forget after not seeing him for a few days, like my brain was editing him to make him seem easier to handle.

But he wasn't. He was intensity personified: a tall, unyieldingly solid man, muscular and strong. His red-brown hair fell in his green eyes as he glared down at me.

'Why'd you run away?' I stepped back, suddenly needing space. I couldn't breathe when I was this close to him. His presence sucked all the air out of the narrow hallway.

'I didn't.' His gaze drifted over my shoulder, to Theo. 'Dunne.'

'Rochester.' Theo's tone was humorous and cutting at once. I'd never heard him sound that way before.

Bas grimaced. Turning back to me, he said, 'You shouldn't be here.'

'I work here.' I crossed my arms. 'Where else would I be?'

His lips twisted as though he was going to snap at me—then he turned away, frowning. 'It would be better if you laid low for now.'

'Laying low means not attracting attention. Disappearing from the job I allegedly desperately need in order to pay rent would not be laying low.'

Well, I actually did need it, because my emergency funds were almost nil. Not that Bas needed to know how much money I had. He thought—rightly—that I was here because I'd been spying on the Iron Fists for Evander Hardwick.

Bas scowled. 'It's like you want to get caught—'

'I don't!'

'Then why can't you just stay home, away from the gangs?'

Ooh, he was asking for trouble. '*And* we're back to you telling me what to do,' I said coldly.

Behind me, Theo snorted. I jolted around to glare at him. 'Don't you start.'

'I'm on your side.' He sauntered up and dropped an arm around my shoulders, smirking at Bas. 'Do explain why Harley should sit tight at home like a good girl whilst you go around getting all the glory.'

I loved him, but Theo was such a shit-stirrer. I pulled away from him.

'It's not about glory,' Bas snapped. 'It was about a successful operation.'

'Which she had no idea was taking place,' Theo pointed out.

'She should have trusted me!'

'*She* is right here!' I snapped. Both of them turned to me. I met Bas's gaze. 'And I don't trust you. I agreed to work with you, but that was it. Trust has to be earned.'

'I'm tired of jumping through hoops,' Bas snapped.

Oh, he was tired of jumping through hoops, was he? Bloody hypocrite.

'And *I'm* tired of being left in the dark. You owe me answers.'

'I don't owe you anything,' Bas snapped. 'If anything, *you* owe *me*—you blew the attack on Hannover—'

'No.' I got right up in his face, my arms crossed as I breathed heavily. 'You could have avoided that situation, too. You could have told me the truth. Instead, you made me chase after you, and then you kept secrets.'

'I didn't want you involved.'

'That wasn't your decision to make!' I snarled. 'It was mine!'

A hand touched my shoulder, but I shook it off.

'Harley,' Theo warned.

'Leave her,' Bas said, his eyes never leaving me. 'If she wants to make her bed, she can lie in it.'

'You're both acting like idiots.' Theo rolled his eyes. 'Anyone could walk around that corner at any moment. Sayle could walk around that corner! And Harley.' He turned to me. 'You're going to be a jobless idiot if you don't get back to work.'

He was right. *Shit.*

I turned to look at Bas. 'I'm not going to just hide at home.'

'Going after Hannover was my job. That was our original

agreement.'

'No, you going to the Black Hands' compound alone was our original agreement,' I said darkly. 'But you never intended to respect that agreement, just like you didn't respect me when I asked you to let me deal with Briggs—'

'He'd have got you killed!' Bas clenched his fists, then relaxed them and shook his head. 'I'm trying to help you.'

'Help me by working with me, or not at all,' I said. 'You decide. I'm going back to work.'

I pushed past both of them, glancing at Theo as I passed. He mouthed, *'Later.'*

Okay, then. I strolled back down the hallway, breathing slowly to try and centre myself. I danced better when I was emotional, but anger made me prone to injuries. Better not. Even if Bas did drive me nuts.

Bloody git.

How dare he be so—so—so caring?

That was the problem. I couldn't even be properly furious at him, because even though he was a totally arsehole about it, he actually cared.

I want to help you.

Briggs would have got you killed.

Damn him. Damn him for taking away my chance to solve my own problems. Damn him for lying to me.

Even if things were easier now.

Damn him.

'Harley!'

Loud footsteps hurtled down the hallway towards me, echoing off the concrete walls. I turned. Bas was jogging towards me.

'What?'

He stopped a few feet away and took a deep breath. 'I'm sorry.'

'What?' *What the fuck?* He was *apologising?*

'I should have been honest.' He avoided my gaze. 'About Hannover. It wasn't my intention to deceive you, but—I viewed working with you as personal, and dealing with Hannover as business. And... maybe I kept them too separate.'

I raised an eyebrow. It wasn't the first time Bas had mentioned keeping business and personal stuff separate, though the first time had been under... very different circumstances. 'So I'm personal?'

He nodded, still studying the walls as though they were fascinating.

'Always.'

'Uh… okay.' The moment felt profound, and all of a sudden my tongue felt clumsy. I had no idea what to say, how to say it. I stared at him, bereft of words, as the seconds ticked by. 'I…'

'Do you think this level of openness is wise so soon?' Footsteps echoing down the hall accompanied a gravelly voice that I recognised.

Jackson.

He had to be just around the corner. Bas tilted his head, then abruptly grabbed my arm and dragged me into a side corridor.

'What—'

'Shh,' he muttered.

We were in a little nook, half concealed behind a section of wall that jutted out. A half-height metal door had a warning sign on it. *High Voltage.*

Bas crowded close to me, blocking my view with his body. He was still holding my arm.

'What are you doing?' I whispered.

'The same thing you always do. Be quiet,' he hissed back.

I pressed my lips together. How did he manage to be so fucking infuriating? What the hell did this have to do with me? I didn't randomly drag people into dark corners and—

Oh, Bas, you dick.

He was remembering the time I'd eavesdropped on his conversation with Jackson. And sure enough, once I focused past my irritation, I could hear several sets of footsteps in the corridor.

'…hardly the moment for them to see our weakness,' an unfamiliar voice was saying.

'But we are weakened. We can hardly deny it.' Jackson sounded angry. 'If they took this opportunity to strike again—'

'None of them can spare the manpower.' The other voice sounded bored, almost. 'We've decimated them.'

'Hardly—'

'Enough.' The new voice sent a chill down my spine. Hardened by years of experience, it was the voice of a man who'd shoot you in the face without batting an eyelash. 'There's no need for bickering. We open our doors to our enemies and show them we are not afraid. That's the way of the Iron Fists.'

Sayle.

I swallowed hard. All of a sudden, Bas's presence beside me was less oppressive and more comforting. If I had to face Sayle, I'd rather have Bas by my side.

'And if they take the bait?' Jackson asked. 'After all, we took out several key players. There'll be people—a lot of them—who want revenge.'

'Then we'll be ready,' Sayle said simply, his voice fading as they moved out of earshot again. 'We are always ready.'

Their footsteps vanished slowly, and silence fell in the hallway. Other sounds filtered in that I'd been ignoring—the hum of the electrical box, the *thud-thud* of my heart, my erratic breathing. Bas's grip slipped off my arm, and I grabbed his hand.

'Wait.'

He froze, staring at me, his eyes dark in the low light.

'Harley?' He sounded confused.

'I…' I'd stopped him without thinking, and now I had to say something. 'What were they talking about?'

Bas frowned. 'The night of the strike on the distillery. Jackson sent out nine teams—we were one of them—to kill key members of the Aces and the Black Hands.'

That had been the plan? Holy shit. There was so much he hadn't told me, I wasn't even sure I had the strength to be angry anymore.

'Did the others succeed?'

'Some of them.'

Some. Not all. Which meant, hopefully, that my interference hadn't got Bas in trouble. And speaking of trouble…

'What about Briggs? Do… Does anyone know about that?'

'They know he's dead—I couldn't hide it.' Bas looked away, but he didn't pull his hand out of mine. 'We told them Hannover took him out. It was the best I could do on short notice.'

'And Ellery…' I wasn't sure how to ask, exactly.

'Ellery will go along with it.' Bas's voice was hoarse. 'He's not happy, but he will. We've known each other a long time.'

Did that mean they'd known each other before Bas had become a slave? I shelved the question for later; now, in this quiet moment in the dark, it didn't seem like the right time to ask.

'I am grateful,' I said. I laced our fingers together; I had to. My hands felt restless, and unease trickled down my back. I was out of my element. 'That you helped. Even if I don't like how you did it.'

'What happened with Briggs is on me,' Bas said. 'He was my teammate. And he got out of control. If you heard the way he talked about you…'

I shuddered. 'I think I can do without that.'

Bas nodded gravely. Then he tugged his hand away. 'You should get back to work.'

Moment over. Without warning, without reason.

I'd probably never understand why Bas did the things he did.

'Okay,' I muttered reluctantly. 'See you later?'

Bas nodded. 'Please keep your head down. I know you want to help, but don't make more problems.' His gaze beseeched me. I squirmed uncomfortably.

'I… I'll try.'

'Things are more precarious right now than you realise.'

'Yeah.' I gestured to the hallway where Sayle and Jackson had just been. 'I got that.'

Bas nodded again. We stood there, staring at one another, as the awkwardness grew.

'You should go,' he repeated.

'You're blocking my way,' I mumbled. His eyes went wide.

'Oh. Uh…' He backed up a step. 'Sorry.'

He turned and fled into the hallway, in the opposite direction to where I needed to go. I watched him leave, suppressing a laugh. Theo was right.

We were idiots.

THREE

THE NEXT COUPLE OF DAYS passed mercifully without incident, though I definitely dedicated more energy than was due to obsessing over Bas.

I'd held his hand.

Which shouldn't have felt like a milestone. And yet, there was an innocent teenage girl inside of me that was absolutely swooning. She kept remembering the look in his eyes, the way his brow had furrowed, how soft his hair had seemed in the low light.

How green his eyes were.

She kept wondering what it would be like to kiss him, too.

The adult part of me was more hesitant. Kissing Bas sounded like an extremely bad idea. Our acquaintanceship was so fragile that it would probably break us. I had a good idea that he wanted to—had probably considered it, at least. But what would happen? Could I kiss him? Could he kiss me?

I'd never felt quite that combination of hope, anxiety, anticipation, and fear before. It made me lightheaded and, strangely, seemed to fortify me against the everyday frustrations of my life. The price of food was less bothersome, my demonic landlady was less fear-inducing, and the military blockade was less irritating.

Even the frustrations of work seemed more tolerable that week.

On Tuesday I worked the morning shift so that I could have dinnertime off—I'd planned a farewell dinner for Maddock after work.

Walking home that afternoon, a weird feeling plagued me. I hated when people left town—we had no way of getting news from the other towns, with the exception of the occasional letter and gossip from travellers. This wasn't just goodbye, it was goodbye forever.

Saying goodbye *sucked*.

I picked up food at the market before heading home. At around six, Savannah let herself in, knocking her boots together to get the dust off. She meandered into the kitchen.

'Oh, you're cooking.'

'Mm-hmm.' I kept my gaze on the food I was chopping. 'Maddock's going to be here in a few minutes.'

'Maddock?'

'Yeah.' I tapped the knife against the board to get the bits of onion off the blade. 'He's leaving town. I invited him for a farewell dinner.'

'Oh.' I turned to see Savannah wearing a pensive look. 'He never mentioned anything.'

'He only told me about a week or so ago.' I shrugged. 'You know what he's like… cagey… tight-lipped.'

'I guess.' Savannah traced a line over the counter. 'How… how was work?'

'Fine. Just the same—we're still full up with the merchants.' I stirred the soup before adding, 'And you?'

'Just okay. Everyone's on edge, because of the soldiers, I think.'

'Have you heard anything about that?' I asked.

Savannah shook her head, still studying the counter. 'Have you?'

'No.'

'Oh, right. I'm going to go change.'

She beat a hasty retreat to the bedroom, leaving me to sweat it out in the kitchen. That had been weird. Did Savannah know something, or was she trying to figure out if I knew something? Frowning, I went back to chopping vegetables. I wanted Savannah as far away from the drama as possible.

A few minutes later, she reappeared.

'Need help?'

'You can set the table if you want.'

'Alright.' As she moved around the kitchen, Savannah asked, 'Is Maddock leaving for good?'

'Looks like it.'

'I always thought he'd stick around. He seemed like the type.'

'I guess.' I chewed my lip, a memory of a long-ago conversation popping into my head. In a way, Anna had been right when she'd said they never stayed. Maddock might have taken longer to leave, but he was still leaving.

I had just finished preparing the food when a knock sounded at the door.

'I'll get it.' Savannah hurried off, and a moment later I heard the door opening. 'Hello, James.'

'Hi, Savannah! Long time, no see.'

'Uh, yeah,' Savannah said tersely. 'Long time.'

Maddock made a questioning noise in his throat. 'Are you angry?'

'Yes!' Savannah cried. 'You never told me you were leaving.'

'I wanted to, but I haven't seen you.'

Savannah huffed. 'That's a terrible excuse.'

I bit my lip to suppress a laugh. Savannah was terrible at acting angry when she wasn't.

'I know. I'm sorry,' Maddock said in a contrite tone. 'I brought beer, though. To make up for it.'

I snorted under my breath.

'Well, alright then, I guess you can come in.' I heard Savannah shutting the door, and then they both crowded into the kitchenette with me.

'Hi, Harley,' Maddock said.

'Hey.' I shot him a smile, though my chest ached. Ugh, this had been a mistake. I hated saying goodbye.

'Here.' Maddock handed out beers to each of us. 'Chin up.' He offered me a quirky half smile and knocked his knuckles against my arm. 'It's nothing to cry about.'

'Losing a friend is always something to cry about,' I said.

'You're hardly losing me. I'll just be… a bit further away.' He smiled, oddly distant. As though he'd left already in spirit, even if his body was still here.

I shivered.

'Where will you go next?' I asked to change the topic.

'Back to Brackfields, for now.' Maddock leant against the counter and took a sip of his beer. 'I'll have to see where they want me after that.'

'It's a bit annoying that they haven't told you,' Savannah said. 'When are you leaving?'

'That's up in the air as well. As soon as they get the paperwork sorted, I suppose.' Maddock's gaze landed on the stove. 'Do you need help with the food?'

'No, it's almost done.' I waved him off as he reached for the pot.

'I feel bad,' he said. 'You've cooked for me twice, and I never returned the favour.'

'It's fine. That's just the way it turned out.' I picked up the spoon to check the soup. 'Besides, you brought the beer.'

'That I did.' Maddock laughed.

'And the company,' Savannah said.

We all smiled, but the good humour faded rapidly into an awkward silence.

'Let's not be sad,' Maddock said. 'I want this to be a nice evening.'

'It's just… we're going to miss you,' Savannah said.

'Yeah,' I agreed.

'I'll miss you too. But I want to leave with happy memories.' He held his beer out. Savannah clinked hers with his.

'To happy memories.'

They both looked at me. Reluctantly, I held out my drink. 'To happy memories,' I echoed.

It was drizzling on Friday when I headed to work, which made passing the blockade even more torturous. None of the taxi trucks wanted to waste time going through, so there was no possibility of driving to work. I had to walk.

As much as it hurt me, I had taken to leaving my nice knife behind and taking a cheap one with me instead. I'd rather temporarily downgrade my defences than let the soldiers confiscate my nice one. It was the best weapon I had ever owned.

Fortunately, I hadn't encountered the two jerks who'd tried to confiscate it again. Instead, Dusty and Bracknell, our regulars, had been there every day this week. As I approached, I could see them standing under a makeshift cover made of canvas and metal poles. They filled the entire space, so I had to stay out in the rain.

'Hello there, little lady.' Dusty was almost seven feet tall, with brown skin and close-cropped curly black hair. He was so big, his ankles and wrists poked out of his uniform a good few inches.

'Hello,' I said formally, stopping just out of reach. Dusty was polite enough, but I didn't like Bracknell. His lips were perpetually turned up in a sneer, and he got way too handsy when he frisked me.

'Open the coat,' Bracknell snapped. 'Arms out.'

I complied without argument. They might be the better option, but

I didn't want to find out the hard way how far they'd go to make my life difficult. Bracknell felt me down—and up—and down again, lingering on my chest.

'I doubt she has a gun in her bra,' Dusty said mildly.

Grunting, Bracknell dropped his hands. 'Just the one knife?'

I nodded.

'Fine. Go.'

Compared to last week, it was practically humane. I bade them a good day and hurried on my way.

The hotel was buzzing with activity when I arrived. Laura and Anna were both on; Laura was running back and forth between the storeroom and the first-floor rooms.

'What's going on?' I asked as I tied an apron around my waist.

'The mayor's doing a speech on the square at four,' Laura said. She avoided my gaze, talking to my shoulder, as she had been doing since our awkward conversation about my dad.

'Tom asked us to open up one of the private rooms,' Anna added.

'The mayor?' I asked.

'Tom thinks it'll be about the military.' Anna wiped her hands down nervously on her jeans. 'You know…'

'People are nervous,' Laura said. 'I'm surprised it's taken this long for him to speak up!'

'That would require being decisive and taking action,' I muttered sourly.

Anna snorted—an odd, sudden giggle. I glanced at her. She covered her mouth. 'Sorry. I just… Sorry.'

'It's okay,' I mumbled, baffled. Anna was acting strangely. 'So…' I turned to Laura. She'd never done a private sitting. 'Want me to show you where everything is?'

'Please,' she said with relief.

We decamped upstairs, where there was a narrow hallway of private lounges. A few of them had been temporarily converted into bedrooms for the staff, as Anna had mentioned. I chose the furthest one which hadn't been converted, a dark room with wood-panelled walls and cushy leather sofas that overlooked the square.

'Drinks are in here,' I said, opening a low cabinet. 'I'll grab another bottle of the top-shelf whiskey—they like it when we open a new bottle. Maybe bring up some ice, too, just in case. Do you mind dusting and opening the windows?'

Laura nodded.

The next hour we were all over the place. Tom came to check on us at a few minutes to three.

'Laura, I need you on the bar to take care of the security crew—no charge, they're on tab. Harley, you'll be up here.'

I nodded.

'Please make sure there's nothing blocking the hall. I noticed people have been storing things there.'

'I'm on it.'

I made several more trips back and forth before Tom deemed our preparations adequate, and by that point people were already swarming the lobby: a few officious-looking men and women in suits and a hoard of security officers in black who were canvassing the square and murmuring into handheld radios. Lou, the receptionist, looked quite harried trying to direct everyone to the right places.

Five minutes later, the mayor's car pulled up by the front steps, and he strode in along with three other men: Richard Godfrey, the owner of a major real estate company in town, was a tall, overweight man with curly blond hair. The second, I knew only by his last name, Rochester. Bas's father.

The man who had sold his illegitimate son into slavery.

A man I felt nothing but disdain for.

I twisted my fingers into my apron, fighting an irrational restlessness which came over me at the sight of him.

He was a broad-shouldered, strong man, with steel grey hair and the same green eyes as Bas. I couldn't help but see similarities between them, even though I knew Bas hated to be associated with his father.

Then the last man entered, and I actually took a half-step back in surprise. He was the oldest of the group, with thinning grey hair and a perpetual sneer on his lips. His posture was stiff and upright as he regarded the hotel lobby with open disgust.

And I knew him.

It was Alastair Dunne. Theo's father.

What's he doing here?

Of course, it wasn't that surprising. Like Rochester and Godfrey, he was one of the wealthy old men who flocked around the mayor. Closed-minded people who manipulated the common folk of the town like pawns on a chessboard for their own gain.

I had a particular gripe with Theo's father, though. He'd disowned Theo when he came out as gay.

Pathetic, small-minded bastard.

If he hadn't done that, Theo might never have joined the Iron Fists. He wouldn't have needed to. There should have been a better future out there for him.

Maybe there still would be. If, or when, we left.

Maybe we could make one together.

I shelved those thoughts as Tom stepped up to them. 'Good afternoon, gentlemen.'

A familiar man cut in from the side. 'Tom. Is the room ready?'

It was Evander Hardwick. I'd forgotten that the mayor's presence meant Hardwick would be here, too.

'Of course. Follow me, please.'

Tom turned and led them up the stairs. The mayor and his cronies followed, along with Hardwick, and I brought up the rear.

Evander Hardwick was the man who had forced me to spy on the Iron Fists. He worked for Percival, the leader of the Aces, and moonlighted as a member of the mayor's security, but I wasn't sure that was all there was to it.

His information was spotty, and he had relied on me to spy on the Iron Fists, even though I was obviously not the best choice.

Who was he really working for?

Tom held the door to the private room, ushering them in. 'Harley will prepare drinks for you—yes?' He tilted his head as Hardwick laid a hand on his arm, drawing him back a step.

Hardwick glanced my way. 'Is there anyone else who could serve us?' he asked in a low voice.

Tom cleared his throat, his tone coloured by confusion. 'Harley's the best.'

Hardwick's expression shuffled through a range of emotions—irritation, frustration, anger—before settling in a blank mask. 'Naturally.'

He stepped back. I hurried in and pulled out a fresh bottle of whiskey. 'Drinks, gentlemen?'

'Yes, yes.' Mayor Darling waved a hand impatiently. He was a squat, balding man who looked remarkably unimpressive in comparison to his companions. I had a sudden, profound impression of a child being humoured by the adults around him.

He clicked his fingers and the impression vanished. 'Ice, too.'

'Yes, sir.'

I poured four glasses, keeping half an ear on their conversation.

'I was surprised you chose to hold this so early,' Rochester was saying. 'Won't most of the citizens be at work?'

'I'm sure there'll be an adequate turnout,' the mayor dismissed. 'After all the changes—'

'Changes they resent,' Godfrey said.

'This is good for them,' the mayor said. 'They'll thank us eventually.'

'No one ever thanks people for making hard decisions,' Rochester replied. 'Yet they have to be made. Hurry up, girl.'

I ground my teeth as I scooped ice into the last glass. 'Sir.'

Turning, I transferred the glasses two-by-two onto the low table between them.

'Now go,' Rochester said. 'Wait in the hall. We'll call you if we need you.'

'Yes, sir.' Not like I had a job to do or anything. Sure, I'd just hang out in the hall like a dog waiting for scraps. *Why not?*

I shuffled out, hoping they'd talk more whilst I could still hear—but they didn't. The door shut behind me, and I found myself opposite Hardwick, who was lurking in the shadows of the hall.

'Harley Benoit,' he said.

'Hello, Hardwick.' I raised my chin and rolled my shoulders back. If he thought I was going to take crap from him, he had another thing coming. 'Thought you'd skipped town.'

He hadn't been there when I'd gone for my usual Tuesday evening meeting with him this week. Turner, the bartender at the Hawke and Tern, had told me to come again another night.

Hardwick raised an eyebrow. 'Why would I do that?'

I examined my fingernails. 'I went by the pub on Tuesday… you never showed.'

'I was otherwise occupied.' In the corner of my eye, Hardwick's expression twisted. Though he quickly masked it, his body language betrayed him; he was tense and frustrated. Something more was going on.

When I'd last seen Hardwick, he had been pressing me to find out information about the Iron Fists' plans for the upcoming strike on the whiskey distillery. The strike had gone ahead, and the Iron Fists had prevailed.

The information Bas had given me played across my mind—the Iron Fists hadn't just prevailed: they'd had their own plan. They had struck back.

Which meant they had a source of information that was much better than Hardwick's. And capabilities beyond the Aces.

Yeah, no wonder Hardwick was sweating right now.

I leant against the wall. 'Nice day, isn't it?'

His eyes narrowed. 'What are you playing at now, Miss Benoit?'

'Me? I'm at work. What are you playing at?'

He glared. I grinned. 'Do you know what they're discussing in there?'

'Nothing for your ears.'

'Why? Afraid I'll tell the Iron Fists?'

'Precisely,' he said flatly. 'You are not as good a spy as you think you are.'

'That's funny—because I seem to recall you needed me to get into Reverie. And I did it.' I raised an eyebrow. 'Unless you've had any complaints?'

His expression contorted with anger. 'You mind yourself—'

The door to the private lounge crashed open. Hardwick stood at attention, and I straightened as well.

'You, girl.' Richard Godfrey gestured to me dismissively. 'Get your boss.'

'Yes, sir.'

He retreated, the door slamming behind him. I hurried downstairs and found Tom in the lobby, tense and alert.

'Harley? Why aren't you upstairs?'

'They sent me to get you,' I said, breathing hard.

'Ah. Very well.' He heaved a sigh and set off. I trailed after him. At the private room, Tom knocked smartly and entered.

He stepped inside. I took up my spot opposite Hardwick again.

'Were your services insufficient?' he asked.

'You tell me. Don't you work for them?'

Hardwick pressed his lips together. 'You're overstepping,' he said coolly. 'Percival is not happy with your work, and neither am I.'

Uh-huh. No one enjoyed having to defer to their boss's authority— unless they were afraid their own authority wasn't up to the task. And

Hardwick seemed like a man who was afraid.

'Aren't you in trouble with your cronies, then?' I asked. 'You didn't get them the information they needed, and the Iron Fists still have the distillery.'

Hardwick took a sharp step towards me. I stared him down, unwilling to back off.

'Mind your tongue.'

'Or what? You didn't take care of Briggs either—I'm starting to think you don't have the power you claim you do.'

Hardwick's cheeks were flushed; he looked furious. He opened his mouth, but the door opened abruptly and interrupted him again.

'As you wish, naturally.' Tom strode out, wiping his hands down on his brown wool trousers. 'I'll notify my staff.'

'Good.' Godfrey was cold as he exited behind Tom. 'Let's get started.'

I glanced askance at Tom as the mayor and the others exited. 'Shall I clean up?'

'Not yet, not yet.' Tom gestured for me to precede him down the hall. 'I need all the staff in the bar. Announcement—right now, if you please.'

'Okay.' A glance at his face told me this was urgent. I hurried to the stairs, thoughts tumbling around my head.

A staff announcement? Now? Why would Tom hold a staff announcement whilst the mayor was here?

And what the hell about?

The hotel ran like a well-oiled machine most days; Tom rarely had to get involved in the day-to-day operations.

I started in the kitchen, then the laundry room, and by the time I doubled back to the bar most of the staff were already there. I squeezed in between Anna and Laura over by the window.

'Do you know what's going on?' Anna whispered.

I shook my head. 'Just that Tom spoke to the mayor.'

'Oh, but...' She reached out and grabbed my hand, squeezing it tightly.

'It's fine,' I muttered. 'I bet it has to do with the speech.'

'Thank you all for coming.' Tom strode up behind the bar. 'Sorry to take you away from your duties. It won't be for long.'

He cleared his throat, his eyes moving slowly around the room as the whispers hushed. 'As you all know, the mayor is about to give a speech on the square. He has asked us all to attend as, ah, a show of support.'

Was it my imagination, or did he look a little sheepish?

Why?

'What do we want to do that for?' Bella called. She was one of the cleaners, a brash woman who always spoke her mind.

'Yeah!' someone else added. 'It's the mayor's fault we gotta go through the damn blockades every day!'

Several other people were nodding.

Tom cleared his throat. 'I understand there may be mixed feelings about the blockade.' He regarded us with an empathetic smile. 'The mayor will be explaining his decisions in the speech, which will be taking place in five minutes.'

He consulted his watch.

'Shall we head out together?'

'Are you going?' Laura whispered.

I nodded. How could I not? I couldn't pass up the opportunity to find out what the mayor was planning.

'I guess we have to,' Anna mumbled. 'Seeing as Tom is asking us to.'

By the conflicted expression on his face, I doubted he would enforce his request. Still, I shuffled towards the door along with Anna and Laura. A decent portion of the rest of the two dozen or so staff members also went, though some of them looked reluctant. Bella and a few others marched back around the bar.

Tom joined us at the door.

'Shall we find out what they have in store for us?'

That was a pretty odd comment—but before I could question it, he was already leading the way through the lobby and down the stairs.

The area immediately in front of the hotel was thrumming with security people, though the mayor was still inside. As for the crowd…

There wasn't much of one.

A smattering of people had turned up: a few homeless guys who were probably hoping for handouts, a couple of workers who'd got off shift and were obviously on their way to the bar for a drink, and a smattering of older people who'd probably turned up out of boredom.

A fantastic showing all round.

Anna, Laura, and I huddled together to protect ourselves against the wind and rain. A few minutes later, the mayor stepped out, Hardwick holding an umbrella over his head.

Lucky bastard.

Someone handed the mayor a microphone. He cleared his throat, the sound echoing shrilly through the speakers.

'Ladies and gentlemen.' His voice was thready. 'Thank you for coming.' He stood up straighter, slowly finding his stride. 'I'm sure you are all aware there have been changes in town recently. For too long, you've laboured—' His eyes flicked sideways, and he seemed to lose his nerve for a moment.

I followed his gaze. Godfrey, hands in pockets, was leaning against the railing wall at the foot of the stairs.

Mayor Darling cleared his throat. 'As I was saying, for too long you've laboured under the oppressive influence of the gangs in our town. Too long!'

He looked around expectantly. A few people hollered.

Silence fell.

'Well, no longer.' The mayor hunched his shoulders. Beside Hardwick, he looked small and unimpressive. 'With the help of the army, it's time to fight back, weed out the influence of the gangs, and assert law and order!'

Someone coughed. Somewhere in front of me, a baby was crying.

The mayor continued, his voice rising and falling. My attention waned. As much as I wanted to listen, it just wasn't interesting. Politics went over my head on the best of days.

If only Theo were here.

He'd get it. He'd make fun of the mayor with me, have a laugh at how stupid and inept he was…

Clap… clap… clap…

I jumped. A couple of people were clapping. Gradually the rest of the crowd cottoned on and applauded as well. The mayor was retreating inside.

Was it over? Already?

We'd barely been out here five minutes.

'What a waste of time,' Benny drawled up ahead. The staff were slowly starting to move, trudging towards the hotel.

'Did he say anything important?' I asked Anna.

'Weren't you listening?' she chided.

I shrugged.

'Not really,' Laura said. She grimaced in my direction. 'A lot of nothing, but the army's here to stay.'

'Great,' I muttered.

There was a bottleneck at the doors. I dropped back behind the other women and found myself next to Tom. He had an odd look on his weathered face—pensive and worried.

'Law and order, indeed,' Tom murmured.

I glanced at him in surprise. Tom was strictly apolitical; he went to great lengths to keep all of the gangs and the mayor happy. And he'd always seemed to enjoy doing it, even though it was stressful as hell for the rest of us to constantly have gang members in the bar.

And yet…

Now he didn't look too happy.

'What's wrong?' I asked.

Tom blinked and glanced at me, as though only just realising I was there.

'Nothing,' he said. 'When you get to a certain age, men with guns start all looking the same, no matter the badge on their jackets.'

'I don't think that comes with age,' I muttered. 'They all look the same to me, too.'

Tom shot me a warm look and patted my shoulder. I stared at him, gobsmacked.

'That's a healthy attitude to have,' he said. 'It'll serve you well. Anyway.' He sighed and pushed his shirt sleeves up. 'Back to the grindstone, eh?'

'Yeah.'

He ushered me back to the bar with a friendly, grandfatherly smile, but it did nothing to wash away the rocks that had settled in my stomach.

It wasn't just me; even Tom saw things for how they really were.

The mayor had finally made his move.

And the military was here to stay.

FOUR

'ALRIGHT, BOYS. PUT 'ER THERE!'

'WOO!'

'YEAH, BOY!'

Shouts and cries rose up around the bar as the merchants clinked their glasses together before downing their pints as though alcohol were an infinite resource. I leant against the bar, exhaustion settling into my bones.

Last night.

It had been such a big deal, and now it was over. Tomorrow morning, the merchants would move on to Crater's Edge. And we would be left alone to survive the winter.

It wasn't even that far to Crater's Edge—a hundred and twenty miles or so—but most days that felt like half a world away.

'Chin up,' Laura said. 'At least they made it here, and we managed to get everything we needed. It could have gone a lot worse.'

'Wish they hadn't brought the fecking army with them,' Dana muttered under her breath. She, like Kayla and me, lived outside the barricade and had to deal with being hassled every day.

I bit my tongue. I knew the full story, but I hadn't told anyone—the less you knew, the less trouble you could get in with the soldiers. They were looking for co-conspirators to the gangs, and I didn't want any of my colleagues attracting their notice.

So I held onto my secrets.

Over by the window, a table full of grizzled old men began waving. 'Next round!'

'Ugh. Duty calls.' Dana rolled her eyes. 'I'll get this one.'

She sashayed out from behind the bar. I followed her, heading to the wall where we had three brave tables of people who weren't associated with the merchants' market. I was surprised they'd stuck it out so long, what with the racket engulfing the room.

'Refill, folks?' I asked, leaning my hip against one table.

'Ta.' A man held out his glass. I paused in surprise, almost slopping water out of my jug when I recognised Dusty, one of the soldiers who manned the barricade on Prospect Avenue.

'Hello,' I said cautiously.

'I've seen you before, right?' He winked.

'Yes, you work on Prospect Avenue,' I said drily. I finished pouring his glass and leant over to fill the one belonging to the man next to him. 'You frisk me at lunchtime every day.'

'Ooooh,' the other guys all crowed. One of them drummed his hands on the table.

'Didn't know you had such a way with the ladies, Dust-man.' His neighbour smirked.

Dusty grimaced sheepishly. 'Ey, ey, just doing my job,' he said. He toasted me with his water glass. 'No hard feelings, right?'

'Course not.' I bit my lip coyly. 'Can I get you gents any more drinks?'

'Another whiskey for me,' said a man with a friendly smile, dark brown hair, and tattoos visible beneath the open collar of his jacket.

'Same,' Dusty said, leaning back in his seat and stretching his long legs out. His colleagues all nodded.

'Four whiskeys?' I asked.

'Please,' Dusty said.

'Alright, I'll be right back.'

'Before you go...' The speaker was one of Dusty's colleagues; he leant in, a smarmy smile on his lips, his blue eyes boring into me.

I paused, biting the inside of my cheek. Nothing good could come of that wheedling tone, that persuasive smile. 'Yes?'

'You seem like the sort of lady who knows what's going on around town.'

Uh oh. 'I'm sorry, I'm really not.' I shuffled my weight, hoping they'd take the hint and let me leave.

'You sure? There'd be money in it for you.' He rested an elbow against the table. 'We're not asking for much—we just want to know if you've heard of any deserters around town.'

'I don't need money,' I said firmly. I had to resist the urge to fidget. 'And I don't spend time with deserters. I don't want any trouble.'

'Then it'd be in your best interest to help us out with this one.' Dusty's friend smirked. 'He's the sort who likes trouble, especially with the ladies. Handsome guy — tall and freckly. Red hair. Nice blue eyes. I reckon you'd know him if you see him.'

'I'm sorry,' I said in a wobbly voice. My heart seemed to be beating far too fast. 'I know several people who fit that description, but I don't think any of them are deserters.'

Dusty's friend's eyes bored into me. I didn't think he believed me. I took a steadying breath and stiffened my shoulders.

'Well, you let us know if you do think of anyone,' he said.

'I don't want to be involved in anything like that,' I replied.

'You watch yourself, girlie. It's amazing how trouble can find the wrong people some days.'

His eyes were blue, blue, blue. I felt sick. That was a threat. Definitely.

'I'll bear that in mind,' I said unsteadily. 'Thanks.'

I turned and hurried away, my fingers trembling against the tray I was clutching.

I was pretty sure I knew exactly who he was talking about. Tall, freckly, red hair, blue eyes. Military deserter tattoo in pride of place on his chest.

It was Greg Talbot.

Savannah's boyfriend.

Thoughts of Greg Talbot plagued my mind that evening as I walked to meet Theo.

I did not like Talbot. He was crude, mean, and unpleasant. Savannah could do way better than him — I didn't understand what she saw in him at all, in fact. Not to mention, he was a member of the Aces, the gang run by Percival who ruled the casinos in the west of the town. He definitely wasn't good company for my sensible, kind-hearted sister.

On the other hand, I didn't want anything to do with the army. They were no better than the gangs, really: men with guns throwing their weight around and disrupting our lives. At least the gangs were from around here — the military recruited from all over the region. The soldiers had no loyalty to Bale Rocks.

And they'd threatened me.

Passing information to them wasn't high on my priority list.

No, it was better to leave it alone.

I passed through the checkpoint to the north under suspicious looks. They relented once they searched my bag and found my dance gear, the two soldiers exchanging smirks.

They thought I was a whore, and that made me worthless in their eyes.

Well, that was fine. If it kept me safe, they could think whatever the hell they wanted of me.

Theo was waiting at our prearranged spot by the barbershop, tapping his fingers impatiently against his steering wheel.

He had his own car back.

'You got your car fixed!' I cried excitedly as I threw the door open.

He turned to me, a small but sincere smile curling up his lips. 'Feels good to have her back.' He stroked the leather steering wheel.

'I bet.'

'Greene even cleaned it for me and fixed up the paint job. I don't think it's looked this good since I got it.'

'Not with the abuse you put it through.'

Theo snorted and reached over to tug a lock of my hair. 'Bitch.'

'Yeah. Your point is?'

We both laughed. I shut my door, and Theo steered us out onto the road. 'So. The merchants are leaving in the morning?'

I nodded. 'You should have seen them in the bar tonight. They were downing ale like it was water.'

'Glad I'm not driving with them.' Theo grinned.

'Me too.' My stomach churned at the thought of Theo leaving again. He was a runner for the gang—one of the people who drove to and from the neighbouring towns and cities, liaising with the gangs there, ensuring supply routes, and stealing supplies.

It was a dangerous job. Between the slavers in the wasteland, law enforcement in the cities, and the rival gangs, there was no shortage of people trying to kill you out there. I hated every time Theo left, and the longer he was gone, the more afraid I got.

'When are you leaving again?' I asked in a small voice.

Theo rolled his shoulders. 'Sayle hasn't said. For now, he's keeping us all here, just in case. But I'm sure he'll send one of us out soon. We have to consolidate our position if we want to keep the Aces and Black Hands on the back foot.'

Whoever controlled the trade controlled the town. It was why the Iron Fists had fought for the distillery—one of the main sources of exports for our town. As long as they could keep the main supply route from Crater's Edge under their control, they could keep the power.

But the mayor and the other gangs wouldn't stop fighting for it—and the Black Hands controlled the supply route from Brackfields, in the south. So the Iron Fists weren't the only power around.

I bit my lip. 'I hope they send someone else.'

'I'm the best.' Theo put his hand on my knee, squeezing gently. 'When I go, you can come with me.'

'Mm,' I mumbled noncommittally.

Theo wanted me to leave.

I didn't know.

We didn't have to decide yet.

I leant against the window, watching the deserted streets slide by. Tall brick houses, subdivided into flats, lined either side of the road, their walls blackened with coal soot and crater dust, the windows boarded up. Our town looked more desolate by the day now that winter was upon us.

I sat up straight abruptly. 'Oh, there was something I needed to tell you.'

'What?' Theo asked urgently.

'Nothing bad. Well…' I shook my head. 'Did you hear about the mayor's speech on the square the other day?'

'Yes. We snuck Kade and Tyler in.'

Kade I knew. He was on the same team as Ellery, Bas, and Briggs—not that I was thinking about Briggs. Kade was an unassuming guy, with a surprisingly gentle nature, considering he worked as an enforcer for the Iron Fists.

'Who's Tyler?'

'New guy. He's young, but promising.' Theo shrugged. 'Same old story. No money, dead parents, needs somewhere to go, didn't mind selling drugs on the streets to work his way up.'

It wasn't just the same old story; it was Theo's story—except for the dead parents, of course.

'Anyway, what did you want to tell me?' Theo asked.

'I saw your dad.'

Theo hissed through his teeth. 'Motherfucker. With the mayor?'

'Yep. They had a super-secret meeting beforehand. In one of the private rooms upstairs. Hardwick was there, too.'

'Should have known.' Theo shook his head. 'My dad always did have his head up the mayor's arse. Did he recognise you? Or say anything?'

'No. Why would he recognise me?' I snorted bitterly. 'No one pays attention to their server.'

'I pay attention to you.'

'Yeah, well you're nice.' I rolled my eyes. 'I didn't hear their conversation. I tried, but they kicked me out of the room sharpish.'

'They're wising up.' Theo flicked his lights to full beam as we left the residential area. 'They know someone leaked their plan to attack the distillery to the Iron Fists, so they're retreating.'

I chewed my lip. I wasn't arrogant enough to think that they suspected me. In any case, the meagre information I had provided to Bas, Ellery, and Theo wasn't enough to be considered leaking their plan. The question was, who was it?

'Do you know who found out?' I asked.

'No.' Theo shrugged. 'Someone high up. Multiple people, maybe? We get information from a lot of places. But it was Jackson who hatched our entire plan.'

'Jackson's in contact with the mayor's office,' I said. 'He met with a guy named Malcolm Brady. Hardwick had me listen in.'

Theo shot me a sharp look. 'When was that?'

'Couple of weeks ago. The night you broke into my apartment. Sorry, it got lost amongst everything else.'

I'd had such a confusing few weeks; some days I still felt like I couldn't breathe for the stress.

Theo clucked his tongue. 'I'll look into it. Does anyone else—'

'—know? Yeah, Bas,' I said darkly.

Theo groaned, just like I'd known he would. 'That guy. Honestly, Harley.'

'Don't start.'

'I won't,' Theo said. 'But for the record, I'd have chosen literally anyone else over him.'

'Like who?' I asked spitefully. 'Briggs?'

Theo sighed. 'Not Briggs. Okay, fine. Fine. It's your life, it's your choice. So, what's the plan? Are you going to date him? Marry him?

Have sex with him? Wait, does he even do sex? I can't imagine it at all.'

'Piss off!' I swatted his arm. 'No, no, no.'

'No?' Theo asked incredulously. 'What, you're planning on pining after him for the next sixty years?'

'What? No!'

Theo laughed. 'Harley, babe, you need to get out of your own head. Either you like him or you don't.'

A weird feeling overcame me, somewhat like how I imagined a cat felt if you stroked it backwards. *Rubbed up the wrong way.* I thought a lot about Bas, but I had never actually imagined us going any further. We seemed trapped in our strange love-hate relationship, forever doomed to circle one another and throw punches and never get close.

'I told him about my mum.'

Theo sighed. 'Yeah, you got it bad.'

That didn't sit well with me at all. I turned to stare out the window, the darkness lit only by the occasional light in a farmhouse window. For all I pretended to be experienced when I flirted with people, I had never been in a relationship before. And somehow I doubted Bas had either. We were two idiots flailing in the dark.

Which, when I thought about it, was what he'd been trying to tell me all along.

Oops.

After a few minutes of driving in silence, we reached the train station. As Theo parked, he said in a low voice, 'By the way, I looked into Hardwick.'

'And?'

'Are you sure he works with the Aces? Because my contact didn't know anything much about him.'

I frowned. 'I met with him and Percival together. At the Lucky 2089 casino.'

'Huh.' Theo drummed his fingers against the steering wheel. 'I'll ask around again.'

'He's friends with the bartender of the Hawke and Tern,' I added.

'Really?' Theo reached for his door. 'That's interesting. I always thought Turner preferred to stay neutral.'

'Maybe friends is the wrong word.' I climbed out and Theo and I started towards the depot. 'Acquaintances?'

'Maybe I should have a chat with him,' Theo mused.

We dropped the subject as we entered the depot, where the Iron Fists had a security guard posted. Alex Greene—an old neighbour of mine from childhood and the guy who had fixed up Theo's car—grinned as we approached.

'Yo, Theo. How's the car going?'

'Good as new.' Theo bumped fists with him. 'Can't wait to give it a good run down to Langford.'

'Just mind you don't get caught in any shootouts this time,' Greene joked.

'Cross my heart.' Theo patted his chest before heading for the ladder. 'See you later?'

'Nah, I'm off soon.'

Greene waved us through, winking at me as I passed.

Once we were out of earshot, I glanced at Theo. The low emergency lighting cast strange shadows across his face. 'Are you okay?' I asked.

'Fine.' Theo reached out and grabbed my hand. 'We're going to be okay.' He laced our fingers together. 'Things are going to get better. Sayle has a plan.'

'When the gangs make plans, things get worse,' I muttered.

'The problem is there's too many groups vying for power,' Theo said. 'If we can thin out the ranks…'

'More death.'

'I know.' He squeezed my hand. 'But you and I will be okay. My car's fixed. Pack a bag for yourself—and Sav, if you want. Be ready to go. I know places we can hide.'

What scared me worse? Staying and watching the life I understood crumble? Or leaving and facing the unknown?

I swallowed.

'Where will we go?'

Up ahead, I could see the weapons check. Theo slowed his stride.

'I know people in Langford. You're talented and you work hard; Sav will be in high demand. Between the three of us, we can make a life.'

I'd have to leave Bas behind.

I swallowed again. 'Okay. Keep me updated though, alright?' I shot him a brave smile. 'I don't like not knowing.'

'I know.' Theo wrapped his arm around my shoulders. 'Keep your chin up.'

'You too.'

The crowd was significantly more energetic this weekend than it had been last weekend. It was also the first time that I really felt like I was getting my form back after the injury which had been bothering me. I could ignore the occasional twinge in my abdomen, so long as I stuck to more conservative moves. The pink scar was easily hidden under my leotard now that I had taken the bandages off.

The tips flowed steadily for the first half of my shift, ebbing as the fights ramped up and drew attention away from the dancers.

When my break came, I climbed off the stage and found Posy waiting for me. 'Do you want to go upstairs and watch the next fight? Looks like Diego's going to be on.'

'Sure.' I arched my back to stretch out the muscles. 'Just let me nip to the toilet.'

'Alright, but be quick!'

I nodded. We headed into the back rooms together; in the main hallway, I left Posy scrambling up the ladder and headed deeper into the warren of tunnels towards the toilets. As I turned the corner, someone jogged up behind me.

'Harley!'

I turned: it was Maddock.

'Hey…' I stared at him. 'What are you doing back here?'

It was strictly staff and members of the Iron Fists only back here.

Maddock stopped in front of me and straightened his shirt. 'Can I talk to you?'

'Uhhh…' I frowned. 'I mean, sure, but I don't think you should be back here. How'd you even get back here?'

'Slipped past the floor manager when he wasn't looking.' Maddock shot me a wry smile. 'He has the peripheral vision of a raging bull.'

'Raging bull' was a pretty good description of Carlos all round. I chewed my lip. 'Let's go back out on the floor. I'll sit with you.'

'I…' Maddock shuffled his weight. 'I was hoping we could talk in private.'

There wasn't much more private than a crowded room—I'd worked in the hotel bar long enough to have learnt that. Crowds made a hell of a noise, which could cover a multitude of sins.

If Maddock wanted to speak in private, then it must really be important.

Which meant, unfortunately, that I couldn't tell him no.

'We can probably find an empty room somewhere,' I said carefully. 'One of the storerooms.'

'What about your dressing room?' Maddock suggested. 'Or are the other dancers on break at the moment?'

'I don't think so.' I rolled the idea around in my mind. Posy was out on the floor, and I'd seen Jana, Suzy, and Tina out there, too. 'I guess it's as good as any.'

'If you don't mind,' Maddock said, staring at his feet.

'Alright.'

I led the way deeper into the maze of hallways that comprised the innards of the bunker. We passed a couple of people, most of them techies who paid us no mind, and finally reached the sturdy metal door that led to my dressing room—a largish, boxy room with tables around the outside and a cupboard where we stored extra dance costumes and towels. I held the door for Maddock and shut it behind us.

'So… what did you want to talk about?'

Maddock strode deeper into the room, skimming his fingers over the metal tables.

'Do you know the history of the bunker?' he asked suddenly.

'Not really.' I shrugged. 'I know it was built before the Crash. And I know Sayle took it over when he moved into town and got it working again.'

'Did you know it has more than one floor?'

'Really?' I frowned, thinking about it. A lot of the tunnels were sealed off. 'I guess it's possible. But what does that have to do with anything?'

I glanced at the door. Posy was waiting for me, and I didn't want to waste my entire break back here.

'Everything, really.' Maddock turned back to me, a smile on his face. A shiver of anxiety ran down my spine. There was something odd in his gaze; the fluorescent lights cast sinister shadows over his face. 'For example, the tunnels are much further-reaching than most people realise. This place has so much potential, and Sayle wastes it—' His voice had grown higher and higher. He cut himself off, sucking in a deep breath, before continuing in a lower tone. '—wastes it on partying.'

'I think it's a bit more than that.' I grabbed the door handle. 'Look, if you don't have anything to discuss with me, then I have to get back before I'm missed. I don't want to lose my job.'

'Not yet.'

I turned back to him with a frown. Maddock was tracing his fingers over my dressing table. He lifted them to his face, rubbing them together. 'I wanted to apologise.'

I could count on one hand the number of times men had apologised to me. My first instinct was scepticism—what did he want from me?

'Uh huh?' I asked slowly.

'You were my first friend in this town.' Maddock dropped his hand, wiping his palms on his trousers. 'Unexpectedly.'

I crossed my arms. 'Such an accolade.'

'I mean it.' Maddock frowned. 'Look, I know things have been… up and down. But I wanted to apologise for involving you in the first place. I wish… I wish things had gone differently.'

What the hell was he on about?

Conversations with Maddock were an exercise in mental gymnastics.

'Look, I'm glad you consider me a friend. But as I've said before, I'm responsible for my own life. I don't need you apologising for how things went.' I bit the inside of my cheek, before adding, 'And I'm glad I got to know you—sorry you're leaving.'

'Yeah…' Maddock scuffed his feet. We stood in silence for several seconds.

'Is there anything else?' I prompted. I was being obnoxious, but I was honestly sick of the weirdness. 'When are you leaving?'

'Soon.' Maddock's gaze drifted back to the row of dressing tables. 'Alright. I should get going. I just wanted to clear the air between us.'

'Great.' I turned back to the door. 'Let's get back to the main hall before you're caught.'

'I'm afraid I didn't mean we'd be leaving together.'

Fear whispered down my spine. I twisted the door handle and yanked the door open, seized by a sudden urge to run.

Maddock was faster. He grabbed my shoulder and his other hand closed around my arm in a punishing grip.

'Get off!' I twisted, yanking my arm up, but his grip held. What the fuck was he doing?

'I'm sorry, Harley. I can't risk you going back and warning anyone.'

'I don't understand—' I jerked a step back, wrenching out of his grip, but Maddock caught my forearm and twisted. I kicked his knee. He shoved me hard, and I staggered—and in that second, he managed to grab my arm in one hand and a handful of my hair in the other, pushing me up against the wall. It was cold against my skin.

'This is for your own good.'

'Fuck you! You're supposed to be my friend!' I writhed desperately, my scalp burning as he pulled my hair. 'What the fuck?'

'It's because we're friends that I'm doing this,' Maddock said. 'You'll forgive me one day. I'm sorry.'

He released my hair and dragged my other arm up, holding them together. I thrashed against him, but I couldn't get any leverage with my arms trapped. Maddock grunted and muttered something, then I felt a prick in my neck.

The world began to swim.

'What the hell?'

I squirmed. Maddock released me and I spun around to face him, but the action threw me off balance. The ground rushed up to meet me—and he threw his arms around me, lowering me gently to the floor.

'I'm sorry.' He stroked my hair. 'Goodnight.'

The world went dark.

FIVE

'HARLEY? HARLEY!'

Someone was shaking me insistently. I tried to wriggle away, but my body wouldn't respond. I tried to tell them to stop, but all that came out was a groan.

'Harley!'

It was dark, and my head was throbbing. 'Nghhh.'

'You need to wake up!'

I opened my eyes a crack, trying to push away the incessant hands. 'Gerroff. Nghhh. Bas?'

My voice came out as a hoarse croak. I had to squint against the bright fluorescents.

Bas crouched over me, so close I could smell his sweat.

'Harley, wake up,' he repeated insistently.

''M awake,' I muttered. 'Stop shaking me.'

He dropped his hands. 'Sorry. You were—' Pause. 'You didn't come back to the stage. Carlos was worried.'

I laughed. The sound promptly dissolved into a coughing fit. I rolled on my side, groaning. 'Urgh. Ah. Water,' I managed. 'Please.'

Bas shot to his feet, hurrying to the makeshift commode where we kept a jug of water. I hauled myself upright. I was on the floor of my dressing room. Nothing was out of place—no, that was wrong. My things had been thrown around as though someone had searched through them. My underwear and shirt were strewn on the floor.

'What happened?' I croaked.

'That's my question.' Bas crouched down in front of me and pressed a glass into my hands. I drank greedily, draining it in one go.

'I don't remember.' I fiddled with the glass. My mind was fuzzy; I could barely keep my eyes open. 'What… what time is it?'

'Half two.'

'My break is over…' That felt important somehow. A second later, it hit me. 'Maddock! I was talking with Maddock, and—and—fuck, I don't remember!' I glanced around, but he was nowhere to be seen. 'Where the fuck is he?'

'*Maddock?*' Bas demanded. 'What were you doing with him?'

'He said he wanted to talk.' I strained to remember, but my mind was as blank and shadowy as the wasteland by night. 'I... I don't remember anything. How... What...'

My chest felt tight, and my throat seemed to close up. I couldn't breathe. 'I—' I sucked in a breath. 'He—'

'Hey.' Bas's hands landed on my shoulders—his face was right in front of mine. 'Harley, calm down.'

His voice was steady, his grip was firm. I grabbed his T-shirt, wrapping it around my fingers as I matched my breathing to his. 'Okay. I'm okay.'

'Take a moment.'

Bas's torso was warm underneath his shirt. His fingers rubbed gentle circles on my shoulder blades.

I let go, turning my head away. My cheeks felt hot with embarrassment. 'I'm fine now.'

Bas drew back a little. 'What do you remember?'

'Maddock wanted to talk to me. He was in the hall.' I screwed my eyes shut, trying to think past the pounding in my head. 'I brought him here—well, I must have, but I don't remember. I think we talked... I don't remember what he said. Damnit!'

'It'll come back,' Bas said. 'You don't have any injuries. He must have drugged you.'

'Yes!' I clapped a hand to my neck at the phantom pinching sensation. 'He injected me—that fucking bastard!'

I shot to my feet. The whole world tilted on its side as bile rose in my throat and black spots played football across my vision.

'Harley!'

Bas sprang up and grabbed me before I plummeted to the ground.

'Woah.' He helped me to a chair. 'Here, sit.'

'Ugh.' I swallowed desperately so I wouldn't puke on his feet.

'Here.' Bas passed me another glass of water. 'Drink.'

I took the glass, but my hands were so weak I couldn't grip it. Bas helped me put it to my mouth, and I took a few cooling sips.

'Fuck,' I mumbled when he lowered it. 'Urgh. I have the worst taste in my mouth.'

'It'll pass.' Bas stroked my hair back from my face. 'How long were you on break before you saw Maddock?'

'Not long, I don't think.'

'And you spoke, and then he drugged you.' Bas glanced around. 'I never saw him back in the hall.'

Why would he come back here just to leave again, anyway? Why drug me? I picked up the water glass, and this time my hands were steadier as I sipped it.

'He wanted something back here.' My gaze settled on my dressing table. 'He's gone through my stuff.'

Bas turned to look. He strode over to the dressing table and crouched down. I stood unsteadily, fighting another wave of dizziness, and stumbled after him, watching as he picked through my belongings: towel, makeup cloths, clothes. He laid it all out.

'Is anything missing?'

'I don't think so.' I nudged the edge of a towel with my toe. The glitter had rubbed off the pair of heels I was wearing. I glanced at the dressing table, frowning.

If he hadn't taken anything, then what the hell did he want? There was nothing valuable in here. I leant against the table, exhaustion washing over me.

'Could he have gone somewhere else in the tunnels?' I asked tiredly.

'Not from this side,' Bas said. 'All of the passageways are sealed off over here. For security.'

'Yeah.' I straightened up and rubbed my temples.

And paused.

I brought my hand down so I could look at it.

Dust.

Covering my fingers and palm where I'd touched the table. It was all over the table, too.

But not the neighbouring tables.

Dust.

'Oh fuck,' I whispered.

'What?' Bas asked urgently, standing up.

'The crawlspace.'

'What?'

I yanked the chair out and used it to climb on the table.

'Harley!' Bas yelped. 'You'll fall!'

'I know where he went.' I reached up over my head and shoved at the false ceiling panel. It came loose, and I manoeuvred it to the side, revealing the entrance to the crawlspace. I looked at Bas—he looked shell-shocked.

'What is that?'

'It's where all the pipes and cooling systems and stuff are,' I said impatiently. 'C'mon, we have to get up here and see where he went.'

I reached for the edge, then looked down at myself—I was still wearing my dance gear. 'Shit, I better change.'

There were all sorts of nasties up there: spiders, sharp edges, exposed cables, the works.

I clambered off the table, losing my balance at the last minute. Bas stopped me from eating concrete.

'You need to sit,' he said flatly, helping me into a chair. I tried to pull away, but he pushed me down relentlessly.

'Don't you want to know where Maddock went?'

'I'll radio it in.' He reached for his belt and stopped short—he was wearing casual clothes. 'Fuck.'

'We can go up and look. Just let me change.'

'You change.' Bas raked a hand through his hair. 'I'm going to go and get my radio. Do not go up there without me.'

'But—'

'Harley, Maddock drugged you!' Bas hissed, his gaze wild. I flinched back, my insides tensing.

'Alright, alright. I'll stay put.' I wasn't sure I could climb up there on my own, anyway. All the moving about had made me nauseous, not that I planned on telling Bas that.

'Get dressed. As soon as I've taken a look, I'm driving you home. You can't dance anymore tonight.'

'My shift ends at four anyway,' I muttered.

Bas shot me a *don't do anything stupid* look and stalked to the door. I waited until he was gone, before toeing off my heels and stripping my booty shorts off.

He had no right to criticise me, anyway. It wasn't as though he was the master of strategic thinking, either. And he wouldn't have known where Maddock had gone if it weren't for me.

But what the hell did Maddock want in the crawlspace?

Ugh, if only I could *remember.* But the more I thought back, the harder my head throbbed, until my stomach churned and I had to give up and put my head against the cold metal of Jana's dressing table.

I felt like I'd been run over by a truck.

After a few moments, I forced myself back into action. With slow, careful movements, I managed to dress myself and lace up my boots. I tied my hair back and wiped off the worst of my makeup. When I looked in the mirror, my reflection was barely human: my tan skin had an unhealthy pallor, sweat shone on my brow, and my hair was an unholy mess.

Knock-knock.

'Come in,' I called. Bas peeped cautiously around the door, before straightening up and striding in. He'd changed into his uniform and had his radio in hand. As he shut the door, Ellery's voice came over the speaker.

'No sign of him in the main hall; weapons check hasn't seen him. Can you get into the crawlspace?'

'I'm checking now. Mobilise teams into the peripheral tunnels.'

'Copy,' Ellery replied.

Bas clipped the radio back to his belt and stopped beside me. 'How much space is there up there?'

'About four feet.'

His lips twisted. He eyed the hole in the ceiling with extreme reluctance, before pulling the chair closer and climbing onto the table. It wobbled in protest.

Bas clicked his torch on and shone it inside, then set it on the lip and put his hands over the edge. In a single, extremely enviable move, he hauled himself up and straightened his arms, then wiggled his body through the gap. A few thuds and rustles drifted down to me before he was out of sight.

'This is where you listened in on my conversation with Jackson from?' he called.

'What?' It took me a second to remember the time Bas had got in trouble for beating up Hannover. 'Oh. Yeah. If you follow the really big pipe, it will bring you to the main hallway.'

I heard shuffling and muffled footsteps. Was he leaving me behind?

'Hey, wait for me!'

Bas's torchlight reappeared. 'No, stay there.'

'No way! I'm coming with you!' As I scrambled up onto the table, Bas's face appeared in the gap and he glared down at me.

'I'm not helping you up here. Stay down there.'

'Like fuck I need your help.'

I jumped and grabbed the edge. A wave of dizziness washed over me, and I squeezed my eyes shut, braced my legs against the wall, and clung on for dear life. It receded slowly. When I opened my eyes, Bas was frowning.

'Harley, you need to rest.'

'Move, or I'll kick you.' I walked my feet up the wall. My boots made it harder—the soles refused to grip the smooth wall, but finally, I managed to get my legs over the lip. I pushed myself the rest of the way up, my arms shaking from the effort, and sat beside Bas. 'See? No help needed.'

'Go back.'

'You could pretend to be a bit impressed,' I muttered.

'We have more important things to worry about,' Bas reminded me. He shone the torch around the space, illuminating decades of dust and an assortment of paraphernalia. 'What is all this stuff?'

'One of the dancers from years ago, Cindy, used to steal things and hide them up here. Carlos caught her and fired her, so she never came back for any of it.' I picked up a little baggie filled with white powder. The plastic disintegrated in my fingers, and the powder fluttered over my hand. 'Ugh, gross.'

I wiped it off on my trousers.

'Careful,' Bas said. 'I don't need you getting high on top of whatever Maddock gave you.'

I pursed my lips at him. 'Give me the torch.'

He tightened his grip. 'No.'

'Oi, come on. I want to see where Maddock went.' I scowled at Bas. His every muscle was tense, his knuckles white where he was clutching the torch. He looked like he wanted to be anywhere but here.

Oh.

Ohhhh.

Bas was claustrophobic.

Oh, fuck. I hadn't seen that coming. No wonder.

'Okay, keep it, just shine it around. Before we stir up all the dust.'

Bas turned his face away from me, but not before I caught a hint of shame in his gaze. Then he was engulfed in darkness as he directed the light away from us and onto the floor.

The dust was so thick it resembled a carpet in some places, but my prediction was right—we'd stirred it up so any tracks were invisible. I mentally compiled our options—Maddock was smaller than Bas, almost as small as me, which meant he could get to the same places I could. Either around the large mains pipe or under a wooden box attached to the ceiling, which I assumed concealed the electric cables. The mains pipe led towards the hall.

'Shine the torch over here,' I muttered, shuffling towards the low-hanging box.

'Don't get stuck,' Bas said.

'I should be fine.' I lowered myself onto my belly, grimacing as a plume of dust went up my nose. I pulled my shirt up to cover the bottom half of my face and wiggled forwards. 'Torch?'

'Sorry.' I heard Bas shifting around, and then the torch illuminated the space in front of me. Beyond the box, I could make out indistinct bootprints in the dust.

'Someone's been back here.'

Bas shifted closer, crouching down beside me. 'Do you know what's back there?'

I shook my head. 'Shine the torch under, I'll check.'

I wiggled further forwards and managed to get my whole body under the box. Two metal poles, bolted to the floor to support the box, bracketed me in. I got my fingers around a ridge in the floor and pulled myself through.

'Careful,' Bas said in a low voice.

'It's fine.' I managed to lift my head on the other side. Bas grabbed my ankle.

'Don't go any further.'

'There's a wall, and it looks like there's another room on the other side.' I kicked my foot. 'Bas, get off.'

'No. Let's go back.'

Ugh was he for real? I wiggled my way back until I could sit up next to him. 'I can get through there.'

'And if you get stuck? Or pass out? *I* can't get through there.'

Under the torchlight, Bas looked strangely old. His eyes were deep and shadowed.

'Alright, alright,' I muttered, crawling back to the open ceiling panel. 'Still. I didn't realise there was anything on that side.'

Mine was the last dressing room in the hallway. There was nothing beyond it except a dead end—so why would the crawlspace extend in that direction?

Bas thumbed through a pile of ancient cigarettes. 'I'm not sure. I'll have to get back to the compound and report this. Can you get down on your own?'

'I'm not a kid.'

'I know.' He scowled and shuffled closer, hovering as I lowered myself down. My arms gave out most of the way down and I crashed onto the table, sending the mirror tumbling to the floor, where it shattered with a tinkling of glass.

'Oops,' I muttered.

'Well done,' Bas said patronisingly. 'Mind so I can get down.'

I climbed onto the floor on wobbly legs, glass crunching under my boots. My cheeks burnt.

How was it that Bas always made me feel like a child? Why couldn't I be as capable around him as I was in all other aspects of my life? I handled rowdy customers perfectly. I cooked and cleaned and paid my rent on time. I had friendships. I was a functional human being.

But around Bas, I only ever managed to show my worst side.

He hopped down next to me, the table groaning in protest, then climbed down onto the ground.

'Alright?' he asked.

'Not going to mock me again?'

Bas sighed. 'I'll drive you home after I've called this in. Let's go.'

Scowling, I repacked my stuff. My stomach twinged in protest as I picked up my bag.

Motherfucking Briggs and his stupid knife.

Who was dead. I bit my cheek, suppressing an odd swirl of emotion. I was supposed to be *happy*.

I was *supposed* to be happy.

I zipped my coat up and turned to Bas. He held the door expectantly. 'Let's go.'

'You sure you don't want me to find out where Maddock went?' I asked.

'I'm sure.' He held his radio up and gestured with his head towards the hall.

We fell into step with one another, and Bas hit the call button.

'Ellery, come in.'

The radio sputtered a little, as though the connection wasn't good.

Finally, Ellery replied, 'Ellery here. What did you find?'

'Looks like he got into the ceiling, but I can't follow. Do you know what's behind the dressing rooms on the north side?'

'Harley's dressing room? Isn't that the end of the hall?'

'It was sealed,' Bas said. 'Why'd they seal it?'

'Search me. What would the guy even want up there? Isn't it just pipes and shit?'

'You can get through to other rooms,' I said. Bas shot me a glare and I shut my mouth.

Dick.

'We'd better mobilise a search—Fuck. Break, break, break.' Ellery vanished. The silence was deafening. It stretched and stretched and stretched, filled only with our slow footsteps.

My slow footsteps. I was struggling.

One foot in front of the other.

'Bas?'

'Copy,' Bas said.

'Intruder alert just sounded in the compound.'

'Maddock?'

'Who knows? Just get to—Break, break, break.'

He was gone again.

And back. 'Mobilising a team to main tunnel. What's your exit point?'

'Station,' Bas said tersely.

'Fine. You can take that side. No one in or out until we have more information.'

'Copy,' Bas said. 'And Harley?'

'Keep her with you until we know more.'

'Hey!' I snarled. I wasn't a parcel to be handed around. 'I can take care of myself.'

'Harley,' Bas warned. He hit the call button again. 'Copy. Heading for station tunnel now. Out.'

He shoved the radio back onto his belt.

'Don't do that,' I protested.

'Harley,' Bas groaned. 'Please, please let me figure this out. I'll give you my car key and you can sleep in the back.'

Sleep through the action? Was he high?

Grinding my teeth together, I sped up my stride. Bas kept pace effortlessly. 'You need to rest.'

'I need to be able to decide what I'm capable of.'

'Okay.' I glanced at him. He was agreeing with me? The hell? He shot me a pointed look. 'You can stay with me.'

'Just like that?' I asked suspiciously.

'If you're with me, you can't go running after Maddock on your own.'

For fuck's sake.

'I'm not going to run after him. I just feel—'

'—like it's your responsibility. Yes.' Bas wrapped his hand around the strap of my bag and pulled it away from me, transferring it to his shoulder so smoothly that I didn't have a chance to stop him. 'I know.'

'Hey!'

He laughed.

He actually bloody laughed.

I could count on one hand the times I'd seen him laugh and—

'*Don't* laugh at me!'

Bas's face straightened out, though I could still see the beginnings of a smile at the corners of his lips. 'Don't be silly, Harley. Maddock's dangerous, and this is beyond your skillset—'

'I'm perfectly capable—'

'—of plenty of things, yes.' His eyes bored into me. 'But not of chasing down an intruder when you're barely keeping yourself upright. You need to learn your limits.'

Why did he have to be so fucking right all the time?

Also, why was he looking at me like that? So… so affectionately. He had to stop doing that—it was making it hard for me to get him out of my head.

'You are so annoying,' I muttered. 'I'm not sitting in the car like a little kid.'

'You can stay in the depot, then.'

We turned onto the main tunnel that led out to the train station. At that moment, Bas's radio came to life, a loud tone blaring around the metal hallway.

'What is that?' I hissed.

Bas's expression had frozen. 'Emergency alert.'

The warning tone repeated and then went silent.

'All channels, stand by.'

That wasn't Ellery's voice. It was someone else.

'Sayle is dead. Repeat, Sayle is dead.'

Bas slowed his pace. For a second, his face mirrored the horror in my heart. Then it shut down, all emotion draining away. Over the radio, someone asked, 'How?'

Through the buzzing white noise in my head, I heard the response. 'Shot. James Maddock shot him.'

SIX

WE WERE NOT SUPPOSED TO bring weapons into the bunker.

That was my first thought, my second, my third. It bounced around in my head. My walk slowed to a halt, and I stood there, paralysed.

After long, long seconds, Bas turned to me.

'Did you know?'

My mouth dropped open. I shook my head frantically. 'Of course not!'

He opened his mouth. Shut it. Opened it again. 'Good. Let's go.'

He believed me!

My knees felt weak with relief. I pressed a hand against the wall to keep myself upright. 'Go where?'

Bas raised a finger to tell me to wait a moment, then hit the call button on his radio again. 'Ellery, come in.'

'Copy.'

'Next steps?'

There was a long moment of silence, before Ellery responded, 'Unknown. It's chaos here. Where are you?'

'Still in the bunker.'

'Can you double round?'

'Negative.' Bas paused, glancing at me. 'I'm going to check out Maddock's flat.'

'Good call. I'll meet you there.'

'No, you need to shut down communication lines. Make sure the news doesn't get out to the other gangs. Get Kade on it, too.'

'Copy. See you later.'

'You too. Good luck.'

Ellery echoed the sentiment and ended the transmission. Bas clipped the radio back to his belt.

'We're going to Maddock's place?' I asked.

'I'm taking you home. Then I'm going to Maddock's flat.' Bas turned and started striding down the hall.

'What? Why?' I stumbled after him, my footsteps ringing out in the wide tunnel. 'I want to help.'

'You were at the scene of the crime, Harley,' Bas said impatiently. 'You need to get home and lay low before someone finds out that Maddock used your dressing room to get into the compound.'

My jaw dropped. I slowed my stride, staring at his back, as shock and horror raced through me like a tornado.

I hadn't even considered that angle.

What if someone thought I'd helped Maddock? What if they thought I'd done it voluntarily?

I sped up again, practically jogging to keep pace with Bas. 'But I didn't want this to happen! You believe me, right?' My voice sounded pitiful to my own ears.

'Yes,' Bas said. 'But not everyone will.'

I swallowed at that thought. We walked the rest of the way in silence, though I was awash in the sound of my own heartbeat, like a war drum in my ears.

If they thought I had helped Maddock, they would kill me.

Had Maddock known that? Had they caught him? Would he give me up? What if he got away? Would he leave me here to take the fall?

What would we find at his flat?

We didn't take the usual exit into the train depot to get out of the tunnels. Instead, about a hundred feet before it, Bas opened a panel that almost blended into the wall. Behind it was a narrow hallway which turned to run parallel to the main tunnel. We walked for several hundred yards before reaching a ladder to a small, round hatch.

'Escape hatch,' Bas murmured. 'I'll go first.'

He climbed the ladder and heaved the lid out of the way. Outside was pitch black. Bas exited, then reappeared, holding out a hand to me. 'Come on.'

My head swam, and my body felt heavy, but I managed to climb high enough to grab his hand. Bas helped me the rest of the way up.

We'd exited further down the train tracks. By mutual agreement, neither of us switched our torches on. Instead, we navigated our way over the tracks and down the embankment by moonlight. At the bottom, we walked the last few dozen yards until we reached the gravel parking area and Bas's car.

I had a thousand questions running through my head that I wanted to ask, but once we were in the car the heat combined with my woozy head took me out for the count. I roused a bit when we passed from the dirt track onto tarmac, then drifted off again, and the next thing I knew, Bas was patting me on the shoulder.

'Wake up, Harley.'

We were at my building.

A huge yawn stretched my jaw. I groaned, covering it with my hand. 'Sorry. What's going to happen now?'

'Now you're going to go to bed,' Bas said sternly. 'Sleep it off. Go to work tomorrow. See if you can stay with any of your colleagues inside the barricade.'

'Tom will let me stay at the hotel,' I said, recalling his offer.

'Good. If you're inside the barricade, they won't be able to get at you, even if they do realise you were involved.'

'But I'll be trapped.' The obvious problem presented itself immediately. 'And Savannah will be outside the barricade, and vulnerable if they decide to use her to get to me. No way.' I shook my head.

Bas sighed. 'Can you let me handle your sister?'

'No!'

'Harley…' Bas let out a noise of frustration. 'Now is not the time to be stubborn!'

'She's my sister!' She was the last family member I had left in the world, and she meant *everything* to me. 'Besides, she won't trust you. She doesn't know you.'

Bas twisted his fingers into his hair. 'I can't worry about you and her *and* heading off an investigation,' he said. 'If you could please just take care of your own safety—'

I shook my head.

'Fine! Then let's speak to your sister now,' Bas said. 'Come on.'

Savannah would love being woken up in the middle of the night by Bas. I suppressed a smirk at the thought. 'Fine.'

We ascended the stairs to my flat. The whole building was dark and silent, but when I unlocked and opened my door, I flicked the light switch and found that the electricity was back on. Small mercies. I motioned for Bas to wait in the main room and headed back to the bedroom to wake Savannah.

She wasn't there.

The door was open, her bed was empty, and her bag was missing.

'Fuck,' I whispered. Of all the nights for her to pick to spend with Talbot.

'Harley?'

I whirled around with a gasp. Bas had followed me and was standing in the doorway.

'How do you move so quietly?' I hissed.

'Where is she?'

'Probably with Talbot.' I grimaced. 'That guy is the fucking bane of my existence.'

Bas's jaw tensed. 'In that case we go with my plan. Go to bed, tomorrow go to work, and then stay in the barricade.'

'No.'

'Harley, I don't have time to argue with you.'

I crossed my arms. 'Do you even know which flat Maddock lives in?'

Bas hesitated. 'First floor.'

'There are two flats on the first floor.'

We stared at each other. I poured all of my determination into my gaze. I was tired of him trying to ditch me. Either we worked together or not at all.

'Fine,' Bas said. 'Come on.'

He turned and marched to the front door. I pumped my fists in triumph, then hurried after him.

We headed back down to the first floor.

'That's the one,' I whispered, gesturing to Maddock's door.

Bas gave it a calculating look for several seconds.

'I have pins. I might be able to pick the lock,' I suggested hesitantly.

'No need.' Bas stepped forward, lifted his leg, and slammed his foot against the door, just beside the lock.

Crash!

The door held fast, but I could see the wood splintering. Two more hard kicks did it in. Bas's momentum carried him forwards, and he almost went tumbling through the broken door.

'Shit,' I mumbled. 'Okay, then.'

My door was the same design as that one. Could it be broken just as easily?

The thought made me shudder.

Bas shoved the broken door open and entered the flat. There was a narrow hallway with three doors off it. I opened the one on the right: kitchen. Beyond that was a bathroom, and opposite was the bedroom. At the end of the hall, it opened up to a tiny living room.

You couldn't swing a polecat in here. I felt claustrophobic just standing in the living room, my knees bumping the sofa on one side and the coffee table on the other.

Apart from the furniture, there was nothing there: the walls were bare, the cupboards were empty.

'He's cleared it out,' Bas said grimly.

'This was planned,' I mumbled. Patchy memories were beginning to come back to me. 'He said something about… No, that's not right.'

I sat heavily on the sofa, staring at the uncovered window opposite me.

'He must have been planning this all along,' I said. 'A few weeks ago he told me his company was pulling him out. But that must have been a lie, made up so that no one would question why he disappeared.'

'Makes sense.' Bas paced down the hall, checking the other rooms again. I heard him moving furniture and contemplated doing the same, but there didn't seem to be any strength left in my body.

'You need sleep.'

I jumped. Bas was standing over me.

'I'm fine.'

'You were asleep, weren't you?' He rolled his eyes. 'Go upstairs, Harley. I'll look for your sister.'

I bit my lip. 'I think we should fetch her tonight. I can't just… I can't just leave her to get in trouble.'

'You can't exactly walk up to the Aces and ask to see her.'

'*You* can't,' I muttered. 'But I might be able to.'

Bas frowned. 'What—'

His radio buzzed. He unclipped it and lifted it to his face as Ellery's voice came over, urgent and terse. 'Bas? Come in, Bas.'

'Copy,' Bas said, turning away from me to look out the window at the street below.

'Where are you?'

'Maddock's flat. But there's nothing here.'

'Copy,' Ellery said slowly. 'This isn't about Maddock. Are you alone?'

Bas turned back to face me. Dread settled over me like a blanket, and my heart sank to take up residence somewhere around the basement. His expression was unreadable.

'Why?' Bas asked.

'Just answer.'

'I'm with Harley.'

A staticky buzz carried over the radio. Then: 'You need to get her out of town. Now.'

'Why? What's going on?' Bas turned back to the window, this time with urgency. I gripped the edge of the sofa, my breath suddenly feeling short.

'Carlos saw her with Maddock in the backrooms. Jackson has put a mark on her—he wants her brought in for questioning. There's a team on the way to her place.'

Where we were. I jumped to my feet.

'Who?' Bas asked tersely.

That's not important! I thought in a panic.

'Matthews, Jenkins, Russel. Just left.'

That gave us twenty minutes, maybe half an hour because of the detours.

'Copy.' Bas dropped his radio back to his belt and turned to meet my gaze. 'Now will you leave?'

'I…' I couldn't think all of a sudden. Thoughts raced around my brain, tumbling over each other, too fast for me to grasp any of them. Bas put a hand on my shoulder and steered me to the door.

'Do you have anyone you can stay with?'

'Not now! I can't leave Savannah.'

'You don't have time to fetch her. Jackson isn't going to give you the benefit of the doubt, Harley.'

'She's my sister.' We reached the stairs. I stumbled, almost falling. Bas gripped my arm, keeping me upright.

'You have an appalling level of concern for someone who doesn't care about you at all.'

'She's my sister!' I repeated, clenching my fists. 'Just because you hate your brother—'

'Don't bring my family into this,' Bas said through gritted teeth. 'I'm trying to save your *life.*'

His words left me dizzy. I pulled away from him and started up the stairs. 'I can't just leave my sister.'

'She's safe where she is; no one's going to storm the Aces' compound to get to her. *You* are the vulnerable one right now.' Bas stomped after me. 'Pack your things and let's go.'

'Go where?' I cried. I was practically running now, the staircase blurring from the tears in my eyes. My stomach roiled like a leaf caught in a storm.

'I know a place.' Bas caught up to me when I stopped at my door. He took my arms, turning me around. 'We can lay low overnight and work out a plan in the morning.'

'Okay,' I gasped. 'Okay.'

'You have five minutes.'

I nodded. I felt helpless. I'd looked after myself for years, but now the rug had been pulled out from under my feet, and I was flailing. I didn't know what to do next. But Bas knew. Bas was calm and steady.

I could listen to Bas.

So I listened. I went to my room and threw a few changes of clothes into my bag. I fished out my knife and gun and strapped them on. I wrapped a scarf around my head to hide my face.

'Ready?' he asked when I reentered the main room.

I nodded.

'Let's go.'

SEVEN

THE DRIVE OUT OF TOWN was silent and strange. Every mile that we travelled made me feel worse. It was as if I'd left an integral piece of myself behind, and the further we travelled, the more the two halves strained to reunite.

Savannah.

I'd left Savannah behind.

I had never been without my twin. Sure, we'd fought. We'd disagreed. She'd threatened to move out dozens of times. Once, she had left to spend a year on residency in Crater's Edge.

But she had come back. She'd always come back.

We were constants in each other's lives. We looked after each other. When I had no one else left to rely on, Savannah was there. As antagonistic and idealistic and… everything as she usually was.

My twin sister.

The one person I knew better than I knew myself.

I'd left her to face the dangers alone.

I was too wired to sleep, but Bas was focused on driving, so all that was left for me to do was peer out into the darkness. We had taken the south-easterly road out of the city, after a lengthy drive around the blockaded centre. In this direction, there was mostly farmland, which eventually petered out into nothingness. The land on either side of the road was empty and dark.

We were further from Bale Rocks than I had ever been before in my life.

A metal sign appeared out of nowhere, illuminated by the headlights. It was so rusted, I couldn't make out much more than a round disk with a red line around the outside.

Bas slowed the car and turned off the main road.

I grabbed the overhead handle, nerves twisting like snakes in my stomach.

Where were we going?

'Bas?' I whispered. The darkness seemed to press in on me; I felt very small all of a sudden.

'What?'

'Where are we going?'

'To a safehouse. It's not far.'

'Oh.' I leant back into my seat, gazing anxiously out the window.

Driving into the wastelands was eerie. The road Bas was following was ancient, and so dilapidated that it was little more than strips of asphalt amidst weeds and gravel. Bushes and scraggly trees pressed in on us from either side, stunted and scrawny, their limbs like hands reaching out to grab us. Twice, I saw a dead tree so white it looked like bone in the headlights.

We seemed to drive for miles and miles, through an ever-thickening tangle of trees. I must have dozed off eventually, because I woke up when the car stopped. I had a crick in my neck, and my shoulder ached from sleeping hunched over. The headlights illuminated a ramshackle two-storey house. It had a wrap-around porch with a broken roof, and the whole place carried a general air of neglect. Flaking paint, sagging steps. Several of the downstairs windows were boarded up. The house sat in a tiny clearing. The trees seemed to have been cut back by humans, but they were threatening to reclaim their territory, their limbs reaching for the house.

'Where the fuck are we?' I muttered.

'Somewhere safe,' Bas said tersely.

'Doesn't feel like it.'

'Would you rather take your chances with Jackson?'

I bit my lip. *Not really.* But on the other hand, *yes.* If it meant Savannah was safe.

'I don't know,' I mumbled.

'Come on.' Bas cut the ignition and opened his door, and I squinted as the light in the car came on. My head throbbed.

Grabbing my bag, I clambered out as well, stumbling on the uneven ground. Without the headlights of the car to see by, I had to feel my way in the almost total darkness. Bas reached the front door first; I heard him opening it and stepping inside, his boots heavy on the wooden floorboards. A light flicked on inside.

'Be careful, the steps are rotten,' Bas warned.

I climbed them daintily and crossed the porch, entering the house.

It was basic but surprisingly functional. I had expected it to be fully abandoned, with torn furniture, mouse droppings, and a bird's nest or two. Instead, there was old, mismatched furniture—all functional— and the kitchen turned out to be stocked with all sorts of food.

Bas headed back out to the car. I pulled my torch out of my bag and used it to illuminate my way up to the first floor. There was a bathroom—with running water—and two bedrooms. I was in the process of picking through the cupboards in one of them when I heard Bas approaching.

'What are you doing?'

The cupboards were full of all sorts of mismatched clothes, most of them truly ancient: tattered blouses with ghastly floral patterns, jeans with more holes than fabric, discoloured underwear.

'Looking around,' I said. 'What is all this stuff?'

'Clothes.'

'Yes, I can see that. But why's it here? Who does this place belong to?'

'No one.'

I frowned at Bas. 'Are you being deliberately obtuse?'

Bas scowled. 'It's a halfway house. There's an—maybe 'organisation' is the wrong word—a group of people who help slaves escape. This is a safe place for them to stay the night.'

'Oh.' Suddenly, the clothes made sense. Slaves would come in with nothing but the clothes on their backs—and maybe not even that. 'Did you use this place?'

Bas's expression darkened. 'Yes.'

'Oh.'

'I don't want to talk about it.'

I nodded and turned away, carefully shutting the cupboard. I could respect that. After a moment's consideration, I said, 'We probably shouldn't take anything we don't need.'

'I have a few things. But we'll need to eat.' Bas's voice was gruff with concealed emotion. I didn't try to read into it—he deserved dignity, especially after everything I'd put him through. Especially considering he was still helping me.

'Let's take stock of what we've got,' I suggested.

'We can do that in the morning,' Bas said curtly. 'Go sleep.'

I hated being ordered around, even if I was tired. But also, I felt too anxious to even consider sleeping.

'Shouldn't we keep watch?' I asked hesitantly. 'I can go first—I mean, I've already slept, kind of.'

'Don't be ridiculous,' Bas said.

'What? I'm perfectly capable of keeping watch!' I said indignantly.

'The drugs are still in your system. *I* will keep watch whilst *you* sleep them off.'

'You have to drive in the morning.'

'We won't be leaving in the morning,' Bas replied. 'It'll be safer for us to travel by night.'

'Fine.' I crossed my arms. 'But you have to let me keep watch tomorrow.'

Bas pursed his lips.

'I insist,' I said.

'Fine. We'll share watches.' He pointed to the other door. 'Now go sleep.'

I grinned in victory. There was no reason to be so happy—we were fucked to high hell and back. And yet, I'd talked him down. I'd got him to agree to equal shifts.

'Stop smirking,' he snapped.

'Alright.' I forced my lips to behave. 'Goodnight, Bas.'

'…Night,' he muttered.

I opened the door. Inside was a dusty but functional bedroom. The bed was a mattress on the floor.

'There are blankets in the cupboard,' Bas said. 'The bathroom is the next door along.'

I nodded, still studying the room. I was picturing Bas staying there on his first night of freedom. He must have been so scared. Scared, but hopeful.

Hope could be a terrifying thing.

But he'd made it, and so would I.

'Bas?' I turned back to him. Bas looked up from his bag. 'Thanks for helping me.'

He scowled. 'Go to sleep, Harley.'

Smiling to myself, I retreated into the bedroom.

I jerked out of a restless sleep, my heart pounding as my dreams slipped away. I'd been running.

Maybe.

The images faded too fast for me to keep hold of them. I opened my eyes, squinting around. The room was dark and shadowy, and the sky was bruise-purple outside the curtainless window. Something had woken me, but what?

I pushed away the nest of blankets and squirmed off the mattress. Crouching, I crept to the window and peered out. The wasteland beyond was like a sea of ink: empty blackness, with the occasional darker shape sticking out. Here a broken wall, there a jagged dead tree. Nothing stirred.

Maybe I'd heard an animal howling? There were foxes—and sometimes larger predators—in the wastelands. Coyotes. And smaller animals like rabbits. Cats by the dozens and feral dogs.

It was probably nothing.

I forced myself to turn away. I'd check on Bas, see how the watch was coming along. Make sure he was awake. He had to be tired, too. Maybe I could take over early—

The door opened a crack. I froze.

'Harley?' Bas whispered.

My heart leapt into my throat. 'Bas,' I choked. 'You scared me.'

'You're awake.' He opened the door enough to slip through. 'I thought you'd be sleeping.'

'I was, but I think an animal must have woken me or something.' I gestured to the window.

Bas shook his head. 'There's someone out there.'

My heart skipped a beat—then lurched into double-time. They couldn't have found us. No. Not yet.

'How do you know?' I whispered.

'I saw headlights,' Bas murmured. In the darkness, I couldn't discern his expression.

'I—I thought you said no one knew this place?'

'A few people do.' Bas hooked his thumbs through his belt loops, his expression grim. 'I just didn't think any of them would be after you.'

I swallowed. 'You didn't think to warn me—'

'Can we argue about this later?' Bas's face was pale and worried in the low light. 'Find somewhere to hide.'

'No.'

'Harley—'

'I can help!'

'Harley, will you please—'

Bang! Bang! Bang!

We both froze as the loud knocking cut through the silence of the wasteland. I stared at Bas, hardly able to breathe around my heart in my throat. 'Was that…' I whispered.

'Stay here.' Bas pulled his gun and flicked the safety off. I followed him to the door and watched as he descended the stairs. What did I do?

My gun!

I darted back into the room and picked it up off the chair, my hands shaking. I'd never used it, even though Bas had given it to me a while back now. Could I use it? Would I have to? I kept my back to the wall and watched through the bannister as Bas pressed his own back to the wall and trained his gun on the door. He reached out and drew back the deadbolt, before twisting the handle.

The door swung inwards. A dark figure stood outside, silhouetted against the purple-green of the grass and trees. They had their hands raised on either side of their head.

'Don't shoot,' the figure said in a low voice. 'It's me.'

That voice…

I pushed off the wall, hurrying to the stairs. 'Theo!'

'Harley!' Bas snarled.

I stopped dead on the stairs. 'What? It's Theo!'

'I come in peace,' Theo said. 'May I please come in?'

'What do you want?' Bas snapped. He was still aiming his gun at Theo's chest.

'I'm not your enemy.' Theo sounded much calmer than I felt; my heart was in my mouth. 'If I wanted to turn you in, don't you think I'd have done that rather than driving out here with no radio signal and no backup?'

'Could have people hiding in the trees,' Bas pointed out.

Theo groaned loudly. 'Harley is my best friend, Rochester. Please just lower the gun.'

'He's on our side, Bas,' I said. 'Let him in.'

Bas didn't move for several seconds. Finally, he lowered the gun. 'Fine,' he grunted.

Theo hurried over the threshold and took the stairs two at a time until he reached me and pulled me into a tight hug.

'I'm so glad you're here.'

'Me too.' I buried my face in his neck, breathing in the soothing scent of his skin: sweat and the coarse bar soap we could buy at the marketplace. 'I didn't do it, I swear.'

'I know.' Theo rubbed my back. 'I knew right away, but by the time I could get to your place you were gone.'

He pulled back, shooting a look down the stairs at Bas, who was watching us with his arms crossed. 'Should have known Bas would be involved.'

'Don't,' I muttered.

'You know my feelings.' Theo shrugged artlessly.

'Bas helped me get out!'

'That isn't important now.' Bas shut the door firmly. 'Were you followed?'

'Of course not,' Theo objected. 'I'm more careful than that.'

'Anyone can make mistakes.'

'Yes, everyone can.' Theo glared at Bas. 'Even you.'

'Guys,' I interrupted. A wave of exhaustion washed over me, I leant against the wall. 'Is this really the time?'

Theo glanced at my face and frowned. 'Fine.' He sighed.

'You should go back to sleep,' Bas said.

'You need to stop telling her what to do,' Theo snapped.

'Guys!' Anger obliterated my tiredness. 'Both of you, shut the fuck up!'

They both stared at me, identical expressions of shock on their faces. I glared back. *Honestly, men.*

I gestured to Bas. 'You said I could take the second watch.'

'You need sleep,' he said stubbornly.

'So do you. So does Theo.' I glanced at my best friend. 'You can take the room I was in.'

Theo crossed his arms. 'We need to talk.'

'We can talk in the morning.' I was done taking their shit.

I'd been done a while ago. But now the feeling solidified in my chest. This was it. They listened or they took a hike.

Theo shuffled his weight, scowling. His shoulders sagged. 'Alright. Will you be okay on watch?'

'Yes.'

He nodded. 'Which is your room?'

I pointed. 'See you in the morning.' After a second's thought, I grabbed his hand and pulled him in for a hug. 'I'm glad you're here.'

'Me too.' He kissed my neck. 'Stay safe. Shoot first, ask questions later.'

'I will,' I promised.

EIGHT

THE SUN ROSE SLOWLY, bringing with it a flurry of noise and activity that I hadn't expected. Birds chirping, rodents scuffling, larger animals calling in the distance.

The wasteland was alive.

I spent the first few hours after sunrise curled up in a sunny spot on the porch. My gun sat in my lap, the safety on. I was exhausted, but sleep was the furthest thing from my mind.

Maddock had killed Sayle.

Sayle was dead.

The entire structure of our town was on the verge of collapse.

It was Sayle who had first brought order to Bale Rocks. He had killed the old mayor, cleaned up the streets, taken control of trade, started offering protection deals.

What the hell would happen now?

Someone would have to take over from him, of course.

But would that person have the same clout? I couldn't think of anyone who had the same reputation and strength that Sayle had.

Even if they did, the other gangs—and the mayor—were going to see this as an opportunity to get their feet in the door. Which meant, at best, that one of the other gangs might take control of the town and distillery, and at worst that we'd be plunged into outright warfare.

Not that it mattered to me—I wasn't there.

That was the other question circling round and round in my head.

What the hell was I going to do now?

I had never suspected that Maddock might be intending to murder Sayle. But would anyone believe me?

Probably not.

Realistically, if it was my word against the Iron Fists, no one was going to take my side—not even Theo or Bas—not if it meant they faced the firing squad with me. I could take cover in the centre of town, behind the blockade, but how long would the military keep me safe? Even if it did, what was going to happen to my sister?

To Theo?

To Bas?

To Brenda, and all the other people I cared about?

My chest felt tight. I rubbed it, swallowing.

What a fucking mess.

The best chance I had was finding out why Maddock had done it—but how could I do that? Could I chase him down? Where had he run to?

And that brought up a whole lot of other worries.

I'd never even been this far out of town. I had no idea how to survive out here. Could I go any further? Could I make it to Crater's Edge or Brackfields? I didn't know the first thing about navigating, let alone finding food, making a fire, avoiding slavers.

Hell, I didn't even know how to drive.

I was fucking screwed.

The panic made me lightheaded. I squeezed my eyes shut and pressed my head against the wall behind me.

No. No.

I could do this.

I had Theo, I had Bas. And I was capable. I'd learn.

One way or another, we'd get through this.

Even if I had no idea what was going to happen now.

Before the whirlpool of my thoughts could drag me under again, I heard a creak from the stairs. Grabbing my gun, I turned my head to look through the open front door.

'Who's there?'

'It's me.'

Theo stepped out onto the rotting porch and surveyed the small clearing around us. 'God, this place is a dump.'

'You knew about this safehouse?' I uncurled my legs and stood, stretching my back.

'There are places like this dotted all over the wasteland. Abandoned houses. Shelters. It's my business to know where they are.' Theo glanced at me out of the corner of his eye. 'But yeah, I knew Bas would come to this one. Everyone follows a pattern, even him.'

My stomach squirmed. 'Why do you hate him so much?'

'I don't hate him.'

Thud-thud.

Footsteps on the stairs. Theo mimed zipping his lips, and I suppressed a groan as Bas stepped outside to join us. *So close, yet so far.*

'I'm going to light a fire,' Bas announced.

'You want people to find us?' Theo asked.

'There's something I have to take care of. This is the easiest way.'

Bas looked as neat and fastidious as usual. His hair shone red in the sun, and his face was set in unyielding lines.

He hadn't shaved, though. The only tiny chink in his armour.

'Guess I'll bring my car round, then,' Theo said. 'May as well present a united front, in case you bring the Black Hands down on us.'

'Are we in Black Hand territory?' I asked uneasily. In town, the lines were clearly defined. Out here, I had no idea.

'Just on the edge,' Bas said. He stepped backwards into the house, his boots scuffing the wooden floor.

'I'll be right back.' Theo shot me a grin before hopping off the porch and sauntering off. He, like Bas, seemed to have woken up ready to go. By contrast, I felt unprepared and terrified.

I followed Bas back into the house and watched as he lit the fire in the hearth and stoked it.

'Why do you have to light a fire?'

'There are people watching for the smoke signal.'

Helpful.

'What people?'

Bas hunched down, throwing more handfuls of kindling into the flames. 'People, people.'

'You know, this working together thing really isn't getting off to a great start.'

He shot me a dirty look. 'The organisation I mentioned. The ones who help slaves.'

Oh.

I bit my lip. No wonder Bas didn't want to discuss it.

'How long will it take them to get here? And why… why do we need them?' I asked carefully.

'An hour or two. Long enough to eat. And,' Bas straightened up, 'we need them to restock the house and to help with the Black Hands. Seeing as I'm not there to do it.'

'Oh.'

He dusted his hands off. 'Can you cook, or shall I?'

'I can cook.' Anything to feel useful.

I managed to cobble together something resembling a meal from the tinned food stashed in the kitchen, and by that time Theo had returned. I passed him a bowl of porridge. 'All good?'

'No sign of anyone for miles.'

That seemed like a good thing, but Theo's expression was dark, his shoulders hunched.

By unspoken agreement, the three of us sat on the saggy sofas in the main room, the fire warming us against the chill wind that crept in around the boards on the windows.

'Can you tell me what happened?' Theo asked.

I took my time over my next mouthful, stalling. What would Theo think?

'Did you know about the crawlspace above the bunker?' Bas asked in a testy voice.

'Yes, of course. Didn't you?'

Bas frowned. 'No.'

'I thought it was common knowledge.' Theo leant back and stretched his legs out. I swatted him on the arm.

'Don't be smug.'

He rolled his eyes. 'Fine. Maddock?'

'He wanted to talk to me.' I bit the inside of my cheek as Theo turned to face me. Another spoonful of porridge. Keeping my eyes on my bowl, resting on my knees, I continued, 'We went to my dressing room. I don't remember exactly what he—It's all a bit murky—' I shrugged helplessly. My memory was blank. The more I thought about it, the more panic choked my throat and shortened my breaths.

Not now.

'Anyway, I woke up when Bas found me.'

'You don't remember anything?' Theo asked.

I shook my head, gripping my bowl to hide the way my hands were trembling. 'Not really.'

'Damn.'

'Short-term memory loss is a common side effect of sedatives,' Bas said.

'I *know* that,' Theo snapped.

'Then why make her feel guilty?'

'I'm not!' Theo slammed his fist on his knee, almost upending his porridge bowl. 'Damnit.' He stood, stalked to the door, then stopped dead. Spinning around, he marched back to his seat. 'No, I'm not leaving.'

'Theo?' I asked hesitantly. What was going through his mind?

Theo turned to Bas. 'You have no right to criticise me,' he said, his voice filled with barely suppressed anger. 'You're the one who didn't fucking believe her, and now you want me to believe you're on her side?'

Bas tensed. 'I am on her side,' he said, though his eyes remained on his food.

Theo snorted. 'You're the most self-serving prick in Bale Rocks. The only side you're on is whatever side gets you revenge on your daddy.'

Bas lifted his head. 'That's not true.'

'Isn't it? We all know that's what Sayle promised you — and look at you now.' Theo's smirk was vicious. 'Running, tail between your legs, because you know Jackson will hand you over to the Black Hands to keep Moriarty happy.'

'Fuck you,' Bas snapped. 'There's nothing stopping me from going back.'

'Guys!' I said sharply. 'Theo, shut the fuck up.'

Theo spun to look at me. 'Do you really want to take *his* side? What do you even know about him?'

'I thought you were supporting my decisions.' My voice came out colder than I'd intended, tapping into a deeper undercurrent of emotion that I didn't want to admit to. I was tired of Theo criticising my choices when it came to Bas; I'd never interfered in his relationships, even back during his entirely questionable crush on Brody Cavanaugh. Softening my voice, I added, 'Arguing gets us nowhere. We're all here together.'

'Precisely,' Bas said in a clipped tone. 'We need to discuss Maddock, and we need to figure out our next actions.'

'You need to go back to Bale Rocks to do damage control,' Theo said. 'I can help Harley on my own.'

'Wait, what?' I started. What did he mean, go back?

'It doesn't make sense for me to go back,' Bas said cooly.

'Wait!' I blurted.

'You were the one who just said you could go back,' Theo said smugly.

He was right; Bas had said that. There was nothing stopping him from going back—or Theo. *I* was the only one in trouble. They were free to leave me here to fend for myself alone. The thought sent a trickle of fear down my spine. I didn't want them to leave.

I didn't want Bas to leave.

'Why does someone have to go back?' I asked.

'We can't just all disappear,' Theo said. 'It smacks of guilt. One of us needs to go back and smooth the situation over.'

'It will have to be you,' Bas said. 'I was the last person with Harley before she left. They'll never believe she got away from me on her own.'

'Hey!' I protested.

Bas shot me a sceptical look.

'I could have,' I protested meekly.

'Aren't you tired of underestimating Harley?' Theo asked.

Bas raised an eyebrow.

'Why can't we all carry on?' I asked. 'It's not that far to Brackfields—we can find out about Maddock and go back. Jackson will—'

'Jackson's going to put a bullet in your head,' Theo said. 'He's not looking for a culprit. He's looking for someone to blame. Make it look like he's taking action, cement his bid for leadership.'

To my surprise, Bas was nodding.

'But I have to go back eventually,' I said. 'What about Savannah?'

'Harley,' Theo said in a strained voice that made me look at his face—properly look. He was frowning, a deep sadness in his eyes.

'No,' I said.

'You can't go back.'

'Yes, I can. Maddock is from Brackfields. I can find out what he was planning and prove my innocence.'

My chest felt tight, my breath raking against the walls of my throat. I couldn't *not* go back. That possibility didn't even exist. Bale Rocks was my *home*.

'I'm sorry, Harley,' Theo said quietly.

'No,' I repeated.

'The best we can do is try and get Savannah out of town. You can meet her in Crater's Edge.'

'No,' I repeated. I swallowed. 'What if Jackson doesn't become the next leader?'

Theo shrugged. 'Then it'll be Moncrief.'

'Right. What about him?' I could barely even bring him to mind—

he'd been at the bunker with Jackson, right? He had curly blond hair.

I knew nothing about him.

'He's arrogant,' Bas said. 'And less strategic than Jackson.'

'There's less chance of him taking power,' Theo said.

'But there is a chance.'

'Harley…' Theo shook his head.

'I can't just give up!' I said, my voice turning shrill.

'It's better this way. Besides, you were planning on leaving anyway.'

'Not without Savannah!' I shrieked. Theo flinched back.

'So Theo can go back and fetch her,' Bas said exasperatedly.

Theo turned to glare at Bas. 'It's not that easy.'

'What, you can persuade the Crater's Edge gangs to give up part of their profits, but you can't persuade one woman to leave her home?' Bas's voice dripped with sarcasm.

'Have you ever tried to have a conversation with Savannah?' Theo asked. 'It's like trying to persuade a four-year-old to eat vegetables.'

'Hey,' I protested.

'You got the Black Hands to release the merchants' market,' Bas said. 'Early—meaning that their strike on the distillery was weakened. Yet one woman defeats you?'

Theo groaned and raked a hand through his hair. 'Yes, okay, you've made your point,' he said. 'You want me to go back? And then what? What are you going to do? You know as well as I do that the only way Harley can go back is if you actually find Maddock. Without him, they'll just execute her instead.'

I shuddered. It didn't bear thinking about.

'So we'll find Maddock then,' I said.

'And how are you going to do that?' Theo asked. 'Do you even know where to look?'

'Brackfields,' I said. 'That's where he said he was from.'

'Yes, that's what he said,' Theo replied. 'But even if it was true, why would he go back there knowing you know that?'

I hadn't thought of that. Shrugging helplessly, I said, 'It's worth a try, isn't it? Someone might know something.'

'And where are you going to start?' Theo asked. 'Do you know anyone in Brackfields?'

I shut up. What could I say? He'd made his point, loud and clear: I knew nothing.

'Bas?' Theo asked mockingly. 'Any bright ideas?'

'I know people in Brackfields,' Bas said stonily.

'People who can help you?'

'Maybe.'

'Maybe,' Theo repeated. 'Sounds promising. Always bet on maybes! Sure way to get yourself killed.'

Bas glowered. 'Then what's your bright idea?'

Awkward pause. Theo crossed his arms. I stared at him. After all that, he'd better have an idea.

Finally, he said, 'I come with you to Brackfields. It's a four-hour drive from here. I can get you in and point you in the right direction. But Maddock's not going to be there.'

'He might be,' I said. 'H-he probably expects me to be dead, so…'

So then I wouldn't be able to come after him.

'He won't be,' Theo said. 'It'd be a stupid risk to take after the lengths he went to.'

'Then what do we do?' I asked in a small voice.

'That depends on what we find,' Theo said. 'But you'll have to make a decision. Brackfields is as far as I can go and still get back to Bale Rocks in a day. I can go back for Sav whilst you wait for me in Brackfields. Or we can go onwards. It's up to you.'

Up to me. A weight settled on my shoulders.

I wasn't stupid. Theo didn't want to go back for Savannah. We were already out of town—we may as well continue on.

But how could I go on without my sister?

And yet, sending him back meant risking his safety.

I stared at my hands. 'We don't have to decide yet. We might find something in Brackfields.'

'We might,' Theo agreed. He scraped up the last mouthful of his porridge, then stood. 'I'll clear up.'

'Thanks,' I mumbled.

Bas took the next watch, Theo went to tinker with his car, and I drifted aimlessly around the house. I was meant to be thinking about food, but I couldn't seem to settle. I felt lost, set adrift.

How could things have got so bad so quickly?

How could I be so stupid?

Maddock had played me from start to finish, hadn't he? He'd picked me out from the very beginning, wrapped me up in his clever little game, and spat me out when he was done with me. And I'd let him.

Fuck.

All this time, and I hadn't even realised that the biggest danger was the closest to home.

Maddock had put me in a worse position than even Dean Hannover. Hannover had wanted me to risk my life—hah! He could take lessons. Losing my home was much scarier.

Losing my sister was the worst possible fate I could imagine.

Had he known?

That was the question that I couldn't shake. I had thought Maddock was my friend. Had he really been playing me from the beginning?

As tough as it was to swallow, I could believe he had. Bas and Ellery had played me for years. But at least they'd protected me during that time—to a certain extent.

Speaking of protecting me…

I trailed outside. Bas was sitting in the chair I'd left out there, methodically cleaning his gun. The floorboards creaked under my feet, and he looked up.

'Harley.'

'Hey.' I shifted my weight from foot to foot. 'Can I ask you something?'

Bas raised an eyebrow. 'Why am I here?'

'Uh, no.' Though I was curious about that, too. 'It's about Ellery, actually. Do you… trust him?'

His brows drew together in a frown. 'Yes,' he said, his tone leaving no room for argument.

'Oh. Good.' I shuffled my feet. 'Because we left town on his word alone… And he sort of… hates me.'

'Marco doesn't hate you,' Bas said.

'I hurt him,' I said uneasily. How much did Bas know?

'Yes,' he agreed. 'But he's my best friend. Marco is loyal.' He jerked his chin towards the house. 'More loyal than Dunne.'

'Theo's loyal!' I protested. 'I've known him since I was four! He'd never betray me.'

'Then you've known him as long as I've known Marco,' Bas said. 'So you should understand.'

I swallowed. 'You knew him before you were a slave?'

'Yes,' Bas said shortly. He looked back at his gun, clicking the pieces together slowly. 'We went to school together.'

'Oh.' It had never occurred to me that Bas would have gone to school. I bit my lip. 'How old were you when…'

'Ten.'

'Oh.'

I stared at Bas. He was very pointedly not looking at me as he finished reassembling the gun and tucked it back into his harness. He reached for his knife and pulled out a cloth to wipe it down.

It felt like I ought to say something… something understanding, but my mind was blank. Even though my mother had been a slave, I'd never really engaged with the topic. I didn't know what the right words were, and what the wrong ones.

I didn't want to hurt Bas.

'Please don't lurk there,' Bas said.

'Sorry. I'll go back inside.' I took a step back.

'You can stay.'

I paused. 'Really?'

'Yeah, just not right behind me,' he said. 'It makes me uneasy.'

I stepped outside again. The edge of the porch was in the sun, so I sat there, folding my legs under me. I glanced at Bas, who nodded and went back to cleaning his weapons.

We sat in silence for a good fifteen minutes or so, before Theo shut the tailgate of his truck and strode over, wiping his hands on his trousers.

'I have enough fuel to get us to Brackfields,' he said. 'Do you know the way back to the road?'

'More or less,' Bas said.

'It'll be easiest if we set off before full dark,' Theo decided. 'We'll be harder to spot in the low light. You can follow me.'

'Okay.'

'Good.' Theo's every word was decisive, but his voice had an edge to it. He was looking for a fight. 'We should discuss what we know. It'll help me decide which contacts to call on.'

'Fine,' Bas said. I glanced at him; he sounded funny. Not quite defensive, not quite neutral, not quite acquiescent. Somewhere in between. His expression was strange, too. He avoided my gaze.

Had I hurt him by asking him about his past? Or was it a response to Theo's aggression? Or just that our location was bringing up bad memories?

Theo headed inside and came back with another rickety kitchen chair. He set it on the grass in front of me and slouched down in it. 'So, Maddock.' He caught my eye. 'Harley?'

'I only know what he's told me, and I have no idea how much of it is true.'

'It's all we have to go on at the moment,' Theo pointed out.

That was true. I chewed my lip for a moment before launching in. 'He told me he grew up in Brackfields. His father was in law enforcement. And he came to Bale Rocks working with a military construction company who were contracted by the Godfreys.' I paused uncertainly. 'At least, I think that's right. He said a few different things about his work. He also…'

I shifted uncomfortably.

'Harley?' Theo asked sharply.

'A few months ago, he came to my flat,' I said carefully. 'He was trying to… recruit me, I guess? He said he wanted help taking down the gangs—at least, that was what I thought he wanted. He wasn't very clear.'

Bas narrowed his eyes. 'Why did you never mention it?'

'I've had a lot going on, in case you'd forgotten,' I pointed out.

'Why would he target you?' Theo asked.

'I don't know,' I muttered.

'The same reason Hardwick did,' Bas said sagely. 'You're able to pass unnoticed in the bunker.'

'Yeah,' I said sourly. 'I was a bit too good at it, wasn't I?'

I couldn't help being bitter. Maddock had been inconsistent and a liar, but deep down I had thought he was a good person. I'd considered him a friend. And he had used me to get where he needed to go, then left me behind to take the fall.

'You made yourself a target by not confiding in anyone,' Theo pointed out. I shot him a hurt look. 'It's true, Harley. The whole thing with Hannover could have been avoided—'

'Don't start!' I snapped. I didn't want to rehash this again. Yes, I should have trusted Theo. Yes, I should have told Bas, earlier. Yes, I had made mistakes. 'I don't see you adding to the discussion.'

'He learnt fighting from a professional,' Theo said.

'Didn't all of you?'

'No. Some of us are self-taught. Others learnt from Jackson or one of the other senior members. Vaughn—you don't know him—he's the one who taught me. And Bas, I'd assume.'

I glanced at Bas. He nodded.

'Oh,' I said. 'So what does it mean that Maddock is professionally taught?'

'He must have learnt from someone, someone with a specific style,' Theo said. 'Which might be a clue we can use. Also, he's gay, so if he's ever been to the brothels, we'll know who to ask.'

'That's not really useful!' I protested.

'Harley baby, whores love to talk.'

I kicked him on the arm. Theo caught my ankle and tugged playfully. 'Watch it.'

'Hey!' I yanked my foot back. 'I'm not going to be the one asking them.'

'I'll do it,' Theo said impishly.

'How self-sacrificing.' I rolled my eyes. Theo grinned at me.

'As charming as your banter is,' Bas said, 'we're meant to be discussing Maddock, not your plans for getting your rocks off.'

Theo rolled his eyes. 'Go on then, you're welcome to contribute.'

'James Maddock isn't his real name,' Bas said.

'Yes, we all guessed that,' Theo said impatiently. 'Why would he go to all that trouble just to get caught because he used his real name?'

'Oh!' I sat up straighter. 'Maybe he chose the name for a reason. Ellery once told me that James Maddock—the real James Maddock— was dead. If we knew who he was—'

'We do know,' Bas said heavily. 'James Maddock, better known as James Bradwell, was the son of Marina Maddock and Galen Bradwell. In other words—'

'The mayor's son?' Theo exclaimed.

My mouth dropped open. 'Wait, what? The mayor is Charles Darling.'

'Not the current mayor,' Theo said. 'The old one, who Sayle killed when we were little. Remember?'

The old mayor had died when I was three. At that point in time, my life had consisted of dance and playing dress-up with my sister. I certainly hadn't cared about the mayor or his son. 'No.'

'I wouldn't expect you to,' Bas said.

I scowled, but before I could call him out for being patronising, Theo said, 'I didn't know old man Bradwell had a son, though. Wasn't he about seventy when he died?'

'Sixty-eight,' Bas said.

'Big difference.' Theo rolled his eyes.

'His wife was in her early twenties.'

'Why would Maddock take the name of the mayor's son, though?' I asked. 'Surely that would get him found out quicker?'

'It served a purpose,' Bas said. 'It caught Sayle's attention, so he got into the bunker faster.'

'He played us.' Theo sounded almost admiring. 'Damn. That's deep.'

'You're meant to be helping us track him down, not praising the guy,' I muttered.

Theo shook his head like a dog shaking off water. 'I will, don't worry,' he said. 'But you gotta hand it to the guy. He was fucking clever. You all knew he was suspicious as hell, and not a one of you clocked his plan.'

'You didn't either,' Bas said darkly.

'I wasn't there.'

At that moment, a faint growl reached us. I froze.

'Is that a car?'

Theo jumped up, reaching for his gun. 'How will we know if it's your contact?' he asked Bas in a low, urgent tone.

'He'll be in a dark blue truck,' Bas said.

'And if it's not?' Theo glanced at me. His jaw was tense. 'Harley, go inside.'

'No!'

'What if they open fire?' The engine was getting louder. A flock of birds took flight from the trees, and I jumped, my heart lurching in my chest.

'Cover us from the kitchen window,' Bas said. 'I'll take the lounge.'

Theo nodded. Bas took my arm and tugged me inside.

'I don't need protecting,' I protested.

'What you need,' Bas said lowly, 'is to learn to follow orders during a crisis situation. There's a time to be independent and a time to work with the team.' He shoved me towards the kitchen. 'This is the latter.'

Bas stalked to the lounge. I stared after him, embarrassment burning in my chest. It hadn't even occurred to me that I might be making things worse. Working my gun out of its holster, I hurried into the kitchen and took cover against the wall beside the window. My breathing came in short, sharp bursts as I listened to the vehicle drawing nearer and nearer.

It stopped.

A door slammed.

Footsteps: heavy boots on dirt.

'Clear!' Theo called.

I sighed, tipping my head back against the wall. We were okay.

Bas and I emerged at the same time. He looked tense and worried, and was still holding his gun. He walked ahead of me, blocking my view.

'…definitely weren't followed?' Theo asked.

'I've been doing this run since you were in diapers, kid.'

The speaker had a low, gravelly voice. It sounded familiar. Bas cleared the doorway, and I finally laid eyes on his contact. Shiny bald head, tall, strong.

Turner. The bartender at the Hawke and Tern pub, where I'd been meeting Evander Hardwick to pass information for the last few weeks.

Turner's eyes widened, and before any of us could react, he pulled his gun and pointed it at my head.

My vision tunnelled.

'Woah!' Theo yelled. 'What the fuck?'

'She's an informant,' Turner said. He turned on Bas. 'You brought *her* here?'

'We're well aware of that!' Theo said.

'I'm not,' Bas snapped.

'It's… it's to do with Tam,' I croaked. 'Hardwick knew about it. He blackmailed me. Please…'

'We trust Harley,' Theo snapped. Turner didn't move an inch. Theo turned on Bas. 'Tell him!'

Bas stared between us for long seconds. Each one felt as long as a lifetime. My heart was going to beat right out of my chest.

'Put the gun down,' Bas said. 'Harley's a friend.'

Turner lowered the gun. I took a deep breath and staggered towards Theo. He caught me and drew me into a hug.

'That was uncalled for,' Theo snapped.

'I'm just doing my job,' Turner said. 'Girl's been passing information to Evander Hardwick.'

'You said you were his friend!' I said. My voice shook.

'That doesn't mean I trust him. He does his business; I do mine.'

I swallowed and clenched my fists. The panic was subsiding, leaving me shaky and cold. 'And what business is that, then?'

'Wouldn't you know? You work for him.'

'I don't!'

'Let's go inside,' Bas said sharply. 'We need to talk.'

'Fine,' Turner said. 'Help me bring the boxes inside.'

He and Bas headed to the car; Theo and I went inside. Theo crossed the lounge to the fireplace. The flames had already died down. He spread the ashes, then piled them on top to smother the fire.

I lurked nervously in the doorway. A minute later, Bas and Turner entered and set two crates down in the hall.

'That should do it for now,' Turner said. He turned to me. 'If you weren't working for Hardwick, what were you doing?'

'He… he forced me,' I muttered. 'He knew something I didn't want getting out…'

'Sounds like him,' Turner said. 'Old bastard. Alright, come on.'

He marched past me into the lounge. I turned to Bas, who was staring at me.

'Don't start,' I said.

'You should have told us.'

I crossed my arms. 'You know why I didn't.'

Bas scowled. 'This trusting each other thing isn't getting off to a great start.'

Ouch. My words thrown back at me. I bit my lip. Bas passed me, and I followed him into the lounge and sat next to Theo.

'So,' Turner said, 'don't you have drama to tend to up in your camp?'

'That's why we're here,' Bas said.

'Hiding?' Turner appraised him. 'No, running. Damn, I didn't think you had it in you.'

Bas flinched. 'It's complicated,' he said.

'It must be, if you're leaving your business unfinished.'

'That's what I need to speak to you about,' Bas pressed on. 'I've been keeping tabs on the NCC branches—I think one of the doctors at the clinic is in on it. Markus Clairmont.'

'That makes sense,' Turner said. 'He's fairly senior, isn't he?'

'I think so,' Bas said. 'I've seen him meeting with Hannover.'

I bit my lip, staring at my knees. *Clairmont.* Where had I heard that name before?

'I'll put my team onto Clairmont; see if we can find out who he's talking to,' Turner said, 'But it will be slow. This isn't like anything we've dealt with before.'

'I know,' Bas said. 'That's why you're going to need help—speak to Marco Ellery. He's been putting together a few trusted men—'

'You know I don't like working with the Iron Fists,' Turner said.

'You can't take on the Black Hands alone,' Bas replied. 'Keep an eye on the NCC. You need to stop them from transferring the slaves they have now. They're waiting until they have enough to justify moving them.'

'Do you know where they're headed?' Turner asked.

'Likely the Gauntlet. That's where Moriarty trades most of his slaves.'

The Gauntlet was even further west than Boughton, beyond the mountains. Racetracks, casinos, the whole shebang. The travellers who stayed at the Kranikovska called it the road to civilisation.

Civilisation being in the opposite direction from us.

'I can try to intercept them,' Turner said. 'But I can't make any promises. You know my team. We're a small operation.'

'That's why you need reinforcements,' Bas said. 'I trust Ellery. He'll help.'

'We'll see,' Turner said. 'But what about the NCC? Even if we intercept the slaves, this is bigger than just one shipment. We need to cut off the head of the snake.'

Shipment. I shuddered. That was a horrible way to describe people.

'Their main office is in Crater's Edge,' Bas said. 'If I make it out there, I'll stop in on them. If not, Ellery will go.'

'You have a way to get messages to him?' Turner asked.

'Long distance radio. Just have to commission it.'

'Fine.' Turner sighed. He stood and strode over to the fireplace. 'I'll do my best. As always.'

'You could speak to Savannah,' I said.

They all looked at me.

'Savannah?' Turner asked.

I felt my cheeks heating. 'My sister. She works at the clinic. She might have information on… on Doctor Clairmont.'

Turner raised an eyebrow. 'Is she aware of the situation?'

I shook my head.

'Better not. The fewer people we involve, the better. But I'll keep that information under consideration.' He nodded sagely. 'I should get back to town. I take it you won't be staying here long?'

'We're heading out this evening,' Bas said. 'I'll clean up before we leave.'

'That would be appreciated,' Turner said. A frown flitted over his face. 'Well, I don't know what made you leave town—and I'm sure I don't want to know—but best of luck.'

'And to you,' Bas said.

'Thanks.' Turner smiled grimly. 'I'll be needing it.'

NINE

I SAT IN THE PASSENGER seat of Theo's car, both of us tense. The car was deathly silent. We'd lost the Crater FM radio station when we started towards Brackfields, and Theo had switched the radio off rather than look for a different station.

'I don't need any distractions,' he'd said.

The truth was, he was angry. He obviously didn't like me trusting Bas. I just didn't know *why*.

Clunk!

The truck bounced as something hit the undercarriage. Theo cursed under his breath.

We were driving along with the lights on low. It wasn't completely dark yet, but the oncoming twilight turned the ground ahead of us to pools of shadow amidst the shapes of bushes and rocks. It wasn't easy to see, and we were driving slowly to avoid hitting anything. Theo had taken most of it in stride, in any case. His preparations had been methodical, and his driving was meticulous.

I had thought I knew Theo, but this was a new side of him. The last time we'd been in the wasteland together like this had been when we were sixteen and skiving off school. The before time. Before my dad had died and everything had changed.

We were different people now.

The silence weighed heavier and heavier on me until eventually I couldn't bear it at all.

'Are you mad?' I whispered.

'Why would I be mad?' Theo asked tersely.

'It's my fault you're here.'

'Not like you told me to come. Not like you told me anything at all.' He jerked the wheel and we cleared the low ruins of some kind of burnt-out building.

I chewed the inside of my cheek. True. I hadn't even thought of

Theo—there hadn't been time, in between Ellery breaking the news and Bas convincing me to leave.

But even so, that felt like an excuse. I hadn't thought of Theo after we'd left, either. My only concern had been Savannah.

'I'm sorry,' I murmured. 'I would have told you if I could.'

'You knew I had a plan,' Theo said darkly. 'We've discussed this.'

I pressed my lips together. Theo had had a plan. We were still a bit murky on the details. But I didn't like his plan, because he didn't want to include Savannah.

Not that it mattered now.

'There wasn't time to—'

'Of course there was time. There were a hundred other things you could have done before letting Bas drive you out of town, and you know it!' Theo took a deep breath, as though trying to calm himself. 'There were other options, but instead you trusted him.'

'What's wrong with trusting Bas?' I snapped. I was tired of Theo hinting around the subject. It was time to get to the bottom of his hatred for Bas. 'He's—'

'He's not safe!'

For fuck's sake, really?

I rolled my eyes. 'None of us are safe, Theo. I'm not safe. You're not safe.'

'I *am* safe,' Theo said.

'Are you?' Before he could reply, I plunged on. 'This is a stupid argument. You weren't there; Bas was. I only had his advice to go on.'

'You could have come up with your own options. You could have insisted on waiting.'

Last night was a blur. I'd been dizzy with fear, sick from the drugs. 'It wasn't that easy.'

''Course it was. You don't want to admit that your crush on Bas blinded you.'

'You don't want to admit that you're a jealous prat who hates that I'm relying on people other than you,' I snapped.

There it was—and it felt fucking good to finally say it. Theo was acting completely irrationally. 'I'm twenty-five. I can make my own decisions. If I want to trust Bas, you need to step aside and let me.'

Theo remained silent; I couldn't make out his features, but he radiated tension. For a while, only the rustling of the bushes accompanied our drive as we both stewed in our anger.

What right did he have to tell me I was blind? He hadn't been there. He didn't know what state I was in.

He didn't know.

The truth of my friendship with Theo.

He just didn't know the struggles of my life anymore.

Theo huffed a sigh. 'Fine,' he said.

'Fine?' I asked in a provocative tone.

'Fine,' he repeated, 'I am jealous. I'm jealous that you chose him when I've been your best friend for years. I'm jealous that you jumped through flaming hoops to win his trust when I'd have helped you out the moment you said you were in trouble with Hannover and Hardwick.'

There we go.

'Noble,' I sneered, unable to curb the rush of rage in my chest, 'but you weren't there.'

'I was—'

'You were not,' I snapped. 'Maybe towards the end. But you're not there, you're never there when I need you. Bas was there. Maybe not perfect, but he was there, and he apologise—'

'I have apologised! How many times do you want me to tell you I'm sorry?'

'At least one more—' The words tumbled off of my tongue.

'Oh, there's always one more.'

'—for telling me what I should have done when I was drugged and scared. Fuck you, Theo. You think you know everything.' I crossed my arms. 'Maybe you should have gone back to Bale Rocks.'

'Is that what you want? You want to go gallivanting across the wasteland on a romantic trip with your boyfriend?'

Wham.

'You're pretty fucking derisive considering that he just gave up everything to help me.'

'Don't fool yourself.' Theo snorted. 'He's running with his tail between his legs because he knows Jackson and Moncrief won't protect him from the Black Hands like Sayle did. Moriarty is salivating over the idea of getting revenge on him.'

For what?

But I refused to take the bait. 'Don't change the subject.'

'I'm here, too,' Theo said, 'giving up everything. But you don't care about that.'

'Of course I care!' I cried. 'I'm just tired of you telling me what I should have done. I get it, I'm an idiot. I made a mess. Now fuck the hell off about it!'

'I'm not telling you what you should have—'

'That's exactly what you're doing,' I snapped. 'It's what you've been doing all along. Why do you think I didn't tell you in the first place?'

Theo pressed his lips together. Ahead of us, the headlights illuminated a new horror: the ashes of a campfire beside a collapsed tent.

No people.

I swallowed as Theo swerved around it. What had happened to them?

Had they abandoned their camp… or had something worse befallen them?

'I don't want to fight,' Theo said quietly.

Could have fooled me.

'Then don't,' I said. 'You can stop at any time.'

'I'm trying to, alright? Listen to me.'

'Not as though I have anything better to do,' I muttered under my breath.

'Thanks,' Theo snapped. He took a deep breath. 'I'm sorry, alright. I'm sorry I wasn't there, and I'm sorry if you felt I was telling you what to do.'

If.

I ground my teeth together.

'I just don't think Bas is going to turn out to be as steady as you think,' Theo warned. 'That guy has some serious unresolved issues— and he will turn you in for a chance at revenge on his father. You mark my words. If you're ever in the way of his shot, he'll go through you, not around, Harley.'

'That's a pretty unlikely scenario.' I crossed my arms, half angry, half trying to hold myself together.

'I wouldn't count on it,' Theo said. He glanced at me, but his face was unreadable in the falling darkness. 'But we're here now. You've made your choice. And I'll always be your friend. So… I support you.'

'Uh huh,' I said sceptically.

'That's it?'

'For now, yeah.' I wasn't feeling particularly giving. 'I'll think on it.'

'Wow, thanks.'

It burnt, fighting with Theo. But no matter how deep I dug inside myself, I couldn't find the desire to forgive him. It was all too fresh.

But I also couldn't seem to hold onto my anger. It drained out of me like sand between my fingers. Finally, as the twilight gave way to the oncoming darkness, I murmured, 'I'm sorry.'

'It's alright.' Theo reached over and squeezed my leg.

We drove a while longer in silence.

'You can see the mountains in the distance,' Theo said suddenly, his voice low.

'Oh.' I squinted. It was dark, and yet the longer we were out here, the more the inky blackness took on dimension. Midnight black skies, dotted with millions of stars. The moonlight painted the edges of the trees, rocks, and gutted buildings silver. The ground was brown-black, and the mountains on the horizon were jagged shapes, the dark grey of stark rock mingled with a blue like spilt ink, capped with glowing white in the moonlight.

'Wow,' I whispered.

'They are pretty incredible,' Theo said.

'Have you been—'

He shook his head. 'Only into the foothills. The mountains are dangerous—if the temperature doesn't get you, the rockslides will.'

There was so much I didn't know about the world. A sudden yearning rose up in my chest.

'I'd like to see them.'

Theo laughed. 'One day out of town and you're becoming an adventurer.'

'Shut up.' I hit him on the arm.

'Wait until after we've run out of fuel in the middle of slaver territory before you decide you want to trade in your city life.'

'Is that likely?' My stomach squirmed. I leant over to glance at the gasometer on the dash.

'It's broken,' Theo said. 'Don't worry, I filled up before I left town. I can get us to Brackfields on the tank—so long as we don't run into trouble.'

'How likely is that?'

'Once we hit the main road, fairly.'

'Oh.'

'Which should be soon.' Theo picked his compass up from the centre console, checking the direction. 'About fifteen minutes, give or take.'

Once again, I was out of my depth. I couldn't have said what direction we had to drive to reach the road, couldn't name the peaks on the horizon, didn't know how far a car could get on a tank of petrol. Functionally, I was useless.

'Sorry,' I mumbled. 'It's my fault you're here.'

'Now you're just being ridiculous.' Theo tugged my ponytail, the car never veering from its course. 'This is where I want to be. Do you think I do the city runs for fun? I like driving out in the wasteland on my own.'

I'd never thought about it, and now I felt stupid. Theo had always been an explorer, even when we were little. Abandoned buildings were his playground. The wasteland was his happy place.

'Yeah.'

Theo sighed. 'I don't want you to ever be scared of me, Harley.'

We'd come full circle. 'I won't be,' I muttered to the wasteland outside my window.

'Don't make that promise until you're sure you can keep it.'

Guilt churned in my stomach.

'I feel so stupid,' I muttered. 'All of this could have been avoided.'

'It's not that easy when you're in the thick of things.' Theo felt along my leg until he found my hand. I laced our fingers together, and he squeezed gently. 'Next time, tell me. I can help you. I could have found a way to help you without betraying the Iron Fists. We've been best friends for two decades. You don't have to suffer alone.'

'You don't, either.'

'I know.' He sounded cheerful enough. When I looked at him, he was smiling.

Then he nodded straight ahead. 'There's the road. Keep your gun in reach and an eye out for other cars, alright?'

'Right.'

'And whatever you do—don't roll down the window or open the door.'

My heart seemed to have migrated to my throat, taking up all the space so I could barely get any air. 'Got it.'

We rolled up an embankment, the car angled sideways against the slope. Coarse stones littered the bank, and a metal railing, broken in several places, lined the side of the road. Theo slid deftly through a broken section, and we glided onto the tarmac.

The silence was sudden and almost deafening. I hadn't realised how loud the tyres sounded bouncing over the dirt until we hit the smoother surface.

The road was uncanny. Built about two yards higher than the surrounding wasteland, it afforded us a view of the empty land around. During the day, I would probably have been able to see for miles. At night, it felt like we were on a causeway in a sea of ink. The road stretched out ahead of us—and behind, too—in a dead straight line.

Theo gestured to the compass. 'Brackfields: south. Bale Rocks: north. Moriarty's compound is about ten miles behind us.'

I swallowed. Far too close for comfort.

'Will they see us?'

'Doubtful. They're more active along the road to Boughton than the road to Brackfields.'

Boughton was another town due west of Bale Rocks. Apart from its location, I knew almost nothing about it.

'Is Boughton in the mountains?' I asked, glancing west once again. The mountains spanned the entire horizon to the west; nothing between us and them except wasteland.

'Not quite,' Theo said. 'I'd say it's in the foothills.' He nodded forwards. 'Smoke.'

Theo had much sharper eyesight than I did. I scanned the horizon until I found the faint glow; it was off to our left, a fair distance into the wasteland. The yellow light illuminated several blocky silhouettes.

'Who's there?' I whispered. Whispering felt appropriate, as though it were forbidden to disturb the peace of the wasteland.

'Slavers, most likely,' Theo said grimly. 'They hunt along this road. It's the main way south. Easy pickings.'

Slavers. Until recently, they'd been a distant evil. Something other people worried about.

And now here I was, out in the wasteland, with nothing between me and them but the car, Theo, and my gun.

I swallowed.

'Will they come after us?'

'They won't try to chase us down.' Theo flicked a lever on his steering wheel, dimming the car's headlights. 'They go after easy targets. But they might have an ambush set up.'

Even better.

I clutched the handle of my gun tighter. If it came down to it—if it was a choice between killing someone and becoming a slave—

I dug my nails into my knees. *Don't think about it.*

Theo kept the car at a steady pace, his eyes on the road ahead. I found myself looking all about anxiously. Where was the danger? Who was lurking in the darkness?

My heart clogged my throat, making it hard to breathe.

Fifty yards ahead of us, a figure burst out of the bushes.

'THEO!' I screamed. He hit the brakes, the tyres squealing. A woman was highlighted in stark relief in the car lights—she was stooped, with long, lank hair dangling in clumps around her shoulders. Her clothes hung off her thin form.

The engine whined as Theo accelerated suddenly.

'What are you doing? We have to help her!'

We hurtled past the woman, so fast she stumbled sideways. I thought—or imagined maybe—I saw her mouth open in a scream. Then we were past. I twisted around to see her. 'Theo, we have to go back!'

'It's a trap, Harley!'

'No!' The woman had collapsed to her knees. Bas's car whipped past her. 'She needs help!'

'It's a trap,' Theo repeated. 'They want us to stop, Harley.' He accelerated harder, brightening the lights to illuminate the long, empty road ahead.

A little sob worked its way out of my throat. The woman vanished from sight, and I twisted to see Theo, his face set with determination. 'How can you be so heartless?'

'That's what it takes to survive out here,' he said coldly.

'But...'

'They plant slaves by the road. We stop to help, they ambush us.

That's how it works, Harley.'

I shook my head, bile burning my throat. She had needed help. I'd seen the desperation on her face. Tears escaped my eyes, stinging my cheeks. 'No.'

'I've seen it happen before. Right in front of me. A car stopped to help, and the slavers descended on them. I almost got caught up in it, too.' Theo shook his head. 'There's nothing we can do.'

Nothing.

For the first time in a while, I thought of my mother. Had she stood by the roadside like that, praying for someone to pick her up? How many people had driven past her when she'd escaped from slavery?

Another sob wrenched out of my throat. 'I hate this.'

'I know,' Theo murmured. 'I know.'

TEN

BY THE BY, THEO SLOWED THE CAR.

'What's happening?' I whispered.

'Rest stop. We can stay here for a few hours. Sleep.'

'I thought you wanted to travel by night?' I glanced around. We were approaching a turnoff; a road jutted off of ours at a sharp right angle to the left. Just past it was an area closed off by an ominous fence. The metal sheets were topped with barbed wire and spikes stuck out in all directions.

'I'll explain once we're in.'

Theo took the turnoff and rolled to a halt in front of a gate in the fence. It, too, was covered in wicked-looking spikes. He tapped the horn lightly, making two short, sharp sounds.

Gravel crunched as Bas pulled up behind us, his headlights washing over us. I squinted, trying to pick him out in his car. His expression was serious.

A panel in the gate slid open to reveal a face that was mostly obscured by a balaclava. Theo rolled the window down.

'Name?' a woman's voice grunted.

'It's Theo.'

'Fee.'

Theo grabbed his gun, made a hand signal to Bas, and opened his door.

'What are you doing?' I hissed.

'Back in a sec.' He slid out and headed for the gate, handing over a thin wad of bills. Then he returned to the car, slammed the door, and locked it.

The panel shut and the gate slid open.

'What is this place?' I murmured as Theo drove us slowly through the gate and into the open yard beyond.

The place was filled with shiny metal caravans, not unlike the ones the merchants' market used—I counted seven. A more permanent shack was off to one side, built of wood and metal. And a large sign mounted on its roof proclaimed: *DIGNITY JONES' REST AND RESPITE FOR THE WEARY TRAVELLER.*

We crawled inside, the gate clanging shut behind us. The dirt track was lined with metal signs.

BEWARE OF SLAVERS

DO NOT LITTER

DO NOT LEAVE FOOD LYING AROUND

DANGER, STAY ALERT

DO NOT LEAVE YOUR KEYS IN YOUR VEHICLE

And the last one: a black silhouette of a gun with a red line through it.

Theo stopped in a makeshift dirt lot next to a trio of picnic benches. Beyond them was another wooden shack with a toilet sign.

'It's safe to get out,' Theo announced. 'Just stay alert.'

'What about the slavers?' I asked, looking around uneasily. There was no sign of anyone else—no, that was wrong. There were two other cars—one outside of the wooden hut, and the second beside one of the caravans. Even so, the idea of standing out in the open made me feel extremely vulnerable, as though enemies could swoop down on us at any moment.

'That's what the fence is for,' Theo said ominously.

We climbed out. Bas had parked beside us, and he descended from his car, too, studying everything as he went.

'This is safe?' he asked.

'More or less,' Theo said. 'Dignity keeps the riffraff out. Come on, I've paid for food.'

He led the way over to the central building. As we approached, the door opened, revealing a figure silhouetted against yellow light. They had a rifle slung over their back.

'Come in, but quietly.' It was the same person who had opened the gate. A deep, soothing female voice. She stepped back, making space for us to troop inside.

We entered directly into a kitchen. A large table took up the majority of the small space; the rest belonged to the counters and stove, which had a large pot bubbling on it. The woman who had welcomed us strode over to the stove. She had voluminous black curls, dark umber skin, and was dressed all in black from head to toe. She had the bearing of a soldier.

'Sit, sit,' she said in a low voice. 'Sorry to whisper—the boys are asleep. I'm Dignity. I know Theo.'

'This is Harley and Bas,' Theo said. He stepped up beside her, taking the plates as she filled them and carrying them over to the table. It was a rich, fragrant soup. Dignity brought a loaf of bread over and set it between us on the table.

'Tuck in,' she said.

We all sat and helped ourselves to bread. Dignity leant against the counter, watching us as we ate. 'You came from the north, then?'

'Bale Rocks,' Theo said around a mouthful.

'Mm-hmm. Clean run?'

'Not bad.' He tore a hunk off his bread. 'There was an ambush set up about thirty miles north of here—though they might have moved it by now.'

'I'll pass on the message if anyone else comes through headed in that direction.'

I dipped my bread in the soup and nibbled on it.

'Any news about the run from here to Brackfields?' Theo asked.

'Nothing recently. Had a few incidents down that way about a month back.' She shrugged. 'Rafael did a supply run a week ago and there was no trouble.'

Theo nodded. 'Thanks.'

I glanced at Bas. Did all of this make sense to him? Was I the only one not following?

Bas's head was bent over his plate as he ate hurriedly.

'I take it you'll be wanting to sleep,' Dignity said.

'If you don't mind,' Theo replied.

'I thought you wanted to drive by night,' I reminded him.

'We can't enter Brackfields until six AM. They close the checkpoint.' He put his spoon down to fold up the cuffs of his jacket. 'We'll catch a couple of hours sleep here and set off a bit before dawn.'

'Oh.' The thought itched at me, making me restless. I didn't like the idea of stopping and waiting, because the unknown pressed in on me. As long as we were moving, I could think about what was ahead and nothing else.

Now, my worries were starting to pile up again.

I pushed them away and forced myself to focus on the food. If something went wrong in the middle of the wasteland, I'd rather deal with it on a full stomach.

While we all ate our fill, Dignity sliced the bread and started putting together sandwiches for us.

'For the road.'

'Do you stay out here all the time?' I couldn't suppress my curiosity any longer.

'Pretty much. Except for the occasional supply run.' She hefted a jug of water onto the table so we could refill our glasses. 'Been out in the wasteland my entire life.'

'Really?'

'My father was a scavenger.'

'Wow.' I couldn't imagine living out in the wasteland my entire life. 'Aren't you afraid?'

'We got the walls and we got our guns.' She smirked. 'Word got around pretty quickly after we set up shop here that we mean business.'

'Wow,' I repeated. *Wish I could be that tough.*

But it seemed to arise from some kind of innate quality that I lacked. No matter how I tried, it was just wrong decision after wrong decision.

'Any news from up north?' Dignity asked. 'Heard you guys had trouble with the merchants.'

'Delayed,' Theo said. 'But they got through. I guess they're in Crater's Edge by now.'

'We haven't had anyone from that direction for a few days.' Dignity piled the wrapped sandwiches on the table. 'And the army? Seems like they're amassing quite a force up in your direction. They planning on invading the northern wastes or something?'

'They're in Bale Rocks at the moment,' Theo said.

'Amassing a force?' Bas asked. It was the first time he'd spoken since we'd arrived. I glanced at him — he was frowning.

'You haven't seen them?' Dignity put her hands on her hips.

'It's not what I'd call a force,' Theo said. 'They have enough men to blockade the centre of town. It's been troublesome, but I'm not sure how long they can hold it for.'

Dignity pursed her lips. 'Huh. That's not what I've seen.'

'What have you seen?' Theo asked.

'Convoys.' Dignity checked her watch. 'It's about the right time. Come on — grab your coats. It's chilly in the watchtower.'

She donned her jacket and put her rifle over her back again, then held the door for us. We trooped back out into the cold night air. Once Dignity had shut up the door behind us, she led the way to the far end of the rest stop, furthest from the road. The watch tower was also a water tower. A rusty ladder provided access to a makeshift platform built above the tank. Theo climbed up first, and I followed him hesitantly.

Would it take the weight of four of us?

But the platform felt sturdy enough, even if our boots made strange, hollow clanking noises as we walked over it. Bas and Dignity joined us, and Dignity flicked her torch off.

'Watch the road,' she said. 'Shouldn't be long now.'

'What are we watching for?' Bas asked impatiently.

'You'll see.'

We waited in anxious silence, our breath fogging the air silver under the moonlight. After about ten minutes, the cold was starting to get to me. I rubbed my arms and the metal creaked beneath me.

'Here.' Theo put his arm around me, holding me close.

'Thanks,' I mumbled.

At that moment, the roar of an engine came from the distance. It grew louder and louder—not one engine—at least two, maybe more. Gradually, the vehicles began to appear along the road from Brackfields, their headlights impossibly bright. I squinted, shielding my eyes with my hands. Three vehicles: two four-by-fours and one pick-up truck with some kind of machinery stowed in the bed. In the headlights, I could make out the camo paint job on the vehicles.

They were military vehicles.

A moment later, they had passed us, the noise receding into the distance along with the lights. They were heading north. Towards Bale Rocks.

Dignity clicked her torch back on. 'They've been going back and forth. One convoy every night, round the same time.'

'For how long?' Theo asked.

'At least a week now. Maybe longer? The boys and I didn't notice them immediately.' She waved the torch towards the ladder. 'Let's get down.'

We clattered down the ladder. Once I was standing on firm ground, my teeth chattering, I turned to Theo. 'What do you suppose it means?'

'Reinforcements,' he said grimly.

A shiver passed over me. 'They won't try to take over Bale Rocks, will they?'

'It seems likely.'

Bas hopped down beside us. 'It makes sense. The mayor can't hold the town with the force he has.'

We exchanged grim looks.

'Should we warn them?' I asked in a small voice.

'There's nothing to be done from here,' Dignity said, jumping down beside us. 'And in the middle of the night, no less.'

'We can try and send a message from Brackfields,' Theo said. 'Come on, let's get some sleep.'

I stared in the direction the cars had gone. Savannah was back there. And the military was coming. If the army clashed with the gangs, there would be collateral damage. People would die. I had to help my sister, my friends.

But yet, I was stuck here.

Powerless to do anything.

'Yeah,' I muttered. 'Alright.'

Theo roused me long before the sun rose. 'Harley, come on.'

'Yeah?' I mumbled, fighting against the wave of sleep that was threatening to pull me under again.

'It's time to go.'

'Alright.' I forced myself up, stumbling a little from light-headedness. I dressed in the dark and headed down to the toilet block to wash my face; there was running water, but it was as cold as ice.

When I exited, Bas and Theo were both waiting by the cars, arguing in low voices.

'...don't have a choice if you want to enter Brackfields,' Theo said.

'It's too risky,' Bas disagreed.

'I do this run all the time,' Theo snapped. He gripped his car door, his shoulders tense with restrained anger. 'Just let me take care of it.'

'What's the matter?' I asked.

'We'll have to go through a weapons checkpoint to get into Brackfields,' Theo said. 'We can't take guns in.'

The thought of relinquishing my weapon made my chest clench

with dread. 'What do we do?'

'I can hide them in my car—'

'I'm not going without—' Bas hissed.

'Do you want us to all get arrested?' Theo demanded. 'Because that is what will happen if you don't get off your high fucking horse—'

'Guys! Guys!'

They both turned their glares on me. I crossed my arms. 'How likely are we to run into trouble on the way?'

'Not too likely,' Theo said. 'Sometimes raiders lurk on this stretch, though.'

'Can we stop closer to Brackfields to hide our weapons?'

Theo opened his mouth… and shut it again. Then opened it again. 'Maybe. But it's best not to stop.'

'But we could,' I pressed.

He nodded reluctantly.

'Then that's what we'll do.'

Theo scowled. 'My way is safest.'

'We're travelling together,' I said. 'We can't do everything your way.'

Theo stared at me. 'You're one to talk,' he snapped. He turned and stalked around the truck to fiddle with something in the bed.

I glanced at Bas, who was watching me with an odd look on his face.

'What?' I asked.

'Nothing.' He, too, turned and went to check his car over.

Great, now they were both acting weird. Groaning, I opened my car door and climbed in.

After that auspicious start, we finally hit the road. Theo drove in tense silence, but, true to his prediction, we did not run into trouble. It was light by the time we reached Brackfields, although the sun hadn't risen above the horizon yet.

Gossiping with the customers in the Kranikovska had not prepared me for the sight of Brackfields. I'd pictured a larger version of Bale Rocks. Not… this.

Thick grey-brown smoke hung low in the air over buildings which were roughly the same colour. Tall, utilitarian apartment blocks crowded close together in the centre, with lower buildings around them. As we got closer, I lost sight of the apartments and instead could see the factories, blocky brown buildings, all of them pumping out smoke. An acrid smell permeated the air in the car.

Theo slowed the car as we drew level with the chain-link fence demarcating the first factory. Ahead on the road, I noticed some kind of blockade. Sturdy concrete blocks lay across the road, and there was a guard hut between the two lanes. It was a more permanent version of the blockades the military had set up in Bale Rocks.

My nerves made a reappearance. 'Are you sure they won't turn us away?'

'No, they're only checking for guns.'

'Oh.' I hugged my knees, watching the checkpoint come closer and closer. 'How do they enforce it, though? Don't they have gangs?'

'There's knife crime, but they don't have gangs. Law enforcement here is extremely strict.' Theo wove the car slowly between the concrete barriers and rolled to a stop at the boom. He glanced at me. 'You're my cousin and we're on our way to Providence, okay?'

I nodded.

A security guard wearing beige camo gear with thick body armour and a buff over his mouth and nose climbed down from the hut and strode over to us. Theo rolled the window down, and the stench of sewage and chemicals redoubled. *Yuck.*

'Morning, officer,' Theo said cheerily. Behind us, I could hear another car idling; I glanced back to see Bas had stopped outside the concrete barriers.

The officer squinted at us. He was in his forties, with a wrinkled brow and small, mean eyes. He radiated distrust, from his firm grip on the rifle to the tilt of his chin.

Lifting a hand, he used one finger to lower his buff. 'What's your purpose in Brackfields?'

'Supplies and refuelling,' Theo said. 'We're on our way to Providence.'

'Uh huh? How long you staying?'

'A day, two maybe. I'd like someone to look at the car—hit a bump a couple miles back and she's scraping the floor now.'

The officer's eyes narrowed further. His eyes roved over the outside of our truck.

'Got accommodation?'

'Not yet. I'll try the B&B off Feltman Avenue. We've stayed there before, haven't we?' Theo shot a smile at me. I nodded.

The officer's eyes drifted to me. 'Your wife?'

'My cousin, actually,' Theo said.

'Fine. Open the bonnet.' He stepped back, waving to the guard hut. Three more men emerged, all similarly dressed in beige camo. One of them was holding a strange contraption which looked like a mirror attached to a long pole.

Theo hit a button and the hood bonnet popped open. One of the guards moved around the car, using the mirror to check the undercarriage, whilst another looked under the bonnet. Once they cleared us, the first guard ordered, 'Papers.'

Theo reached into the glove compartment and pulled out a bundle of papers, which he handed to the guard.

'Out the car. Hands where we can see them.'

Heart in my mouth, I climbed out. One of the guards waved me away.

'Gotta search you, lady. This is a firearms-free zone.'

'Okay.' I nodded, swallowing. He patted me down professionally. When I turned so he could search my back, I could see that one of them was going through the car. Theo had put our guns in a secret compartment beneath the footwell of the back seat.

Would they find them?

Two of the guards conferred briefly. Oh God. Had they found something?

'You're good, lady,' said my guard.

'Th-thanks.'

'No need to worry. Just standard procedure.' He stepped back and Theo moved over to join me.

'You alright?'

I nodded.

A moment later, the guards stepped back, and the first one waved us over. He passed Theo the papers. 'You're good to go.'

'Thank you, sir.'

I held my sigh of relief until we were back in the car. Once the window was up, I asked, 'Do you do that every time you come here?'

'There are other ways in.' Theo shrugged as he fired up the car again. In front of us, the boom rose slowly. 'This is the easiest way, though.'

'This is *easy*?' As we rolled past the guard hut, I glanced back. Bas was pulling up to take our place.

Theo laughed.

'Yeah, this is pretty painless. Don't worry about him, Harley. He'll be fine. He's a big boy.'

I made a face. Was I really that transparent?

We cleared the last concrete barrier, and Theo gunned the engine, picking up speed. On either side of the road, tall walls and fences closed us in. Beyond them were the factories I'd seen as we approached: megaliths that pumped black smoke into the sky. Even though it was still early, I could see people wearing hard hats on the sites.

Brackfields. The place where we would hopefully find information on James Maddock.

I crossed my fingers in my lap. *Please.*

Once the checkpoint was out of sight, Theo pulled over. 'Lean in the back and grab my gun.'

'You aren't afraid of getting in trouble?'

'Harley baby, I've done this hundreds of times before.'

Right. I'd almost forgotten.

By the time I had fished Theo's and my handguns out, Bas had joined us. He rolled the window down.

'Where to?'

'There's a motel on Twelfth. It's grungy but safe,' Theo said.

Bas nodded, rolled his window up, and set off.

Brackfields was overwhelming. The further we drove through the city, the more I realised how small Bale Rocks really was. You could have fit half the population of our town into two streets here, or so it felt. Tall buildings rose on every street, balconies crowded with drying laundry; grocery shops, bakeries, and newsagents had queues out the doors; cars filled the streets. People stood talking to one another, or walking from place to place.

And there were police.

Uniformed men stood on every street corner. I watched them every time we passed a group, my heart thudding against my ribcage. Even though we weren't here to break the law, I couldn't shake the feeling that they were watching me.

'What happens if they catch us with weapons?' I asked.

'Then we get kicked out of the city,' Theo said. 'Well, not us. Samantha and Mark Banners do, though.'

'Who are they?'

'Those are the names on our papers.'

I stared at the side of his face. 'How did you manage that?'

'Greene made the papers for me.' He shrugged and slowed at a corner, turning off. 'I thought we might need them.'

He really had thought of everything.

'What about Savannah?'

Theo sighed. 'Don't ask questions you don't want to know the answers to.'

Exhaustion washed over me. I was so tired of Theo hating Savannah. For all her flaws, she was my sister. Besides, I was flawed, too. Why should he forgive me, but not her?

'I do want to know,' I said.

'I… Greene is sorting them out.'

'Why aren't they done yet?'

Theo shrugged. 'I told you not to ask.'

I pressed my lips together. He hadn't requested them originally. Of course not.

'I'm not letting this go,' I said.

Theo sighed. 'They'll be done, Harley. Worry about where we are now.'

Before I could reply, he performed a hair-raising turn, cut across an empty lot, and jammed on the handbrake.

'We're here.'

It took me several seconds to regain my equilibrium after that manoeuvre. Finally, I looked up. 'Here' was the greyest, dullest building I had ever seen. Unlike the Kranikovska, the room doors opened directly to the outside. Most of the building was covered in graffiti.

'Charming,' I muttered.

'It's Brackfields.' Theo shrugged. 'I'll go sort out rooms.'

He dropped the keys into my lap and jumped out the car. I watched him until he vanished through a door. Was I supposed to stay here? Could I get out?

My legs ached from sitting for so long.

Fuck it.

I flicked the lock on my door and opened it, then slid my legs out. Damn, that felt good. I'd never driven for this long before in my life. I felt all stiff and sore from sitting.

Rolling my shoulders, I looked around. The parking lot we were in was a wide-open space surrounded on three sides by tall buildings. The fourth, the motel, was a low, squat structure. I counted around half a dozen cars, all battered and dirty.

The air smelt of dust.

A moment later, Bas arrived, his car engine grumbling as he parked beside me. He climbed out.

'What are you doing? Where's Dunne?'

His terse tone made me scowl. He stretched, his neck clicking.

'He's sorting out rooms for us.'

'Good.'

Bas turned away and started fiddling in his car. I bit my lip.

I'd thought we were making progress, but suddenly it seemed like we had nothing to say to each other.

'Look, about the Hardwick thing—'

'It's water under the bridge,' Bas interrupted coldly.

'But—'

'Forget about it.'

I stepped back, smoothing my hands down my legs. 'You know what? Fine. We don't need to discuss it.' I turned around. To my relief, Theo was jogging back towards us.

His footsteps crunched on a few loose stones as he reached us.

'Alright,' he said, tossing me a key. I fumbled to catch it against my chest. 'I've got us rooms. Let's freshen up and then we can go see what we can dig up about James Maddock.'

ELEVEN

WE ENDED UP IN A CASINO.

I had never been in the front end of a casino before, but I had imagined them to be slightly more… boisterous. A few customers were playing half-hearted and subdued card games. Lights flashed in the arcade section, but most of the machines seemed to be broken. The floor was covered in dust and littered with empty drink bottles.

'I didn't take Maddock for a gambler,' I muttered.

'Desperate people are the first to cave,' Theo said.

He and Bas stood out terribly in their fatigues, but even in my torn jeans and fraying jumper, I was less shabby than ninety percent of the people here. A man slumped at a table clutching a mostly empty beer bottle. Two women, slender to the point of frailty, were bickering quietly over a slot machine. Even the music was lacklustre, a woman in a stained red dress playing an untuned piano in the corner. Theo led us over to a counter that was protected by a mesh barrier. A woman dressed in a shabby black and gold uniform stood behind it.

'Buying in?' she asked with a shadow of flirtiness in her voice. Mostly, she sounded—and looked—tired. Her makeup couldn't quite hide the bags under her eyes.

'Looking for the floor manager, actually,' Theo replied.

The woman set a small stack of chips on the table. 'We only allow people to stay if they're playing.'

Sighing, Theo laid a twenty NP note on the counter. The woman passed him the chips. 'Enjoy your evening.'

'I will,' he said brightly. As we turned away, he put an arm around my waist. 'Sam, baby, why don't you go get yourself a drink whilst Seb and I play a round or two?'

I shot him a look. No way I was waiting around whilst he did all the work.

Theo kissed me on the cheek. 'Let me handle this.'

He headed for the tables, Bas skulking after him. We weren't going to find out anything if Bas didn't improve his mood—unless Theo planned on intimidating the information out of the other players. But then again, I kind of shared Bas's sourness right now. Left to hang out at the bar like a good little girl whilst they did all the work. I'd have expected it from Bas, but from Theo?

We're in his element now.

But even so, that didn't mean I couldn't help out. I knew the rules of blackjack.

'You hanging out here all night, sugar?' the chip lady asked.

'No,' I muttered. I turned and headed for the bar. The bartender was a grey-haired man who was wiping down the taps with a dirty rag.

Bartenders make the best spies.

I would know. I'd done that job for two years.

I bit the inside of my cheek as a plan began to form in my mind.

The bar consisted of a laminate countertop, a rather sorry-looking collection of bottles, and a mirror which had suffered water damage and leant a brown cast to everything. I slid onto a stool with a collapsed red cushion and waved to the bartender, who ambled over.

'Whatcha having?'

'Whiskey.' I leant forwards. It would have been nice if I'd been wearing something sexier, but I had to work with what I had on. I slid my hand over my chest, casually flicking the buttons there open, and discretely tucked my shirt in to pull it taut against my chest and abdomen.

The bartender's gaze slid over my chest. *Gotcha.*

'Coming right up,' he said.

He fetched a bottle and glass, setting them in front of me to pour. I put my elbows on the bar top.

'You get a lot of business around here?'

He raised an eyebrow, enjoying the proffered view down my top. 'Some.'

I rested my head on my hand. 'Anyone interesting?'

He set the bottle down. 'You ain't flirting with me, girl.'

'Pretty sure I am.'

The bartender shook his head. 'I saw the boys you came in with.'

Damn.

'My cousins,' I hedged.

That earned me a smirk. 'Nah, not the way that one's watching you.'

He jerked his head. I followed his gaze and saw Bas, staring at me intently.

Look away, idiot.

But he kept his eyes firmly on me, a frown marring his lips.

'He's just making sure I'm safe,' I said.

'Ah-hah.' The bartender rolled his eyes. 'Sure, I believe ya. So, what can I getcha?'

I frowned and nodded to the bottle beside his hand. 'Whiskey?'

'I heard your drink order. You ain't here to just hang around whilst your boys gamble.'

Well, shit. I'd lost that round. So much for flirting a bit and getting him to open up—he probably dealt with plenty of women who tried that same trick. So… fess up, or go try someone else?

Bartenders make the best spies.

I sat up straighter. 'You're right, I'm not here to hang out. I'm looking for someone.'

He returned to pouring my glass and finally slid it over to me. I passed him a fiver to cover. 'Lemme guess. Lucy?'

'Who?'

Come again, now?

'Information, right?' He waggled his brows. 'Lucy's the one who'll help you. For a price.'

Lucy. Well, I had a name now. Which was more than we'd walked in with. *Take that, Theo.*

Fiddling with my hair, I asked, 'What price?'

'Depends on what you want to know.'

Of course it did. 'And where can I find her?' I shot a discreet look around the room. Was she here? None of the other patrons looked particularly knowledgeable—about anything other than what the bottom of a bottle looked like.

'Don't be impatient.' I glanced back at the bartender, who smirked at me. 'Finish your drink.'

I rolled my eyes. Was that how he wanted to play it? I'd just fled my home and was stuck with two guys who refused to get along. I wasn't in the mood for games.

I picked my glass up, tilted my head back, and downed it.

Oh, yuck. My eyes watered. Cheap-arse whiskey, that was for sure. Should have known. Still. I set the glass down and looked the bartender in the eyes. 'There.'

He laughed.

'Can you blame an old man for wanting company? Alright. Go speak to the lady in red. She'll put you through.'

I glanced around, even though there was only one lady in red. I'd noticed her when I entered—the pianist.

'Thank you,' I told the bartender.

He winked.

Summoning my courage, I crossed the room. The pianist was tinkling away, an expression of rapture on her face. Was it put on, or did she truly enjoy her job? Glancing around, I couldn't imagine actually enjoying working here.

I had intended to wait until she finished her song, but she paused when my shadow fell over the piano keys.

'Hello,' she said quietly. 'Can I help you?'

Here goes nothing.

'I'd like to request a song. It's called 'Lucy.''

'I don't know that one.' She had a soft, breathy voice. The kind that you couldn't imagine raised any louder than a whisper.

'Really?' I dropped my voice to match hers. 'It's my favourite.'

'Well…' She glanced at the bartender and a moment of unspoken communication passed between them. Then she looked at me. 'Lucy's not here tonight. You'll have to come back tomorrow.'

Tomorrow. Maybe we could wait, but it didn't feel like it. 'I'd prefer tonight. It's somewhat urgent.'

The pianist blinked, her lashes brushing her cheeks. Up close, she was very pretty. The makeup hid the tired lines around her eyes. 'Metalworks,' she said finally.

'Metalworks?' A factory? That sounded unlikely.

'It's a club on Fortieth Street. You can't miss it. You have to ask for a VIP table…' Her expression turned calculating. 'If you can afford it.'

'I'm sure I'll manage,' I said flatly. 'Thank you for your help.'

'Oh, it's my pleasure.' She closed her eyes, and her fingers began to dance over the keys once more.

I watched her for a moment. She really seemed to be enjoying herself. Huh, maybe she just loved music.

Enough that she didn't mind working here.

I stood and headed for Theo's card table. He was leaning on his elbows, staring at his cards with a look of rapt concentration. I slid in between two men opposite him, cocking my hip.

Theo glanced up at me.

'Ready to go?' I asked.

Theo frowned. 'No.'

'Well, I am. Come on.' I jerked my head towards the door.

One of the other men chortled. 'Don't think your lady likes it here.'

'I'm *busy*,' Theo hissed.

'Busy losing?'

He skewered me with a glare, then tossed his cards down. 'I fold. Come on, then.'

He stood, almost knocking his chair over. Bas followed him up. I headed for the door, and they fell into step with me.

'What's going on? We're here for a reason, Har,' Theo hissed.

'I got the information we need. Lucy. Metalworks. It's a club on Fortieth Street.'

'I know it,' Theo replied. 'We won't get anything there. That place is always packed—and pricey as hell.'

'That's what they told me.'

'Who?'

'The bartender and the pianist.'

'The bartender and the pianist,' he echoed incredulously. 'And you know that because…'

'I asked.'

'You just asked. Forget subtlety, forget being discreet—' Theo shook his head. 'Harley, what are you doing?'

'Getting information,' I said. I had a sudden urge to cross my arms and stamp my foot. I quelled it. Why was Theo doubting me? He'd never done that before.

'That was meant to be my job,' Theo snapped. 'I know the people here—'

'We don't have specific jobs,' I said. 'We're working together. I got what we needed. I'd have thought you'd be glad to be out of that place.'

Theo crossed his arms. We reached the weapons check, the cold air from outside washing over us. 'Fine,' he said. 'But just so you know, if they're wrong, this is going to be a very expensive mistake.'

'Do you think they're wrong?' I asked.

He shrugged. 'You're the one who spoke to them. Do you think they're lying?'

My information, my responsibility. Right. Annoyed, I snapped, 'They don't have any reason to. And besides that, no. I don't think they did. So let's go to Metalworks, and if it works, it works, and if it doesn't, tomorrow's another day. Okay?'

'Fine.' Theo marched ahead, displeasure radiating from his tense shoulders. I glanced at Bas. He was watching me—again—but with a different look now. I couldn't figure it out, so I raised an eyebrow.

'You got a problem, too?'

'No,' he said.

'Fine,' I muttered, following Theo to retrieve my knife.

Bas drove the three of us across the city, following Theo's directions. As we travelled, the buildings grew taller. They were also built closer together, lending the centre a cramped feeling, as though the buildings were pressing in on us. Fortieth Street was a narrow road lined with a haphazard collection of buildings, each one with wildly different architecture and signage, so that they looked more like they'd been placed there by a giant child playing a game than built with any kind of intention. We turned off beside a squat two-storey building with a brightly lit sign that encompassed the entire second floor.

SPICE HOUSE

best food in the West Rim

I'd have thought it a lofty claim, but there was a queue out the door.

The narrow alley Theo had directed us to led to an open lot behind. We weren't the only ones out on the town tonight—the lot was filled with cars of all shapes and sizes, from tiny vehicles that looked unfit for purpose, to pick-up trucks even larger than Theo's. Bas reversed into a parking space and we climbed out.

'It's just around the corner.' Theo led the way back to the street. 'When we get there, let me do the talking.'

I frowned. After our disagreement earlier, that didn't sit well with me. 'You know, I was the one who found her in the first place.'

'We need to present a united front, Har. That means only one of us does the talking,' Theo insisted.

And why not me? But even I wasn't a hundred percent confident in my own information-gathering abilities. So I scowled but nodded.

'Fine, then.'

'Thank you,' he said.

I looked at Bas. How did he feel about all of this? If he had any objections, they weren't obvious. He strode alongside us, looking as steady and determined as always.

Metalworks was in a two-storey building that took up an entire block. Even before we joined the queue, I could hear the music thumping, a pounding bass that seemed to thrum through my veins. It reminded me of the bunker, and I felt a sudden pang of nostalgia.

I'd hated working at the bunker, but it was home.

Somehow, I missed it.

We shuffled forwards. The queue moved fast. When we got to the front, I opened my coat and knotted my shirt beneath my breasts. If there was one thing I knew, it was how to get into clubs. The bouncer's gaze drifted over us. He frowned at Theo and Bas, but I got an immediate nod.

'They're with me,' I said.

Theo slid an arm around my waist, then traced his finger over the bouncer's arm. A bundle of cash was tucked into his fingers, and he transferred it discreetly to the bouncer. 'You don't mind, do you?'

'In you go, then.' The bouncer waved at the door, already looking at the group behind us. We headed inside, entering a narrow room with lockers down both walls.

'Weapons in a locker,' a woman said. 'And the fee to me.' She was sitting at a folding table.

Theo had given me a tiny stiletto which I could hide in my boot, but even so, checking my hunting knife felt wrong. It had been with me through so much; I hated to be parted from it. Still, I obligingly put it in a locker with Theo and Bas's assortment of weapons.

'We need a VIP table,' Theo said.

'Thirty NP,' the woman replied in a bored tone.

I grimaced—Theo had been right, it was pricey. He paid with a frown on his face, and the woman drew a cog on the back of each of our hands before allowing us through a set of swing doors at the end of the hall.

I'd expected it to be like the bunker, but once we got inside I discovered that it was anything but. Where the bunker was spread out, with minimalist furnishings and coloured lights that made everything seem alien, shiny, and futuristic, Metalworks was the opposite. They appeared to have converted an old factory, and most of the machinery was still there. The conveyor belt had been turned into a bar top; some hulking metal contraption was the stage, and the catwalk above was the VIP area. The whole place was cramped and industrial, reminding me irrepressibly of the bottling plant.

And Gabriel Tam's untimely demise.

I hadn't thought of that since we'd left, but now Briggs wandered back into my mind, his leering face reminding me of my sins.

I'd killed Tam in a factory just like this.

Bas had killed Briggs to keep him quiet.

And now here I was, in a place just like that.

A feeling of uneasiness crept into my stomach.

Theo led the way through the main room and over to the metal stairs. Our heavy boots clanged on the steps, though the noise was lost amidst the pounding music. At the top of the stairs, Theo turned to Bas.

'Can you keep watch?'

Bas nodded sharply and broke away from us to lean against the catwalk railing. Theo and I continued across a narrow walkway and entered a room with one glass wall overlooking the dancefloor below. Tables had been set up around the room, and there was a second bar across the back wall. A woman leant against the wall beside a door marked *'Staff Only.'*

Three of the tables were filled. Theo pulled out a seat at one near the wall. 'This'll do.' He motioned for me to sit. 'I'll grab us a drink.'

I nodded. Theo headed for the bar, and I looked around, nerves making my stomach churn. Here we were. At Metalworks. What if this was a dead end? What if it was a trap? Or Lucy couldn't help us?

I couldn't help but feel exposed, even in the small, dim room. It wasn't our location, so much as the distance from home.

This was unknown territory.

Theo returned, setting a beer in front of me. 'House speciality, apparently.' He sat opposite.

'And now?'

'You tell me.' He sipped his beer.

I grimaced. 'I don't know. The pianist just told me to come here.'

'You couldn't have got more specific—' Theo cut himself off. The woman in the corner had pushed off the wall and was approaching us with a slow, sultry gait. Her gaze was appraising. She stopped at our table, pulled a chair out, and sat with her elbows resting on the backrest and her legs crossed.

'Hello, dears. What brings you to my club?'

She was the club owner? She wasn't what I'd have expected a club owner to look like—oh, she had the confidence, the seductiveness, but she was a squat, strong woman with bulging muscles and an alert air that made me think she'd be more at home in the military that running a club. Her brown hair was cut in a neat bob, and the only makeup she was wearing was dark red lipstick.

'Are you Lucy?' Theo asked.

'Depends on who's asking.'

She leant forwards, her white button-down shirt slipping open enough to expose a lacy bra.

'I am,' Theo replied, taking a sip of his drink.

'And you are…'

'An interested party.'

The woman smiled superciliously. 'I see. I am, in fact, Lucy.'

'We were told you could help us,' Theo said.

She raised an eyebrow. Her gaze moved from Theo to me. It was an effort not to squirm.

Finally, she turned back to Theo, and her tone turned business-like. 'I only take cash or information.'

Theo and I exchanged glances. 'What sort of information?' Theo asked.

'The interesting kind.'

Unhelpful.

'Really.' She smiled. 'Fascinate me. Intrigue me. I hate being bored. And the world is so boring these days.'

Boring? Was she joking? That had to be a joke. I lived in constant danger—it was anything but boring.

'We've come from Bale Rocks,' Theo said. 'The military has taken over.'

'I know about that.' Lucy twirled a lock of hair around her finger. 'Old news.'

'The mayor is—'

'*Old news,*' she repeated. 'Come on, you'll have to try harder than that. You think I don't know these things? I'm the most important woman in Brackfields.'

'We could—' —*pay her*, I started to say, but Theo cut across me.

'Eduard Sayle is dead. What is that worth?'

Lucy's lips curved up in a smile. 'Now that—that's worth my while. Fine. We're in business. Tell me what you want to know.'

Theo leant back, taking a slow sip. Making her wait. Lucy's mien never faltered.

'We're looking for someone,' he said finally.

'Someone?'

'A man by the name of James Maddock.'

'Mm-hmm.' Lucy hummed. 'Can't say I'm familiar.'

'It might be a false name,' Theo replied. 'He claims to be from Brackfields, working for a construction company.'

'We have a few of those,' Lucy said. 'Do you have anything more concrete to go on?'

'He's around twenty-four,' Theo said. 'Dark hair.' He rattled off Maddock's description, but Lucy's expression remained politely blank. We could be at this all day and she'd never know who we were talking about. How many hundreds of thousands of people lived in the West Rim? Millions, even?

No, we needed something more. Something that she would recognise. Something like—

'He's the former mayor of Bale Rocks' son,' I blurted.

Theo shot me an absolutely scalding glare, but Lucy's eyebrows had risen, and there was a knowing glint in her eyes. She knew who I was talking about.

So does that mean it's true?

'In that case,' Lucy said slowly, 'I'm terribly sorry, but I am unable to help you.'

She didn't sound sorry—no, she sounded delighted. No doubt, word was going to spread that we'd been here, and we couldn't leave empty-handed.

'You know who we're talking about,' I said forcefully.

'Yes,' she said. 'But I still can't help you.'

'We paid upfront,' Theo said.

'So you did, so you did. Yet the person you seek cannot be found here. He passed through, from Langford.'

'That's not good enough,' I said. 'You need to give us more than that.'

'Like what?' Lucy crossed her arms, the movement emphasising her chest. Did she think we cared how she looked?

'About Maddock.'

'I can't tell you what I don't know.'

'Something that would interest *us*, then.' I had nothing else—and I had to say something. I could tell Theo was mad because I'd spoken up after promising he could do the talking.

'Something that would interest you…' Lucy assessed me, her eyes narrowed. 'Are you heading home soon?'

The question threw me. 'I… I don't see how that's any of your business.'

'Oh, of course not.' Lucy tilted her chin. 'Only I'd have thought you'd want to be there. There might not be much to go back to, what with what the army is planning.'

'The army?' Theo's eyes narrowed.

'Oh yes. We had a few of their boys in town just recently.' She hummed. 'They had all sorts of stories up their sleeves. Advanced weapons, an elite force. You name it. They were heading north.'

And she smiled.

'To Bale Rocks?' I asked.

'Sorry, darling, you only get what you paid for.'

My mouth dropped open. 'What we gave you is worth way more than that stupid hint!'

But I'd misspoken. Lucy's expression closed off suddenly.

'I've given you what you paid for. Time for you to go, I think.' She glanced over her shoulder, and I realised belatedly that she wasn't alone. Several sturdy military types lurked in the shadows, watching us. Lucy's backup in case a deal went bad, presumably.

I looked at Theo; he'd noticed the same thing.

'You know what?' He pushed his chair back and stood. 'I quite agree. A pleasure doing business with you.' He shot her an amiable smile.

'Any time,' Lucy replied, watching us closely.

We stuck close together as we left, Bas joining us as we headed down the stairs. I couldn't help but look back; Lucy watched us from the catwalk until we reached the door.

TWELVE

WE WENT STRAIGHT TO THE ROOM Theo and I shared when we got back to the motel. Two small beds, walls a dirty shade of beige, and a tiny window framed by motheaten curtains. I barely took any of it in as I collapsed onto one of the beds, sending up a cloud of dust.

'We have to go back to Bale Rocks.' The words burst out of me like water out of a blocked hose, I'd been holding them in so long.

'Go back? Harley, we're here to keep you safe!' Theo said.

'We're here to get information on Maddock so that we can go home.' I shook my head. 'This changes everything.'

'It doesn't change anything!'

I glanced at Bas. He was standing stiff and silent by the door, but after a moment he strode over and sat beside me.

Did that mean he agreed?

'We can't not warn them!' I pressed. 'That's our town!'

'We're a hundred and fifty miles away,' Theo said. 'And the military is way ahead of us. What can we even do?'

'We have to go back then—' I started.

'And get killed? We've been gone three days, Har. We're traitors now.'

'We can sneak in—'

Theo shook his head.

'Well, what other option do we have?' I cried. 'My sister is there. Our friends. Theo, we can't just abandon them to… to whatever the mayor has planned!'

Theo squirmed uncomfortably. I glanced at Bas, whose face was set in a frown.

'You said you could contact Ellery,' I said.

'Long-distance radio.' Bas hesitated. 'It's not a guarantee.'

'Do you have a radio that'll reach that far?' Theo asked.

'No. But I know where the transmitter stations are,' Bas said slowly.

'We could get a message back…'

'If we can get to a station. If we can get someone to receive the message. If that someone is able to take action,' Theo said pointedly. 'That's a lot of ifs.'

'Or we go back and warn them,' I said, leaning in. 'That would guarantee that we got the message through. If we leave now —'

'They're going to be on the lookout for us,' Theo said. 'We'll need different cars, for starters. Some kind of disguise. It's a logistical nightmare. And what if Lucy calls in her slip-up? The mayor will know the message is out.'

'Even more reason for us to go!' I said hotly.

'It's too dangerous!' Theo shook his head angrily. 'Let Bale Rocks go, Harley.'

'I won't,' I snapped. 'My sister lives there. My friends. It's my home!'

'Not anymore.'

'It is until I decide it isn't.' I clenched my fingers, digging them into my knees. My eyes stung, but I took a deep breath and pushed on. 'I'm not giving up on my sister. I don't care what you say. You can ask me anything else, but not that.'

Theo looked away, his shoulder stiff. After a long moment of silence, he muttered, 'Fine.' He stood sharply and rifled through his bag, pulling out a bundle of paper. 'Here.'

As he unfolded it, I realised what it was: a map. Printed in rough ink, it depicted our little pocket of civilisation.

Theo spread the map over his bed. 'Right. Here we go. You want to contact Bale Rocks? This is how it's going to work.'

He pointed to Brackfields, which occupied a spot in the centre of the map. North of it: Bale Rocks. Northeast: Crater's Edge and the crater itself. West: Boughton. South: the three cities.

'This is the West Rim,' he said. 'We're here, obviously. To send a message back to Bale Rocks, we need two transmitter stations.' He glanced at me. 'Long distance radio stations.'

'I get it. You don't have to explain,' I snapped.

'There are multiple problems with this.' Theo tapped his fingers against the edge of the map, making the paper rustle. 'I don't know where the transmission stations all are — that's the first problem. But I'm going to assume — this is the second problem — that like the one in

Bale Rocks, they're all maintained by the army.' He indicated a spot to the north of Bale Rocks. 'The closest is in the northern outpost.'

My heart sank. *The army?*

'What do we do?'

'I have friends who can intercept the message at the base,' Theo said. 'But that will complicate things. Wording a specific message so they get it but no one else does—and this is all assuming they're even on the base at the moment, and not posted in Bale Rocks.'

I twisted my fingers into the covers of my bed. This was sounding less and less likely.

'Then we have to go back—'

'There's another station,' Bas said.

I twisted to him. 'Really?'

'On Marco's farm. In Freetown.' He gestured to a spot northeast of Bale Rocks.

'Since when is there a transmitter station in Freetown?' Theo asked disdainfully.

Freetown was a farming community about ten miles north of Bale Rocks. Reeling, I asked, 'Ellery has a *farm?*'

'Yes,' Bas said.

'But—'

'Does the transmitter work?' Theo asked.

'It should do.'

'That's not a guarantee,' Theo snapped. 'These things need constant maintenance—'

'And Marco will be prepared for me to try and contact him through it,' Bas replied steadily. 'That's been our plan for a long time.'

'Plan in case of what?' I asked.

'No one cares about your revenge planning,' Theo cut over me. 'We need to know if the radio will work in an emergency.'

'Marco will have made sure it works as soon as we left town.'

Bas sounded certain, but I wasn't. Ellery hadn't proven so reliable when I'd needed him. Theo looked similarly sceptical.

'Fine, but that doesn't solve the problem of how we're going to actually get the message to him. Unless you happen to know where all the other transmitter stations are in the West Rim.'

Bas met Theo's gaze head-on. 'Camp Moraine, Mount Beaker Camp—'

'That's on the other side of the mountains,' Theo said.

'Fort Laughman—'

'In Providence. It'll take at least a day and a half to get out there.'

'Langford Base, Brackfields Base—'

'You have got to be joking.'

'Camp Echo.'

'That one's been taken over by TSE in Crater's Edge,' Theo snapped. 'They're all military bases. You want to break into a military base? You're fucking crazy.'

Bas crossed his arms. 'The only other option is going back.'

'I'm not going back,' Theo snapped. 'If you two are so determined to do that, you can go back and I'll take Harley—'

'Theo,' I hissed. 'We're not abandoning our town!'

'We can't break into a military base, Harley!' Theo threw his hands up. 'We'll all get killed.'

'Well, how else are we going to do it?' I demanded. I stared him down, determined not to give an inch. 'Seriously, go on. What's your bright idea?'

'I…' Theo opened and shut his mouth.

'Abandon them,' Bas said. 'That's his plan. Take you, run, and never look back.'

Theo crossed his arms. 'You'd do the same.'

'I don't abandon my duties,' Bas said.

'My duty is to Harley!'

'You say you want to protect her, but you don't understand her very well, do you?'

'I can talk for myself!' I blurted.

They both twisted to look at me.

'I'm not abandoning Bale Rocks,' I said emphatically. 'Theo, if you don't want to help, Bas and I can find a way in ourselves.'

Silence followed my declaration. I glanced from one of them to the other. Bas nodded, but Theo avoided my gaze.

'Is warning the town really more important to you than your life?' Theo asked.

'Yes.'

He stood and walked to the window, peering down at the dismal concrete lot. After a while, he sighed. 'Brackfields Base is the closest.'

'That's the one Lucy said the troops were coming from,' I said.

'Right, so they'll be operating with a skeleton staff. Unless they've brought in reinforcements from another base, but we'll have to hope they haven't yet,' Theo said. 'Even so, getting in won't be easy. We're going to need help.'

'Do you know anyone on the inside?' Bas asked. His tone was businesslike. We were back in his comfort zone: planning action.

'No, but I might know someone who can help anyway,' Theo said. 'Only we'd have to go to Langford to find him.'

'How much longer will that take?' I asked anxiously. We couldn't afford to lose any more time than we already had.

'Not long.' Theo sighed. 'It'll be quicker if I go straight there and meet you at the base.'

My eyes jumped to Bas against my will. That would mean I'd drive with him.

Alone, with him.

For the first time since we'd fled Bale Rocks.

I swallowed, suddenly nervous for reasons I didn't fully understand. 'I guess that would be okay. Do you know where we're going, Bas?'

Bas looked at Theo.

'I have a spare map,' Theo said. 'Alright then, let's go.'

'Now?' I asked, taken aback.

'When else? I thought we were in a hurry.'

'It's late. I thought we couldn't get in and out of the city at night.'

'In, no. Out, yes.' Theo moved back to his bed and started folding the map with brisk movements. 'Besides, we'll want to hurry. I have a feeling Lucy is going to regret being so open with us sooner rather than later.'

There were no words to describe the profound awkwardness of climbing into Bas's car an hour later. The last time I'd sat here, we'd been running from Bale Rocks. Urgency had got us through. Now, with my hair damp from a last-minute shower, the cold air chilling my skin, and fear weighing down on my shoulders like bricks, my stomach squirmed at the thought of sitting in a car with him, with nowhere to escape to.

Theo finished his last-minute checks and came over to my window.

I rolled it down. His face was pale with worry in the moonlight.

'Here.' He thrust a map at me. 'I've marked the route out from the main road. I assume you know how to navigate with a compass.'

'Yes,' Bas said.

'Good. If you miss…' He paused. 'If you reach the train line, you've gone too far. You shouldn't miss the junction, though.'

'We'll be fine,' I said. 'You worry about finding your contact.'

'It's not finding him that's the problem; it's convincing Mirko to let him go.'

'Mirko?' I asked.

'He's a gang leader in Langford. The guy we need works for him.'

'Will he let him? What are you going to tell him?'

'Let me worry about that.' Theo reached through the window and squeezed my hand. 'I'll see you at the fork in the road, an hour before sunrise.'

I nodded. Leaning out of the car, I hugged him. 'Love you,' I mumbled into his hair.

'You too, Harley baby.'

Theo stepped back, looking past me at Bas. 'Keep safe,' he said seriously.

'We will.'

Then my best friend loped off and climbed into his car. He gunned the engine and pulled out of the parking lot.

Silence fell. I glanced warily at Bas.

'Ready?'

'Ready,' he confirmed.

Theo had given us a list of supplies, and we needed to refuel. He'd also insisted we leave the city by a separate route, just in case. Bas found a service garage on the west road out of the city, and whilst they were filling up extra canisters of petrol, I headed inside to pick up the list of supplies. Bolt cutter and wrench, the brightest torch I could find, several tins of non-perishable food, and three balaclavas.

'Robbing a bank?' the clerk joked when I set the items on the counter.

My heart leapt into my mouth. 'N-no,' I stuttered. Fuck, that wasn't suspicious at all. I cocked a hip out and pasted a smirk on my face. 'Freeing slaves, actually.'

The clerk, a young, weedy guy, frowned at me. 'You insane?'

'Yeah, probably.' There wasn't much else I could say to that.

He snorted and rattled off the total.

Theo had given me two hundred-NP notes. I passed them over, and the clerk's smile turned to a frown as he pinched them between his fingers.

'Don't get many of these through my shop.'

'Can you change them?' I asked. If he couldn't, I didn't know whether I had enough small change.

'Yeah, sure.' He squinted at my face. 'These aren't stolen, are they?'

'What? No!' I smoothed my hands down my thighs, suddenly anxious. 'Look, can you hurry it up? My—my boyfriend is waiting for me.'

'Uh huh.' He seemed to take forever to count out the change, but finally he slid it onto the counter. I grabbed the heap of bills and coins and shoved them in one of the bags.

'Thanks.' I turned to leave.

'Safe travels out there!'

'Yeah. Thank you.' I hightailed it out to the yard, where Bas was leaning against his car, waiting. He pushed off and strode over to meet me.

'Got everything?'

'Yeah.' I pushed the heaviest bag into his arms. 'Let's go.'

Bas's eyes narrowed. 'What's wrong?'

'Nothing, just—' I tossed a glance over my shoulder. The clerk was standing in the doorway, watching us. 'I just think Theo's right. The sooner we're out of Brackfields, the better.'

We stashed everything in the boot, and finally, we pulled out of the yard. According to the directions Theo had given us earlier, we were only a short drive from the checkpoint. But when we got close enough to see it, Bas slowed the car and my heart leapt into my throat.

A swarm of people was milling about the checkpoint. I counted at least four cars, all of them military-issue four-by-fours.

We rolled to a halt.

'Do you… think they're waiting for us?' I asked.

'It's possible,' Bas said.

'Should we… Can we…' I swallowed. 'Should we try a different way out of the city?'

'Not sure there's a point.' Abruptly, Bas began driving again. I dug my fingers into my thighs.

'Bas! What if they are looking for us?'

'Then they'll be looking for us at every checkpoint,' Bas said.

'Theo said there were other ways in and out.'

'Well, I don't know them.' He steered us around the concrete barriers. The men who were milling around seemed to back away, and by the time we reached the checkpoint, a uniformed guard had exited the guard hut and was approaching us.

Bas rolled his window down. I couldn't breathe.

Shit, we're going to get arrested.

'Evening,' the guard called as he strolled over, one hand resting on the butt of the rifle slung over his shoulder.

'Good evening, officer.' Bas was a study in politeness. I could hear my heartbeat in my ears.

'Late to be heading out,' the guard said. I couldn't make out too much of him, even under the floodlights. His helmet and buff obscured his face.

'I prefer to travel by night,' Bas said.

''Course you do, 'course you do.' The guard rested his free hand on the window. 'And where are you headed, if you don't mind me asking?'

'Langford,' Bas said.

'Uh huh? What for?'

'A wedding.'

Pregnant pause.

Bas slid his arm around my shoulders, stiff as a lamppost. 'Our wedding.'

Oh boy.

I pasted a silly smile onto my face and leant into him, half burying my face in his neck. 'That's right.' I giggled.

Bas tensed even further.

Why the fuck had he picked this charade if he wasn't willing to play it?

I worked my hand between his back and the seat and massaged his hard muscles. 'We want to be with our family. My daddy's from Langford originally.'

'You're getting married,' the guard said, his tone dripping with scepticism.

'We are!' I shifted my head so I could catch his eye, beaming. 'In three days' time! Isn't it exciting? I've always wanted to get married, and I have the prettiest dress—made it myself. I'm a seamstress. Can't afford anything fancy, but we make do, right?'

The skin around the guard's eyes puckered. He lowered his buff, his mouth open to speak. Panic washed through me.

Then he pressed his lips together in a frown, staring at us. 'You're marrying him? Not much of a catch, is he?'

I squeezed Bas's shoulders.

'Love conquers all.' I giggled again. I sounded like a fucking airhead.

He raised an eyebrow. 'I see.'

Panic washed through me. 'Are you married?' I blurted.

'I am,' he said slowly.

'What's she like? Or he, obviously.' I needed to shut up. Really, really. But he was still frowning, and I had a sudden, desperate need to get him to smile. If he smiled, he'd let us through.

'Quiet,' he said flatly.

'Oh. Well…' I had run out of words. I scrambled for something else to say. 'That's great.'

The guard shook his head, but the frown was sliding off his face. He looked between us a few more times, smiling wryly, then said, 'I need to see your papers.'

'They're in the glove compartment. Won't you get them…' Bas cleared his throat. '…love?'

'Sure!'

I fished out the bundle of papers from the glove compartment and leaned over Bas to pass them to the guard. He stiffened again, his breath puffing against my neck. The guard studied the papers for a long time and stared at our faces for even longer.

He was going to turn us back.

I bit my tongue, keeping myself still and my smile firmly in place. I couldn't afford to show a single sign of nerves.

He turned and signalled something to the guard hut. My heart shot into my mouth.

This is it. We're done for—

'You're good to go.' He handed the papers back to Bas. 'Wait until the light turns green. And have a safe journey. It's dangerous out there.'

Relief flooded me, so suddenly and sharply that I could have puked from it. I felt lightheaded. Bas dropped the papers in my lap.

'Thank you, officer.'

The guard nodded and retreated. Bas rolled the window up.

'Shit,' I whispered.

The boom rose, and Bas drove us agonisingly slowly through and past the concrete barriers on the other side. Three—two—one. We were out. We were free. The open road stretched ahead of us.

'Don't ever do that again,' Bas said.

I turned to look at him, my mouth dropping open. *What the fuck?*

'Do what? Help you out?'

'Drape yourself all over me like some airhead.'

Was he joking? Without me, we'd have been caught for sure!

'You could say thanks, you know,' I snapped.

'*Thank you?* For molesting me?'

'Molesting you?' I crossed my arms. 'You could have fucking warned me you planned on pulling something like that!'

'I could handle it,' Bas said coldly.

'Yeah, you were handling it so well,' I sneered. 'You wanted him to believe we were going to get married, and what? You're so miserable over your fate that you can't even muster a smile?'

'I'm perfectly capable of smiling. I didn't need you throwing yourself at me.'

'Throwing myself at you? Are you kidding? I was trying to sell the act!'

'You could have done it without touching me!'

He sounded angry, but there was a note of desperation in his voice that made me pause. In the ambient light from the city, I could see that he was gripping the steering wheel hard. His shoulders were tense.

Uncertainty filled me. Had I triggered some kind of trauma?

I swallowed, forcing my anger down to a simmer.

'I'm sorry,' I said, my voice small. 'I was just trying to help.'

Bas jerked his shoulders as though he could throw off the memory of my touch. Then he accelerated, carrying us away from Brackfields and into the inky darkness.

THIRTEEN

THE SILENCE IN THE WASTELAND was absolute. My breathing sounded like a landslide as I sat alone in the dark car in the middle of nowhere.

Thud!

I grimaced and hunched my shoulders to make myself as small as possible.

Okay, so I wasn't totally alone, nor was I technically in the middle of nowhere. Bas was here, currently laid out on top of the car so he could get a good view of the road to Langford. We were parked about a hundred yards off the junction where we'd agreed to meet Theo, only Theo wasn't here.

He was late.

He'd said an hour before dawn. Dawn was approaching, the first light brightening the horizon, and he still wasn't here.

He'd said he would be here.

Thud! Crunch!

I jumped as Bas hopped to the ground beside my window. Yanking the handle, I opened the door.

'Shit, you scared me!'

Bas turned, his hand on his gun. 'Harley! Keep the door shut!'

'Can you see Theo?'

'No, not yet. Shut the door.'

I made a face but complied. Since we'd left Brackfields, Bas had spoken to me about four times, each time barking some kind of order. Do this, do that, don't do this, don't do that.

In short, our 'working relationship' had completely regressed. I'd tried to bring up why, but he'd brushed me off.

Bas opened his door and climbed in.

'Should I keep watch?' I asked. My breath fogged the air.

Bas shut the door, closing out the chill wind. 'Stop worrying. He's only half an hour late.'

'He said he'd be here!'

'So things didn't go exactly according to plan,' Bas said. 'There's no point in worrying yet.'

'I don't get how you can be so calm,' I muttered. Except I did. Bas was calm because he didn't care if Theo was okay. 'How would you feel if it was Ellery and he was late?'

'The same,' Bas said. 'Because I trust Ellery to get the job done.'

I scowled. 'You could at least try to understand where I'm coming from.'

Bas shrugged again.

Fan-fucking-tastic.

I leant my head against the window. 'Can we turn the radio on?'

'No, it will run the battery down.'

'What?'

He shot me a frown. 'Don't you know anything about cars?'

'I know they run on petrol.'

Bas's expression was scathing. 'That'll serve us well if we break down.'

'I've never even been out of town before, okay? When the hell was I supposed to learn?'

Bas locked his jaw and turned away. 'Sorry I didn't have a cushy upbringing like you did.'

'Cushy?' I hissed. 'You think my life was *cushy?*'

'Dance classes—two parents who doted on you—a fancy school. How else would you describe it?'

'You fucking—'

At that moment, the grumble of an approaching car reached us. I cut myself off hastily, turning back to the road.

Was that Theo?

Bas shielded his eyes and peered out into the darkness. I squinted against the headlights as the car pulled off the highway, bouncing down the embankment to come to a stop beside us.

I reached for my door. 'That's him.'

'Wait!' Bas snapped.

I froze. 'What?'

'Don't just throw your door open every time you see someone you think you know! What if someone else is driving his truck?'

'And they knew to stop here?' I rolled my eyes. The door of the truck opened, and Theo slid out, hand on his gun.

'See? It's him.' I threw my door open and jumped out. 'Theo!'

'Hey.' He caught me as I hugged him tightly.

'You're late. Where were you?' Against my will, my voice shook.

'There was a bit of trouble convincing Mirko. But it's fine. I'm here, and Rhett is with me.'

'Rhett?' I stepped back, peering into the cab of the truck. A figure sat in the passenger seat, but it was too dark to make out any details.

'I'll introduce him in a minute,' Theo said. 'We need to get away from the road.'

'Alright.'

He went around to Bas's side of the car, and the two of them conversed in low, urgent whispers for several seconds. I couldn't catch more than nonsensical snippets before Bas nodded. 'Fine, that's what we'll do.'

Theo stepped back. 'Follow my car.'

'Alright.'

Bas rolled his window up, and Theo retreated to his car, switching it on. He waved to me out the window before rolling off into the wasteland. A moment later, Bas and I followed, the car bouncing on the uneven surface.

'What is the plan?' I asked.

'There's a dry riverbed near here. We can hide the cars there.'

'And then?' I peered out into the brightening morning. The wasteland here was different to the terrain further north. Warped trees poked up out of the dirt, with wide open spaces between them. Large rocks and hunks of concrete—those were the same as around Bale Rocks. But there were no scrubby bushes threatening to grab your ankles and trip you.

'Then we walk.'

'Oh.' I swallowed. Walk? In the wasteland?

'Aren't there... wild animals?' *And slavers? And a million other dangers?*

'You wanted to do this, Harley. I can also drop you in the nearest city and leave you there.'

Ouch.

I hugged myself, keeping my eyes on the wasteland as my stomach churned. Bas had brought me here. Was he really having regrets now?

Hadn't we been aligned on doing what we could to help Bale Rocks?

The sun rose on the horizon, turning the sky red.

'*Red sky in the morning, shepherd's warning.*'

Something my dad had always said.

'*Red sky at night, shepherd's delight.*'

The sand was yellow. Around Bale Rocks, our sand was red.

I felt very far from home all of a sudden.

We drove for maybe twenty minutes, though it felt longer because we had to stick to a crawl to navigate the loose sand. Every time the wheels lost traction, the engine would roar as Bas revved it to get us moving again—and my heart would skip a beat. What if someone heard us?

We were definitely the loudest thing in the wasteland that morning.

Finally, Theo's truck vanished from sight, and a moment later Bas and I followed him between a narrow gap in a cluster of bushes and down a steep bank into an overgrown riverbed. Bas parked beside Theo and opened his door.

'Come on.'

I climbed out, staring around me. I'd never seen anything like it—bushes crowded in on us, with strange wax-like leaves. The sand was damp and firm underfoot, though when I stepped back my feet threatened to sink in. I hastily moved away from the soft spot.

'This is stable, right?'

'It'll be fine,' Theo called. He hopped down from his truck, landing with a thud on the hard sand. 'Right, did you get the supplies?'

Time for business, then.

But it was better than thinking about Bas and what the hell I'd done to piss him off now. I rounded the car and opened the boot.

'Here.'

'Thanks.' Theo took the bags. 'Did you get out of Brackfields alright?'

I glanced at Bas, who was approaching us. 'Fine,' I murmured. 'You?'

'They were searching cars, but they didn't find anything.' Theo shrugged. 'I've had worse. I doubt it was us they were looking for. Come on, let's get this packed up.'

He swung the tailgate of his truck down and laid out our gear to check it. As he worked, he murmured, 'I need to warn you about something.'

'What?' I asked warily. *More trouble?*

'Rhett. He's… difficult.'

'Difficult?' Bas echoed, swinging a bag onto the tailgate beside Theo.

'He can do the job,' Theo said. 'I promise. Just try to ignore him, okay?'

Ominous. I glanced into the cab of Theo's truck. Rhett seemed to be sleeping, his head against the window.

Once he'd packed everything up, Theo handed me a small backpack. 'Are you alright to carry this?'

'Yes.'

'Thanks.'

At that moment, Rhett's door opened and he stumbled out, almost kissing the dirt. We all turned to watch him. He grabbed his door to right himself and stared back at us.

'What you all looking at?'

He wasn't that old, but the years hadn't been kind to him—or rather, I suspected he hadn't been kind to himself. He was unshaven, his hair lank and unwashed, and his eyes unfocused. In short, he was drunk. He proved it as he stumbled towards us, swaying.

'You brought a girl,' he slurred.

'Problem with that?' I snapped.

'Yeah.' He looked me up and down. 'You gonna walk miles through bushland in those pants, darling?'

'Great, drunk *and* misogynistic. That really makes my day.'

Rhett burst out laughing. He fell against the side of the truck, banging the metal. 'Oh, she's mouthy, too.'

'Leave Harley alone,' Theo said.

Rhett just snorted.

'Are we leaving or not?' Bas asked darkly.

'Yep,' Theo said.

'Wait,' I muttered to him. 'Should I change?'

He glanced at my jeans. 'Doesn't matter what you wear so long as you're comfortable. I have cargo pants in the truck that should fit you though.'

I'd been wearing these jeans so long they were practically becoming part of me. But if we were going to be walking… maybe I should change.

'Please.'

I had to duck behind the bushes to change. When I came out, Bas swept a gaze over me. 'Done being a princess?'

Fuck you too.

I marched past him and grabbed my pack. 'I'm ready.'

Our trek didn't begin well. The bank itself was the first hurdle. The loose sand kept making my feet slide out from underneath me, and I had to haul myself up by grabbing a tree branch.

'Need help?' Theo asked, holding out a hand to me.

I glanced at the others. Even Rhett had managed it without difficulty.

'No thanks,' I said, dragging myself the last way up on my own strength.

'Alright,' Theo said and turned away.

Once I'd survived the bank, the land flattened out and the only trouble was the loose sand, which seemed to grab at my boots and somehow worked its way between the laces to grind between my toes. As the sun rose higher, it warmed up enough that I could take my coat off.

Rhett kept up a steady drunken chatter. His pack clinked as he walked, and twice I saw him drinking from a hip flask.

This was the guy we were entrusting our mission to? He could barely walk straight.

A glance at Bas told me that he shared my feelings. His lips were pressed into a thin line, and his brow was wrinkled from scowling. But he wasn't saying anything either.

About half an hour in, Theo distributed rations bars. Rhett snatched his and wolfed it, before burping.

'Ahhh.'

I grimaced and turned so I couldn't see him as I unwrapped mine and took a bite.

'Ugh—that's—' There wasn't even a word for it—it was at once dry, chewy, and sticky. Worse, it left an ashy sludge on my tongue and teeth. *Disgusting.*

'I know, but food is food,' Theo said.

I swallowed and forced myself to eat the rest in three big bites. When I paused to stash the wrapper in my pack, I caught Rhett smirking.

'What are you looking at?'

'Don't like the provisions, princess?'

'No one asked you for your opinion,' I snapped.

He chortled and fished his flask out of his pocket again. I turned away again. *Gross.*

'Ignore him,' Theo muttered.

'I know.' But I couldn't resist scowling at his back as we marched in through the punishing sand. If there was one thing I hadn't missed about working in the Kranikovska, it was misogynistic drunks.

A pang shot through me. I hadn't even thought about the Kranikovska in… ages. Maybe even not since I'd left. How were my colleagues doing? Was the military getting them down?

Did they miss me?

I had disappeared without a trace. They had to be worried.

And what about Savannah?

Don't think about it.

But I'd opened the floodgates, and now the worries were rushing in. Was Savannah okay?

Maybe Ellery had managed to get her a message?

But even as I thought it, I knew he probably wouldn't do that for me. No—Savannah had no idea where I was.

I'd left her alone.

'Let's stop here,' Theo announced, cutting through my thoughts. 'I'll scout ahead.'

'Are we there?' I asked, glancing around. There was no discernible difference to the wasteland: more trees, more sand, more rocks.

Theo nodded to a silvery construction that glinted in the sun, just visible above the treeline. 'That's the transmitter station. We're not too far away.'

'Oh.'

Seeing it brought back all of my nerves. We were here—the next step was getting in. No big deal: it was only a highly secure military compound chock full of armed men who'd probably shoot us on sight.

No big deal.

'I'll be back in a bit,' Theo said. He handed me his pack and slipped off between the trees.

My nerves redoubled, my heart rate picking up. Truth be told, I had no idea what lay ahead. Armed men, for sure. But what else?

'Nervous, girlie?' Rhett asked.

'None of your business.' I turned to Bas and, trying to sound efficient and business-like, asked, 'What's the plan once we're in?'

'Find the transmitter station, send the message, and get out,' he said flatly.

Great. Absolutely super.

'You know, you could be a little more helpful,' I hissed.

Bas glared.

'So, you two are boning and you don't want your mate to find out?'

We both spun to face Rhett. He was smirking like the cat that caught the canary.

'Where the fuck would you get that idea?' Bas snapped.

'I dunno.' Rhett waggled his brows. 'Fact that you've barely looked at each other all morning?'

'We're not!' I hissed. 'Shut up!'

Rhett laughed. 'Oh, you definitely are, girlie. I can practically smell the awkward car sex on you.'

Great, just great.

'It's not possible to smell something that isn't there,' I said. 'Though with the amount you've drunk, I wouldn't be surprised if you were hallucinating.'

'Judgy-judgy,' Rhett chuckled.

I bit my tongue. There was no point in arguing with him; he'd turn anything I said into ammunition. I shot a glance at Bas, who had his arms crossed and was glaring into the distance.

Car sex. Ugh.

Bas and I could barely have a conversation. There was zero chance of us ever managing to have sex.

Not that I wanted to, or anything.

Definitely not.

For fuck's sake. Now he'd gone and put the idea in my head.

I ground my teeth together and moved a few steps away from the men, peering between the trees to see where Theo had gone. All I could see was more trees.

'Don't go too far, girlie,' Rhett called. 'Wouldn't want you to get lost.'

I whirled around. 'Shut your mouth or I'll punch it.'

It was an unusually violent threat for me, but I felt like something had snapped deep inside. All the worry, all the fear… I was stuck here in the wasteland, hundreds of miles from anything I knew, and he was making dickish comments. *Fuck him.*

Rhett burst out laughing. He doubled over, slapping his knees. 'Oh, that's good. That's just too good. Sure, babe. I doubt you've ever punched a man in your life.'

'Of course I—'

'*I have though.*' Bas's voice was quiet, but it cut through Rhett's laughter and my retort. 'And I've hit much smaller targets than your big mouth.'

Rhett shut up, appraising Bas with a nervous look. He opened his mouth.

'If you're not boning her, can I have her?'

He swept his hip flask out of his pocket, tipping his head back to take an arrogant sip. Bas snatched it and dumped the alcohol out at the base of a tree.

'Oi! That's mine!'

'We're here to work,' Bas said. 'Next time you pull a bottle out, I'll break it over your head. Now I suggest you take a walk.' He mimed walking with his fingers. 'Before I decide to just break your head instead.'

Rhett glared at him. 'You ain't nearly as fun as Theo is.'

'Didn't realise I was expected to be.' Bas's expression was completely unyielding.

Grumbling under his breath, Rhett retreated to a tree about four or five yards away and slumped down in its roots, his arms crossed. I glanced at Bas.

'Thanks.'

'Don't thank me. That had nothing to do with you.'

Ouch.

'Fine,' I snapped, 'I don't thank you, then. You're a dick with an attitude problem, and it's always a good day when you find someone to direct it at who's not *me.*'

Bas glared. 'Good for you.'

He turned on his heel and marched off between the trees, leaving me alone to guard the packs.

Honestly.

Theo returned about half an hour later. I was in the middle of having a sip of water—our most precious resource, as we hadn't passed a single stream, or even a puddle, since we'd started walking—when he slipped between the trees. Bas materialised about two seconds later, as though he'd been there all along.

'So?' Bas asked.

'They've cleared the perimeter of trees, so we'll have to approach in the open,' Theo said. 'We can get to about seventy yards away from the fence, at a guess.' He narrowed his eyes at Rhett, who ambled over to us.

'Our approach is from the south,' Rhett announced. 'Riverbed. Poor visibility. There's a stormwater culvert. It's always been a blind spot.'

'Right.' Theo swung his pack on his shoulder and glanced my way. 'Ready to walk again?'

I nodded.

We walked with more purpose this time. Theo periodically scouted ahead, making sure we were staying well back from the treeline as we headed for the southern end of the base. It was further than I'd expected. By the time he called a halt, my feet ached, and the sand had rubbed at least one blister on my toes. We were standing at the top of the bank, but here the riverbed wasn't completely dry. A stream trickled sluggishly down the very middle, leaving crevasses in the grey sand.

Theo passed a canteen around. I sipped the icy water, then handed it to Bas.

'You're up,' Theo told Rhett.

Rhett staggered to the edge of the bank and leant over the side, grabbing a sturdy tree branch to hold himself up. After a moment, he heaved himself back and stumbled to a spot a bit further along. This process was repeated twice more before he suddenly pitched himself down the bank and vanished from sight with a thud.

I glanced at Theo. 'Are you sure he's capable?'

'Give him a chance,' Theo muttered.

I was rapidly running out of chances to give—at the rate Bas was using them up, there were barely any left over for mister alcoholic misogynist. Fortunately, at that moment, he called out, 'Found it!'

We all hurried to the edge. Rhett was in the riverbed, picking at the branches of a large bush. 'Mind coming down. Concrete's a harsh mistress.'

Theo raised an eyebrow at me, but I wasn't in the mood for an 'I told you so.' I scoured the edge, grabbed a branch, and started to walk myself down into the riverbed.

A few minutes later, we all stood on the damp sand, in a loose huddle around our entry point: a concrete pipe with a broken metal grate blocking the outlet. It was half-covered by thorny bushes, and the stale smell of stagnant water emanated from it.

I pulled my scarf up to cover my nose and mouth. 'You cannot be serious.'

'Deadly serious, princess,' Rhett sang.

'It stinks.'

'We can always leave you behind if it's too much for you, princess.' Rhett smirked.

I gritted my teeth. 'No, I'm coming.' No question about it—I wasn't waiting here for the men to do the hard work for me. This had been *my* plan.

'Fine.' Rhett gestured ostentatiously. 'Lead the way, princess.'

Dick.

Not to be outdone, I wrapped my scarf around my face more securely and climbed up into the mouth of the culvert. It was wide enough that I could stand at my full height, though I guessed Bas and Theo would have to duck. Rhett wasn't too much taller than me—not that I cared if *he* hit his head.

The metal gate appeared to just be leaning against its hinges. I grabbed it and pulled, and the whole thing keeled towards me.

'Oof!' I heaved it sideways and managed to lean it against the side of the culvert. Not elegant, maybe, but it was out of the way. I glanced back at the others. 'Let's go.'

The weak sunlight hardly reached ten yards into the tunnel. I pulled my torch out and shone it ahead as Theo joined me at the front.

'Alright?' he asked, his voice echoing weirdly.

'Yeah,' I mumbled, gripping the torch harder to hide how my hand was shaking.

The culvert sloped upwards, mostly gently, but at times steeply. Twice, we had to climb a ladder in single file. Most of my energy was focused on not thinking about the fact that we were *underground*.

Deep underground.

In a *small* tunnel.

With tonnes of heavy earth above us.

Okay, I was exaggerating slightly. Eventually, we would have to surface. Eventually, and hopefully at our destination.

After what felt like miles and miles of traipsing through a layer of muck, the tunnel levelled out. Amidst the drips of green gunge, I could pick out notches on the sides of the pipe—1m, 1.5m, and so on. And every so often, there were nooks in the side of the pipe, large enough for a man to stand in, with ladders leading up to access hatches.

Rhett pushed his way to the front, snatching Theo's torch and shining it into each alcove. 'Should be somewhere here.'

Theo tucked his hands into his pockets. 'Make sure we come out in the right place.'

'You doing the job, or am I?'

I scowled at his back. Did he get off on being a jerk or something?

We walked on, our footsteps clanging loudly. The only other sound was our breathing—I could hear Bas behind me, his breaths short and sharp.

Realisation struck me.

Of course—I kept forgetting Bas was claustrophobic.

And it hadn't even occurred to me that he might have trouble coming in here.

I felt like such a shitty human being.

Turning back, I offered him a sympathetic smile. 'Are you okay?'

Bas's eyes narrowed. 'Stay focused, Harley.'

Of course.

Right, then. I turned back to the front, picking up my pace. If Bas didn't want sympathy, I wouldn't give him any. He could look after himself.

A moment later, Rhett stopped abruptly. I pulled up a second before I collided with him.

'I think this is it,' he said.

'You think?' Bas echoed incredulously.

'Ey, it's been a while since I was here.'

'Yeah,' I muttered, 'we can tell.'

'Less cheek from the peanut gallery, yeah? I don't have to help you.'

Then don't, I thought savagely. Not that I'd say that out loud. But I definitely wouldn't miss Rhett once we said goodbye to him.

Rhett put the torch between his teeth and slipped into an alcove. His boots rang against the metal rungs as he climbed the ladder.

'Crowbar,' he demanded.

Theo fished a crowbar out of his pack and passed it up. Rhett heaved and grunted, and a shower of dust rained down on us. Finally, a scraping noise echoed down the alcove.

'Got it!'

Rhett tumbled off the ladder, hitting the walls and floor with a litany of clangs and thuds. Grabbing the ladder, he hauled himself upright.

'I'm alright, I'm alright, don't worry.'

I pressed my lips together.

'Maybe one of *us* should scout ahead,' Bas said.

'Have at it.' Rhett rolled his eyes. 'Hope you get shot.'

Bas gave him a withering glare before grabbing the ladder and climbing up. He vanished from sight, and a few tense moments later, his voice reached us.

'All clear!'

'You go next,' Theo told me.

I nodded and slipped into the alcove. When I touched the ladder, rust flaked away. I climbed up and through a small manhole, emerging into… a shower block.

The stink of sweaty human hit me, and I wrinkled my nose. *Charming.*

There were four stalls along one wall and sinks on the wall opposite. Bas stood off to one side, next to the door, gun in hand.

'All good?' Theo called.

'Yeah.'

He started up the ladder. I joined Bas by the open doorway, then pulled my gun and peered around it.

'Careful,' he said.

'I am being careful.'

There was no one in sight. The base seemed strangely deserted, nothing moving in the still winter day.

'Where is everyone?' I whispered.

'Can you see the transmission station?' Theo joined us, a hand on his holster and his eyes alert. I could hear Rhett clattering up the ladder.

'Maybe we should leave him behind,' I muttered.

'We might need him to get us in the station,' Theo said. 'Just ignore him.'

'Easy for you to say. You're not the one he keeps harping on at!'

'Just let it wash over you. He's not important.'

'Who's not important?' Rhett joined us, his whiskey breath washing over me. I turned away.

'It's nothing,' Theo said. 'Let's move out.'

Rhett took the lead, against my better judgement. Mostly, I was annoyed at Theo. There must have been a better option.

Yet we were stuck with this guy.

Fortunately, he'd got one thing right: he had brought us out on the north end of the base, and the transmitter station wasn't too far away. I could see it now, a beige building with a tall metal tower protruding from the top.

And armed guards around the base. I could see two men, both holding rifles.

'What's the plan?' Theo asked as we pressed our backs into the service entrance of a low brick building.

'I'll draw their attention away from the building, then someone can sneak behind and knock them out,' Rhett said. 'Slave boy over there can help me.'

Bas immediately covered his left wrist with his right hand, glaring at Rhett. 'That's none of your business.'

'Don't worry, I don't care about your deep dark mysterious past.' Rhett rolled his eyes. 'You should be no stranger to danger though. Come on, boy.'

Bas looked ready to commit murder, but he nodded sharply. 'Lead the way.'

'Do you take other orders, or—'

'And keep your mouth shut, or I'll shoot you in the back of the head,' Bas added.

Rhett's lips quirked. 'Gotcha.' He turned and sauntered off around the edge of the building. Bas followed, gun held at the ready.

A moment later, they were out of view. I peered around the corner, but Theo pulled me back.

'Trust them, Harley.'

Rhett didn't exactly inspire confidence, though I supposed Bas did. We waited in tense silence, and I stroked my fingers idly over the handle of my gun. It was reassuringly solid, but it suddenly made me wonder if I could really shoot a man.

'Intruder!' someone shouted.

I peered around the corner again, right in time to see Bas clock one of the guards over the head with the butt of his gun. The other guard was out of sight.

Bas vanished around the side of the building, fleetfooted and silent.

'Harley,' Theo warned.

I pressed myself harder against the building, but I couldn't bring myself to look away. Where was he—

'All clear!' Rhett hurried towards us, holding what looked like a lump of stone in his hand. As he reached us, he threw it aside. 'And no one dead. Quite the achievement.'

'Let's go,' Theo said briskly. 'We can't afford to wait around— someone might have heard the call go up.'

'We'll hear a siren if word gets out.' But Rhett turned as well and set off at a steady pace towards the radio station. I followed them, every muscle in my body tense. If anyone had seen, we were screwed…

We reached the base of the tower. The door was locked with a keycode. Rhett squinted at it as Bas joined us.

'Should be…' He tapped a few keys. The keypad made a dispirited beep. 'Ah, guess not. Let's try…'

He hit a few more keys.

Beep-beep.

The door slid open.

'Still got it, boys!' Rhett beamed at Theo.

'Yeah, yeah, well done,' Bas snapped. 'Let's hurry it up, shall we?'

Rhett's expression darkened. 'After you, then, sonny.'

We all filed in. The radio station was a large, round building. Bas crept up a flight of stairs, then vanished from view. A moment later there was a grunt from upstairs.

'Clear,' Bas called.

When I reached the top, he was laying a man in military gear out on the floor.

The transmitter station looked like something from another planet. Entire counters and walls were covered in all sorts of devices, buttons, levers… I couldn't even name half of them, let alone guess what they were for. I ran a finger over one of the panels. The buttons were labelled, but the paint had faded so I had to squint to make out the letters. I was afraid to touch anything in case I broke it.

Bas took a seat in a swivel chair with a torn leather back and turned to what I assumed was the main console, which was covered in more lights and buttons.

'You know what you're doing, boy?' Rhett asked.

'You're welcome to take over,' Bas said without looking up. He was pressing buttons with an efficiency that elevated my confidence somewhat. A few lights blinked, and then he pressed a large grey switch. 'Freetown Station, come in. Freetown Station, come in.'

We waited in tense silence. It stretched out, seeming to fill the room and draw out all the air. I could hardly breathe.

Bas bent forwards. 'Freetown Station, come in. Freetown Station, come in.'

More silence. Then—something. A faint crackle, maybe. It cut out a second later.

'Ellery, come in,' Bas said.

'It's not working, boy,' Rhett taunted.

'The problem could be on either end,' Bas said. He studied the console as though it might yield the answers. Maybe for him it did, but it certainly wasn't for me.

Pressing the talk button again, he said, 'Freetown Station, radio check.'

This, too, was met with silence.

'It shouldn't be a problem on this end,' Theo said. 'The army maintains this station.'

'We have no way of knowing that.'

'So we test it then.' Theo hit another button. 'Radio check.'

A voice came over the line.

'Basecamp, this is Station Mike-Bravo. Reading you loud and clear.'

We all froze. Bas opened his mouth—and hesitated.

Rhett leant in. 'Station Mike-Bravo, this is Basecamp. Thank you for confirming.'

'Roger that. Mike-Bravo out.'

Rhett backed off. 'Very clever. Now they know we're here.'

'This station was manned anyway,' Bas said. He glared at the console. 'So the problem is on the other side.'

'Ellery must not have got it working,' Theo said.

Bas set his jaw.

'What do we do?' I asked.

'We—' Theo shook his head.

'We can't stay here forever, kids,' Rhett warned.

'We need time,' Bas said. 'Maybe it is working, but there's no one there to receive the message.'

Theo shook his head. 'It's not working.' He straightened up. 'I'm calling it. Let's go.'

Bas gripped the edge of the counter. Silence reigned.

'Let's go,' Theo repeated, heading for the door. 'Harley, come on.'

I stayed where I was, staring at Bas. After what felt like forever, he stood and stalked to the door. As he passed me, he shot me a scowl. 'Well? Get a move on.'

'Yes, sir,' I muttered, turning to follow him back the way we'd come.

FOURTEEN

WE MADE THE THREE-HOUR journey back to the cars in heavy silence. By the time we got there, Rhett had drunk his way through a whole bottle of whiskey. I knew because he'd chucked it at a tree about two miles back, laughing boisterously when it shattered.

When we found the cars, we climbed down into the riverbed. Rhett staggered straight into the bushes, and I heard the unmistakable sound of him vomiting.

Gross.

'What are we going to do?' Theo asked, voicing the question that I guessed was on all of our minds.

'What are our options?' I clenched and unclenched my fists restlessly. I was no stranger to helplessness—I'd experienced it every day of my life. But this was a new kind of helplessness, separated by hundreds of miles from Bale Rocks, with the army bearing down on them. There was nothing we could do from here—the radio had been our only hope.

'We either go forwards, or we go back,' Bas said.

'What's forwards?' I asked.

'Langford,' Theo said. 'The Langford Army Base. But if the problem is with the transmission station in Freetown, then going to a different base won't make a difference.'

He was right, of course. I chewed my lips.

'And back is Bale Rocks,' I said needlessly. If we went back, we could warn them. But I had no idea what we—what I—would be returning to.

Which only left one other option: we split up.

But who went back, and who went forwards?

'If we split up...' I started uncertainly. 'If... if two of us went to Langford to look for Maddock, and one of us went back...'

'Harley,' Theo groaned. 'You're obsessed with this idea of finding

Maddock. The guy's gone. Why can't you give up on him?'

'Because I want to go home!' I cried. 'Bale Rocks is my home!'

'You were quite happy to leave when we were plotting to kill Hannover. What the hell changed?'

'Oi, pipe down over there!' Rhett stumbled out of the bushes, wiping his mouth on his sleeve. My stomach heaved. 'Can't a guy get some peace around here?'

I turned my back on him. 'What changed is that I would never have left without Savannah,' I said. 'And you knew that from the start.'

Theo set his jaw. 'Well, Savannah's not here.'

'No, she's in Bale Rocks,' I said. 'My *home.* You know what? I shouldn't have to defend this to you. Bale Rocks is my home! It always has been. I'd have left then if I had no choice—I did leave—but that doesn't mean I don't want to go back.'

'So I'm not enough of a reason for you to want to leave,' Theo said.

I swallowed. 'That's not what I—It's not a choice between you and Savannah, Theo.'

'No, it's fine.' He shook his head. 'You've made your feelings more than clear. I'll go back to Bale Rocks and warn them. Then I'll fetch Savannah and we can meet in Crater's Edge.'

'Theo…' I said helplessly. *Yes. No. Don't do that. That plan sucks. But yes.*

I felt selfish, but I was relieved at the idea of Theo fetching Savannah. He was the only person I trusted to keep my sister safe.

'Okay,' I said softly, avoiding Theo's gaze.

'Fine,' he replied. 'In that case, we should rendezvous in Crater's Edge in, let's say, five days. That gives me enough time to get there and do what I need to.'

I nodded.

'And you'll have that long to find out what you can in Langford. It's a day's drive from here to Crater's Edge, so—'

'Can you check out the transmission station in Freetown?' Bas asked suddenly.

'What's the point?' Theo replied. 'If we're meeting—'

'If anything goes wrong—'

'You can let us know you arrived and what the situation is,' I interrupted. 'We don't know how far things have progressed in Bale Rocks. There might be trouble.'

'I've dealt with more trouble than both of you put together,' Theo snapped. 'I can handle it.'

'You're not working alone,' Bas said. 'We need to keep each other informed.'

'Fine. Fine!' He turned away, glaring into the bushes. 'I will get a message to Ellery telling him to sort out the transmission station. We can make contact in five days and—assuming you don't totally blow this plan to hell as well—we can rendezvous in Crater's Edge six days from now.'

I bit my tongue to keep from replying sarcastically. This was goodbye. I didn't want to be nasty—even if Theo wasn't holding back.

'Thank you,' I said.

Theo grimaced. 'You're welcome.'

'Where are we meeting?' Bas asked.

'Red Rock Inn. You'll find it—everyone knows it.'

Bas nodded. Then he frowned. 'And Rhett?'

We all glanced over to where Rhett was slouched against Theo's truck, apparently sleeping upright.

'Rhett has to go back to Langford,' I said, though the thought of sharing a car journey of any length with that man filled me with horror.

'Rhett is coming with me,' Theo replied. 'It's what I promised him. But on that note—you need to be careful in Langford. Do not mention my name. If Mirko finds out you know me, he'll come for you.'

'What have you done?' Bas asked suspiciously.

Theo jerked his head towards Rhett. 'Rhett's indebted to Mirko, and Mirko isn't going to be pleased that he bailed.'

'Fantastic,' Bas muttered.

'It shouldn't be a problem if you stay out of the east side.'

Theo spent the next ten minutes showing us the route on his map and advising us on where to stay. 'When you reach the farm with the red windmill, you're about two miles out. The city will start up quicker than you expect—there's a police checkpoint, but it's not usually manned. This street has cheap accommodation, if you don't mind that there's a brothel opposite…'

Finally, he closed the map and handed it to me. 'Be smart,' he said.

'I will.'

'I'm serious, Har. It's not Bale Rocks—you don't know everyone there.'

'I'm well aware.' He meant well, but I couldn't help but feel patronised. I hadn't started off knowing everyone in Bale Rocks, either. And I knew how to fend for myself.

'Fine.' Theo's eyes darted away. Then he took a deep breath and looked back at me. 'I guess this is goodbye, then.'

I swallowed. 'Yeah… I guess.'

Theo held his arms out. I hugged him tightly; my throat ached suddenly, and I had to blink fiercely. *Don't cry. Not now.*

This was stupid. I'd chosen this. Warning Bale Rocks was the right thing to do. So why did it feel so final?

Maybe because deep down I knew Theo wasn't happy. He didn't want to go back, and I was forcing him.

He pulled away and turned to Bas. 'Keep her safe.'

Bas nodded stiffly.

'I can keep myself safe,' I muttered. 'You worry about you.'

'I'll be fine.' Theo shrugged. 'See you in six days. Seven PM at the Red Rock Inn.'

'See you then.'

With one last glance my way, Theo turned and loped to his car. Rhett pushed off as he approached—not as asleep as he had wanted us to believe.

'We blowing this joint?'

'Yes.' Theo swung himself up into the cab. 'Let's go.'

'See ya, princess.' Rhett waved to me and clambered up as well. Theo turned the truck and the engine roared as he climbed the slope back up out of the riverbed.

Then he was out of sight. Feeling hollowed out, I turned to Bas. 'Ready to go?'

'I wasn't planning on hanging around.'

Charming. 'You could be a bit less antagonistic, you know.'

Bas scowled. 'Let's just go. The sooner we get on the road, the sooner we get to Langford to go on your harebrained quest.'

'Harebrained?' I glared at him. 'I didn't hear you coming up with a plan.'

Bas turned and stalked to his car, throwing open the driver's door and climbing in. A second later, he slammed it.

Guess we weren't talking, then.

I climbed up into the car. Bas followed in Theo's tracks, up onto solid ground, and we set off towards the road. I couldn't keep myself from periodically throwing glances Bas's way. He drove in absolute silence, his expression the picture of concentration. It was as though I didn't exist.

He was mad at me again.

But why?

I couldn't even think what the hell I'd done this time. I was trying — really! But we'd all been tense since we left Bale Rocks. It was hardly my fault that things weren't going perfectly.

'Harebrained plan.'

What did that mean? Had Bas changed his mind about looking for Maddock? Thinking back, I couldn't even remember if he'd wanted to in the first place. Maybe he didn't want to go back to Bale Rocks either.

Maybe it was just me who wanted to go home.

Or maybe it was something else. The scene I'd made when we left Brackfields?

Or…

I had no idea.

He'd been short with Rhett, too, so maybe it wasn't me. Maybe it was something else entirely.

But then there was that thing in the car earlier. What was his deal, honestly?

My life had been anything but cushy. Even when Mum and Dad had been alive… our life had been small.

How dare he describe it as cushy?

The more I thought about it, the more I felt anger heating my blood. But arguing with him now would get us nowhere. We were both stuck in this car for the next however many hours. No, it was better to bite my tongue for now.

I balled up my coat and used it to cushion my head against the window, staring outside at the yellow-grey sand and letting the movement of the car lull me to sleep.

Langford was… grungy.

Somehow, after everything I had heard about the cities, I had expected more. Bigger buildings, newer, cleaner. Instead, Langford seemed like a larger version of Bale Rocks. Decrepit three- and four-storey buildings were built of dirty brick, with boarded-up windows, broken roof shingles, and a general air of neglect. The nearer we got to the centre, the more cramped the buildings were: tall and narrow terraced buildings, seeming to lean against one another as though they were propping each other up. The streets were dirty, rubbish piled up in alleyways, and the people walked with a hunched gait, as though the weight of the world was pressing down on them.

The hotel Theo had directed us to was in an extremely seedy area. Eyes watched us from shadowy alleyways, and the buildings bore signs advertising all manner of sexual services.

Madame Merlot's Dancing Delights—the best dancers in town
Nokturnal Pleasures—Feast your eyes for only 4NP
Jiordan's Gents—Enrich your mind and body—only 20NP full
experience

Bas stopped in front of a narrow building with the name painted directly onto the door in flaking white paint:

Dina's B&B
12NP single
15NP double
No whores

'This is it?' I asked sceptically.

'Apparently.'

'Okay.' I eyed the nearest alleyway nervously. This was not the sort of place I'd be safe walking around at night.

'Can you go in and ask where we can leave the car?' Bas asked.

I nodded.

When I climbed out of the car, I discovered the air was muggy and smelt of refuse. *Gross.* I hurried across the pavement and knocked on the front door of Dina's.

The door cracked open, revealing a suspicious-faced woman. 'Yes?'

'I'm looking for a room.'

She eyed me up and down several times. 'Fine, come in.'

She only opened the door a sliver, forcing me to squeeze through a tiny gap. Inside, the narrow hallway was dark and gloomy. The walls were mottled grey, and the carpet squelched slightly underfoot. The woman locked and bolted the door, then led me into the first room off the hall, which featured a saggy brown lounge set and a reception desk.

'Name?' she demanded.

'H—' I bit my cheek. *Names. Shit.*

'Huh?'

'Hannah,' I improvised. 'Hannah and… Ben. Jones.' *Smooth, Harley.*

The woman's wrinkled brown face showed every ounce of her scepticism, but she wrote the names down. 'Hannah and Ben Jones. Double?'

I swallowed. 'Two… two rooms would be better.' Bas probably wouldn't want to share. 'Four nights.'

'I only have one room available.'

Shit.

'Fine.' I glanced around for inspiration, found none, and added, 'That's fine.'

'Right then. Cash upfront.' She set a key on the counter. I fished through my coat and came out with a few notes, the change I'd never returned to Theo. Oops.

'Here. Um. We have a car—'

The woman waved. 'Straight down the road, turn left, left again, and on the right fifty yards on is the parking garage. Pay the boy. He works hard.'

Pay the boy?

She dropped my change in front of me and pushed the key across the counter. *Scrape, scrape.*

'Knock to get in. If you're out after nine, you're out until morning. And don't let your brother bring any whores in. You got that?'

Brother? Oh. She assumed that—Oh.

'Right,' I muttered, taking my change. 'Thanks.'

I hurried back out to Bas, who was watching for me impatiently. When I climbed in, he said, 'Well?'

'I got us a room, and the parking is just around the corner.' I directed him with half my brain, the rest focused on the room dilemma. 'Left, left, then right.'

Bas set off.

'They only had one room.'

He grunted.

'Is that okay?'

'Harley, I'm concentrating.'

Fine. Then I'd assume it was okay. I directed him into an underground parking garage filled with cars. I'd never seen so many in one place—so many that they needed an entire hall dedicated to them.

Bas pulled us into a parking space.

'She said 'pay the boy.''

'Who?'

'The woman in the hotel.' I cast a glance around. Sure enough, a tiny, dirty-faced boy was approaching us, a hat pulled low over his head. I rolled my window down.

'Six,' he said.

'For what?' I asked.

'I watch your car and make sure no one tries nuffing.'

'And if we don't pay?' Bas asked.

'Then I don't watch.'

Ten to one it was his mates who would 'try things' if we didn't pay. I gritted my teeth. 'Four a day, and we're here for several days.'

'Five.' He crossed his arms, tilting his chin up. I knew that look. It said, *'I'm not going any lower.'*

'Four and we pay up front,' Bas said. 'Four days.'

He shuffled his feet. 'Four-fifty.'

I scooped through my pockets and managed to put together eighteen new pounds. Daylight robbery.

'Pleasure doing business with you, ma'am.' The boy shot me a toothy grin and sauntered off, tucking the cash into his patched coat.

'You should have opened with three,' Bas said.

'You're welcome to take the lead next time,' I snapped. I was fed up with his attitude. 'Come on, we need to be inside by nine or she's going to lock us out.'

'I suppose you didn't bother to negotiate on that, either?'

I shot him a dark look, snatched my bag off the back seat, and jumped out—then slammed the door. Immature, maybe, but it was satisfying.

Walking over to the hotel, I felt very exposed. We seemed to stand out amidst the Langford residents, as though we were somehow indefinably different.

The receptionist frowned at us as we passed through the lobby and up the stairs. Our room was on the top floor, tucked away under the roof. The ceiling slanted so that we couldn't stand on one side.

And there was only one bed.

Awkward.

'Sorry,' I said. 'It was all she had.'

'It's fine. I'll sleep on the floor,' Bas said.

Oh.

Not that I'd been looking forward to sharing with him, exactly, but that seemed like a bad solution.

'I don't mind sharing.'

'It's fine.' Bas dropped his bag against the wall. 'I'm going to wash up. You can come up with a plan.'

'Okay. Yeah.'

The showers were communal—and unisex—and I wasn't ready for that adventure, so I washed in the sink in our room. The water was icy cold, and when I looked in the mirror, I didn't recognise myself. Sure, those were my features, my brown hair and tan skin and brown eyes, but I felt different somehow. Like someone had taken me apart and put me back together, but I wasn't quite right anymore.

How, I wasn't sure. But it wasn't.

When Bas came back, I sat on the bed and watched him warily. He was too big for the room. Bas always seemed larger than life, and that impression was worse here, in this shabby room. His every movement was precise and targeted, nothing like our worn-down, patched surroundings. This felt more like my world than his.

'Plan?' he asked.

'Do you know anyone in Langford?' I asked.

'No.'

My heart sank. I didn't either. Which meant… we were on our own.

I glanced out the window. The sun had set, but the city was still light. Thousands upon thousands of people.

How the hell were we going to find Maddock amidst all of them?

'I guess we start by asking around,' I said. 'The receptionist might know something?'

Bas shrugged.

Irritation flared in my belly. 'Okay, can we please talk about what the hell your problem is?'

'I don't have a problem.'

I gritted my teeth. 'If you don't want to be here—'

'I want what you want,' Bas said. 'A way home. Maddock is not that way home.'

'Then what is?' I snapped. 'And why didn't you say something earlier?'

'You didn't ask.' Bas pulled his gun out and started disassembling it.

'I did—'

'You made the plans. We're here. Don't complain that you got what you want.'

I clenched my fists around the bedcovers. 'You've been in a bad mood for longer than that.'

Bas gestured imperiously to the door. 'Go on.'

Fuck you too. I stood sharply. 'You can come with me.'

'No.'

'If that's how you want to play it, then fine.' I crossed my arms. 'If you want to act like I made all the decisions, and you never got a say: that's not true. But if that's what you want to pretend, then I will make all the decisions. You're coming with me. I don't know how safe this place is for me alone.'

Bas stared at me, his green eyes burning like a thousand suns. Oh, he wanted to eviscerate me. There was no doubt about that. But after a few seconds, he set his gun aside and stood. 'Lead the way.'

I pulled the door open and stalked to the stairs. Bas followed like a silent, angry shadow.

The receptionist was filing her nails, her lips pursed in concentration. But she was alert. Before I got to her desk, she called, 'Can I help you?'

I approached warily. 'Yeah…. Um… We're looking for someone. I wonder if you might recognise him?'

The receptionist raised one bushy eyebrow. 'Girl, you think I know everyone in this city?'

My confidence faltered. 'I… No… But…'

'Exactly.' She rolled her eyes. 'You outsiders are all the same. Go back to your room and stop bothering me.'

'I haven't even described him yet!'

'I won't know him, girlie. I barely know my neighbours and I see their ugly faces every day. Now, get. I'm busy.'

'Harley,' Bas said.

Scowling, I followed him to the stairs, kicking the scuffed carpet as I walked. I paused on the bottom step, remembering what Theo had said. *Whores love to talk.*

'Can you… at least point me to a brothel? With… with male prostitutes?'

The woman shot me an incredulous look. 'There are seven on this street alone. You're wasting your time, girl.'

'I'll be the judge of that,' I snapped. I turned and stomped up the stairs to where Bas was waiting, one floor up.

Such friendly fellows here in Langford. And I had thought Bale Rocks was unwelcoming.

Hah, we were practically warm by comparison.

FIFTEEN

SAM'S WAS NOT EXACTLY the classiest establishment in the West Rim. The clientele was a healthy mix of men and women, the majority of whom wore shabby work clothes and carried themselves with stooped postures. They stared at Bas and me suspiciously as we entered.

The bar itself was nothing to write home about either. The floor was scratched and unpolished wood, and the bar counter was covered in linoleum that was bubbling up in places. A dirty mirror reflected our faces as Bas and I took seats at the bar.

The bartender, a whip-thin man in his thirties with an impressive moustache and a lecherous stare, set two glasses in front of us and poured each of them full of obviously watered-down whiskey.

'Fiver.'

Bas paid. I picked up my glass, grimacing at the chips in the rim and dirt marks on the outside. No way I was putting my lips on that; I'd probably get a disease.

'It's just whiskey, sugar.'

I looked up at the bartender, grimacing. He was eyeing me like I was the hottest thing he'd seen in months.

Bas cleared his throat, and the bartender turned to him.

'Whiskey's the only option here.'

'We heard you might be able to help us find someone.'

This was the first concrete tip we'd managed to get after three days in Langford. Without Theo, I had quickly discovered that we had no leads and no ways to access information. What I had thought would be a matter of asking around had turned out to be an impossible task.

Langford was a big city. People didn't just know each other.

Finding out about Maddock was like finding a needle in a haystack.

'Me?' The bartender raised an eyebrow. 'Not sure you got the right person, mate.'

'You,' Bas said. 'But I suppose if they were wrong we can go somewhere else.'

'Now hold on just a minute…' He rubbed the back of his neck. 'What exactly are you wanting help with?'

'We're looking for someone,' Bas said. 'Travels a lot. Goes by the name of James Maddock. Spent a while in Bale Rocks recently and got himself in some trouble.'

'I don't know anyone by that name,' the bartender replied, scratching his chest. 'We don't get a lot of travellers through here, in case you couldn't tell.' His gaze darted around the room before settling back on us.

I leant forward, resting my elbows on the counter so that I squeezed my breasts together. 'Are you sure?'

He looked, of course. Then he glanced at Bas and backed off a step. 'I—I'm sure.'

I followed his gaze. Bas was scowling.

Uh oh, not again. He'd been in a foul mood the last few days, which he'd stubbornly refused to explain, and I was just sick of it. My play might have worked if Bas hadn't gone and ruined it.

We needed that information.

'You know what? We're done here.' I stood, pushing away my untouched whiskey. 'Let's go.'

Bas jumped up and marched to the door, forcing me to trail after him. As we hit the street, I hissed, 'What is your problem?'

'What's yours?' Bas set a punishing pace down the street. I had to take two steps to his one.

'I was just trying to get information!'

'I get it, you want every man in the city to salivate over you. You do what you have to do.'

'That's not true!' I felt as though I'd been slapped. What the hell was he on now? 'I don't want a guy like that salivating over me at all! I just wanted to know what he was hiding.'

'Then go ask him.' Bas waved a hand over his shoulder. 'And stop bothering me.'

He sped up, though I had no idea where he thought he was going. I had the room key.

I followed him at a slower pace, stewing in my own fury. Bas was driving me crazy.

He was waiting for me outside our room when I got to the hotel, leaning against the wall with his arms crossed. I pretended I hadn't noticed his presence as I unlocked the door. I marched across the room, still ignoring him, and picked up my bag.

Bas could throw all the tantrums he wanted. I wasn't entertaining them.

I'd nicked Theo's cargo pants by accident, and with a bit of sewing thread and some patience, I could make them fit me without a belt.

So that was what I'd do.

Theo could get another pair. I, however, was starting to think I needed a more practical wardrobe.

I settled on the bed and threaded the needle. Bas stomped around the room, gathering his toiletries. Then he left, and five minutes later he was back, hair damp from the shower.

More stomping.

Wasn't he a twenty-eight-year-old man? He was a bit old to be throwing a tantrum like a five-year-old.

Stomp. Stomp. Stomp.

My temper snapped. I dropped my mending in my lap and turned to him.

'Can you stop that?'

'I'm not doing anything,' Bas growled.

'You know what? I'm done. Tell me what your problem is or you can get out. I paid for this room, and I'm not letting anyone in it who talks to me like that.'

Bas glared at me. 'You don't want to know what I'm really thinking.'

'Is this about something I did in Brackfields? Or is it before that?'

'Before.'

Great. That helped. Not.

'Could you maybe be a little more spec—'

'You don't want that.' Bas stepped closer, looming over me. I stood suddenly, my mending tumbling to the floor.

'Yes, I do.'

We glared at each other, neither of us willing to give an inch. Finally, I pointed at the door. 'If you don't want to be here, then leave.'

'I don't *want* to leave,' Bas spat, sounding very much like he wanted nothing more.

'Then tell me what's going on!'

'I—' He broke off, turning away from me and raking a hand through his hair. 'For fuck's sake, Harley.'

I was close, so fucking close, and this time I pushed him intentionally.

'Are we just going to ignore this forever?'

Bas turned back to me. Opened his mouth—and shut it again.

'I can't read your mind, you know,' I pressed. 'Or—or is it that you're scared?' I advanced a step and this time he backed away. 'Scared of telling me the truth?'

'I'm not scared,' he snarled.

'I mean, I don't think it's necessarily better to be a raging arsehole. At least if you're scared then you have an excuse,' I said loftily.

His eyes narrowed. 'Fine, we'll talk,' he said. 'What shall we start with?'

'The fact that you've been nothing but a dick to me for the last few days, for absolutely no reason?' I asked.

'What about the fact that you're continually reminding me about the differences in our experiences?' he asked.

What?

'That's not—'

'Or the fact that you flirt with every guy you come across, indiscriminately, except me?'

What the hell?

'You said you didn't—'

'What about the fact that the whole time you were working against me, and then you blamed me for not telling you the truth?' He glared down at me, panting for breath. I seized my moment to get a word in.

'Don't you think I might have been more inclined to tell you the truth if you'd believed me the first time I tried to tell you?'

'Don't you think I'm maybe tired of being tested over and over again?' He took a step forwards, sudden and sharp, and I backed up, wariness creeping down my spine. 'If you come out with a story and expect me to just believe you without checking—'

'Except you did check and you preferred to believe their lies over my truth!'

'I apologised for that!'

'Just apologising isn't enough!' I snarled. The words came from deep in my chest, a culmination of weeks and months of emotion I'd been struggling with. That was it. I appreciated his apology, but it wasn't enough. It didn't erase the hurt, the powerlessness that I'd felt.

'Then what *do* you want?' Bas hissed, his eyes wild. 'Do you want me to get down on hands and knees and beg for your forgiveness?'

'No!'

'Shall I follow your every order unthinkingly?'

'No!'

He stalked towards me; I backed up again. My breaths came short and sharp. 'I just need time.'

'Time,' Bas parroted, as though the notion were ridiculous. 'Of course, how could I not guess? Harley Benoit expects all of us to conform to her schedule—'

'Oh, fuck you,' I hissed.

'I should have known from the start,' he mocked, glaring. 'You always were pernicious and—'

'Fuck. You,' I repeated. I stepped towards him, put my hands on his chest, and shoved. Ineffective, as always. Bas was as immovable as stone. He grabbed my hands, yanking them off him.

'If I pushed you around like that, you'd tell me to take a walk off a steep cliff.'

'Right,' I sneered. 'And if I spoke to you the way you are to me? Told you to just 'get over it'? You're a fucking hypocrite and I'm so sick of it.'

'Right, and you're the queen of righteousness.' He rolled his eyes. 'Looking down on all of us, and for what? Because we're men. You think you're better because of an accident of birth—'

'Accident of birth?' I choked. 'You don't know shit about what it's like to be a woman in this world. Always being pushed around, told what to do, never having the power to control your own life—fucking let me go!' I shook my hands, trying to dislodge his grip from my wrists, but of course he held fast—of course, because I could never make him do anything. That was Bas; he defied my every attempt to keep him in check.

He dragged me closer and lifted my hands above my head. 'No.'

'What… what are you doing?' I asked, unease displacing my anger.

'What I want to do.' He stared at me, intent and angry. 'I'm sick of fighting.'

'What?' I yanked harder on my wrists. Bas released them, but before I could turn to escape, he dropped his hand to the back of my neck, leant in, and kissed me.

I froze. My thoughts sputtered out like a candle in the wind.

Bas…

Bas was kissing me…

My breath stuttered as panic tightened my throat. Prickles ran down my spine. I was hyper-aware of every sensation. His hand on my neck. His stubble scraping my cheeks. His lips. Soft. Warm. Gentle.

I—I can't—

Stop!

Bas pulled back, his grip on my neck hardening. 'Harley?'

His lips were so full and soft. How had I never noticed?

'I'm sorry.' He stepped back, his hand sliding off me. 'I shouldn't have—'

'No.' I wrestled with myself. I needed words, but I couldn't find them. So I stepped forwards and grabbed his shirt. Going on tiptoes, I kissed him.

Our lips met. His opened, and I pushed my tongue in, tangling with his, pouring every feeling I couldn't put into words into that kiss. *Take everything I have. Find the words that I can't.* I kissed him hard. Our teeth clashed. His arms wound around me, and his fingers dug into my shoulders, the sensation on the border between pleasure and pain.

It wasn't enough.

I clawed at his shirt, pulling it up until I could get my hands on his skin. He was warm, solid, *strong*. Everything I wished I could be. I leant into him and dug my nails in, scratching lines into his skin. He bit my bottom lip, sending a jolt through me.

Heat pooled in my stomach.

Yes.

More.

I broke the kiss, gasping for breath. My hands were on his chest; his hands were in my hair. There wasn't an inch of space between us. I couldn't tell where I ended and he began.

It was too much.

I pulled back, sliding my fingers over his skin, before dropping them to my sides. 'I… I need to…' My brain was blank. He'd flicked a switch in my head, redirecting all conscious thought to noticing the stark lines of a tattoo on his hip, the sweat visible on his collarbone, how swollen his lips were. 'Space. I need space.'

Bas nodded.

'I'll be back in a sec.'

He nodded again.

Frustration welled in my gut. 'Say something!'

Bas tilted his head. 'Are you okay?'

Not what I'd wanted him to say. Because I didn't know. I didn't fucking know.

'Maybe? Probably.' I rubbed my forehead. 'Sorry, I... I'm not good at this stuff.'

'I know.' Bas consulted his watch. 'I'll go see if I can find food. Take your time. We can talk later.'

Later. The thought filled me with dread. But at least he was giving me space.

'Thanks,' I said.

I managed to access the roof by wiggling out onto the window ledge and hooking my fingers around the drainpipe. I lifted one leg up, then my upper body, and hauled myself the rest of the way onto the slanting corrugated metal.

Success.

It felt reasonably sturdy, but I wasn't brave enough to try standing, so I crawled away from the edge on hands and knees, rust flakes rubbing off onto my clothes. Once I was a decent way up the incline, I lay on my back, cushioning my head on my arms, and stared up at the darkening sky. The horizon still held the last traces of red and pink, but the rest of the sky was dark blue. Twilight.

Bas had kissed me.

It wasn't as though I'd never been kissed before. I'd fooled around with my fair share of guys back at school. But as an adult, my experiences were limited to Bas... and Ellery.

Whom I hadn't thought of since I'd left town.

But the thought of him didn't evoke any strong feelings anymore, only vague concern. Would he be angry that I'd kissed Bas?

Did it really matter?

Ellery and I wanted different things. What I wanted...

Bas's face swam before my eyes.

He was infuriating. We took one step forwards and ten steps back.

He held grudges over things I'd said that I didn't even remember. He didn't listen.

I should hate him.

And yet, in those rare times when we met on the same level, we just clicked.

If only they came more frequently.

If only I knew what he wanted.

God! He drove me crazy. One minute, he was my friend. The next, he hated me. Then he was kissing me. Where had that even come from?

Was it possible that he felt something for me? Something more than… begrudging respect?

I ran through our past interactions in my mind. There'd definitely been something. I'd thought he was going to kiss me, once, in the bunker… and then we'd never spoken about that moment again. Which was how it always went—Bas got close, and then he backed away.

Would we be back to picking fights tomorrow?

I wasn't sure I could take it anymore. The constant fighting, constantly being on edge. Today had only scratched the surface of the tensions I was carrying. If we went any deeper, there'd be an explosion… and I didn't know if I'd be able to live with the consequences.

Groaning, I rolled my neck and stretched my back. *Fuck.* How had I ended up here? What was I going to do now?

Go to Crater's Edge.

But then? Get a job and stay there? Could I do that?

If Theo brought Savannah, there'd be nothing tying me to Bale Rocks anymore. Except for my history, but how important was that? I loved my parents, but they were gone. There was nothing left of them except my memories, and I could carry those with me to Crater's Edge.

So…

Worry about it when you get there.

The sky turned purple, then faded to black. It was impossible to see the stars here; the city was too bright. How did people cope with the constant light and noise? It was driving me crazy, and I'd only been here a few days. But even now I could hear cars hooting, people shouting, music…

'Harley?' came a muffled voice from below.

I sat up. Bas was back.

'On the roof,' I called.

I heard scuffling, and a moment later he pulled himself up over the edge. He made it look much easier than it had been for me.

'What are you doing up here?'

'Thinking.' I shrugged.

Bas glanced around.

'It's so loud,' I added.

'I don't like the smell,' he confessed. 'Reminds me of—then.'

Then? When he'd been a slave? I stared at him, trying to read the answers on his face, but in the darkness he was closed to me. He shuffled closer on hands and knees, then knocked his fingers against the metal.

'This doesn't feel sturdy.'

'As long as you don't move, I think it will be fine.' I glanced down. 'We'll only land back in our room, anyway.'

Bas snorted. He reached where I was sitting, and lay down beside me, resting his head on his hands.

What should I say to him? Did he expect me to bring up the kiss? After a moment, I said weakly, 'No stars.'

'Too much light pollution from the city,' Bas replied. He turned, and I could tell he was looking at me, though I still couldn't really make out his face.

I bit my lip. 'Do you want to talk?'

'Only if you're ready.'

Oh, okay. The ball was in my court, then. I hated that. Unfinished things set my teeth on edge. 'I—'

'When you're ready,' Bas repeated.

'I'm ready.' I had to be. 'I… I liked the kiss.'

'Me too.'

I couldn't remember anything I'd thought about earlier—his presence had sent my thoughts scattering like rabbits in the wasteland. 'Um… do you want to do it again?'

'If you want to.'

I traced a ripple in the metal roofing. 'Do you want to?'

Bas stared, his eyes like dark pools. Finally, he said, 'Yes.'

I sighed in relief. Okay. Okay. 'Me too.'

'Now?'

'Uh…' There had been other things I wanted to say to him—hadn't there? But my mind was empty. 'Yes.'

Bas frowned. 'I don't want to hurt you.' His intent gaze moved from my eyes to my lips.

I *wanted* to kiss him again.

I'd never felt this way before, not even back when I'd had a crush on Ellery. My desires had revolved around spending time with him; I'd enjoyed the way he made me laugh. Sure, I'd been younger then, but the lack of sexual attraction to Ellery was a marked difference to how I felt about Bas.

I wanted to touch every inch of his body.

I wanted to kiss him.

I wanted to find out what little noises he'd make when I pleasured him.

It was more than I'd ever wanted before, and it both scared and excited me.

'I think…' I cleared my throat, wrestling for words amidst the storm of desires. 'I think I need things to be slow.'

'Me too.'

'Good.' I smiled up at him. 'But I'd like to try.'

'Alright.' Bas smiled, a slow grin that lit his eyes up like stars in the night sky. He leant in, his every movement clearly telegraphed, and cupped the back of my head, guiding my lips to his.

My heart leapt, and heat flooded my body.

Kissing Bas was everything—heat, need, a dizzying rush of emotion. It was almost too much. I clung to him, unsure if I wanted him closer or further away. I needed air, but I also needed him. I dug my fingers into his skin, and he rolled over me so his knees were on either side of my hips.

Enclosing me.

Tension coiled in my belly.

He pulled back. 'Okay?'

I took a deep breath. Then I nodded, tracing a finger over his chest. I could feel his warmth. 'Yeah. I'm okay.'

Or I would be. There was a steady familiarity to Bas's presence that was stronger than my automatic fear. He wouldn't hurt me. I wasn't entirely sure he was capable of it. For someone so strong, he was much more vulnerable than I was.

He pressed his lips to the corner of my mouth, his stubble scratching my cheek. I turned my head, trying to catch his lips, but he resisted, kissing over my chin and down my neck, until he found a particularly sensitive spot.

'Bas! Fuck!' I gasped.

Bas hummed, tonguing that spot again. I wrapped my arms around his back, dragging him closer, and he kissed me again. This time was more heated, our tongues tangling. I dug my nails into his back, and he lowered his weight onto me. 'Harley—'

His words were lost against my lips. He rocked against me, and the roof sheeting groaned.

At once, Bas scrambled back, leaving a chill everywhere he'd been touching me. I sat up, shivering. 'Maybe we should take this inside?'

Bas smoothed a hand over his hair. 'Maybe, yeah.' His voice was husky. Not that mine sounded any better. My heart was racing. I shuffled to the edge and peered down at the windowsill.

Bas settled beside me. 'I'll go first and help you down.'

'I can do it…' I paused, biting my lip. My default response. *I can do it on my own.*

But if Bas and I were going to try this whole thing—whatever it was—then I couldn't do everything on my own anymore. There had to be give and take.

'Yeah, okay. Thanks.'

Bas watched me for a second, as though waiting for something. Abruptly, he shifted to the edge and slithered down, deftly lowering himself to the window ledge below. I followed him and knelt on the edge. The street below had come alive since we'd arrived; people milled about outside of a nightclub, streetwalkers lurked in doorways, and the windows in the building across the road were lit up red. Women gyrated in them, dressed in skimpy clothes. A brothel.

'Harley?'

As I glanced away, something caught my eye. I looked back at the red windows. The left-hand one… the woman looked vaguely familiar. She'd just turned her back, waggling her bum. She had long blonde hair and wore a glittery silver dress that was basically just a tiny square of fabric which covered her butt and left her back bare. At that moment, she turned again, and my heart sprang into my throat.

I did recognise her.

In fact, I knew her.

Her name was Cindy Dawson. She had been a dancer at the bunker when I first started working there. In fact, she was the dancer who had clued me in to the existence of the crawlspace—and the entrance in the dressing room.

Which Maddock should have had no way of knowing existed.

Unless someone had told him. Perhaps even the same someone who had told me.

'Harley?'

I looked down. Bas was leaning out the window, frowning up at me. 'Are you coming?'

'Yeah.' I turned onto my stomach and eased a leg over. Bas caught my hips and lifted me down until I could stand on the windowsill.

'Thanks.' I jumped in beside him. 'I know who we can speak to.'

'Who?'

'Cindy Dawson. I just saw her working in the building across the road. We can catch her when she goes off shift.'

'Who's Cindy Dawson?' Bas asked cautiously.

I smiled. 'The person who told me about the crawlspace in the bunker.'

SIXTEEN

'BYE!'

'See you tomorrow!'

Cindy squeezed out of the back of Madame Merlot's brothel and shut the heavy steel door behind her before turning to face the alleyway. Her breath fogged the air in front of her. She had donned a thick coat, which looked comically oversized on her thin, tall frame. The effect was made even more prominent by her tall heels. As she strode towards me, she lit a cigarette.

I pressed myself back into the shadows as she passed.

Cindy stopped, her hand going to her hip. She spun deftly, despite the heels. 'Who's there? What are you doing here?'

Damnit. 'I don't want any trouble.' I stepped out of the shadows. 'Just to talk.'

'Talk?' Cindy echoed in a high, shrill voice. She lifted her hand — she was clutching a knife in her fist. 'As if I'd buy that. What do you want? I don't have any money.'

'I don't want money.' I eased into the puddle of light at the entrance to the alleyway, holding my hands by my shoulders. 'I'm not armed. It's Harley — we used to work together.'

'I don't remember anyone called Harley,' she snapped.

'At the bunker. In Bale Rocks.'

Her shoulders hunched, and she held the knife higher. 'Get away from me! I don't want anything to do with you people!'

Fuck.

I was meant to follow her home, not get into a knife fight in a dingy alleyway.

'Cindy, please! Let's just talk. We can go out on the street — in public — I'm not armed, see?' I wiggled my fingers. 'I was a dancer just like you. I just need to ask you —'

'*I'm not answering any questions!*'

She lunged at me, hitting me bodily. The impact sent me stumbling into the street. I threw my hands against her shoulders. Shit, this was all wrong. She was going to get us both killed with the wild way she was waving the knife. I jabbed my foot into her knee and threw my forearm against hers at the same time, forcing the knife away. She staggered. I grabbed her wrist and twisted it until her grip strained and the knife clattered to the floor.

'NO!' she shrieked.

Bas jogged up at that moment, sliding his hands under Cindy's arms and lifting her away from me. Relieved, I relinquished my grip on her. She screamed and writhed.

'Let me go! Get off me!'

'We want to talk,' Bas said. 'You can do this the easy way or the hard way, but you will do it!'

'The easy way! The easy way!' Cindy sobbed loudly. 'Please, I'm pregnant, please just don't—don't hurt the baby!'

Fuuuuck.

I backed off as Bas dropped her like a hot potato. He stared at me, his eyes wide. Cindy scrabbled for the knife, and I hurriedly put my boot on it.

'We really do just want to talk,' I said. 'We have no intention of hurting you.'

'No one ambushes a person in an alleyway if they don't mean to hurt them,' Cindy sobbed.

She had a point, and I felt like the biggest arsehole. We'd let our goals cloud our reason.

'Sorry.' I bent down and picked up the knife. 'Let's find a place to chat. Your choice where.'

Cindy stared at both of us, tears glinting in the streetlights, her chin tilted up defensively. Finally, she said, 'There's an all-night café just down the road.'

'Lead the way,' I said, tucking the knife inside my coat.

I'd half expected Cindy to lie and try to get rid of us, but there was indeed an all-night café around the corner, the kind that was obviously positioned to catch people coming out of the brothels and tempt them with cake, maybe, or a milkshake. It was an open, square room, with red plastic booths and a counter down one wall—it was also brightly lit, which did nothing to improve the aesthetic.

Cindy relaxed as we entered. Did she know someone here?

'Can you get a table?' I asked Bas. 'I'll grab drinks.'

He nodded and headed for a booth. I led Cindy to the counter.

'Hullo, Cindy,' the waitress called out. She was a curvaceous woman with thick makeup, her figure stuffed into an obnoxious pink uniform, but she smiled at Cindy before nodding at me. 'Friend of yours?'

'No,' Cindy said.

The woman's smile faltered.

'I'm an old colleague,' I said before Cindy could make things worse. 'We just want to have a quick chat. Can I get two coffees, and—' I glanced at Cindy. 'Get whatever you want.'

'The green shake and a slice of honey cake,' she said without skipping a beat.

She'd done exactly what I would have done—ordered the most expensive items on the menu. I pressed my lips together and handed over a twenty-NP note. At least the cake was worth the money; it was huge. I couldn't imagine Cindy finishing even a quarter of it.

Maybe she planned on throwing it at me before she made her getaway.

For now, however, she played along. We left the waitress to fix our orders and walked over to Bas.

'He your boyfriend then?' Cindy asked.

'Who?'

She jerked her chin towards Bas. 'Tall, dark, and moody.'

'Oh.' My cheeks heated. Bas. My boyfriend. Fucking weird thought. And yet…

'Yeah. Yes, he is,' I said. Butterflies erupted in my stomach. Oh, that was really weird.

'Huh. He a gang member?' Cindy smirked. 'Oho, you two ran away! Eloped! And now you think you're going to make a life here, away from the gangs.' She burst into mocking laughter.

'That's not it!' I hissed.

'Oh, this is too good,' Cindy crowed. 'You want advice? Someone told you I was here and could help you? Well, here's my advice: you're fucked! Should have stayed home and married a good guy.' She laughed so hard, tears smudged her makeup.

'You're wrong,' I snapped. 'That's not why we're here at all.'

'Oh, sure, that's what they all say.'

'We're going to go back—'

'And that, too! 'As soon as things die down.' That's what they say.' Cindy shook her head. 'I give it three months. He'll realise you have no skills except spreading your legs. Then he'll get jealous and leave you for someone else. That's what they do. That's what they *always* do.'

A hand seemed to have closed around my chest, squeezing my heart. I felt cold all of a sudden. 'That's not going to happen,' I gasped. 'We're not here to elope.'

I met Bas's gaze. He stood and strode over to us.

'Time to get this show on the road,' he said. 'Sit.'

'Don't order me about,' Cindy snapped. 'You ain't my man.'

Bas gestured sharply to the table. 'We're not here to stand around.'

'Though if you ever get bored of her…' Cindy made bedroom eyes at him.

'I don't pay for hookers.'

She rolled her eyes and waved at me. 'What is she, then?'

'My friend.'

My mouth dropped open. What?

'That's not what she said.'

Bas glanced at me. I stared at him, my chest aching. *Friends?*

'Our relationship is none of your business,' he said flatly. 'Sit. It's time to talk.'

Snorting, Cindy flounced into the booth. 'Shagging your friends is a really bad idea.'

'I'd rather sleep with a friend than a whore.' Bas nudged me into the booth. I had to force my feet to move. 'At least I respect my friends.'

I wasn't sure if that made things worse or better. Bas sat next to me, but far enough away that we never touched. Had I been demoted already? Did I suck at relationships so much that I'd misread what had happened between us?

Or had he decided that 'taking things slow' meant we had to be friends first?

Friends.

Somehow, I'd never considered calling Bas a friend. I'd called him a lot of other things—*arsehole* came to mind—but never a friend.

The waitress delivered our drinks, and Cindy attacked the wedge of honey cake. Bas glanced at me expectantly. I raised an eyebrow.

We hadn't discussed what happened next beyond just agreeing to ask her questions. But clearly he expected me to do the talking.

I cleared my throat.

'We're looking for a guy named James Maddock.'

'Never heard of him.'

Her response was rapid, slightly muffled by her mouthful, and utterly deceitful. Her eyes flicked away, and her shoulders tensed.

'Uh huh,' I said. 'He's a little taller than me, fighter's build, black hair, tan skin. Good manners.'

'We're four hundred miles from Bale Rocks, Harley. Why the hell would I know this guy?'

'Word on the street is that he's from Langford,' Bas said, his voice soft, yet somehow threatening.

'So? There's a million people here. Maybe more. Probably more.'

She was sweating. Rambling. I glanced at Bas.

'Press the advantage,' his gaze said.

I swallowed. 'You were fired from the bunker for stealing,' I said.

Cindy tensed. 'I—That's—'

'You hid things in the crawlspace above our dressing room.'

'So? Everyone knows that.'

'A few days ago, James Maddock used that same crawlspace to get through the bunker into the Iron Fists compound and murder Eduard Sayle. They're looking for the culprit—' And I was a terrible human being. '—and there's no way Maddock just found the crawlspace by accident. Someone has to have told him.'

I fixed her with a pointed look.

Cindy's face crumpled.

'Alright, alright!' she said. 'He was my roommate, alright? I did tell him—but please don't tell! I didn't realise he was—was planning anything like *that!*'

I crossed my arms. 'Tell us everything you know, and I promise I'll take your involvement to the grave with me.'

Cindy stared at the table. Then she pushed her cake away, curling her arms around her. 'I knew him as James Doherty,' she mumbled. 'He travelled a lot and needed a place he could come back to. We—we're four in my flat. Five made it easier to afford the rent, and he was never there, so it was a win-win.'

'And he was nice,' I surmised.

'Exactly! So well-mannered.' Cindy grabbed her fork again. 'Not like the other guys who groped on us all the time. He'd buy us food whenever he was there, kept his stuff neat. He even got the landlord to back off when he was threatening Mary—' She shook her head. 'Are you sure it was him? I can't imagine Jim killing anyone.'

'It was him,' Bas said.

Cindy flicked her eyes to Bas, then back to me. 'What are you going to do if you find him?'

'That… that depends,' I said.

Her lips thinned. 'He's my friend.'

'I thought he was my friend, too,' I said. 'Turns out, he wasn't.'

Cindy scowled. 'I don't know what else I can tell you, anyway,' she said. 'I didn't know him that well, just spoke to him a few times when he was there.'

'You told him about the crawlspace.'

'He was interested! One of the other girls told him I was from Bale Rocks. And he said *he* was from Bale Rocks originally, so we talked about it. He wanted to know about how the town had changed since he left, so I told him.' She shrugged, her voice turning whiny. 'I didn't think anything I told him was harmful.'

I glanced at Bas, a frisson of excitement shooting through me. Maddock was from Bale Rocks? Or had he lied to Cindy about his origins, too?

Bas frowned.

'Did he leave anything at your flat?'

'A few things, some clothes and stuff.' Cindy squirmed. 'You can take a look if you want, but I doubt you'll find anything there.'

'Fine,' Bas said. 'Finish your cake and we'll head over.'

'What, now?' she asked.

'No time like the present.'

Cindy scowled and jabbed her fork into her cake. Then she looked at me.

'You really have a way of picking 'em, don't you?'

SEVENTEEN

CINDY'S FLAT WAS IN A newbuild with dirty whitewashed walls and the same outdoor hallways that some of the Godfreys' apartment blocks had in Bale Rocks. The landing was littered with an assortment of junk, from dirty shoes to children's toys to saggy old sofas. I could hear shouting emanating from one door that we passed; another was open to show a hoard of small children in various states of undress, screaming and giggling. Finally, we stopped in front of a door that had been painted brown, the paint chipping off to show the white beneath. Cindy unlocked it and held the door for us.

We entered directly into the main room of the flat, which appeared to be kitchen, living room, and dining room all squashed into one small space. It was crowded with furniture, to the point that Bas entering forced me to stumble against the sofa. Cindy squeezed in behind us and shut the door.

'Cindy?' A woman appeared in the hallway that led, I assumed, to the bedrooms. She had very long brown hair and a pale, angular face.

'Hey, Solange.' Cindy edged past me into the kitchen area.

'Who are they?' Solange asked, eyeing us warily.

'People from Bale Rocks. They're looking for Jim.'

'Jim?' she echoed. 'What for?' She stared at both of us, me first—with disdain—and then Bas, with interest.

'Apparently he killed someone.' Cindy shoved the leftovers of her cake in the fridge. Solange wrapped her arms around herself.

'Killed someone? Jim?' Her eyes went wide. She glanced around as though an axeman would leap out of one of the shadowy doors behind her. 'Who?'

'No one you would know,' Bas said. 'We just want to look through his things.'

Solange glanced at Cindy, who shrugged.

'Better let 'em. The faster they do it, the faster they're gone.' She shot a glance at Bas. 'Well, you can stay.'

'Just show me where his room is,' Bas said.

Cindy rolled her eyes and marched down the hall. 'I have better tits than her.'

'I don't care.'

'I bet she's never even put out if she's making you be friends first.'

I bit the inside of my cheek. *Don't let it bother you.*

But it did.

This whole thing with Bas was like a newly hatched baby bird. I wasn't ready to let it out into the world for people to criticise or shoot down yet.

'I fail to see how that is any of your business,' Bas said stonily. He gestured to the door Cindy had stopped at. 'Is this it?'

'What you gonna do if you find him?'

'Take him back to Bale Rocks to exonerate myself and Harley,' Bas said.

'So you'll dob him in to get yourself out of trouble.' Cindy crossed her arms. 'We don't like snitches here.'

'I will find him with or without your help.'

'Well.' Cindy trailed a finger over her ribcage. 'You could at least make it worth my while.'

Bas turned away, disgust written across his face. 'Harley, let's go,' he barked.

I stared at him, baffled. *Say what, now?*

'Are you serious?' Cindy demanded.

'I'm not sleeping with you for information,' Bas said flatly. 'Let's go, Harley.'

The thrill inside of me was totally irrational. I knew it, but I couldn't stop smiling. 'Yeah, okay.'

'By the way,' Bas said, 'if Maddock comes back, you'd better not tell him we were here.'

'Yeah, you can fuck right off,' Cindy snapped.

'He left Harley to take the fall for him quite readily. I'd hate for him to decide you know too much.'

Cindy squeaked. Solange, who was still watching from the entrance to the lounge, whispered, 'Just let them look around, Cindy.'

A pregnant pause ensued, before Cindy finally snarled, 'Fine! You can look. Just get it done, alright.'

'Thank you,' Bas said, as though he hadn't just threatened them. He took my hand and tugged me past Cindy into a small, basic room.

Cindy scowled as we passed. 'He'll dump you for someone prettier eventually,' she hissed.

'He can hear you,' Bas retorted. 'Shut the door behind you.'

Cindy retreated, leaving the door ajar. I shook my hand free of Bas's and turned to survey the room. Bas caught my shoulder. 'Harley.'

'What?' Try as I might, I couldn't help the note of hurt that crept into my voice.

'She's just jealous.'

'Yes, obviously,' I snapped.

Bas stared at me, rolled his eyes, and kissed me.

Oh.

Yeah, that was nice.

Also, weird. I still wasn't used to it—to this. To the feel of his lips on mine, the suddenness, the possessiveness. When he pulled back, I wasn't used to the breathlessness, either.

'What was that for?' I asked, with less heat than I intended—or at least, different heat than I intended.

'I'm here with you,' Bas said.

'Yeah, and we argue all the time, and now you just said we were friends.' There was the familiar anger, rising up in me again. 'Friends!'

'You are my friend.'

'I don't want to be your friend!'

'No?' Bas took a step towards me. I backed up—and hit the door, slamming it shut. *Oops.* 'I'm much nicer to my friends than to my enemies.'

His voice was low, husky. Needy? He was flirting. I swallowed.

'I—I think I'm good with you not being—uh—nice...'

Bas smirked. He traced a finger over my lip, his expression half playful, half curious. As if to see what I'd do.

The doorhandle rattled.

We jumped apart like kids caught stealing cookies. The door swung open, almost clocking me in the shoulder. Bas pulled me away.

'What are you doing?' Solange asked. She was holding a wooden tray, hard enough that it looked like she might hit us with it if needs be. 'Why was the door shut?'

'My bad,' I said. My voice was croaky. Solange stared at me, and I suddenly felt like our activities were written across my forehead. God.

Fuck. I'd never been that girl. What the fuck was Bas doing to me?

'Right,' she said sceptically. 'Well, it's like four AM, so if you could do whatever you're doing quietly? Cece and Mary are asleep.'

'Right.' I cleared my throat. 'Sorry.'

I turned to the room. 'Basic' was the only possible word that came to mind. There was a bed, two wooden crates which had been turned into shelves, and a chest of drawers with the top two drawers missing.

I heard Solange withdrawing.

'Cece,' someone muttered. 'Go back to bed.'

'What's going on?'

Furious whispers travelled up the hallway.

'—about Jim—'

'—should tell them—'

'He was always nice to me!'

'—but that one time—'

'You tell them, then!' That voice, I recognised—Cindy. 'I'm going to bed.'

A door shut with distinct finality.

I glanced at Bas. He was staring at the chest of drawers, frowning. 'Bas?'

'Where would you hide something if you were Maddock?'

'Uh…' I surveyed the room. 'In my flat, I hide things under the bed.'

He shot me a smirk.

'Alright, alright, I know it's predictable.' I grabbed the mattress and heaved. It was heavier than it looked, but I managed to tip it up.

'He never leaves anything here.'

I dropped the mattress, sending a cloud of dust straight up my nose. 'Fuck!'

Coughing and spluttering, I turned to the door. A new person was standing there. She was around my age, if I had to guess, with fine blond hair that hung to her shoulders and eyes that were just slightly too far apart, giving her a dazed look.

'Hi,' I said cautiously. The way she clutched the doorframe made her seem skittish, as though she might spook and run off if I moved too suddenly. 'I'm Harley.'

'I'm Cece.'

She looked at Bas and then, when he said nothing, back at me. 'The others don't want me to tell you this,' she announced.

'Tell us what?' Bas said sharply.

Cece backed up a step.

'Bas,' I hissed. I shot him a look, and he turned back to the chest of drawers. I sat on the edge of the bed and patted the spot beside me. 'If you want to get something off your chest, I'm happy to listen,' I murmured.

Cece crossed her arms. 'Solange said you're looking for Jim because he killed someone.'

'That's right,' I replied.

'That's not the first person he killed,' she said. 'Least, I don't think so. He came back one night with blood on him. I was awake—I get back late from work sometimes.'

'It wasn't his own blood?' Bas cut in.

Cece glanced at him again. Then she edged into the room. 'No. I'm a nurse. I tried to look at him, but he refused. He said it wasn't his blood. And he made me swear not to tell anyone.'

She caught my eye as she said it, almost pleading.

'It's okay,' I said. I felt useless. She was scared of something, but I didn't know what. I didn't know if it was a specific fear—Maddock— or more of a metaphorical fear—men with guns. 'He's not here.'

'I know.' Cece shuffled her weight. 'He was nice,' she said, tilting her head thoughtfully. 'But there was always something about him. I only saw him angry once—it was after that night. Solange moved something of his—a shirt, maybe? I don't remember. But he got angry, and for a second he looked like he'd hit her. Then he stopped and left the flat. And we didn't see him for a few weeks.'

'I'm sorry,' I murmured.

'It's okay.' She shrugged. 'He wasn't here much.'

'Do you know where he went?'

'He said he had an uncle in Crater's Edge.' She frowned. 'Solange might know. They were closest.'

'I do.' Solange shuffled in—evidently she'd been lurking out in the hall, eavesdropping. 'That's what I found that he got angry over. In his trousers, there was a note with an address. 42B Galley Lane, Crater's Edge.'

Bas and I exchanged glances.

'Do you know what's there?' Bas asked. He was still over by the chest of drawers. I got the feeling he was an interloper in this flat—

Solange could sense that he was dangerous.

'No?' Solange rolled her eyes. 'Why would I have been to Crater's Edge? I've barely been off this street since I was born.'

I bit my lip. So close, yet so far. In this case, literally. How far was Crater's Edge from here? Three hundred miles?

'He said that's where his uncle lived,' Cece insisted. 'His uncle raised him after his parents died.'

'In Crater's Edge?' Bas asked.

'Well...' Cece started. They exchanged glances.

'He said he grew up here,' Solange muttered.

'Maybe his uncle moved there later on?' Cece asked.

They both stared at me hopefully. Was I supposed to confirm that? Tell them he hadn't lied to them? They both struck me as so naïve—I had never been that naïve, had I?

God, I hoped not.

'Maybe,' I said, smoothing my fingers over the faded bedspread. Maddock had told so many lies. Even if I wanted to, I couldn't have told them what was true.

'We should go,' Bas said.

'Yeah.' I stood. Cece and Solange clustered together, blocking the doorway.

'If you find him...' Cece murmured.

'Don't hurt him!' Solange blurted. 'He—he's our friend.'

He hurt you, though.

'He killed someone,' Bas said.

'But he was good to us,' Solange insisted, wringing her hands. 'Most people aren't *good* to us.'

I could see where she was coming from all too well. There weren't that many people who were good for no reason. *And then again...* I glanced at Bas. *Everyone has two sides to them. Good and bad.*

Two sides of the same coin.

Even me.

Even Bas. Especially Bas.

'We'll make sure to do the right thing,' I said firmly. 'Whatever that turns out to be. It will depend on what he says when—if—we find him.'

Cece and Solange stared at me. Finally, Solange nodded. 'Okay.'

She stepped back. Bas and I exited, and Solange trailed us to the door. 'Be careful out there.'

'You too,' I replied.

We picked up breakfast at the same twenty-four-hour café that Cindy had taken us to earlier, then headed back to the hotel.

'So,' I said once the door was shut. I stared at Bas, shuffling my weight from foot to foot. 'Uh…'

We needed to talk plans, but every time I looked at him, I thought about kissing him. Which was making it a bit difficult to focus like an adult.

'Crater's Edge,' he said.

'Well,' I cleared my throat, 'we were going there anyway.'

Bas nodded. 'I need sleep. It will take… six hours, from here to the army base, all things going smoothly.'

'Midday, then.'

He strode over to his things, shucking his jacket as he went. 'You should sleep, too.'

It made sense—we'd been up all night. But at the same time, I felt too wired to even consider it.

Bas continued stripping his outerwear off: boots, trousers. In his briefs and T-shirt, he approached the nest of blankets he'd made on the floor.

For the first time, I didn't avert my eyes. Why? He'd kissed me. Surely that allowed me the liberty of watching him.

'Harley.' He paused.

'Yeah?' I asked, suddenly breathless.

'Go to sleep.'

'Yeah, yeah.' I turned away and started taking my clothes off. The bed loomed in front of me. 'We could share, you know.'

'I thought you wanted to take things slow,' Bas replied, his tone fraught with wry amusement.

I swallowed, heat rushing through me. 'I do.'

'Sharing a bed wouldn't be slow.' I heard his blankets shifting. 'And also not conducive to sleep. Which I need if I'm going to drive.'

Oh. There was a promise in those words, and I *wanted* it.

Badly.

Unfortunately, he was probably right. We both had to sleep. We needed to be fresh when we reached the army base, or we'd get caught.

'Fine.' I sighed gustily. 'I'm going to bed.'

'Good.' I could hear the laughter in his voice. I turned to shoot him a scowl. Bas was watching me. Openly. I glanced down at myself. I'd washed my clothes in the sink on the first day, but I didn't exactly make a pretty package anyway, in my ragged jeans and old shirt, with my hair in a messy ponytail. And yet, he looked plenty admiring.

'That isn't conducive to sleep, either,' I muttered.

'You're right.' Bas smirked. Then he rolled over. 'Sleep well.'

Damn, should have kept my mouth shut. Yet, a fizzy sort of happiness was bubbling inside me, irrepressible despite our circumstances. Bas and me. We were together. Sure, we still had a thousand and one problems. But suddenly none of them seemed so big. We could overcome them together.

I was sure of it.

I crawled into bed, and still smiling, finally let myself drift off.

It wasn't long enough, of course. I felt like I'd just closed my eyes, and then Bas was already shaking me awake.

'Harley. *Harley!* We have to go.'

'Ugh,' I groaned, blinking furiously. 'Fine, I'm up.'

'You can sleep in the car.' Bas dropped my bag beside the bed. 'Pack up.'

Exhaustion weighed heavily on me as I threw my things into my bag and washed up in the bathroom. Last shower before Crater's Edge. All things going well, we'd arrive there tomorrow.

All things going well.

Back in the room, I grabbed my bag and slung it over my shoulder.

'Ready to go?' Bas asked.

'Yeah.'

'Alright.' He headed for the door.

We returned our key to a girl half my age, who watched both of us curiously, but said nothing outside of the usual pleasantries. 'Have a safe journey.'

'Thanks,' I replied.

It was cold outside—the temperature had fallen last night—and I shivered as we walked back to the parking lot.

'Harley,' Bas said suddenly.

I glanced at him; he radiated tension. Alarm filled me. 'What?'

'We're being followed,' Bas murmured out of the corner of his mouth.

'What?' I turned my head.

'No—don't look,' Bas hissed. 'Keep walking. Don't speed up.'

The moment he said it, all I wanted to do was run. I studied the street out of the corner of my eye. No one looked out of place. There were plenty of people around, but none of them were paying us any attention.

'Who?' I whispered. 'And why?'

'No idea. We need to get to the car.'

'We're almost there.' I could see the ramp, forty yards ahead. Thirty. Twenty. Ten.

We reached it and descended into the humid parking garage. I breathed a sigh of relief as we reached the car. The boy whom we'd paid to watch it materialised out of the shadows.

'Not even a scratch,' he announced proudly.

'Very good.' To my surprise, Bas slid him a couple of extra coins. The boy grinned toothily.

'You leaving now?'

'Yes,' Bas said.

'Okay. Come again soon!' He ran off, joining a couple of other boys who seemed to have set up a little camp about halfway down the long room.

Bas threw the boot open and we put our bags in. As we did, he glanced around discreetly.

'Anything?' I asked, squeezing my fingers around the sleeves of my coat.

'No. Let's go.'

He shut the boot.

A car engine roared.

Bas spun around. 'Harley, get in the car!'

I sprinted for the passenger door, yanking the handle. Before I could swing myself up, a car pulled up behind us and blocked us in. A second vehicle stopped immediately behind that one. Both were black, with dark windows. The passenger door of the front one swung open, and a man climbed out. Tall and slender, with dark brown skin and a bald head. He wore a charcoal grey suit that immediately set him apart from the dirty, downtrodden residents of Langford.

I walked slowly back over to Bas. His lips were pressed together in a thin line, and he had his hand on his gun. The bald man approached us.

'Bas and Harley, I presume?' He had a smooth, deep voice. Reassuring.

'We don't want any trouble,' I said immediately.

'Neither do I.' He doffed an invisible hat. 'My name is Parker. I work for Miroslav.'

'Miroslav?' I echoed. Were we supposed to know who that was?

'You may know him by his nickname: Mirko.'

I glanced at Bas. He looked calm, except for the beginnings of a frown between his eyes.

'We have no quarrel with Mirko,' Bas said.

'Yes. Unfortunately, that's not true of one of your associates, I think.' Parker smiled, an oddly genteel and friendly smile that set every warning bell in my head clanging. 'All Mirko would like is to talk to you.'

'We're on a bit of a tight schedule,' Bas replied.

'That's unfortunate. But I'm sure we can come to a… speedy agreement.' Parker nodded to his car. 'If you'd come with us, we can settle things in a manner beneficial to all of us.'

Oh, this was bad. The more he spoke in that calm, even tone, the worse the prickling up my spine got. There was a threat hanging in the air—the sort of threat I hated. At least if someone was holding a gun, you could see the danger. But right now it was intangible, unplaceable. All I could think was that Theo had warned us to stay away from Mirko. We had to get away. But how?

'I don't think that's going to be possible,' Bas said.

Parker's smile fell. 'I was afraid you'd say that,' he said apologetically. 'I am sorry, but…'

He nodded to the car, and three other men emerged, all of them big, burly, and holding guns.

There it was.

Four of them, two of us, and our escape route was cut off.

Bad odds.

'If you could please get in the car,' Parker said. 'The lady first.'

I glanced at Bas. His jaw was tense. After a second, he nodded.

'Do as they say, Harley.'

I swallowed and inched towards the black sedan. One of the men slammed the butt of his pistol into my shoulder, sending pain jolting through me.

'Hurry it up, girl!'

'Now, now,' Parker interjected, waving his henchman back. 'We promised there would be no violence.'

I shot both of them a scowl. Rubbing my shoulder, I climbed into the car and slid over the torn leather seats. I glanced back at Bas, who took a step towards me.

And the door slammed shut.

'What? No!' I lurched towards the door, but the driver gunned the engine.

'Sit tight!' he barked.

'No! Where are you taking me?'

'Mirko wants to see you.' Tyres squealing, engine roaring, he made a tight turn and sped towards the ramp. A moment later, we exited the garage into the winter afternoon.

Leaving Bas behind.

Leaving me alone.

Fuck.

EIGHTEEN

THE CAR RIDE LASTED EIGHTEEN MINUTES.

There was a clock on the dashboard—functional, albeit showing completely the wrong time. But still, I could use it to tell how much time had passed.

That meant two things:

One, I was now an eighteen-minute drive away from the only person I knew in this city.

And two, despite taking Theo's advice, Bas and I had never been out of Mirko's reach.

We were such idiots.

Had we tipped him off somehow?

Why was he interested in us in the first place? We'd never even been to Langford before.

I'd initially thought we were driving out of the city, but eventually, we slowed in an industrial area and the car pulled through a set of steel gates into a yard. We stopped in front of a large warehouse, its roller doors raised. The inside thrummed with activity: people moving boxes, loading up a truck, and unloading another one.

'Out you get,' the driver snapped. 'And don't try anything funny.'

What the hell did he think I was going to try? I still had my gun, but it wasn't going to do me much good, not when I could count a dozen armed men around me, between the men in the car, the men overseeing the packing activities, and the security on the gates.

I climbed out of the car, and Parker joined me, gesturing towards the open roller doors. 'This way, please.'

Silently, I walked beside him into the warehouse. It was a veritable hive of activity, men and women hurrying around, shouting to one another, or chattering in huddles. We cut through the middle to a second, smaller hall. An array of boxes was stacked against the far wall, each of them stamped with an unfamiliar logo. A group of people waited in the middle: two armed bodyguards, and between them an unassuming man, a little taller than me, with tanned skin, dark hair, and a goatee. He had his hands tucked in the pockets of his dress pants, and he was smiling.

I'd bet my right arm this was Mirko.

Parker led the way over to him. He ran his eyes over me, frowning lightly.

'This is her?'

Parker nodded.

'Good. Put her in the cell. We'll negotiate with her friend when he arrives.'

Sexist git. 'How do you know I'm not the one you should be negotiating with?' I snapped.

Mirko glanced disinterestedly at me. 'Do you know who I am?'

I could guess. 'You're Mirko.'

'That's right. This is my city. Nothing happens here that I don't know about. Including two no-names from Bale Rocks sneaking in and staying at Dina's B&B.'

Fucker.

'You've got the wrong people! We don't have anything you'd want.'

'Do you know a man named Theodore Dunne?'

I flinched. Mirko smiled.

'Yes, I see that you do. Theodore Dunne has run off with someone who owes me a great deal of money. Now you pitch up, from the same place he's from, working for the same organisation. You can pay his debt instead.'

How the hell could he know that?

My surprise must have shown on my face, because Mirko continued, 'I see you're wondering where I get my information.' He tilted his head towards the side of the hall. I glanced over and saw a woman standing in the shadows.

Cindy.

My heart sank. We hadn't even considered that Cindy might sell us out—but she must have gone straight to Mirko after we'd left.

What for? To protect Maddock? Because Bas had threatened her? Or maybe simply to improve her own standing with the local gang. It didn't matter. She'd done it, and now we had to face the consequences.

Mirko cleared his throat. 'I consider myself a fair man, Harley,' he said gravely. 'I don't extort people. I don't demand things they're not willing to give. All I ask for is my dues. My cut… But I definitely don't like it when outsiders come into my home and interfere with my business. That's not on.'

I glanced at Cindy. She crossed her arms, lifting her chin stubbornly.

'Take her upstairs,' Mirko said.

There was no point in fighting—I'd never make it out. Two men grabbed my arms and hauled me to a metal staircase which led up to a narrow catwalk along the side of the room. At the end of the catwalk, they pushed open a door, revealing a room that looked like it might once have been an office. They'd pulled all the furniture out and installed a row of steel bars that divided the room in half.

A third man stepped up to me. 'I'll have to take your weapons.'

'I'd rather keep them.'

He smirked. 'I think not. Arms out.'

Scowling, I complied. He frisked me up and down with rough hands, getting in under my clothes. I tensed as his hands ran over my chest and down the insides of my legs. He removed both my knife and gun, and even found the stiletto Theo had leant me. *Crap.* Finally, he stepped back.

'Belt off.'

I unwound it and passed it to him. 'I need that, you know.'

'You'll get it back when you leave.'

I crossed my arms. 'If I get to leave.'

He gestured towards the open cell. 'If your boyfriend can come up with Mirko's money, then you'll be let go.'

I stalked into the cell. I could have cursed Theo. Nice of him to warn us.

'This has nothing to do with me or Bas!'

'If he brings us the person we want, you will be let go.' He shut the door with a clang.

For fuck's sake.

Rhett and Theo were back in Bale Rocks. And there was no way to contact them.

I sat on the floor. At some point, the carpet had been ripped up—I assumed when they'd installed the bars—so I was forced to sit on freezing cold concrete. My guards conferred before they all left the room.

'Be good,' one of them called, and the others laughed mockingly.

The door shut, and I was alone.

Fuck. What was I going to do now?

Time ticked by. Several times, I managed to fall into an uneasy sleep, jerking awake whenever my guard poked his head in. Other times, I stared at the ceiling, fear sliding through my veins.

We were going to miss our check-in with Theo.

He would worry.

I had no real idea of how much time had passed. My only means of tracking it was the skylight: it was still light. It was still day.

Why, oh why didn't I wear a watch? My old one had broken years ago, and I'd told myself I'd get it fixed, then never bothered. Now, it seemed like a stupid oversight.

Not that it would help.

Even so.

I rolled onto my side, trying to find a more comfortable position on the concrete floor. How long would it take for Bas to figure out a way to rescue me?

Or would he even?

Sure, we were dating now… but did that mean he'd come for me? It was too new to be sure. I hoped he would; we'd travelled this far together.

But…

No, he will.

Bas was honourable. That much I knew for sure. He wouldn't leave me.

But he also wasn't going to be able to come up with the money—I knew that, as well. Unless he had a secret moonlight job as a thief. Which I was confident he didn't. So…

Rescue mission.

Or… or I could take the opportunity to prove that I was capable and… deserving of his respect. I could get myself out.

That was an idea.

I remained lying down, casually shifting my position so that I could study my cell. For lack of better words, it was a cage, built directly into the office. The bars connected to a perpendicular metal strip which was bolted to the floor. It was rusted and didn't look terribly sturdy, but I probably wasn't strong enough to break it, either. The bars didn't seem to go all the way up to the ceiling. Could I squeeze through the gap?

In a pinch, maybe. But there was another option: the skylights. The office was directly under the roof of the warehouse. The only trouble was that I couldn't reach the windows from the ground. I was too short.

Pursing my lips, I studied the bars again. There was a crossbar about two feet off the ground and a second one two feet from the ceiling. If I could get up there…

That might work.

I waited until my guard poked his head in again, feigning sleep. Satisfied, he withdrew. As soon as the door shut again, I sat up and worked my boots off. After knotting the laces together, I hung them around my neck. Then I tied my coat around my waist.

Time to get out of here.

Breathing slowly and evenly, I set one foot on the crossbar. Then I reached above my head to grab the bars and lifted the other foot up.

One of my boots swung, hitting the bars with a soft thud.

Crap!

I jumped down. Would the guard check? I hastily lay down again and counted my breaths. Two, three, four, five.

The door remained shut.

Okay, okay. That had cost me time. I'd be more careful this go around.

Once more, I climbed onto the crossbar. I shifted my boots so they were hanging down my back, then clamped my legs around one of the bars and shimmied up.

The metal was rough and rusty—hard on my palms, but the way it snagged on my jeans prevented me from sliding down. *Perfect.* I hauled myself up until I managed to get a grip on the higher crossbar. That was the first hurdle.

The second was getting my legs up there.

It took a hell of a lot of manoeuvring and muffled grunting, but I managed to swing one leg up, then the other, so I was crouching on the upper crossbar, my knees to my chest. The skylight was about a foot behind me and above. I took a deep breath, then let go with one hand and reached for it, feeling about until my fingers touched smooth glass.

Gotcha.

How long did I have before my guard checked on me again? Why hadn't I thought to measure how frequently he came by?

No matter now—I could only go forwards. I found the handle and pushed the window open. Cold air rushed in, chilling the back of my neck. I twisted to look.

That was a small gap.

Fuck.

I'd never get through there.

Damnit.

I looked down at the ground, several metres below. I had no other options. It was this or stay trapped.

Swallowing, I turned back to the window and shoved it as hard as I could manage. It wobbled. Could I force it further open?

I tried again, this time watching what I was doing. It was loose on one side, and further examination showed me that the hinge was broken. If I could pry it up somehow… But I didn't have anything to use for leverage.

Damn. Could I get the other hinge off?

It was fastened by a screw. They'd taken my weapons when they had shoved me in here, along with everything else useful I'd had on me. They'd even taken my belt. But what they hadn't done was take the pins out of my hair. I worked one out and clamped it between my sweaty fingers.

This has to work.

Using the back end, I put it between the grooves of the screwhead and twisted.

The pin popped free and slipped out of my fingers.

No, damnit!

Gritting my teeth, I worked a second one out of my hair. I wiped my fingers down on my jeans and took a deep breath.

Focus, Harley.

I set it in the grooves again, twisting slower this time. Slowly, ever so slowly, the screw began to turn.

Yes!

I worked it a few times until I could get my fingers around it and unscrew it by hand. Finally, it came loose and I shoved it in my pocket. I pushed against the window, and it swung up.

Gotcha!

Now I just had to get out.

Take it slow. You can do it.

Clenching my knees around the bars, I took my second hand off the bars and worked it over to the skylight. Without the hinges, the window wouldn't stay open either. I pushed it up as far as it would go, balancing it so it didn't fall on my hands. Then I gripped the edge and slowly turned myself so my back was to the ceiling.

Step one.

Now to get my legs through.

I clamped my hands around the edge of the window frame, took a deep breath, and pushed myself off the bars. For a second, I was swinging through space. Then I used my momentum to haul myself up. I got one leg through.

The window fell on my head.

'Ah, fuck!' I snarled. I froze.

Shit.

Behind me, I heard the door opening.

'What's going on in—SHE'S ESCAPING!'

Shit. Shit, shit, shit.

With renewed urgency, I yanked my other leg up. My thighs cramped from the awkward position. The window pressed down on me. My arms strained.

Then my knees were on the roof. I shoved the window away and scrambled clear.

I had done it.

I sagged, weak with relief. I was out. I'd overcome the first hurdle.

Now I had to figure out how to get out of the compound.

My hands shook as I relaced my boots and pulled my coat on again. The metal roof bowed in protest as I made my way to the edge.

I was high up—way too high to jump.

Was there another way off?

I made my way along the edge. *Come on. Ladder. Something. Please.*

A second warehouse bordered the one I was standing on. The gap was only around a yard and a half.

I heard shouts from the yard beneath me.

Fuck it, no time to hang around.

I took a run up and leapt over to the other warehouse.

'Ouch, shit!' I cursed under my breath as my knees hit the metal. At least I was across. I was still on Mirko's land, though.

I crawled along the edge of the second warehouse. Didn't these stupid things have fire escapes? Why was there no ladder? I spied a pile of boxes on the asphalt below and hastily manoeuvred myself to a spot above them.

It was about a ten-foot drop to the top of the crates. Would they hold my weight?

'STOP HIM!'

I whirled around. A group of men had emerged into the yard. Abruptly, one broke away, throwing a punch that knocked another guy to the ground.

Bas.

He twisted like a snake, throwing more punches. A crack reached me across the yard, and I shuddered. Sweeping my gaze around, I found the gate. Time to get out of here.

I jumped.

My stomach lurched as I fell. Then I hit the crates with a thud. I scrambled down the pile and dropped to the ground. I sprinted for the gate.

'BAS! LET'S GO!'

'THERE SHE IS! STOP HER!'

I couldn't look—didn't dare, lest I trip. I kept running, my heart pounding like a drum in my ears.

'CLOSE THE GATE!'

'Harley!' Bas sprinted up beside me. 'Car—this way.'

We made the gate with seconds to spare as the mechanism slowly clanked shut. Bas pushed me out first then squeezed through and grabbed my arm. 'This way.'

I stumbled after him around the corner. And—there. The best sight I'd laid eyes on all day. The car. I could have wept as we closed the gap and Bas unlocked it. Footsteps pounded on the pavement behind us. I scrambled up as Bas climbed into the driver's side. A car engine cut through the stillness.

We weren't going to make it.

CRACK!

A gunshot tore through the silence.

'Get down!' Bas hissed. He put pedal to metal as I threw myself into the footwell. Another gunshot went off, and the car swerved. I turned to see Bas aiming his own gun through his window.

Bang! Bang! Bang!

A yell reached me, and then Bas was accelerating. The engine snarled in protest as we shot down the road and took a corner at a hair-raising speed. I waited, my jaw clenched, but no more shots were fired. Finally, Bas slowed the car.

'It's safe,' he said. 'You can come out now.'

I crawled out of the footwell and collapsed into my seat. 'Shit.'

'Are you alright?' he asked.

'Yeah, I think so. Where have you been this whole time?' I clicked my seatbelt into place.

'Trying to rescue you.' A small smirk played about his lips. 'Apparently, I needn't have bothered.'

'What, did you want me to wait around for you to play knight in shining armour?'

'Definitely not,' he said.

'Good, because I wasn't planning on it.'

NINETEEN

THE FURTHER WE GOT FROM Langford, the sicker I felt.

'Maybe we should try and get a message to Theo,' I said. 'We could—'

'We'd lose an entire day,' Bas said. 'And he won't be waiting.'

'I know but—'

But nothing. I had no solution. We'd missed our meeting with Theo. Which meant we moved to plan B: rendezvous in Crater's Edge. As we had decided.

That was where we needed to go anyway.

I just felt so powerless. The distance stretched between us, a chasm that I couldn't see across. Theo was on the other side.

And we had missed our deadline.

What would he think had happened to us? What fears were going through his mind?

Were any fears going through his mind?

He was probably just as calm and collected as Bas was about the whole thing.

It was just me. I couldn't cope with the pressure. I wasn't cut out for travelling the wasteland with no contact with the people I loved.

'I'm going to teach you to drive,' Bas announced.

I turned to look at him. 'What?'

'It's more than four hundred miles to Crater's Edge. I can't drive the whole way without breaks.'

'Oh.' An odd feeling twisted in my belly. I'd never driven before. No one had ever even offered to teach me, and I had never been able to afford to pay anyone for lessons. 'When?'

'Right now.' Bas pointed to the ignition, his key dangling down. His keychain was the shell of a bullet, as long as my index finger. 'This is the ignition. Turn it to switch the car on.'

'I know that!'

'You have to start from first principles.' Bas pointed to the gearstick. 'The gearstick changes gears. Always start in first.'

I crossed my arms. Bas continued to explain the workings of the car, taking me through what the different pedals did and what gear I should be in at what time.

'Lower for accelerating, higher for cruising.'

'What gear do I use for outrunning slavers?'

'I'll drive once we reach Brackfields,' Bas replied. 'You can take over now.'

Shit.

My heart leapt into my throat. 'Right now?'

'No time like the present.'

He slowed the car and stopped by the side of the road. I glanced around warily. We were on the edge of Langford. Though not in the city, there was still visible evidence of civilisation. I could see a farmhouse just off the road, smoke rising from its chimney. 'You want to get out the car here?'

'I'll get out. You climb over.'

This had not been on my list of things to do before I died. Learning to drive was something you did in the city, where breaking down wasn't a matter of life or death. Not in the middle of the wasteland with slavers hiding just out of view.

'I… I don't think this is such a good idea,' I mumbled.

'You'll be fine.'

'How can you be so confident?' Confident was the opposite of how I felt. More like *we were going to die.* I rubbed my sweaty palms on my trousers.

'I'm here,' Bas said. He leant back to grab his gun from the back seat, then opened his door.

'Bas!'

He slammed the door. I was alone in the car. I was—

Meant to be climbing over to the driver's seat. *Right.* I scrambled over, the gearstick digging into my knees, and collapsed, trembling, into the driver's seat.

The driver's seat.

Oh God.

I was way too far from the wheel, and this was such a bad idea—

Knock-knock.

I gasped and twisted around. Bas stood by my door, an amused smile on his face.

Shit, I'd forgotten to unlock it. Hastily, I leant over and flicked the lock. Bas climbed in.

'Thanks.'

'Sorry,' I muttered.

'You need to relax.' He shut and relocked the door. 'You're too in your head.'

What?

'Where else would I be?' I asked in a strangled voice.

'Compartmentalise,' Bas said. 'You feel too much. It stops you from thinking logically.'

'Is this your way of telling me I'm being a stupid emotional woman?' I asked darkly.

'No?' He glanced at me. 'If you're in your head, you can't respond to threats as quickly as you need to. You react with fear instead of logic.'

'I don't know how else to be.'

'Calm.' He rolled his eyes. 'Lock your door.'

I'd forgotten to do that, too. I hurriedly locked it. Then I took two deep breaths. Calm. Yeah, no way that was happening. I was the opposite of calm. My fingers trembled and my knees jiggled.

'Harley.' Bas put his hand on my knee, stilling it. 'You can do this.'

I wished I could share his confidence. 'I'm not so sure.'

He reached over me, his body totally in my personal space. I pressed my back into the seat. 'What are you doing?'

'There's a lever here. Use it to move the seat forwards.'

'Oh.' He pulled back. I pressed a hand to my chest, rubbing it over my heart. It was racing. 'Okay.'

I moved the seat forwards, then forwards again, until I could reach the pedals. There were three. I'd already forgotten what they did. 'Uhh…'

'Check the car is in neutral.' Bas tapped the gearstick, making it wiggle. 'Then switch the car on.'

Patiently, he talked me through the whole process again. I managed to get the car on, depressed the clutch and put it in gear. Then I tried to start driving. The car jerked, and the engine went dead.

'What happened?' I cried. Shit—I'd broken it—

'You stalled. Start again from the beginning, slower this time.'

'Stalled?' This was way more complicated than I'd realised.

Everyone made it look so easy.

'Mm-hmm.' Bas looked amused. I was pretty sure he was trying not to laugh at me. I must look so stupid.

Take two worked. I got the car rolling forwards—at a snail's pace—with me gripping the steering wheel tightly.

'Now accelerate and go up a gear,' Bas said.

'Um.' I wasn't ready for that!

There seemed to be way too much to remember. For about five minutes, we progressed in fits and bursts, the engine making moans of protest as I failed to change gears smoothly. Finally, we were rolling forwards, somewhat steadily, and as long as I didn't have to stop, we'd probably be fine.

'Now brake,' Bas said.

I groaned.

By the time we'd left the farms behind us, I could go up and down the gears without the engine making its horrible scraping noise. And I wasn't mixing up the pedals anymore. I drove us steadily along the straight road.

'See, that wasn't so hard,' Bas said.

'Are you joking?' I was gripping the steering wheel so hard my fingers ached.

'You can relax now,' he said.

'You can fuck off now,' I muttered under my breath.

Bas laughed. 'It worked, didn't it?'

'What did?' I would rather focus on his comment than on his laughter. It made me want to look at him, see the smile on his face, and if I did that, we'd probably go off the road.

'I got you to forget about your worries for a bit.'

My mouth dropped open. 'You—That—You did that to distract me?'

'Of course.'

'You—you—Argh!'

Bas laughed again. This time, I did look. He was smiling, his green eyes bright with mirth. Happy. He was happy, because of me.

The car swerved.

'Harley!'

I looked straight ahead, yanking the wheel. 'Sorry!'

'Focus,' Bas said. 'If you crash my car, we'll be stuck here.'

'Don't distract me then!'

He snorted. 'Don't worry, I won't. I'm going to sleep.'

'Wait, what?'

'So I can drive later.'

'But what if something goes wrong?'

'Then you can wake me up,' he said. 'You'll be fine. Put the radio on if you want.'

So much for distracting me from worrying.

I ceded the wheel back to Bas when the ugly brown smudge of Brackfields appeared on the horizon. I had managed to drive in a straight line for several hours, an experience which had taught me that driving was, in fact, terribly boring. Almost sleep-inducing.

Still, I'd managed to do it without crashing or waking Bas too often. We'd gone through potholes a few times, and he'd stirred enough to grouch at me not to break his car.

Now, he took the wheel again and I curled up in the passenger seat. 'Are we going through Brackfields?'

'No, it's too risky.'

How had I known he'd say that?

'We'll go east,' Bas said. He looked west, to where the sun was dipping down in the sky. 'We need to camp. I can't drive through the night in the wasteland like Theo can. I don't know the terrain well enough.'

Camp.

'Uh… maybe it would be safer to just spend the night in Brackfields,' I said tentatively.

Bas consulted his watch. 'We have twenty-one hours to make the rendezvous in Crater's Edge. We can't afford to get held up.'

I swallowed. The nerves I'd been holding at bay surged up again, stronger than ever. He was right. And if we missed that rendezvous… we'd have a big problem. Bigger than I could imagine.

Get to Crater's Edge. Meet Theo. Find Maddock.

Worry about everything else later.

'Okay.' I steeled my shoulders. 'How do we camp in the wasteland?'

Bas's demeanour shifted. He'd convinced me—now on to the next order of business. 'We need to find somewhere sheltered. Preferably with a water source nearby. Keep a lookout once we're off the road.'

'Right.'

Five minutes later, Bas found a spot where the barrier had broken, and we descended the embankment into the wasteland. The sun was directly behind us, turning the hard-packed dirt and stunted trees red and gold. I squinted into the oncoming darkness, searching for anywhere we might set up camp overnight. Bas set a slow pace, zigzagging around obstacles.

After about twenty minutes, he murmured suddenly, 'There's a watchtower straight ahead.'

'Where?'

Bas gestured with one hand. A tall metal tower glowed red in the light of the setting sun.

'Who are they?' I asked.

'I think they're military. Stationed in Brackfields. They're checking for people trying to approach the city from the wasteland.'

'To stop them sneaking in?'

'Yes.'

'Why is Brackfields so well defended?'

'It's a valuable target. That's where most of the industry for the region is. Control that, and you can exert power over the government in Providence.' Bas steered us around a cluster of bushes. 'So the government stations most of their men here to protect their investment.'

'Like the distillery in Bale Rocks for the Iron Fists,' I said.

'Exactly.'

I'd never considered that the gangs in Bale Rocks were just playing a smaller version of the political games that played out across the entire West Rim. But of course—there was nothing new under the sun. Why would anywhere else be any different?

Just more money, more men, more guns.

These men with guns, however, didn't bother us. Periodically, we saw them in the distance, the setting sun glinting off their binoculars. I assumed they wouldn't do anything unless we tried to approach Brackfields, but Bas kept us on a steady course, with the hazy brown clouds above the city to our left.

Eventually, it passed behind us.

'We have to make camp.' Bas's voice was soft but urgent. 'We're losing the light.'

'I'm looking.'

'We can't afford to be fussy.' Bas's eyes skimmed the horizon. Finally, he turned us away from the track we'd been following. We bounced through the bushes and came to a stop near the shell of a burnt-out building.

'This will have to do.'

I glanced around. Shadowy wasteland surrounded us. 'This… doesn't feel safe.'

'We'll sleep in the car,' Bas decided. 'You can sleep first. I'll take the first watch.'

We ate a cold dinner out of tins Bas had stashed in the back. He had all sorts of gear with him—I'd never realised what it took to survive in the wasteland.

Nor how prepared you had to be.

'Why do you have all this stuff?' I asked around a mouthful. 'I mean, you can't have expected that we'd need to run.'

Bas shrugged. 'I like to be prepared.'

'To leave home?' Was I the only one who hadn't been ready to abandon Bale Rocks at a moment's notice?

'In case the situation changed.' Bas tapped a finger against the tin, his gaze sweeping over the dark, empty landscape. Brackfields glowed on the horizon.

Maybe it was just me. I hugged my legs, shivering. We were sitting in the back, amidst boxes and bags. Bas had cleared enough space for us to sit face-to-face and produced an electric lantern. Now, he rifled through a box and pulled out a blanket.

'Here.'

'Thanks,' I mumbled, drawing it around me.

'You should get some sleep.'

'Yeah.' I eyed the darkness beyond the car. Inky black. Anything could be hiding out there.

'You'll be fine.' Bas rolled his eyes. 'That's why I'm keeping watch.'

'What if slavers come?'

'Then I'll shoot them.'

How did Bas manage to make everything sound so simple? Didn't he worry about the unknown, the things he couldn't control?

I finished my tin of beans and sausage, and we rearranged the back so there was space for me to lie down and Bas to sit beside me. When he stretched his legs out, they touched mine.

'Do you want me to switch the lantern off?' he asked.

'No, it's fine.'

The darkness outside the car seemed to press in on us. Every rustle, every wing flutter, every unexplained noise seemed amplified a hundred-fold.

I didn't think I'd sleep a wink. I couldn't remember falling asleep, but then Bas was shaking me gently.

'Harley. I need you to keep watch.'

I sat up, alertness washing through me. Scrubbing my hands over my face, I glanced around. It was pitch black outside the car, but Bas was illuminated by a small torch. He had his own blanket wrapped around his shoulders.

'Did the lantern go out?' I yawned.

'I put it out. The light seemed to bother you.' He held out the torch. 'You can turn it back on if you want.'

I nodded. We switched places, and Bas nestled down amidst the blankets. I kept one to ward off the winter chill as I took his spot by the door.

'My gun is to your right,' Bas said.

I glanced down. The metal shone in the torchlight.

'You know how to use it, right?'

'Yes.'

'Good.'

He pulled the blanket over his head, and a moment later his breathing evened out. Asleep. I hugged my knees and stared out into the darkness. It was the deep of night, when the silence seemed to take on a different quality. It was heavier, somehow. I felt as though even breathing cost me more energy than during the day.

'Bas?' I whispered.

He didn't stir.

I stretched my feet out until I could burrow them under his blankets and touch his leg, the way he'd done to me.

The night seemed to last forever. Thoughts circled like vultures in my brain. What would we find when we got to Crater's Edge? What were we going to do about Maddock?

And then there was Theo—what must he be thinking?

And I'd see Savannah again.

What would they say about Bas and me?

Did I even care what they had to say?

I groaned under my breath and adjusted the blanket, trying to clear my mind, but all that happened was Maddock popped up again. What would we find? Who was his mystery uncle?

And most importantly: was he really the son of the old mayor? Lucy had seemed to think he was. But Bas and Theo had thought it was a con. And I had no idea what I thought about the whole thing.

The questions went round and round until I thought I'd drive myself to distraction. I was dying to walk around, but too afraid to get out of the car. I peered out into the darkness.

Nothing stirred. Nothing except my thoughts.

We hadn't agreed on what time I should wake Bas, but it ended up not mattering. When the low light reached the car, he stirred on his own and sat up.

'Morning,' I said.

Bas glanced around and blinked at me. His hair was mussed, his eyes half open. I had to smile. Half-awake Bas was cute. 'Harley?' he croaked.

'Sleep well?'

'Yeah.' He rolled his shoulders, shaking off the sleepiness. 'We should go.'

Spending several hours sitting in a freezing car wasn't exactly my idea of a fun time. Besides that, I was dying for a shower. 'Yeah, let's.'

TWENTY

CRATER'S EDGE WAS A RAGTAG tangle of low-rise buildings—mostly houses, but as we approached the centre squat, long four-storey apartment blocks were added to the mix. Although most of the buildings were painted either white or cream, a thin layer of red dust covered everything, turning them a sort of washed-out terracotta.

Bas drove through the city with the confidence of someone who had been there before, bypassing the crowded centre and eventually arriving on a street of ramshackle terraced houses. Standing alone halfway down, separating the two rows of terraces, was a single building made of whitewashed brick.

Red Rock Inn

The sign, gold paint on dark red, swung in the winter breeze. The parking lot beside it was packed with trucks and cars, so we had to stop on the street.

'Looks like they're full up.' I surveyed the mass curiously. After spending time alone in the wasteland, it was weird to encounter evidence of so many people in one place.

We entered via a side door with a chalk sign:

Rooms

7NP per night no food

10NP with breakfast

15NP premium

Inside was similarly full. Every seat at the low wooden tables was occupied, and chatter drowned out the music system. The place was dimly lit, open, and cosy. The walls were white, though on the far one an artist had rendered a detailed painting of cliffs made of red rock.

Is that the crater?

I couldn't take my eyes off it as we approached the low bar.

'Stunning piece, hey?' the bartender called.

'What?' I turned to look at him; he was an older man with a thatch of white hair and crow's feet around his bright blue eyes. He grinned as we reached him.

'The painting. My daughter did it.' He nodded to the nearest stretch of wall. 'That's the view off the cliffs.'

'Wow,' I said.

'You after a room?' he asked. 'Or food? I'm Smith, by the way. Just Smith. We don't get fancy about names round here.'

'Harley,' I replied. A second later, I remembered that I'd intended to give a fake name. *Shit.* His smile was just so disarming.

'Nice to meet you, Harley and…'

'Bas,' Bas replied.

Smith nodded, already reaching for a bottle of whiskey. 'You been driving long?'

'Since Langford,' Bas said.

'Helluva drive.' Smith started filling two glasses. 'Looks like you could use this.'

He slid a glass to each of us.

'Thanks,' I murmured, taking a sip and glancing around. The crowd was oddly familiar: sturdy men and women in well-worn work gear.

Bas coughed up the money. 'Do you have rooms?'

'Sure do. Single or double? Will you be wanting breakfast?'

'Double, no food,' Bas said. He forked out another note. 'We're only staying one night.'

'Righty.' Smith took a key from a hook board on the wall. 'You'll be across the way. Sorry about that, but we've got a big group from the merchants' market.'

I glanced at the crowd again, understanding dawning. Of course—I'd forgotten. The merchants' market had travelled straight here from Bale Rocks. It felt like so long since we'd left Bale Rocks; it was hard to believe they were still in the area.

'It's easy enough to find,' Smith continued. 'Straight across, four doors to the left. There's a sign on the door. You'll be on the second floor. All the way down the hall.'

'Thank you.' Bas pocketed the key and took a hefty sip of his whiskey. 'And the car?'

'Leave it outside. We don't get much crime on this street. They boys make sure of it.' He nodded to a pair of bouncers that I hadn't even noticed. They were sitting discreetly at a table near the door, as though they were customers, but now that I was looking, I realised that they were alert and their table had a perfect view of the whole room.

This place must be doing good business if they could afford in-house security.

Once we'd finished our drinks, Bas and I walked down to the building across the road. When we entered, I discovered that what I'd thought was a row of terraced houses, was actually a single building, the walls knocked out and each room converted to a hotel room. Ours was at the end, overlooking the street. I threw myself dramatically onto the bed.

'Ugh, that's so good.'

'Harley Benoit doesn't like camping. Noted.' Bas smirked.

'Piss off.' I waved dismissively at him. 'You're male. These things are easier for you.'

'You can just say you don't like it.' He dropped his bag on the floor and sat beside me. 'The world won't end if you admit to being spoilt.'

'I am not spoilt!'

Bas laughed. I glared up at him, but the heat in my veins ebbed. He looked happy. And deservedly. We'd survived Langford. We had a lead. We'd meet Theo tonight, and hopefully the dread that lay heavily on our shoulders would finally lift. It already felt easier being here, closer to home. On territory that Bas, at least, was familiar with.

I touched his thigh, tracing over the seam of his trousers. 'What are we doing now?'

Bas caught my fingers and set my hand gently on the bed. 'We have about nine hours before we have to meet Theo.'

'Time to go to Galley Lane,' I said.

'And to head to the NCC office.'

I bit my cheek. I'd forgotten that Bas had promised Turner we'd check the office out. 'Do you think we'll find anything?'

'Probably not,' Bas said. 'But I wasn't planning on just asking.'

'Okay.' My heart sped up a bit. More lawbreaking. It was becoming pretty commonplace for me.

'I at least want to see if we can get information on Markus Clairmont,' he added. 'If he's dirty, he might be the key to exposing the entire network.'

'You think there are higher-ups involved in this?' I theorised.

Bas nodded.

'There must be. Or people would have figured it out already.'

'Yeah.' A long-forgotten conversation with Savannah popped into my head. 'Savannah didn't know anything about the NCC being dirty.'

'Why would she? She's just a nurse, isn't she?'

'Doctor,' I corrected. 'She's a doctor.'

'Has she mentioned Clairmont before?'

I shook my head. 'Don't think so. She doesn't really talk about her colleagues. Only her friend, Nina. She's—'

I cut myself off abruptly.

She's also a doctor.

She was more than that though.

'Nina Clairmont,' I said. 'That's her name.'

'A relative of Markus?' Bas asked, sitting up straighter.

'She must be.' There weren't so many people in our town that there'd be more than one Clairmont family. 'No, wait, she's married.' I bit my lip, probing the depths of my memory. 'Sav went to her wedding. She told me about it. Nina married some lower government guy… I think his name was Nick. Nick Clairmont.'

'He works for the mayor?' Bas asked.

'Maybe. I'm not sure.' I sat up, suddenly restless. 'Do you think Nina knows about the slaves?' A new thought occurred to me, making my heart race. 'Do you think Savannah is in danger?'

'Probably not,' Bas replied. He caught my shoulder. 'Harley, calm down.'

I took a deep breath, smoothing my palms down my thighs. 'She's my sister—'

'She can take care of herself. She's done it this long.'

'No, I take care of her!' I said shrilly. I jumped up, pacing the length of the room. 'We have to go back!'

'We don't know if Nina Clairmont is even related to Markus Clairmont,' Bas said. He stood and caught me mid-stride, putting an arm around my shoulders. 'Harley, relax. Savannah's twenty-five. She can cook. Clean. She works a job that requires her to be extremely capable. I know you helped her, but that doesn't mean she doesn't have the skills to survive.'

'But—'

'*Harley.*' He shot me a pointed look.

'You don't even know her,' I muttered meekly.

'I have met her, actually.' Bas smirked. 'In the pub. You two are remarkably similar.'

'You haven't! When?' Savannah had never mentioned that.

'Around when I met you. As I recall, she got rather intoxicated. I walked her home.'

I stared at him, open-mouthed. 'Savannah was drunk? Wait, is that how you knew where I lived? I wondered about that!'

'Yep.'

'Oh my God.' I pulled away, shaking my head. 'All this time, and you did know my sister. Oh man. What was she doing in the pub?'

'She said she was with colleagues.'

I shook my head again and turned to the window. A car rolled by on the street below. The sky was dirty red from the dust. I could smell it in the air.

'Savannah will be okay,' Bas said. 'I know you're worried. But she can survive a week without you. When we're alone, we discover skills we didn't realise we had.'

'Maybe you do, but I don't,' I muttered.

'Fishing for compliments doesn't suit you.'

'I'm not fishing!' I turned back to him, putting my hands on my hips. 'You make everything look so easy!'

'Says Harley Benoit, queen of pole dancing.' Bas rolled his eyes. 'Who took to self-defence considerably faster than I did. Come on.' He waved me over to the bed. I shuffled over. He grabbed my wrist and sat, forcing me to take another step that put me between his legs.

'Hello.' His voice was husky suddenly.

'Uh… hi.'

'I'm going to kiss you.' He dropped my wrist and grabbed my belt, pulling me closer. I expected him to lean up, but instead, he pulled my shirt out of my trousers and kissed my stomach.

'Bas!' I squealed.

He laughed, his breath tickling my skin.

'What are you doing?' I hissed. 'I'm dirty—I need to shower!'

'Spoilt.' He traced a line over my abs with his nail. I squirmed. 'Ah! Stop!'

'The showers are just down the hall,' he said.

'Stop tickling me.'

'You can step away any time.'

I pulled away, making sure to step on his foot. Bas prodded me in the stomach. 'You're not heavy enough to hurt me like that.'

'I'm sure I could find a way,' I grouched. I stooped to rifle through my bag. 'Once I'm done, we can talk to Smith.'

'Don't I get to shower?'

'Oh, did you want to?' I shot him an angelic smile. 'And here you were, calling me vain…'

Bas laughed.

Smith was unfailingly friendly. I kept expecting him to break character, but he genuinely seemed to be a nice guy. He fed us for free—'I always do one free meal for everyone who stays. Life's tough out in the wasteland.'—and provided directions to both Galley Lane and the NCC office. We headed to Galley Lane and found more of the same squat, whitewashed apartment blocks that we'd passed on our drive into town. The dust was thick in the air; as we parked up and climbed out, Bas commented, 'The crater's only about a mile from here.'

'Can we go see it?'

'I didn't realise this was a sightseeing trip.' But he was smiling.

'Oh, come on.' I elbowed him gently. 'Aren't you curious?'

'I've seen it before.'

'When?'

Bas took my shoulder, steering me towards the door of 42B. 'When I was seven, Marco and I took his father's car and drove there. He was furious.'

'You and Ellery stole a car?' I gaped at him. 'When you were seven?'

'We were very naughty.'

'You don't say!'

I was discovering a whole new side to Bas. He'd stolen a car when he was seven? What the hell else had he got up to?

'Did you live in Freetown?' I asked as we stopped at the glass and metal front door.

'Yes.'

'How come?'

'My mother was friends with Marco's mother. She offered for us to stay.'

'Oh.'

'My mother thought it would be safe.' Bas studied a line of doorbells and pressed one at random. 'And it was.'

'How did you…'

Bas pressed another doorbell, then another. He was going down the line.

'How did I?'

I cleared my throat. 'Get caught?'

'He lied to her and told her he'd marry her.'

He pressed the last two doorbells.

'That's horrible,' I said.

'It was Rodney's fault. He recognised me. He wanted to be friends.' Bas spat every word. He turned away, scowling, every muscle in his body tense. 'Never trust the Rochesters. They're snakes.'

Rodney had wanted to be friends with Bas? I couldn't see it.

'I'm sorry,' I said.

'Don't be,' he snapped.

'I am,' I pressed. 'Because that shouldn't have happened to you. You deserved better.'

'You don't know me that well, Harley,' Bas retorted.

'I'm pretty sure—'

The door swung open. A little old lady stared at us, a floral shawl wrapped around her stooped shoulders and wrinkled neck. 'Can I help you?'

'Hi.' Bas's voice softened so suddenly that it practically gave me whiplash. 'I'm sorry to disturb you. We're looking for someone in this building.'

She looked us up and down. 'I don't think I can help you, sorry.'

She stepped back, making to shut the door.

'Wait!' I cried. She paused, staring at me. 'Wait. My friend—his uncle lives here. He… he asked us to check up on him. My friend, that is—Jim. He hasn't heard from his uncle in ages. He got worried. And we were in town.' I made my eyes wide and bit my lip. 'We won't be any bother, we just need to make sure he's alright.'

Her brow wrinkled in a frown. 'We don't have anyone like that here.'

'Are you sure?' I stepped towards her, trying to fill my voice with desperation. 'Jim was really worried.'

She sighed gustily. 'Come in, then.'

The hallway was drab, and the woman's flat similarly so. As she prepared tea, she introduced herself as Mathilda.

'There's old Jenkins,' she said, 'but no one ever visits him. And the two men in 104, they're middle-aged. Could have a nephew your age, I suppose. They have family in and out at all times.'

'Maybe you'd recognise the nephew?' Bas asked. He looked about as out of place as it was possible for a person to look, in his black fatigues amidst Mathilda's floral sofas, floral curtains, and floral plates on the wall.

'I see lots of people.' Mathilda set the tea on the round wooden table, atop a crocheted doily. 'My flat overlooks the door.'

I glanced at Bas, who was lurking by the window. I was betting that was the first thing he'd noticed. He nodded to me.

My turn.

'Jim is about my age,' I said. 'Dark hair, brown skin. Not too tall.' I paused to collect my thoughts.

'Oh, you mean the Bradwell boy!' she said.

'Bradwell?' I echoed.

'Yep. Owns the flat at the end of the hall. Don't know anything about an uncle, though.' She shrugged, dislodging the shawl off one frail shoulder. 'Maybe somewhere else in town? This is where he stayed when he was here.'

I exchanged glances with Bas. He strode over and picked up his tea. 'What was his first name?'

'Something funny... with G, maybe? Gareth? No, that wasn't it. Graham?'

'Galen?' Bas asked.

'That's the one! Galen!' She nodded as though she'd thought of it herself. 'Galen Bradwell. Odd name. Nice boy, though. Always polite.'

Galen Bradwell. Hadn't that been the mayor's name? Theo had mentioned it, but now I couldn't remember for sure.

'Can you show us which was his flat?' Bas asked.

'Of course.' But a frown crept onto Mathilda's face. 'Why, though? He's not here at the moment... Didn't you say you were with—Wait, where are you from, anyway?'

'Langford,' Bas said before I could get a word in. 'We should go.'

That, he said to me. I nodded, setting my barely touched cup of tea on the table. 'Thank you, Mathilda.'

'Wait, where are you going?' Her eyes darted between us. 'You just got here.'

'Well, if Galen Bradwell's not here, and neither is his uncle, then we have no business here,' Bas said.

'Oh.' She looked at my cup of tea, then Bas's, both still full. 'You haven't finished your tea.'

What was happening? I caught Bas's eye. He glanced around the flat. It was aggressively floral, small, pokey. Mathilda fit in very well here.

Too well, in fact. There was no sign of anyone else living here.

She was lonely.

Understanding dawned on me.

'Why don't you head to the NCC office?' I suggested. 'I'll hang out with Mathilda for a bit.'

'We can both stay,' Bas said, much to my surprise. I'd have thought he would want to leave. 'The NCC office will still be there in the morning.'

'The NCC?' Mathilda asked. 'What do you want with them?'

'Just business,' I said.

'What sort of business?'

Lonely… and nosy, apparently.

'We're looking to negotiate a sales opportunity,' Bas said smoothly. Then: 'Harley is. I'm just security.' He winked.

Mathilda tittered.

Was I dreaming? What was this easy-going side of Bas that I'd apparently never noticed before?

Had it been there all along, and he'd just never let me see it?

'I can't imagine you in sales,' she told me.

I picked up my tea and took a sip, stalling for time. 'Uh… I clean up alright when I'm dressed for work. I think.'

'Definitely.' Bas shot me a smirk.

Was he really flirting? Now?

And then it hit me: he was talking about the outfits I wore to dance at the bunker.

Oh my God.

Heat washed through me. I hid my surprise with a cough. *What the fuck?*

'Didn't think you'd noticed,' I shot back.

'You can't have been looking very hard. It was obvious.' His grin broadened. You could have fried an egg on my cheeks. I put my tea down and gripped the edge of the table.

'Oh, young love.' Mathilda fanned herself.

I cringed, but Bas looked incredibly pleased with himself. *Dick.*

I'd get him for that. Later. Somehow.

'Sorry,' I told Mathilda. 'That was… uh… inappropriate.'

'No, no. It's so nice to see young couples these days. My husband passed. Years back, now.' She smiled a small, sad smile. Lifting her chin, she added, 'How did you meet?'

Huh. How to answer that one?

'It's a long story,' I hedged.

'She kept flirting with my best friend,' Bas said. 'And my brother. And everyone else except me.'

'It was not like that!' I said.

'Oho, I see.' Mathilda grinned. 'Clever, clever. You know how to get them hooked, don't you?'

'No!' I exclaimed. 'That wasn't it at all! He—he helped me out of a bad situation—'

Bas waved dismissively. 'That was afterwards. The flirting came first.'

'That wasn't it!'

They both laughed. I scowled, rubbing my hands over my knees. That was not how it had gone. He made it seem like I'd been intentionally making him jealous! All I'd done was respect *his* wishes. He was the one who'd told me not to flirt with him.

'Anyway, anyway,' Mathilda said around an impish grin. 'Langford, eh? That's a long drive with just the two of you alone in a car…'

We entertained Mathilda for a full hour before Bas finally, with uncharacteristic politeness, cleared his throat. 'I'm afraid we should probably get going. We've a few things to do still today.'

'Of course, of course.' Mathilda sighed. 'Well, it was fun. Thank you for humouring me.'

'Any time,' I said, pushing out of my seat. 'Thank you for the tea.'

'You're most welcome, dearie.' Mathilda rewrapped her shawl and led us to the door. As we descended the stairs, Bas said, 'If you hear anything about Jim in the next day or two, could you get a message to the Red Rock Inn for us?'

'I can certainly try.'

Bas shot me a pointed look. I bit my cheek.

'Won't you at least tell us which is his flat so we can ring the doorbell? Just in case?' I pried gently.

Mathilda frowned, hesitating inside the front door. 'Well… I don't see what it could hurt.'

'We'd be very grateful,' I added.

'Certainly.' She opened the door and pointed to one of the buttons, flat number 206. 'That's the one.'

I hit the bell, and we all waited for a few tense seconds.

Nothing.

'I guess there's no one there,' I said.

'We'll speak to Jim when we get home,' Bas said. 'We'd better head out. Thank you for your hospitality, Mathilda.'

'No, no, thank you.'

She stood aside so we could leave, and remained there watching as we crossed the parking lot. Bas unlocked his car and climbed in.

'We're not going to look inside?' I asked, scrambling into the passenger seat.

Bas shot me a look. 'What do you think?'

Of course we were. Bas had a plan, as usual.

Under Mathilda's watchful gaze, we pretended to depart. Bas drove around the block and found a parking spot on the street behind. 'We should be able to get in from here.'

It took a bit of finagling. We had to climb a wall to get to the back of block 42B. Once we were in, Bas counted the balconies.

'It should be this one.' He gestured to a second-floor balcony without any furniture.

'You want to climb up there?' I asked nervously.

'I'll boost you up, then follow you.'

This seemed like a horrible idea. Bas crouched down, lacing his fingers together. I stood on his hand, and he raised me until I could grab the bars of the first-floor balcony.

'Can you pull yourself up?'

'Yes.' I walked my hands up to the crossbar, then lifted one leg until I got my boot between the bars. Straining my muscles, I pulled the other leg up and clambered over the bars. Bas followed, walking his feet up the brick wall. Which, in hindsight, would have been a much better idea. *Oops.*

Once we were both on the first-floor balcony, I glanced around nervously. The curtains of the flat were shut tight. More importantly, however, there was no obvious way up to the next floor. 'What now?'

'I'll go first.' Without any sign of fear, Bas climbed on top of the railing and hauled himself up to the next floor using the same technique as the first. A moment later, he hissed down, 'Can you grab my hand?'

'I hate everything about this idea!'

'You can stay there and wait for me if you want.'

I hated that worse. 'No, no way.'

I scrambled up onto the railing, adamantly keeping my eyes on his arm. I grasped his hand, and he lifted me until I could get a grip on the bars.

'Good?' he asked.

'Yeah,' I grunted. I followed his lead, walking up the wall, and he held onto me until I'd managed to half-climb, half-fall over the railing to stand beside him.

I looked around. The balcony was empty. There were no curtains, so we could see directly into a sparsely furnished living-dining room.

'What now?'

Bas pulled a screwdriver out of his pocket and started fiddling with the door.

'I noticed in Mathilda's flat. The doors don't have a lock.' He wiggled the screwdriver into the gap, slowly widening it until he could get his fingers in and shove it open. 'There.'

We stepped into the flat. After how empty and devoid of personality Maddock's places in Bale Rocks and Langford had been, I wasn't surprised to find the same here. The furniture was minimal and functional: a single sofa, a table, and one chair. The kitchenette was covered in a layer of dust. A short hallway led to the front door and two other rooms: the first was a bathroom, and the second was the bedroom.

The bedroom walls were covered in papers.

I paused in shock in the doorway.

'What is it?' Bas asked.

'Look.' I entered the room and headed for the nearest wall. A hand-sketched schematic covered most of it. After a few seconds, I realised what it was. The bunker.

He'd surrounded the floorplan with all sorts of notes. Profiles on members of the Iron Fists, a detailed timeline, notes on the bunker's security. Lists of names.

Mine jumped out at me.

Harley Benoit. Kranikovska (IF contact to ask about fights)

'What the fuck?'

'What is it?' Bas was bent over a desk in the corner of the room, rifling through papers.

'My name is on here!'

Bas hurried over to study the wall. After a moment, he determined, 'So is mine. And Marco's.'

I skimmed the lists. Bas's profile was sparse.

S. Rochester. 'Bas' (loyal to Sayle, avoid if possible)

Ellery's read:

Marco Ellery, team lead, origin Freetown (family as potential weak spot? runs network of informants, may pose a threat)

'This is freaky,' I whispered.

'He knew everything.' Bas traced his fingers over the timeline.

Make contact at Kranikovska

Enter fights at The Arsonist—deliberate loss?

Slow build, target three weeks

He'd plotted the entire course of his time in Bale Rocks, right down to planning his exit.

Depart with merchants' market

'All of it was fake,' I said. 'He only came to Bale Rocks to kill Sayle.'

'Who could have told him about you?' Bas asked. When I looked up at him, he was frowning.

'Who else knew I was passing info?'

'Me, Ellery, Dunne—I guess. Kade and Briggs.' He grimaced at the last name, as though it left a bad taste in his mouth. 'One or two of the other teams, maybe. Not many people. Ellery arranged it under the table.'

'Huh.' At the time, it had felt like everyone knew.

'Someone has to have told him,' Bas mused, striding back to the desk. 'One of us. This information—it couldn't come from anywhere else.'

'What does that mean?'

'I'm not sure.' He lifted a bundle of papers whilst I studied the schematic. Maddock had marked my dressing room and labelled it *'entry point.'*

The next wall was less interesting. Lists of companies that had offices in Bale Rocks. A few names that meant nothing to me. I mouthed them to myself, trying to memorise them, in case they might be important.

Months of planning must have gone into this.

'Harley,' Bas said urgently. I turned to look. He was holding a piece of paper out to me.

I took it.

Rendezvous ten days after the strike. 4 pm at the old mill.

—A.S.

'A.S.?' I asked.

'That's today,' Bas said.

'What?'

'The rendezvous. It's today.' He checked his watch. 'In half an hour.'

A chill ran down my spine. 'Do you know where this old mill is?'

'I think so.' Bas met my gaze and cleared his throat. 'It's on the road to Bale Rocks. I've driven past it before.'

'We have to go.'

He nodded. 'Grab anything you need.'

I turned to look at the wall of papers. What did I need to take? These were the scribbles of a madman—a man obsessed. That was what Maddock was. And none of this held the answer to why—only he could answer that question.

I shoved the paper I was holding in my pocket. 'Let's just go.'

We took the front door—riskier, but speed was of the essence. As soon as we piled in the car, Bas pulled out and set a harried pace through the city. He seemed to know where he was going, and I didn't dare distract him, so I stared out the window as we raced towards our destination.

What would we find?

Maddock appeared to have a mysterious collaborator. Someone who had given him the names—and details—of all the important players in town.

Including my name.

A shiver ran down my spine. I'd never considered my small role as a part-time informant important before. I was no one.

But I'd wondered, at the time, how he'd known to approach me to ask about the bunker. Would I finally find out?

We left the city behind, trading the apartment blocks for farms—

mostly cattle farms, by the looks of things. Ten minutes later, the road met a small, fast-flowing stream, and we followed that until it split from the road again and Bas turned off onto a dirt track.

About two hundred yards in, he stopped the car behind a clump of trees.

'We'll have to go the rest of the way on foot. They'll hear the car.'

'Alright.'

I swung myself out of the car, reflexively checking for my gun—oh yeah, I'd lost it in Langford. *Fuck.*

I felt naked without it.

We hurried through the underbrush, dead bushes and dry twigs crackling beneath our feet and tangling with the noise of the rushing stream. It wasn't long before the mill appeared, a brown building with a sagging roof. The wheel had been removed and lay rotting on a patch of dead grass in front of the door. Two cars were parked beside it—a large four-by-four that I immediately recognised as Maddock's car and a sleeker black sedan.

Whose car was that?

I'd seen it before—or a similar one—parked on my street. I was sure of it.

More importantly, though: two cars, two people. The rendezvous was happening right now.

'We made it,' I muttered, hurrying forwards.

'Harley!' Bas's urgent whisper brought me to a halt. I glanced at him. 'Let's look for a back way in.'

'Alright.'

I fell into step behind him as we crept around the building. We'd barely made it three steps when—

BANG!

A gunshot rent the air.

I froze, not even breathing. Bas spun to stare at me. He looked at the building.

'Hide,' he hissed.

I couldn't move—my thoughts scattered. Who had shot? Why?

'Harley!' He grabbed my arm and hauled me behind a cluster of bushes, not a moment too soon, as we heard heavy footsteps. I clutched Bas's arm, my breath coming in short sharp pants. Who—

A short, dark-haired man exited the mill. He had broad shoulders and brown skin, and he wore black fatigues.

It wasn't Maddock. No, in fact, it was someone else familiar, someone whom I hadn't thought about since leaving Bale Rocks.

Anton Sorokin, my landlady's son. And a member of the Iron Fists.

TWENTY-ONE

A.S.

A.S. was Anton Sorokin. A.S. was a member of the Iron Fists. Which meant… All along, Maddock had been in contact with the Iron Fists.

But he'd killed their leader.

Anton moved out of sight. A moment later, a car door slammed. The engine roared, and the dirt crunched as it drove away. Once it had faded from hearing, I turned to Bas.

'That was—'

'Anton,' Bas said, his voice low. He frowned. 'But what is he—No. Anton couldn't have planned this. Someone else must be pulling the strings.'

'You think—' *—Anton's a traitor?* My head was spinning. I glanced around, desperate for something to cling to, but there were only winter-bare trees and the decrepit mill building. *Maddock.*

I turned and hurried to the door, almost falling when I accidentally stepped on a loose stone. I pushed the remains of the door aside.

'Harley, be careful,' Bas warned in a low voice. 'You don't know what you'll find.'

His warning came too late.

Maddock lay sprawled out on the dirt-strewn cobbled floor. A dark stain was spreading over his chest. Was he—? No, as I hurried over, he stirred slightly, his eyes blinking open.

'Har—ley?'

'Hey.' I tumbled to my knees beside him. He squinted blearily at me.

'You… you're a dream…'

'I'm not. I'm here.' I pushed his jacket open and clawed his shirt up. It stuck to his skin. *Come on, come on.*

There was so much blood, I couldn't even see the wound beneath it. Maddock's eyes fluttered.

'Harley,' Bas said in a low voice.

'He—he needs help. He—' My voice broke on a sob. I shrugged my coat off, then pulled my jumper off and wadded it against his chest. 'I don't know what to do.'

My hands shook. I pressed the jumper harder against Maddock's chest. It was getting soaked—too fast. What did I do? I had no idea how to treat wounds.

If only Savannah were here…

What would she do?

'F-first aid,' I sobbed. 'We need—we need to stop the bleeding.'

'Harley,' Bas said softly. *No.* I hated that tone. *No.*

'Please!' I gasped.

Bas looked at me with eyes full of regret. 'There's a first aid kit in the car, but—'

'Get it! Go!'

He turned and sprinted for the door. I looked back at Maddock, my eyes hazing with tears. Blood had bubbled at his lips.

'Stay with me,' I choked.

'It's… okay…' he mumbled, his lips barely moving.

'No, don't talk. Save your strength,' I said.

'I want to…' Maddock groaned. 'S-so-sorry.'

'Shhh, it's alright.' I didn't even know what I was saying. 'Bas will be back in a minute. You're going to be alright.'

'N-no.' His eyes fluttered shut. Panic seized my chest.

'Maddock? James, open your eyes!'

His eyes slid open, unfocused. He took a rattling breath.

'Stay with me,' I repeated. 'Please. Just a bit longer.'

'Harley…' he mumbled.

'Shh, shh.' I found his hand and squeezed it.

He stared at me. 'I… I had to do it… I'm sorry…'

'It's okay.' I pushed his hair back from his face, stroking gently, swallowing against the sobs that were trying to break free. 'It's alright.'

'No. Th-they—they killed—' He broke off, shivering.

'Killed?' I prompted gently.

'M-my par—' He coughed, a wracking cough that seemed to wrench through his entire body. His eyes fell shut again.

'James!' I cried.

'S-sorry, H-H-Har…' He turned his head to the side as his breaths grew shallower. A sob was stuck in my throat like a stone.

'James. James, please.' I grabbed his hand, squeezing as hard as I dared. 'James!'

But his eyes remained shut. He took one last breath, and as he exhaled, it seemed like something else had left along with the air. His body sagged in on itself.

'NO!' I took his chin and turned it, putting my cheek to his face. 'Come on, breathe. Breathe! Bas is almost here! Come on, please.' He didn't stir. 'Please…'

I collapsed over him, sobbing. His blood was sticky under my fingers, congealing rapidly in the cold air. His body was still—too still. I staggered to my feet and stumbled to the wall to throw up. Tears stung my eyes, bile stung my throat. Anger stung my heart.

Fucking Maddock! Why?

Why couldn't he hold on?

I balled my fists and punched the wall, pain jolting up my arms.

'FUCK!'

'Harley?' I spun around. Bas stood in the doorway, a first aid kit in hand.

'It's too late,' I said, the words like ash in my mouth. 'It's… it's too late.'

The dam burst and tears flooded down my face. My anger went with them, like water draining down a plug hole, leaving me empty. I wrapped my arms around myself, and a moment later Bas reached me and pulled me against him.

'It's not your fault,' he whispered.

I buried my face in his chest. 'It's not fair!'

'I know.'

He rubbed circles on my back as I cried, and cried, and cried. Whenever I thought the tears might stop, a stray thought would bring them back. Maddock drinking in the Kranikovska, Maddock fighting Theo, Maddock having dinner with Savannah and me.

Maddock, Maddock, Maddock.

Dead.

I shuddered.

'You're cold,' Bas murmured.

'No, I'm fine.'

'Harley…' Bas drew me back, his fingers gentle on my shoulders. He stared into my eyes for a long moment, before sighing. 'Come on.

I'll help you bury him.'

'Alright,' I whispered.

I stared at my whiskey, or more accurately, at my hands wrapped around my whiskey. A few hours earlier, they had been covered in blood. I'd showered it off, but I could still feel it. Sticky. Slowly growing cold.

'Drink,' Bas prompted quietly. He'd been infinitely, *horribly* gentle since we'd left the mill. He'd been the one who'd made me take a shower, who'd scrubbed the blood out of my clothes, who'd put the whiskey in front of me.

It made me want to scream.

Instead, I took a gulp of my whiskey.

It burnt the whole way down, an alive feeling that made me even angrier. Because Maddock wasn't here.

Maddock was dead.

And even though he'd left me to take the fall...

I still cared.

Bas covered my wrist with his hand. His expression was pained. 'Harley... if you want to talk...'

'Not really,' I said.

'Alright, well, if you do...'

'Because...' I sipped my whiskey. 'Because he was a fucking lying arsehole.' Tears stung my eyes. I blinked furiously. 'He doesn't deserve my sadness because he would have let me die for his stupid revenge that didn't even mean anything in the end.'

Because it looks like someone else was pulling the strings all along.

A tear escaped. I dashed it away angrily. 'Maddock's not worth all this anyway.'

'He was your friend,' Bas said.

'I need better friends.'

'Maybe. Maybe not.' He shrugged. 'Ellery and I have killed people.'

Briggs flashed before my eyes. The way his eyes had opened in surprise, how slowly he'd seemed to crumple to the floor. The wet, squishy sensation of having his blood and... other stuff splattered on me. I'd been standing the closest. My ears had rung for hours afterwards.

'That's different,' I muttered. 'You never left me to take the fall.'

'We manipulated you.' Bas rested his elbows on the table. 'You said so yourself.'

'Maybe.' I looked away. That conversation felt like it had taken place years ago. Yes, they had manipulated me. Put me in the Kranikovska to spy for them. Did it even matter anymore?

'You've killed people, too,' Bas said quietly.

I swallowed. Tam. Another moment I tried not to think about. Another moment when I'd had blood on my hands.

And that time it was my fault.

'What are you getting at?'

'That we aren't the sum total of a single deed,' Bas said. 'You were friends with Maddock based on the information you had at the time.'

'He manipulated me so easily.' I scowled. 'And so did you and Ellery. Is that—Am I? Am I easy to manipulate?'

Bas raised an eyebrow. 'Not especially.'

'Are you just saying that?' I snapped.

'Half the time you do the opposite of what I ask just to be contrary.'

'I do not!' I hissed indignantly.

He stared at me, both eyebrows almost at his hairline. *Smug arsehole.*

I looked away. 'Anyway, it's not about me. It's about Maddock. He lied to me.'

'Maybe.'

'What, you think he was telling the truth?' I asked. 'If I had agreed to work with him, would he have let me in on the plan?'

Bas frowned. 'Possibly.'

'I doubt it.' I took a sip of my drink. 'He was just using me, just like everyone else does.'

'You're being hard on yourself,' Bas said. 'You can't act on information you don't have.'

I looked away. 'I should have dug deeper.'

'I don't think you'd have gotten anywhere. His plan was too airtight for you to stop him.'

I pressed my lips together, fiddling with the glass between my fingers. *Stupid Maddock.*

Stupid, dead Maddock.

Fucking hell.

'Do you think it was true?' I blurted. 'Do you think Maddock was the son of the old mayor?'

Several seconds ticked by. When no answer was forthcoming, I forced myself to glance at Bas. He was frowning, his brow wrinkled.

'Hard to say,' he said. 'It depends on who fed him the information. Maybe they found out his identity and took advantage. Maybe they just made a scapegoat because they needed one. How would the mayor's son have survived anyway? He was an infant when the mayor was killed.'

'Anyone could have snuck him out,' I said. 'A member of staff, a relative, one of the mayor's friends.'

'Possibly,' Bas said. He drained the last of his whiskey. 'We might never know.'

'Yeah.' Shame that didn't help with the hollow feeling in my belly. I drank more whiskey, trying to fill it, but it didn't want to be sated.

When I looked up again, a man was marching over to us, heavyset and wearing work overalls. I tilted my head at him, and Bas immediately dropped his hand to his gun.

'Evening,' the man greeted. He eyed Bas. 'Easy, son. I'm just a merchant. I don't want trouble.'

Bas laid both hands on the table. 'What do you want?'

'Couldn't help but overhear. You were talkin' about a Maddock?'

Pain erupted in my chest, robbing me of breath.

'Why?' Bas asked.

'That wouldn't happen to be Jim Maddock, would it?'

I stared at him.

'How would you know him?' Bas asked.

'He joined us on the drive over from Bale Rocks. Nice fella—was looking for security on the drive. Don't blame him, what with how things have been lately.'

I recalled the notes in Maddock's flat. *Depart with merchants' market.* So that was what that meant—of course, it made sense. Leaving with them had ensured he wouldn't be noticed escaping town whilst everyone was on high alert.

I leant in.

'Did he… say anything about where he was going next?' I asked. Not that it mattered now. But I couldn't help but wonder if he'd had any plans after his ill-fated meeting at the mill.

'Wasn't sure. He said he might stay here.' The merchant shrugged. 'He seemed a bit lost, if you ask me.'

Lost. Because he'd fulfilled his purpose? I remembered the look on his face at the end. Almost… accepting.

'Anyway,' the merchant gestured over his shoulder, 'I better get back to the others. Just wanted to ask. You seen him lately? He doing alright?'

Bas and I exchanged glances.

'Yeah,' Bas said. 'He's doing alright.'

I swallowed.

The merchant grinned at us and lumbered off. I put my elbows on the table.

'We should eat,' Bas said.

'I'm not really hungry.'

'Try,' he said. 'You'll see your sister again soon.'

Savannah!

Amidst everything, it had almost slipped my mind that we were meeting her, too. I instantly felt bad. How could I forget my own sister, even for a moment?

'Let's eat when they get here,' I said.

Bas shrugged. 'Alright, I'll get us another drink.'

He loped off to the bar, and I sat back, hugging myself. I'd have to tell Savannah—and Theo—what had happened. And what now? Maddock's death had probably blown our chances of going back to Bale Rocks. Then again, if Savannah was coming here, I didn't need to go back. I could stay here. She could get a job at the hospital, and I could ask around to see who was hiring. I had dancing experience and waitressing experience—someone would want me.

That was it.

The plan began to blossom in my head. We'd find a flat together, just like in Bale Rocks. And Bas and I could explore this thing growing between us.

Bas and I.

Oh God, Theo and Savannah would never approve, would they?

Worse, what if Bas didn't want to stay in Crater's Edge? I couldn't exactly force him. He might leave. Go back to Bale Rocks, or join Ellery in Freetown. What then? Would he consider staying for me?

I swallowed.

'You're fretting again.'

I looked up. Bas had returned without me noticing. He passed me another whiskey and slid in beside me. 'Penny for your thoughts.'

'Uh…' I lifted the glass to my lips to stall for time. 'Just thinking about what happens next.'

'Next, we meet your idiot friend and your sister, then go back to our room and get a good night's sleep in a proper bed,' Bas said.

Against my will, a smile pulled at my lips. 'Hah, I knew you didn't enjoy sleeping on the floor!'

Bas frowned. 'It was fine.'

'Just admit it. You hated it,' I crowed. 'You were cutting off your nose to spite your face, and you know it.'

'I wasn't.' Bas sipped his whiskey, scowling. 'It was the right thing to do. We'd have killed each other if we had to share the bed.'

'You think? We might have ended up snogging much sooner.'

Bas shook his head. 'Definitely not.'

'Why not?' I demanded.

'You're too stubborn.'

'*I'm* too stubborn?' I gaped at him. 'Are you joking? You're the definition of stubborn!'

'Me?' He had the gall to look offended. 'I'm very flexible. No, you're definitely the stubborn one.'

'I'm not stubborn!' I prodded him in the arm. 'Just for that, maybe I'll make you share with Theo tonight, and I can share with Savannah.'

'Absolutely not!' Bas said in a tone of express horror. 'I'd rather sleep in the car again.'

'Alone? You'll get cold.'

'Exactly. And you wouldn't want me to get cold, would you?' He flashed me a roguish grin. 'So the only option is for me to share with you… Unless you want me to crawl in with your sister…'

'No way!' I swatted his arm. 'Bas!'

'Then it's settled. We're sharing.'

Behind him, the door swung open, letting in a flurry of cold air. I looked up, excitement blossoming in my chest. Was that—

But no, two burly security types strolled in and headed for the bar, the door falling shut behind them. I looked back at Bas.

'They'll be here soon,' he said.

'I hate waiting.'

'I'll add 'impatient' to your list of qualities.'

'You're such a jerk.' I rolled my eyes. 'Maybe I should list your flaws. Rude, insensitive, angry, volatile—'

He swallowed my rant with a kiss. I gasped into his mouth.

'Bas—mmph!'

His hand slid behind my head, gripping firmly. I clutched the collar of his jacket. A moment later, he pulled away.

'What was that for?' I hissed, glancing around to see if anyone had noticed. A guy two tables over winked at me.

Ugh.

'You're cute when you're flustered,' Bas said.

'Cute?' I huffed. 'I am not cute.'

'Adorable.'

'No!'

Bas grinned. 'I'm going to see about food. If I have to wait any longer, I might eat you.'

'E-eat me?' I spluttered.

He tossed me a saucy smile and left for the bar again. I stared after him, open-mouthed, my cheeks burning. *What the fuck? What the actual fuck?*

I had thought I could handle anything, but I had just been proven resoundingly wrong. Bas's flirting was beyond my talents. I didn't think anyone on the planet could handle that level of intensity.

The door opened again, the cold wind blissful against my hot cheeks. I looked over hopefully, but it was more merchants, trickling in for dinner after closing the market for the evening.

I rubbed my chest.

Bas was flirting with me. Somehow, for reasons beyond my comprehension, he liked me. I liked him.

We hadn't even argued since leaving Langford.

It was weird.

When Bas returned, I smiled up at him. He hesitated as he pulled his chair out.

'What?'

'Nothing.' I bit my lip. 'Can't I smile at you?'

'Of course you can.' Bas stared at me a second longer, before breaking into a grin of his own. 'Whenever you want.'

'Well, good.'

My smile lasted until we got our food and through two more groups entering the front door. After swallowing a mouthful of stew, I asked Bas, 'What time is it?'

He checked his watch. 'Seven-fifteen.'

My heart dropped like a stone.

Theo was late.

No.

He'll be here. He's probably just been held up on the road.

My stomach seemed to have shrivelled up. I picked at my food as seconds, and then minutes, crawled by. Half an hour. Bas finished my food. An hour. The crowd started to thin as the merchants retired to bed.

Two hours.

Three.

We were the last ones in the bar. Eventually, Smith wandered over to us.

'Bar's closing.' He wore a vaguely apologetic expression. 'I'm afraid you've gotta head out.'

I gripped the edge of the table. We couldn't go. Theo was meant to meet us here tonight!

'Can't we…' I trailed off, shooting Bas a pleading look.

'We're meant to be meeting someone,' he said.

Smith raised an eyebrow. 'Anyone I'd know?'

'Maybe. His name's Theo.'

'Oh yeah, I know Theo. Stays here when he's in town. Occasionally meets his fella.'

'Fella?' I parroted.

'Yeah, you know, roundabouts your age, not too tall, brown hair. Always wears it like this.' He mimed slicking his hair to the side. 'Posh accent.'

No, I didn't know. I had no fucking clue.

'Theo's never mentioned anyone,' I said.

'Huh.' Smith shrugged. 'Guess maybe it was too fresh for him to share? Anyway, I haven't seen him in about… a month, maybe? Maybe a little less.'

That was about the time Theo had returned to Bale Rocks. But it didn't help us right now. Where was he?

'Can't we wait just a little longer?' I pleaded. 'My sister's meant to be with him.'

Smith's eyes softened. 'I really can't, I'm sorry. I have to close up the bar—can't risk leaving it open at night.'

'But…' I stared at the table, my eyes stinging. *What if they don't come? What if they're…*

Don't think it.

'Harley, let's get some sleep,' Bas said quietly.

Smith cleared his throat. 'Look, if he comes by I'll direct him to your room, alright?'

'Okay,' Bas said, standing up.

'No, but—'

'Harley, let's go to bed. He probably got held up, and he'll leave first thing in the morning.' Injecting a humorous note into his voice, Bas added, 'Your sister probably held him up.'

'Probably,' I mumbled. Even so, I felt rooted to the spot. Theo had promised. We'd promised. Red Rock Inn, seven PM, tonight.

We'd promised.

But he wasn't here.

Bas held his hand in front of my face. 'Come on,' he said gently. 'It's been a long day.'

'Yeah.' I took his hand and let him pull me to my feet. 'I guess it has.'

TWENTY-TWO

IT WAS A LONG NIGHT, TOO. I tossed and turned, unable to settle. Thoughts chased one another round and round in my brain.

Where was Theo?

What if something had gone wrong?

What if something had happened to Savannah?

The more I thought about it, the tighter my chest felt.

Eventually, I did fall into an uneasy sleep. I woke when Bas got up and watched through half-open eyes as he got dressed and headed out for his morning run. Once he was gone, I crawled out of bed to do my stretches. If nothing else, yesterday's balcony-climbing exercise had proven that I couldn't afford to let my fitness lapse.

Yesterday.

Maddock.

I breathed through my stretches. *In-two-three-four, out-two-three-four.* I lowered myself into the splits, my thighs burning. It had been a few days—my own oversight. But the pain was welcome, as well. It gave my mind something else to focus on.

In one day, Maddock was dead and Theo and Savannah had missed their rendezvous.

I dug my fingers into the carpet, fighting a wave of grief.

In-two-three-four, out-two-three-four. I leant over my front leg, my back and thighs straining.

My chest felt hollowed out, the sensation making me almost nauseous. Despite how he'd treated me in the end, Maddock's death had left a hole that I didn't know how to fill.

I covered my face. *In-two-three-four, out-two-three-four. Change positions.*

I swapped my left leg to the front. What would Bas say?

'Compartmentalise.'

Of course.

But how could I? Between the grief and the worry, I was being torn apart.

I scrubbed my hands over my face.

Finish stretching, then shower. It's a new day. You'll survive this one, just like you have every day up to now.

By the time I finished showering, Bas was back from his run and had also washed up. He flung his towel over a hook by the door. 'Breakfast?'

I bit my cheek and nodded, crouching to lace my boots up.

'Do you think Theo will arrive today?' My voice came out small.

'Only one way to find out,' Bas said briskly.

The main bar of the Red Rock Inn was full of subdued chatter. The merchants were eating an early breakfast before heading to the market hall, I assumed. We wove our way through the room to the bar, to see Smith, his arms loaded with plates.

'Have a seat,' he called. 'I'll be with you in a moment.'

I chose a table with a view out the window, not that it helped. All I could see were the sides of two parked cars. When Smith finally reached us, he set two plates down.

'If you pay up now, I'll change your room charge to include breakfast.'

'Yes please.' I sifted through my pockets for the money; Bas beat me to it.

'Any news on Dunne?' he asked.

'Who?'

'Theo,' I explained.

'Ah. No, 'fraid not. We didn't have any arrivals during the night.'

My heart sank.

'If you're hanging around, just mind that I need you out the room by lunchtime.'

'We'll keep that in mind,' Bas said.

'Great.' Smith headed off. Bas tucked into his breakfast, but I prodded mine unenthusiastically.

'He'll be here soon,' Bas said. 'I'm sure your sister is just giving him the runaround.'

I forced a chuckle, thought I felt like my stomach was filled with rocks. 'Yeah.'

I eventually ceded my untouched breakfast to Bas, and after

finishing it, he persuaded me to come with him to the NCC office.

'We have to check. I promised Turner.'

'Yeah, alright.' A distraction would help—hopefully.

Bas provided me with another distraction; twenty minutes after we climbed into the car, he stopped in a cramped parking lot. 'Hop out.'

'Are we there?' I glanced around, searching for something that might resemble an office, but we were surrounded by single-storey houses with corrugated iron roofs.

'No. There's something I want you to see.'

Curiosity fought its way through the cloud of negativity in my brain. I climbed out and trailed Bas down a narrow road which abruptly spat us out of the cluster of buildings onto a narrow path with a fence along one side. And nothing beyond except red rock and brown sky.

Bas put a hand on my back, steering me to the fence. I looked down. *Holy shit.*

It was the crater. It was ten times—no, a hundred times—bigger than I had ever imagined. A steep drop fell away from our feet just beyond the railing. If I looked to either side, the buildings of Crater's Edge lined the rim of the crater as far as the eye could see. Ahead, the slope eventually grew shallower at the base of the crater, easily over a thousand feet below us, maybe even more. Vegetation had started to take over, greyish-green trees breaking up the endless red.

'Wow,' I whispered.

Bas leant against the railing beside me. 'It's impressive, isn't it?'

'It's much bigger than I realised.' How big must it have looked to Bas the first time he saw it when he was seven? Impossibly large. 'Do you know what was here before?'

Bas shrugged. 'Some say mountains, others say a city. I don't know.'

'A city?' I gaped at him, horror twisting in my belly. An entire city, wiped out in an instant. 'That's horrible.'

'We might never know.' Bas pushed off the railing. 'I've heard people say that the whole of the West Rim used to be a lakebed in a mountain valley, and that's why the soil is so fertile now.'

'A lakebed?' The whole West Rim under water? I couldn't even imagine. 'What do you think?'

'It doesn't matter,' Bas said. 'It's history, and we live now. How does knowing what was here help us?'

I scowled. 'I'm just curious.'

'I know.' He held out his hand. I stared at it. Bas wiggled his fingers. 'Come on.'

Realisation struck me. He wanted to hold hands. *Holy shit.*

I grabbed his hand before he could change his mind. Bas folded me into his arms.

'I thought you didn't like being touched,' I muttered.

'I'm working on it.'

With me. For me. Soft as a butterfly's wings, happiness fluttered in my chest.

Bas had to finally coax me away from the crater. 'We have to get back to the inn in time to check out.'

I sighed. 'Fine, let's go.'

The NCC office was back in the centre of the city, in a tall building amongst the cluster of concrete behemoths which almost seemed to touch the sky. We climbed the stairs to the third floor and entered a reception area: two plastic benches, a linoleum floor that was grey with dirt, and a counter that sagged on one end. A woman sat behind the counter, an expression of boredom engrained on her face.

'Hello.' I pasted on a smile.

She didn't look up from picking at her nails.

'Excuse me!'

She glanced up, her eyes sliding over us. 'What do you want?'

Bas stepped forwards. 'We're looking for information on the NCC's operations in Bale Rocks.'

Her eyebrows rose, as though to say, *'Whatever for?'*

'Right, you want Timothy.' She pointed through a doorway. 'Third row, second cubicle.' She went back to picking at her nails.

If this was the front the NCC was putting forwards, I wasn't surprised they were corrupt as all hell.

Bas and I headed through the door and emerged into a large room filled with desks. There had to be at least thirty of them, though most were unoccupied. Two women were gossiping with one another at a desk in the front row. We passed another desk that was covered in plant pots containing small, scraggly plants. Down the third row, we finally found Timothy, a short man with large glasses, wearing a stained blue shirt. He was bent over a form, filling it in with slanted handwriting.

'Timothy?' Bas asked.

He shot up, his glasses dropping off his nose.

'Ah-hem.' He pushed them back up and stared at us. 'Can I help you?'

'The receptionist sent us here. We want to ask you about the NCC office and clinic in Bale Rocks.'

'Bale Rocks?' He raised an eyebrow. 'There is no NCC office in Bale Rocks.'

'The one on Blackwall Street,' Bas clarified.

Timothy shook his head. 'We shut it down, oh, a year back. The government pulled their support. Embezzlement, apparently. Dunno what the fuck funds they think they were appropriating—we never had any to start with.'

'But there's a clinic,' I said. 'And a church that runs a soup kitchen.'

'Oh, those, yeah. Those are still ours. There's a woman in the church who handles the paperwork. And we send monthly deliveries to the clinic.'

I exchanged glances with Bas. What did that mean?

'Who do you communicate with in the clinic?' he asked.

'You mean, who does the ordering?' Timothy flipped through his papers. 'Uh, that'd be... Hey, Nancy, who's our contact in the Bale Rocks clinic?' he called to the next desk.

A woman glanced up, brushing her hair out of her eyes. 'Markus Clairmont. He's their liaison with the mayor's office.'

'That's the one,' Timothy said. 'Never met him—he always sends a driver to drop off order forms.'

This was sounding all shades of not good. Clairmont was in charge of ordering? There was no NCC office in Bale Rocks?

Except I'd seen it—it had their logo in the window!

'Have you had any supplies go missing?' Bas asked.

'Missing?' Timothy raised an eyebrow. Nancy stood and wandered over. She had crow's feet around bright blue eyes and sun-bleached blonde hair.

'Sorry,' she said. 'Can't help but be interested. Where'd you say you're from?'

I glanced at Bas; he'd taken the lead so far.

'Bale Rocks,' he said. 'We had some questions about the NCC office there.'

'But there isn't one.'

'That's what I said.' Timothy waved a hand. 'We shut it down a year ago.'

'There's still an office, though,' I pressed. 'With your logo. Office hours. I've seen trucks moving supplies.'

'We send a truck once a month to the clinic,' Nancy said.

'But we have had one or two go missing,' Timothy said. Nancy shot him a look, and he sealed his lips.

Huh, interesting. I cast about for something else to loosen their tongues. A conversation I'd had with Savannah popped into my head.

'What about the new storage facility?' I asked. They all looked at me with varying degrees of curiosity. 'My sister works at the clinic; she mentioned that a new storage facility had been built. She seemed really happy about it.'

Timothy and Nancy glanced at each other, frowning.

'That didn't come out of our budget,' Nancy said slowly. She leant against Timothy's desk, her gaze turning distant. 'Maybe you should… tell us everything.'

Opening up to them hadn't been in the plan. I raised an eyebrow at Bas. He shrugged.

'We have reason to believe they're collaborating with slavers,' he said.

Nancy gasped.

'Not the NCC,' Timothy said firmly. 'We're a charity. We help people!'

'The NCC office in Bale Rocks seems to be the centre of the operation,' Bas continued. 'Possibly, after you shut it down, someone else moved in.'

'That… that would explain the requests,' Nancy murmured.

'Requests?' I asked.

She shook her head. 'I didn't give them a second thought. Sometimes we get requests—NCC stamped—for medical supplies. Shortfalls. We thought the gangs were stealing supplies on the roads and that was why the clinic needed extra.'

Bas tapped his fingers against the desk, looking uncharacteristically grave. 'Did you approve them?'

'If we had the supplies. Not always.' She shook her head.

My heart was flip-flopping in my chest. If those supplies requests had come from the NCC office, and the NCC office was a front… then the supplies had really been going to… the Black Hands.

All this time.

Shit.

This was really bad.

'This is impossible,' Timothy said firmly. 'Our people are good people. We do our best.'

'Even good people will do bad things,' Bas said.

'I know the people who worked in that office!' He shook his head, desperation written in the set of his shoulders and the frown on his forehead. 'No!'

'I'm sorry,' I said quietly. 'But we have evidence. I followed an NCC van to the Black Hands' compound and saw them transferring people.'

Timothy shook his head again. Nancy leant over the desk, gripping the edge as though to hold herself up. 'We… we'll have to notify someone,' she said. 'The higher-ups will want to look into this.'

'What can they do?' Timothy asked bitterly. 'We don't run the office. Maybe we never did.' He stared off into the distance.

'If anyone from your office does come to Bale Rocks,' Bas said, 'I can tell them who to get in contact with. We have a man on the ground, investigating.'

'Yes,' Nancy said fervently, looking up. 'That… that's good. A contact. Someone who knows the lay of the land.' She nodded.

'I'll write it down.' Bas found a pen and paper and scribbled Turner's name—*Malcolm Turner, Hawke and Terne pub.* 'He'll help you.'

'Thank you.' Timothy snatched the paper, clutching it like a lifeline. 'Thank you. We'll look into it. Thank you.'

They were either terribly good actors or genuinely concerned. I glanced at Bas, but whatever he was thinking, his face gave no clues.

'Thank you for helping us,' he said solemnly.

'Of course, of course,' Timothy said. 'Any time.'

'Safe travels,' Nancy said.

'Thank you.' Bas headed for the door, and I followed him out of the office.

'Do you think they were genuine?' I asked as we descended the stairs.

Bas hummed. 'I don't think they knew,' he said finally. 'But I also don't think they'll help.'

'They wanted to.'

'Good intentions are rarely as useful as one might think.'

I snorted. Wasn't that so true?

Five minutes later, we climbed into the car. Bas started it up, but he made no move to drive off.

'Where are we going now?' I asked. 'Back to the inn to wait?'

Bas glanced at me, frowning lightly. 'I think we need to drive back to Bale Rocks. They need us.'

I swallowed. 'But Theo…'

'We can't give him forever, Harley.' Bas touched my wrist. 'If he's on his way, we'll pass him on the road.'

'Fine,' I muttered. 'Can we at least leave a message with Smith?'

Bas nodded.

It was a surprisingly short drive from Crater's Edge to Bale Rocks. Bale Rocks had always felt like it was on the edge of the world, a million miles from civilisation. A tiny spec on the map, isolated from the rest of humanity. In reality, it was only a two-hour drive through farmland, and there were signs of civilisation almost all the way along the route. Around one and a half hours in, the bales started to appear: enormous hunks of yellow-grey rock, oddly rounded, that sat in the farmers' fields looking like giant hay bales.

Those rock formations had given our town its name. No one knew where they'd come from, but they were by and large too heavy to move, so they had stayed.

When the terrain became familiar, I knew we had reached the eastern reaches of the town: burnt-out husks of buildings were scattered amidst still-functioning factories that seemed strangely small to my eyes now that I'd seen their bigger brothers in Brackfields.

As we approached the outskirts of town, a sign appeared.

MILITARY CHECKPOINT 1000 YARDS

Bas slowed the car.

'That can't be right,' I said. 'The checkpoint was way in from here.'

'They must have moved it,' Bas said.

A fist closed around my chest. 'What does that mean?'

'I don't know. But we can't risk trying to enter without knowing the lay of the land.'

Bas glanced behind us, then manoeuvred into a turn.

'Wait, no!' I hissed. 'We have to go into town and find Theo.'

'Let's go to Freetown first.'

'No!'

'He was supposed to go there to check on the radio.' Bas was frustratingly calm. I scowled. 'They'll be able to tell us when he left. And explain what's going on in town.'

I bit my cheek. Damnit, he was right.

'We could just go straight to the clinic,' I said.

Bas shook his head. 'I know you want to see Savannah, but we can't risk driving into an unknown situation. We don't know if the Iron Fists are going to be after you.'

'Fine.'

I hugged myself as Bas steered us north. Freetown was about ten miles out of Bale Rocks. We drove cross-country for a while, until we joined a tar road speckled with cracks and potholes.

Although I knew of Freetown, I had never actually been there. It was too far from town to walk, and I had no reason to drive there, seeing as the only thing there was about half a dozen large farms.

At least, that was what I'd thought. But as we approached, I discovered that I couldn't have been more wrong.

A sturdy chain-link fence had been reinforced with metal sheets, barbed wire, and a whole host of other DIY defences. The gate consisted of two corrugated iron sheets and was guarded by a tower on either side. Only one was manned, that I could see; the figure looking down on us from it held the distinctive shape of a hunting rifle.

Bas stopped at the gate and rolled his window down.

'Who goes there?' the guard called. He was young; his voice hadn't changed yet.

'It's Bas,' Bas called back.

There was a moment of silence, then, 'Bas? For real? OPEN THE GATE!'

The gates slid back. The metal sheets were mounted on rollers, and they rattled loudly as they were shifted. Once they were open wide enough to admit the car, they stopped. Bas drove us in, and I got my first look at Freetown.

It was bigger than I'd realised. Directly ahead of us, I could see a cluster of buildings. To the left, the road ran along the edge of a field. To the right, there were more buildings.

Bas rolled to a halt as several children came jogging over and crowded around his window.

'It's you,' said one, who was no older than ten and had a hat pulled low over his head. 'It really is!'

'Who's she?' a girl with a dirty face demanded.

'Where have you been?' another boy cried.

'Oi, you lot, get outta here.'

This was the boy who'd been manning the guard tower. He stomped over to the car, and the smaller kids scattered—not that he was much older than them, though he certainly was taller. If he was that tall already at twelve or thirteen, he was going to be a giant one day.

He peered into the car, flashing us a grin. 'Marco told us to look out for you.'

'Is he here?' Bas asked.

'Want us to check? Jill, run to the Ellerys and tell them Bas is here,' he commanded over his shoulder.

'No need,' Bas said. 'We'll drive straight there.'

'No way! You've got to come catch up with everyone.'

Bas grimaced. 'I'll have to catch up later, Jonah. I need to speak to Marco as soon as possible.'

Jonah frowned, but then he straightened. 'Of course! I'm sure it's super important. I can't go off guard anyway—I'm supposed to be watching out for the soldiers.'

'You'd better get back to it, then,' Bas said solemnly.

'Will do!' Jonah saluted him and ran off, waving the hoard of small children to follow him. Bas rolled the window up and steered us towards the buildings.

'They know you really well,' I said.

'Everyone knows everyone here,' Bas replied.

We passed a low building made of dark brick with a corrugated iron roof. Recognition pricked at me—the collection of buildings looked markedly similar to the ones we'd seen in Brackfields, down to the same faded green paint on the metal roofs.

'Is this an old army base?' I asked as we drove by a long building with a green metal door. '*MESS*' was painted in faded white on the door, though a sign over it now read '*schoolhouse*'.

There was a school here? I'd never realised.

'Probably,' Bas said, 'but if it was, the army abandoned it years ago.'

'Makes sense,' I said. 'Why build new stuff when there's buildings already here?'

I thought Bas would stop at one of the buildings, but he continued through and turned us onto a dirt track. We bounced through deep ruts left by tractors and swerved to avoid two dogs and, later, a cat. All three were well-fed and, I presumed, belonged to the community, unlike the mangy strays we sometimes saw in Bale Rocks. Finally, Bas stopped outside a large house constructed of a haphazard mix of building materials, from three different sorts of bricks, to breezeblocks, wooden boards, and metal sheets.

He tonked the horn once before sliding out.

'What was that for?'

'To warn them we're here. It's a big farm.'

I glanced around. The fields were empty for winter. Some kind of barn stood about three hundred yards to our right.

The front door swung open to reveal a tall woman in her early twenties with blonde hair holding a shotgun.

'Claire.' Bas strode over. I hastily followed him.

We're walking towards a woman with a gun. No big deal.

Her face twisted into a scowl. 'Oh, it's you.'

'Is Marco here?' Bas asked.

'Of course not.' Claire jerked her chin towards me. 'Who's she?'

'Harley.' Bas waved distractedly to me. 'Harley, this is Claire. Marco's sister.'

Ellery had a sister. On top of all of the revelations of the last week, this hardly even fazed me.

Claire shot me a glare as though I'd personally offended her, before turning the dark look on Bas. 'Marco's not here. Leave.'

'It's important.'

'Who's there?' a second voice called. Claire's lips twisted in a scowl as she turned to the dark hallway behind her.

'Stay inside. I'll deal with it.'

'I heard voices.' A familiar voice reached us a moment before a redhead popped out of an open doorway. She laid eyes on me, and her jaw dropped.

'Oh my God, Harley!'

It was Laura—my colleague from the Kranikovska. I stared at her in shock. 'Laura? What are you doing here?'

'Harley!' She pitched herself at me, throwing her arms around my shoulders. I stumbled back a step at the sudden weight. 'Where have you been? We thought you were dead!'

Dead? A cold feeling wormed its way into my belly.

'I had to leave town. Laura—what are *you* doing here?'

Last I'd seen her was at work—hadn't she been staying in the Kranikovska with some of the other waitresses? What was going on in town?

Laura drew back a little, dabbing at her eyes. When she looked at me, she smiled brightly.

'Marco brought me here.'

'Ellery?' Why would he bring Laura here? 'Why?'

'There was a problem with some of the soldiers.' She twisted her fingers into her skirt. 'They've been going after the women… But where have you been? We were so worried. Your sister came in, and even she didn't know where you were, and we thought—Well—But then the gang came in looking for you, and—'

'Which gang?' Bas asked sharply.

'The Iron Fists. They wrecked the place—Tom was furious. We're all fine, but they almost shot Benny—'

'The Iron Fists? Are you sure?' I asked. They'd gone looking for me? I bit my cheek—I'd never imagined my friends might be hurt because I'd left.

'Marco was there.' Laura grinned, the sheepish grin of a woman with a crush. 'He apologised afterwards.'

'Of course he did,' Claire muttered under her breath. 'He wants to bone you.'

Laura shot her a tart glare that looked all wrong on her face.

Claire crossed her arms. 'Anyway,' she said loudly, 'what are you doing here? You know Marco lives in that compound. He's not here.'

'When will he be back?' Bas asked. 'It's urgent.'

'How would I know?' Claire arched an eyebrow.

'He's been coming here every night for dinner,' Laura volunteered. Claire shot her a scathing look. 'If you wait, he'll probably be there tonight.'

'Fine,' Bas said.

'No, not fine!' Claire snarled. 'Go find him in town. You're not waiting here.'

'She's right,' I said. 'The sooner we speak to him—' I shot Bas a significant look. He nodded.

'Fine.' He turned.

'Wait!' Claire said, her lips twisting into a grimace. 'Why—why'd you come here in the first place?'

Bas turned back, and for a second I caught a tiny smile on his lips. 'We're looking for a friend of ours. He was meant to come here.'

'I haven't seen anyone.' Claire crossed her arms.

'Are you sure?' I pressed. 'He might have—'

'Claire?'

An older woman appeared around the side of the house—clearly Claire's mother. They were the spitting image of each other, but thirty years apart. She strolled over to us.

'Are we all just standing around, then?'

Claire gestured angrily towards Bas and me. 'They just showed up looking for Marco.'

Ms Ellery turned to us. 'Goodness gracious me, Bas!' She pressed a hand to her chest. 'Marco said you were out of town.'

'We had to leave for a while,' Bas said.

'And you didn't think to just come here?' She tutted.

Bas frowned. I bit my cheek. After everything, could we have just come straight here?

'We'd have had to leave, in any case,' Bas said. 'There were things we had to do.'

'Well, you're here now. Are you staying? Or are you going to join in the gunfights with my idiot son?'

Bas grimaced. 'I'm not sure yet. Has anyone else come here looking for Marco?'

'Not that I'm aware of. Who would that be?'

'Theo Dunne.'

Ms Ellery glanced at Claire, who shook her head. 'We haven't seen anyone else. They're not letting strangers in at the gate anyway.' And she shot me another glare.

'Harley's with me,' Bas said.

'She's still a stranger.'

'No, she's with me.' There was a flat note to his voice. By the way Claire thinned her lips, I knew she'd picked up on it, too.

She scowled.

'Whatever. Anyway, we haven't seen your friend.'

I caught Bas's eye. He frowned.

If Theo hadn't come here… I dug my fingers into my knees. *Where are you, Theo?*

Could something have happened on the road?

But Theo was an expert at navigating the wasteland. He did it all the time. He was the last person who would get into trouble out there…

'Have you tried asking around in town?' Ms Ellery asked. 'The soldiers are giving everyone the runaround. Maybe he got held up.'

That seemed… vanishingly unlikely, for Theo. He slipped out of trouble like sand through your fingers.

'That's where we're heading next,' Bas said.

'You'll have to be careful,' Ms Ellery warned. 'There are blockades left, right, and centre these days.'

'Go in from the north,' Laura blurted. We all turned to look at her, and she flushed under the scrutiny. 'That's what Marco said; he said it was the only way in. The Iron Fists are holding the north.'

I shot a look at Bas. That seemed even more risky than trying to go through the blockade. I doubted the Iron Fists would be pleased to see us right now.

Bas nodded. 'Thanks.' To Ms Ellery, he added, 'Can we come back… later?'

'Of course. Don't be silly. The more the merrier.'

Behind her, Claire was scowling.

'But remember, if you stay, you work,' Ms Ellery added. 'And your friend, too.'

'Yes, ma'am.'

I had to suppress a smile. Bas was like a naughty schoolboy being told the rules. It was incredibly sweet.

'Let's go,' he said, pulling out his keys.

'Take the truck,' Ms Ellery suggested. 'It'll get you through the barricade. They're used to the farmers coming and going.'

'Thank you,' Bas said. He raised an eyebrow at me.

'One sec.' I glanced at Laura. 'You said you saw my sister?'

'Oh, yeah. She came into the bar about two days after you left—she was really worried? Angry? I don't know. She said she was going to be staying with some guy over on the east side and made Benny promise to bring her a message if we heard anything.' Laura frowned. 'Is she always that… forceful?'

'Savannah's Savannah.' This time, I let the smile blossom on my face. It sounded like Savannah was okay—hopefully. That still left Theo, though. What had happened to him?

'Anna and the others are staying inside the blockade,' Laura continued. 'They might know what happened to your friend.'

'I'll see if I get a chance to speak to them,' I said.

'Tell them I miss them? If you see them?' she asked hopefully.

'Sure,' I replied.

TWENTY-THREE

THE TRUCK'S STEERING PULLED NOTICEABLY to the left, and for the first few moments, Bas had to focus on driving. Once we'd got off the farm track and he seemed a bit more relaxed, I finally allowed myself to voice my fears.

'What do you think happened to Theo?'

'I don't know,' Bas said.

'Laura saw Savannah.' I swallowed and forced myself to go on. 'So that means Sav's still in town. As of a few days ago, anyway. And Theo never came here.'

'Don't speculate,' Bas warned. 'We can't know what we don't know.'

'He's my friend!' I couldn't not worry. 'If something happened—'

'—then we'll find out and handle it. He wouldn't want you worrying yourself sick over him.' Bas swerved around a gash in the road.

'I can't not. I'm not like you.'

'You don't have to be. But if you can't put the worry aside to think straight, how will you help Theo?'

The words hung in the silence between us. I stared out the window at the passing fields, stung. It just wasn't that easy for me. I'd never learnt to put my emotions aside. I'd never had to.

'Harley.' Bas's tone was soft. I gritted my teeth against a wave of irritation. 'You can do it.'

'You want me to be cold and unfeeling and—'

'I never said that.' Bas cleared his throat. 'After you were… assaulted—' He cleared his throat again. 'This isn't the first time you've had to… set aside your emotions in order to survive. Pain and fear and… those things. They aren't useful.'

'I can't make myself stop feeling them.'

'No, but you can set them aside, temporarily. Focus on what needs to be done.' He slowed the truck as we approached the cluster of buildings.

'What needs to be done?' I asked reluctantly. He was right, of course, but it just wasn't that easy. And he had no right to bring me being assaulted into this conversation. That was a no-go zone.

'We'll ask around town. Tonight we speak to Marco and find out what's going on with the Iron Fists. Then we can make a plan.'

'To find Theo?'

'To do whatever you want to do. If you want to fetch your sister and go back to Crater's Edge, we can do that, too.'

I couldn't now, not without knowing what had happened to Theo. But I did want to see Savannah in person, to know she was okay. To get her out of town. Could I bring her into Freetown?

She was a doctor. Probably anywhere would take her, with her skills.

Something else occurred to me. I bit my cheek. 'What do you want to do?'

'I don't mind,' Bas said.

'No,' I pressed, tracing the seam on my trousers. 'You must have something you want to do.'

'I can stay here.' Bas hesitated. 'Or I can go with you.'

We slowed to a halt in front of the gate. Bas rolled his window down and signed something to the kids who were waiting to open it for us. When he turned to me, I met his gaze. His green eyes were impossibly intense. What did I say to that? What could I say?

'Let's… let's speak to Ellery,' I muttered.

Bas nodded sharply and turned back to the road, putting the truck back in gear. Just like that. Orders received and acknowledged.

Did it really not bother him? That I hadn't answered? Or was he just not showing it?

I felt like a coward.

Why is it so hard to make decisions?

I should have just told him I wanted him to stay with me. But the thought filled me with terror that paralysed my limbs and robbed me of breath. The only person I'd ever wanted to stay with was Savannah. Bas was an unexpected addition. I felt too much, and it was moving too fast. I wasn't ready for that decision. Instead, I sat in silence as we left Freetown and started towards Bale Rocks.

It didn't take long before we reached the eastern outskirts and the signs appeared.

MILITARY CHECKPOINT 1000 YARDS

MILITARY CHECKPOINT 500 YARDS

MILITARY CHECKPOINT 100 YARDS

When we reached it, I found they'd created a similar setup to the checkpoint in Brackfields. We had to weave between concrete barriers at a crawl, finally coming to a halt at a metal railing. Bas cut the engine and rolled the window down.

A soldier jumped down from the guard post, rifle over his shoulder.

'Out the car,' he called. 'Hands where I can see them.'

This was nothing like the original checkpoints in Bale Rocks. The soldier's movements were brisk and efficient; he screamed professionalism. Nothing like the guys who'd run the checkpoint on my street.

A second soldier frisked us. I had nothing since I'd lost my weapons in Langford. Bas came back clean as well. They checked the back of the truck, then one of them turned to us.

'Where you from?'

'Freetown,' Bas said.

'Destination?'

Bas hesitated.

'The grocery store on Prospect Avenue,' I said.

The soldier turned to me. 'Have you got papers?'

'Papers?' I asked, alarm making my fingers tingle. Ms Ellery hadn't mentioned anything about papers!

'We're residents of Bale Rocks,' Bas said. 'We do regular supply runs. Why would we need papers?'

'New regulations.' The soldier shook his head. 'We'll let you pass this time, but make sure you have them next time. Got it?'

Bas nodded.

'Good.' He beckoned to the other soldiers. 'Wait until we give you the signal before you turn your engine on.'

Two of them shifted the metal railing, and the third waved to us.

Bas drove us slowly through and away from the checkpoint, before speeding up. I gripped the edge of the seat and bit my lip.

'This feels so weird.'

'The question is why,' Bas said.

'Why?'

'We're not a high-value target like Brackfields. There's no reason for this level of military involvement.'

'There's the distillery,' I said tentatively.

'The distillery is important to the mayor,' Bas said. 'But not the military. The military cares about food, raw materials, and weapons. Our food supply is barely enough for Bale Rocks, and most of it's in Freetown, which they haven't taken over.'

'Huh.' Bas knew a lot more about the topic than I did. I subsided into silence, turning those thoughts over in my head. To me, the military had always been an amorphous mass that represented danger: more men with guns. They'd come into town occasionally on their breaks and usually spent the time getting drunk in our bars and gambling in our casinos. But Bas was right. They had no real reason to care about us.

So why were they here?

More changes became apparent as we drove into Bale Rocks proper. Our streets had always had a deserted, rundown feeling to them, but that feeling had worsened in my absence. More shops had boarded-up windows, and several seemed to have closed down. In places, the buildings and streets seemed to have been damaged: cracked asphalt, bullet holes in the buildings.

'It wasn't an entirely peaceful takeover,' Bas remarked.

I dug my fingers into my knees. 'I hope everyone is okay.'

Bas remained silent. What could he say? 'Okay' was relative. People would die, but the town would survive, because that was what we'd always done.

We cleared the remnants of a second blockade, which was now abandoned, and Bas stopped by the side of the road.

'Where to?' he asked.

'My flat?' I paused, considering, then leant over to check the time on his watch. 'No, Savannah will be at work right now. Unless you can think of a better place to check?'

'Theo's flat—but it's in the compound.' Bas grimaced in frustration. 'We'll never get in.'

'Could we get a message to someone?' I asked.

'Not quickly.'

We lapsed into silence, pondering the issue. Finally, Bas pulled off and turned towards the clinic. 'We can't go any further north than that. This is risky enough as is.'

'Do you think the Iron Fists will realise we're here?'

'I don't know.' He tapped his fingers against the steering wheel. 'Who was Laura talking about? She said your sister was staying with someone.'

'Oh.' I thought back. 'Talbot, maybe? I hope not.'

It would make sense. On her own, Savannah wouldn't have a hope of covering our rent. Besides that, with the soldiers, she might need extra security. But Talbot… He was a deserter. If the army found her with him, there was a good chance they'd shoot first and ask questions later.

My stomach churned.

'I thought she was cleverer than that,' Bas said.

'Me too,' I grumbled.

A few minutes later, we pulled up outside the clinic. 'I'll run in,' I said as I pulled the doorhandle. I had to lean my weight into it to get it open—the wind was blasting outside.

'Be quick,' Bas said. 'If there's any sign of trouble, leave.'

I nodded.

I hurried across the road. The weapons check outside had a new guard station. My heart sank as I realised who was on duty: it was manned by two burly soldiers.

Damnit, not again.

One of them, a blond man with small blue eyes, seemed vaguely familiar. A customer at Krani's, maybe? The other, I didn't recognise.

'Halt,' the blue-eyed soldier called. 'Purpose?'

'I'm here to see the doctor.' I couldn't keep the sarcasm out of my voice. What the fuck did he think I was here for?

'You don't look injured,' he sneered.

Neither do you, but I'd love to rectify that.

I pasted a grimace on my face. 'I'm in terrible pain, actually. Do you mind?'

'We have to search you.'

I submitted to that without argument, not that it mattered—I was unarmed. Finally, they let me through, and I poked my head in. The clinic was a hive of activity, but there seemed to be fewer patients… or rather, there seemed to be fewer civilian patients. I counted three soldiers in for treatment.

Interesting.

But I cared more about finding Savannah. I wove between the people and rounded the curtain to her cubicle—only to find someone else on. A small, pale woman with long dark hair. Nina Clairmont.

'Sav—oh, Harley!' She gaped at me. 'What are you doing here?'

'Looking for Savannah,' I said.

She continued to stare for several seconds, before shaking her head. 'Are you crazy? She's been so worried!'

'I'm sorry.' I shrugged. 'I'm here now. Is she on?'

Nina shook her head. 'She has the afternoon shift today. She should be here soon.'

Damnit.

'Alright, well thanks.' I backed away a step.

'Wait!' Nina called. 'Where have you been?'

There was no harm in telling her—unless Turner was right, and her father-in-law was working with the slavers. Then there might be a lot of harm. I swallowed. 'Away, but I'm back now. I'll see you around.'

I turned and fled.

I rushed out into the street and hurried past the soldiers.

'Oi, what's the hurry?'

'Nothing.' I forced myself to slow my steps and shoot them a smile. 'Just didn't see the person I wanted to.'

'But you said you needed to see the doctor.'

'I did. She's my sister.' I paused a few feet inside the chain-link fence. So close to freedom… But I wasn't going to risk picking a fight with a soldier. 'I don't like being treated by anyone else.'

'You sure?' The blue-eyed soldier stepped closer to me. 'Sounds to me like you're here to make trouble and now you're making excuses.'

'I'm not!' I backed up a step—mistake—he reached for his holster. *Fuck.* I froze.

At that moment, a rumble reached my ear. Car engines. And not one—there were several. They roared around the corner towards us, and Blue-Eyes swung wildly towards the street, as his partnered grabbed a radio.

'Gang incoming!'

I whirled around. Four cars had pulled up, and as I watched, several men descended from them, all in black fatigues, all with a fist painted on their jackets.

Oh shit.

My gaze met Bas's across the street.

'HARLEY, RUN!' Bas yelled.

There wasn't a moment to think. I sprinted past the chain-link fence and hurtled down the road.

Bang!

A shot whistled past me. My foot hit a crack in the pavement, and I slammed to my knees. My stomach lurched—I couldn't seem to draw in a breath. Footsteps approached.

'Try anything and I'll shoot. Stand up slowly with your hands in the air.'

My breaths rasped in my throat. It took a few tries before I could get my limbs to cooperate. I stood shakily and turned to see a man standing in front of me, gun trained on my face. My vision swam. I recognised him, but I couldn't remember his name.

'Please…'

'Jackson wants to see you.' He jerked his head towards the car. 'Off you go.'

One shaky step after the next, I stumbled towards my fate.

TWENTY-FOUR

THE CAR ROLLED THROUGH THE gates to the Iron Fists' compound. I'd been here before, but only ever to Ellery's flat. Never to the long, low building at the back of the compound, where Sayle—and now Jackson—had his centre of operations. That was where we stopped now, and my driver—a gang member I recognised, but whose name I couldn't for the life of me remember—swung himself out the front of the car.

He opened my door, and the second man, sitting beside me, prodded my arm with his gun.

'Out you get.'

'I haven't done anything!'

'Jackson will be the one to determine that.' The driver reached in and grabbed my arm, hauling me out onto the asphalt. I stumbled and grabbed the door to steady myself.

His hand slipped to my bum, squeezing casually.

My stomach turned.

The second car drove up and stopped perpendicular to us. Mr Gropey stepped away, and my guard nudged me at gunpoint towards the other car. Bas climbed out with a guard of his own, scowling up a storm.

'Leave Harley out of this.'

'Jackson wants both of you,' one of the men snapped. 'Get going.'

They marched us through a doorway. Bas fell into step beside me, his arm brushing mine.

'Alright?' I whispered.

'Yes. Are you?'

I nodded. I couldn't say it aloud—I wasn't sure if I could pull off the lie. My stomach had twisted itself into knots, and my breathing was too shallow and fast. Bas touched the back of my hand.

'Let me handle this,' he murmured.

'Okay.' I grabbed his hand and squeezed it lightly.

Fingers intertwined, we walked along the endless grey hallway. Every so often we passed metal doors, most of them shut tight. Occasionally, we saw other people, both men and women, who stared at us as we passed. What did they think of us? Did they recognise Bas?

Finally, one of our guards stepped past us and opened one of the doors, holding it for us.

'In.'

Bas dropped my hand and stiffened his shoulders. I copied him, and we entered the room.

I had been expecting an office of some sort, but we entered a bar. There was a stage on one side of the room, with round tables scattered around it, each surrounded by wooden chairs. The opposite wall served as the bar, though currently there was no one on duty. Instead, members of the Iron Fists mingled between the tables, waiting for us. I recognised several of them: Ellery, leaning his hip on a table, a grim look on his face. Kade, the youngest member of Ellery and Bas's team. Roswell, Jenkins, and Tanner, who all hung out at the Kranikovska occasionally.

Now, they all watched with dark looks as we were led in. Tension twisted in my stomach.

We're fucked.

Jackson sat amidst them all, a compact, bald man with weathered brown skin. His chair had a high back and red cushions, and he sat with his back straight and his chin lifted, surveying us haughtily.

He looked, for all the world, like a king on his throne.

One of our guards split off from our group and strode over to him, leaning down to whisper something in his ear. A range of emotions flickered over Jackson's face: confusion, frustration, and then acceptance. He wiped his expression blank and nodded, and the other man stepped back.

Jackson turned to us, his small eyes narrowing as he took us in from head to foot. I was seized by the urge to run as far away as possible.

Instead, I dug my nails into my thighs.

'So, Sayle's pet wolf has returned.' Jackson leant back, surveying the room, before his gaze settled on Bas. 'I hear you have information for me?'

'I do,' Bas said. 'We tracked down James Maddock. He was hiding out in Crater's Edge.'

'Is that so?' Jackson leant forwards, gripping the arms of his chair. 'And I suppose you brought him here to stand trial?'

He knows.

I couldn't have said how I knew, but the certainty filled me from the top of my head to the tips of my toes.

'He's dead,' Bas said.

'So you have no evidence?'

'Only my word and what I saw, sir.'

'And what did you see?' Jackson asked softly.

We were being led down the garden path. A glance at Bas told me he'd realised it, too. His eyes darted around, looking for a way out, but there was none. At least a dozen armed men surrounded us, not to mention Jackson himself, and even if we did manage to give them the slip, there were probably dozens more around the compound. We'd never make it out alive.

Bas shifted a little closer to me.

'Anton Sorokin killed Maddock,' he said. 'We caught up with him in Crater's Edge, but before we could interrogate him, Anton arrived and killed him.'

I frowned. What was he doing?

Jackson smiled.

'Is that so?'

'Yes. I believe Anton is a threat to—'

Jackson chuckled. 'Of course Anton killed Maddock. I ordered it.'

My mouth dropped open. Bas cleared his throat. 'Sir?'

'You did well.' Jackson clasped his hands in his lap. 'It's just a shame that none of that matters anymore.'

'Sir?' Bas repeated, slow and careful.

'You see, Sayle is dead. I'm in charge now. What came before… well, it's over. There's a new regime in place.' He jerked his chin towards someone lurking in the shadows. My heart seized in my chest.

Hannover stepped forwards.

What the hell was he doing here? A member of the Black Hands in the Iron Fists' compound.

'I believe I promised you an execution,' Jackson said.

Oh shit. Oh shit!

'So you did.' Hannover smiled. 'Perhaps even a dual execution.'

'I think we can swing that.'

Fuck.

Understanding hit me far too late.

He meant us.

'Put them in a cell.' Jackson gestured carelessly. Several of the Iron Fists strode over—I caught sight of Kade, his expression apologetic; Russel and Matthews, both of whom I knew from the bunker; and Ellery, blank-faced. I turned to Bas, desperate.

'Don't fight,' he mouthed.

What? What the fuck?

Of course we had to fight—they were going to kill us!

Before I could think of a single solution, they grabbed me. Kade locked my arms behind my back as Matthews twisted Bas's arms.

'Don't even think of trying anything,' he snarled.

Bas cast his gaze downwards, his shoulders slumped.

He'd given in.

Sick to the stomach, I let Kade push me towards the door. My skin crawled everywhere he touched. We'd been—well, not friends, but certainly acquaintances. Friendly acquaintances. Respectful.

This was so wrong.

How could things have changed this much in the few short days we'd been away?

I was going to die.

They marched us out into the hallway. Whitewashed walls, raw concrete floor. It was uneven and my boots were coming unlaced. I stumbled again and again as Kade pushed me. Around a corner. Through a doorway.

A flight of stairs loomed ahead.

The lights died, plunging us into darkness.

I froze; Kade pushed. I stumbled, my shoulder slamming into the wall.

'AH!'

'The fuck?' a man grunted.

Someone brushed past me—and then flesh hit flesh.

Smack!

'STOP HIM!' someone bellowed.

'LIGHTS!'

The light flicked on. I squinted as spots flared on my vision. No one was where they should have been, and I couldn't see a damned thing with Kade pressing me against the wall—

Pressing me?

I shoved against him; he grunted.

'Stay where you are.'

Someone crashed into us. My head thunked against the wall and my ears rang. A scream of pain cut through it, and then a thud as someone tumbled down the stairs.

'Fuck—ARGH!'

Silence.

Kade stepped back. Ellery and Bas were standing shoulder-to-shoulder. One man was collapsed at their feet, another lay slumped against the door, and the third was at the foot of the stairs. All of them unconscious. Or worse.

Ellery dusted his hands off. 'Time to blow this joint?'

'Way overdue,' Kade said.

'Excellent.' Ellery strode to the door, kicked the unconscious guy out of the way, and hauled it open. 'Coming, Harley?'

I pushed off the wall, rubbing the back of my head. *Well, that was unexpected.*

TO BE CONTINUED

WHAT'S NEXT?

Dear reader,

Thanks for giving REDEMPTION a chance! I hope you enjoyed reading about Harley's adventures as much as I enjoyed writing them.

I'd love it if you could take the time to leave a review on my Amazon and Goodreads pages. Reviews are the best reward an author can receive.

If you want more from this world, please join my mailing list. You will receive a free short story, as well as updates about my writing, sneak peeks at new projects, and freebies from other series.

And if you want to explore my other books, check out my website.

You can also follow me on my socials to learn more about me.

See you in the next book!

REVENGE

THE IRON FISTS #4

Harley and Bas's adventures conclude in REVENGE.

Hunters are supposed to hate vampires—but everyone will betray their people for a price. Nathan is about to discover his.

Nathan is a vampire hunter on the cusp of graduation. He's been training for this his entire life: the moment he qualifies and joins the rest of his family in their noble calling.

If only it were that simple.

His grades are a mess, his social life is a disaster, and what's worse, his best friend is a witch! Add to that, his vampire uncle is back in town and his crush might just be supernatural too, and you have one big melting pot of potential parental disapproval. Nathan doesn't think he can take much more, and then the dark mages come to town.

As bodies begin piling up in the streets, Nathan finds himself pulled deeper into political intrigue and a deadly plot that will pit him against his own family. When the girl he likes comes under threat, Nathan races against time to solve the mystery... well aware that with every step he takes, he comes closer to his father exposing all his secrets.

ACKNOWLEDGEMENTS

Once again, we reach the end of a book, and as always, I'd like to thank the team who support me and make this career possible.

My cover designers, MiblArt, for bringing my characters to life.

My alpha readers, for being pedantic gits. (Joking, they were great.)

My editor, Cameron, who helped corral my stray commas and bonked me over the head every time I made a bad decision.

My dad, who continues to support me in every way. And my brother, who lent me his flat and his kitties during the editing. It wasn't distracting at all.

My kitties, for doing zoomies at 3am and reminding me that normal humans sleep at that hour.

And most importantly, my mum, who fills in all the gaps, organises my weirdness, rocks the last-minute technical stuff, and is just generally awesome.

Margot de Klerk is a British author who writes fantasy and science fiction for teens and adults, with a bit of comedy, a dash of romance, and a whole lot of plot. She is most often found in her favourite coffee shop typing furiously on her computer with an iced latte at hand. When not writing, she enjoys photography, travelling, sewing, and various sports.

Follow her on social media, subscribe to her mailing list, and get information on new books: